LIKE

The

SASSAFRAS TREES

LIKE
The
SASSAFRAS
TREES

AURORA STENULSON

For my mom. Your example taught me how to overcome adversity and let the past grow us, but not allow it to define who we are.

AUTHOR NOTE

Some themes and descriptions may be triggering for
sensitive readers. Please be advised that there are depictions
of domestic violence and mentions of animal cruelty.

ALSO BY AURORA STENULSON

Four More Words
Your Drowning Heart
The Consequence of Audrey

Scan the QR code or go to www.aurorastenulson.com
to visit the Aurora Stenulson author website to subscribe
to her newsletter and receive a free book!

CHAPTER ONE

Trinity

September 1997

ELP

    Help is the word I write with my finger across the condensation building on the inside of the car window. The car that I'm literally trapped in because the passenger's side door is broken, and I can't get out even if I tried.

He leans over me as he speeds down the county road to our house and wipes my desperate message away with one fierce swipe of his hand.

"Don't write that," he says with a grunt as he sits back in his seat and focuses on the road. "You know I hate when you touch my windows."

You know I hate you, I want to say.

But instead, I say nothing. Mostly because my lip is so swollen that I probably wouldn't make any sense if I tried to speak. But also because I'm done talking to him.

I'm done with his control.

I'm done with his fist.

I'm done with his manipulation.

I'm done with *him*.

I twist the golden band tightly wrapped around my finger and imagine how good it's going to feel when I take it off for good.

We pull up to the house and I wait for him to get out so I can crawl across the center console of his black Oldsmobile. My head is begging for my pillow. And the throbbing my brain's doing is calling for an Advil, a glass of water, and sleeping in until tomorrow afternoon.

He finally turns the car off and opens his door. I shift in my seat, readying myself to get out but he's not leaving. He's just sitting with his eyes fixed on the windshield.

It's quiet, aside from the lone frog croaking in the night. So when he finally exhales, it's consuming. I can tell he's still angry by the subtle way he side eyes me, even though his mouth is curled upward on one side into a strange, twisted grin.

He grazes my cheek with the back of his finger, causing me to wince, and an apologetic expression falls over his face. "I didn't wanna hit you," he finally says in a low voice. The underlying tone of regret he's portraying would be convincing to anyone else. But I'm not anyone else. I'm an expert when it comes to decoding the false pretense in every word he says. "You know that, right? I didn't mean to hit you."

I pull my gaze forward, looking away from him and out the windshield at our home. Refusing to answer him and give him what he wants. And what he wants is for me to make him feel better for punching me in the face.

I bring my hand up, gently touching my lip to see if it's bleeding. It is. Not much, but enough to leave a shiny layer of dark liquid on my finger. I slowly wipe the blood onto my pants. Still refusing to speak to him.

He clicks his tongue in frustration at my lacking response. "Trinity…," he says my name with warning, "don't make this hard for yourself." He's threatening me with more abuse.

Honestly, I'm beginning to wonder what's taking him so long to get annoyed with me. When he's like this, it doesn't take much for him to snap from my lack of obedience.

What he doesn't know is that I don't want to continue accepting his apologies anymore. If you can even call what he's saying an apology.

I *can't* keep accepting the empty apologies because each time he hits me, it gets more severe. One of these days my children are going to wake up and find me dead. And I won't let them grow up without a mother like I had to do.

Without hesitation, he jerks around to face me. Gripping one hand on the steering wheel and digging his fingers into my face with the other as he squeezes my cheeks in his hand until my clenched teeth are forced open.

"Did you hear what I said?" *There's the familiar rage I was expecting.*

"Let go of me!" I struggle to release his grip from my face.

He blinks once when he releases me, and his mouth parts slightly. As if my reaction was surprising. I'm sure the fight in me caught him off guard since I've never stood up to him before.

An orange glow illuminates the side of his face as the porch light suddenly flicks on. He's yelling at me, but I tune it out to focus on my thoughts. And my thoughts are telling me to call out for help.

Chills sprinkle down my arms as I prepare myself for whatever is going to happen after I do what I'm about to do. Because I know West isn't going to make this easy. Nothing West ever does is easy.

"Martha!" His mother's name erupts out of my throat in a shriek. "Martha! *Help me!*" I cover my head with my arms as I feel the instant blows of the anticipated power from West's clenched fists. And even though I was expecting the abuse, something about this feels…different.

This feels eerily more intense than the prior beatings I've endured. Maybe it's because it's been nearly three months since he's hit me. Maybe there's more anger built up in him. I don't know, but one thing is for certain, he's unrelenting.

I continue screaming for Martha to no avail. Then I give up calling out to her since West is dragging me out of the car by my hair now. Surprisingly, it doesn't hurt. Nothing does because my adrenaline has overridden my entire nervous system.

I'm fearless.

Which makes me do the bravest thing I've ever done. Or the most reckless thing I've ever done.

Flipping around, I stagger to my feet as I stumble behind him, trying to keep his pace while he continues to pull me by my hair on his way inside the house. I gather enough momentum to lunge at his legs just as he begins to scale the porch steps. The unexpectedness of it causes him to tumble over and release me as he reaches down, catching himself with his hands.

In the split second that I have to decide what to do while West is on the ground, I choose to flee.

And I run. I mean, I *run* like I've never ran before.

I hear my feet hitting the ground so fast I'm half expecting to take off like an airplane. I hear my pulse hammering in my ears. I hear my grunting voice mixed with my quick breathing. Then, I hear West.

"Get back here, Trinity!"

I run harder.

I breathe faster.

I pump my arms, driving myself forward through the dark night.

I'm going to get away.

I have to get away because I've made him angrier than I ever have before. I *have* to get away from him.

But West is a police officer, farms our cornfield, and is in better shape than I am. Not to mention just one of his strides is longer than two of mine. Then, I hear his breath before I feel his hand grip the back of my jeans and tug me backwards.

It takes only seconds for him to catch me.

Seconds to verbally threaten me.

Seconds to turn those threats into painful reality.

Seconds to toss me over his shoulder and haul me into the house. And there's only one thing running through my mind the entire time. *He's not going to get away with this.*

All I have to do is *survive.*

CHAPTER TWO

Knox

"A little late for coffee, isn't it?" Constance says as she fills a glass of water at the sink.

I tighten the lid on my thermos and take my gear belt from the counter. "Graveyard shift."

She gives me one nod and sets her glass down after taking a sip. "All you do is work. Don't you want to meet some people? I mean, aside from other police officers and criminals?"

I shake my head. "Not in this town."

"We're not going anywhere." She crosses her arms. "Try to meet a girl, that'll get you to stay."

"Yeah?" I look down to lock my gear belt into place against my hips. "Where am I gonna meet a girl around here?" The population of Mount Vernon, Texas is just under three thousand. Which means, there's cliques that have been here since before I was born. History I'm not aware of that's woven between each of the people that grew up here. And the women my age are married to the guys they shared a lunch table with during elementary school.

I notice a small, stifled grin hit the corner of her mouth which causes a similar grin to emerge on my own face. It's nice to see her smile after what she's been through, even if it is one she's trying to hide.

"There's girls everywhere." She shrugs. "The library, the animal shelter, the grocery store. Maybe she'll be on the side of the road waiting for you to help her because her car broke down in this God forsaken heat. I don't know, she could be anywhere. You just need to look." Her face goes flat. "Except the bar." She points a stern finger at my chest. "Do not go looking for a girl at the bar."

I fold my mouth in and narrow my eyes at her with a short nod to satisfy her. Too bad the only places to eat around here are sports bars and dive bars, or else I wouldn't associate with them at all if I could help it.

She returns to her glass of water as I turn my radio on. When I begin lacing my boots, she says, "You can't make coffee up there?" She's referring to the studio apartment I live in above the garage.

"Nope." I stand up and cinch my belt before taking my thermos and keys to exit. "Water's off again."

She mumbles something about the defective plumbing while she heads back to her bedroom.

"I'll fix it tomorrow," I say as dispatch blares through my radio. "Don't call a plumber."

She tosses her dark braided hair over her shoulder until it slaps at her back. "Thanks, Zio." She's called me this nickname since we were kids.

And I gave her a nickname too, just to make her head spin. "You got it, Kid. See you in the morning."

I lock up and radio in to dispatch. "A 10-9 for Santino."

Dispatch responds with, "Call in for domestic violence on County Road 228. The husband is getting pretty rough with the wife."

I let out an irritated exhale. "10-4." I get the address and call in for back up. Next to child abuse, nothing makes my blood boil like a man harming his wife.

Thankfully Mount Vernon is a small enough town that it only takes me a few minutes to find the place. Just as I pull up to the house, I see Chandler's squad car behind me in my rearview mirror. I quickly assess that the car parked outside the home has the driver's side door wide open. Next to it is a squad car that I assume is another officer that beat me to the scene. Although there doesn't seem to appear to be another officer besides Chandler.

An older blonde woman with a grown-out bob comes running out of the house to meet me before I'm completely out of my squad car. I'm assuming it's the wife. I radio in my arrival and hold my hand up to make sure the woman keeps her distance when I ask her what happened.

She's hysterical when she reaches me. So much so that I can't make out what she's saying through her blubbering.

"Ma'am," I say, subtly searching her face and person for evidence of foul play. "Take a breath. I can't help you if I can't understand what you're saying." Not only do I need to find out what I'm walking into, but I can hear a dog barking inside. And I don't want to enter the house without knowing if the dog is territorial or aggressive.

She covers her face with her hands to calm herself just as Chandler approaches us.

He gives me a look of anticipation, assuming I've got a report for him.

I shake my head as my brows knit together with a slight disturbance. "I can't understand what she's saying, she's crying too hard."

Chandler gives me a nod and places one hand on the woman's shoulder to console her. "Ma'am, I'm Officer Chase Chandler and this is Officer Knox Santino." Chandler's much better at the personable side of things than I am. "Are you hurt?"

The woman shakes her head and looks up at Chandler. Her voice is breathless when she says, "No, I'm not hurt. I made the call." When her quivering expression faces the house, her tone drops to an eerie disturbance as she speaks in a hoarse whisper, "But I'm afraid he's killed her."

The woman's statement is enough reassurance for me. She's not the wife I'm looking for and more importantly, I need to get to whoever the wife is immediately.

Any concern I had about the barking dog evades me as I lunge up the porch steps and enter the house. "Mount Vernon Police Department!" I call out as I enter the home in haste.

I've redirected arguments before. Even ended assault situations.

But when I see him straddling her limp body, the body that's positioned face down…

When I see him lift the back of her head by clenching a wad of her hair in his bloody fist…

When I see him slam her face into the linoleum of the kitchen floor…

I.

Lose.

It.

In half a second, I've tackled him and pinned his chest to the floor with his arms behind his back. He yells in agony when I feel a pop from one arm as I handcuff him and dig my knee into his back. I know I'm being rough with him but compared to what he's just done to his wife, this is nothing.

He lets out an agonizing roar, followed by a plea. "Left arm! Left arm! I've got a metal plate in my shoulder!" His statement comes out in a muffled voice since my knee is pressed into the back of his neck now. "I'll do whatever you want, just don't pull on my left arm, man."

I shake my head. Stunned by the audacity he has to plead for mercy after he's shown none to the unconscious woman he calls his *wife*.

I'm not gentle when I lift him up—it's no accident that I use most of the force on his left arm to raise him to his feet either. And in doing so, I finally get a glance at his profile and realize I know this guy.

"West Laurel?" I recognize West's stature, but I don't want to believe a police officer is capable of doing something so horrific. And not just any police officer, but one running for a promotion. In a couple weeks West is supposed to be the new sergeant at the station. We'll see how the promotion plays out after this stunt.

Chandler is radioing in for an ambulance when he enters the house.

I shove West toward Chandler and say, "Get him in the squad car."

When Chandler takes a look at West his face falls in disappointment. "Oh, West. You didn't."

West swings his head in my direction. "She attacked me first!"

I take three abrupt paces into his space and clench my hand into a fist at my side. "It doesn't matter, West. You don't treat a woman like that. You never hit a woman. Ever!"

"It was self-defense." His expression is astonishingly convincing, but since he's three times her size, I'm not buying it. Not to mention I just pulled him off her defenseless body.

I harden my expression with my forced exhale as I pull myself away from West's face, making sure I don't do anything that will get me written up. "Get him out of here, Chandler."

Chandler takes West's arm and guides him out of the house before I rip into West any further.

I back pedal, remembering something. "Chandler?"

He's holding West's handcuffed wrists when he faces me. "I dislocated his left shoulder."

He cocks his head to the side, then adjusts his glasses before exhaling and shaking his head. If it was anyone else, I'm certain Chandler would give me an earful about getting written up for being too aggressive. But since it's West we're dealing with I know Chandler is on the same page as me.

When I bring my attention to West's wife on the floor, I notice that the barking from the dog stopped once I pulled West from her. Now the dog is lying its head between the woman's shoulder and jaw. I'm not sure if its protecting or comforting the woman.

So when I kneel down, I'm careful not to invite an attack from the K-9. It seems harmless with its widened fear filled eyes. I slowly lift the back of my hand near the dog. It sniffs my hand briefly then lays back down. I give it a gentle pet on the top of its head and say, "Don't worry. I'm not gonna hurt her." I keep petting the dog with one hand and slip my other around the woman's wrist to check for a pulse. "I'm here to help." I'm not sure why I'm reassuring a dog, but it seems to ease both of us.

I release a heavy exhale with the relief of the woman's strong pulse against my fingertips and give the dog a reassuring look, hoping it trusts me enough to let me further inspect its owner. To my surprise, the dog backs off just as the woman begins to moan quietly.

"Ma'am?" She's trying to lift her head, and I'd like to get her flat on her back to avoid furthering the damage done to her. I wouldn't be surprised if West cracked her skull with that last blow to her head. "Try not to move, you have some serious injuries." Blood drips to the floor from her nose as she raises her head. "Can I get you to lay on your back?" More blood leaks from her hanging jaw.

I'm trying to brace her when she begins lifting herself off the floor.

"Ma'am, I'm going to help you onto your back. It's safer until the paramedics arrive."

She moans again but it sounds like she's trying to speak. I'm sure she was knocked unconscious if not before the last of West's blows that I witnessed, then definitely after it.

Chandler enters the home again, followed by the hysterical older woman. He drops down beside me, rolling West's wife over into a safer position. He's gently pulling her hip and shoulder as I kneel at her head and brace her neck in my hands to stabilize her better, just in case she has a spinal injury.

When we get her adjusted, she continues to let out painful moans with her hair matted to her face. The sound she makes is sort of gurgled.

The older blonde woman approaches and looks down at the battered woman. "Is she going to be okay?" I can hear her fearful breathing intensify when she asks this.

Chandler looks down at the assaulted woman then back up to the older woman. "Martha? Didn't you say that was your name?"

She nods with a terrified expression. She must have told him her name when they were outside.

"Well, Martha, we won't know the extent of her injuries until she gets checked out by a doctor." Chandler's keeping the wife's shoulders still as I continue to cradle her head in my hands.

I keep my eyes fixed on the woman's red stained hair hiding her face when I speak to Martha. "What's her name?"

Martha's voice is meek when she says, "Excuse me?"

I look up at Martha and with a disgusted expression I say, "What's *her* name?" tilting my head down toward the woman.

"Trinity," she says immediately. "Her name is Trinity. She and West are married."

"And who are you?"

She drops her gaze and covers her face with her hands, choking on her sobs.

I'm beyond irritated. "*Martha?*" I spit her name out. "Are you the neighbor? How do you know West and Trinity?"

She lets out a sob into her hand. Then when she uncovers her face, she hurls the words out like a confession, "I'm West's *mother!*"

I clench my jaw so tight I can hear my teeth grinding before I say, "Are you kidding me?" with disappointment in my voice and an expression full of revulsion. Because I realize that this foolish woman let her son treat another human with such complete and utter disrespect.

Chandler gives me another look as if he wants me to take back what I've said. Before either of us can defend our position on the matter, the ambulance sirens blare in the distance as they approach the house.

I have several choice words I'd like to say to Martha. But I drop her into the compartment of my mind where I could give a rat's ass about her.

Instead of allowing my anger to consume me, I concentrate on keeping the woman in my hands safe. I gently peel away the hair stuck to Trinity's face and place the bloody strands at the sides of her head. And in doing so, I reveal a woman that is unrecognizable as a human.

"What kind of person does this?" I say, mostly to myself.

But apparently Martha has a response since she says, "West is a good man. He's never done this before." She shudders an inhale, then, "Is he going to jail?"

I don't hold back when I plow my words into her. "You have to be *the* dumbest woman alive. You know damn well he's going to jail." The anger and disappointment in humanity I'm battling with consumes me again with her stupidity. "And I have half a mind to send you right along with him for assisting in a battery. You watched him do this to her. That's a Class A misdemeanor and a one-way ticket to jail."

Chandler sighs, knowing I'm exaggerating her fault to infuse fear into her. I don't think I'm in the wrong for scaring her though. If she's not going to jail with her garbage-bag of a son, she should at least stand there for a few minutes tormented by the idea of going to jail.

The ambulance and a few other police officers finally enter the home. While the paramedics are adjusting the gurney, I notice Trinity relax in my hands and begin to move her swollen lips. I place my ear closer to her face and hear her saying, *"Take me with you. Please, Mom, take me with you."*

When I face her again, I can't tell if her eyes are open or closed since there's so much blood and swelling. But I focus on what I can see of her eyes and say, "Hey, Trinity. Stay with me.

We're gonna take good care of you." Her eyelids part and I can see the bright green color of her irises. "You're safe." There's nothing about this situation that's giving me any reassurance about her condition. I especially hate that she's talking to a person that's not in this room.

As the paramedics begin transferring her to the gurney and wheel her out, she takes hold of my hand.

"Hang on a second," I say to the paramedics as I place my other hand over her grip.

They stop wheeling her and I crane my neck down in front of her face.

She's more alert now and her eyes seem to be screaming up at me in terror.

I'm gripping her hand in both of mine when I reassure her with, "You're safe now, Trinity. Nothing is going to happen to you." I place her hand back at her side on the gurney, but she keeps her grip tight on my hand. I look down at her stiffening grasp then back to her panicked face. "These guys are gonna take you to the hospital where you'll be taken care of, okay? You're safe."

Her grip is still tight as if I haven't given her enough peace of mind. When I realize what sort of reassurance she's looking for, I say, "And West is going to jail, so you don't have to worry about him anymore."

And with that, she finally relaxes her grip.

For her sake, I hope he stays in jail for a long time.

Officer Ballard takes Martha outside to get a statement while Chandler helps me check out the rest of the house. I notice the dog's still inside the home. I thought the dog would've followed Trinity, but once she left in the ambulance truck, the dog sat in the corner of the kitchen facing the lazy susan cabinet.

"Nice house," Chandler says. "You never suspect something like that to go down in such a nice place." His voice drops when he adds, "Or from an officer."

I flick the light on in the bathroom and pull the shower curtain aside. "Yeah, well abuse doesn't discriminate." I turn the light off. "Bathroom's clear."

"Kids' bedrooms on this side are clear too." With the click of his tongue, he says, "Strange. I didn't know West had kids."

I don't bother commenting on that. Since I've lived in this town, I haven't worked the same shifts as West Laurel. But from the interactions I did have with him, I didn't care to get to know him more. He's the kind of guy that thinks the louder he talks the more impressive he is.

Chandler follows me past the kitchen to the other side of the house. "You know his dad's the mayor?"

I shake my head. "I didn't." In fact, not only do I not know about the intricate facts and tangled gossip in this town, but I don't care to know it.

"Yeah, he's always helping West get out of trouble."

I enter the master bedroom and check the closet and other side of the bed.

I don't care to ask what sort of trouble West gets into, but Chandler doesn't seem to pick up on my silent cues since he says, "It's stupid stuff. Open container, DWI's, using his badge to intimidate." He's looking around the dresser. "Weed."

"Smoking or selling?"

Chandler turns to face me. "No, I meant," he says, throwing a thumb over his shoulder. "There's a blunt in an ashtray on the dresser."

"Better ask West if he's willing to do a tox screen."

Chandler lets out a breath of laughter. "Yeah, that's going to go well."

After we clear the bedroom, we pass the kitchen on our way out. I double back when I see the dog still sitting in front of the lazy susan.

"What're we doing with this dog?" I say to Chandler.

He stops in the entrance doorway and drops his head to one side in thought while his eyes fix on the dog. "See if Martha will take her."

I draw my head back, unsatisfied with his suggestion. "That dog is better off at the pound."

He turns to exit and throws his hands up. "Take her to the shelter then."

I fold my arms over my chest and shift to face the dog again. "How did he know you were a girl?"

Turning only her head, the dog faces me with the same pleading expression she gave me when she was comforting Trinity.

"You wanna keep me company for the rest of my shift?" I approach her and squat down to pet her golden head of fur. And as soon as I do, she perks up with excitement and licks my hand. Then she begins to whine and paw at the lazy susan.

"What is it about this cabinet?"

Then, the sound that releases from behind the cabinet door makes my pulse stop. Because it's a sound I recognize. It's the sound of a small child coughing.

I rise to my feet. "Hello?" I say with a gentle tone. Unsure why there's a kid in a cabinet.

I radio in to let the other officers know what I've found as I keep my attention at knee level.

Squatting back down, I give the cabinet a gentle knock with my knuckle. "My name is Officer Santino. Do you want to come out?" There's a subtle shaking of the cabinet before the lazy susan begins turning. "Come on out, I'm not gonna hurt you."

I gently push my hand on the wood, assisting the rotation of the cabinet until I see not one, but two small, wide-eyed children. I drop my head back between my shoulders and exhale, containing my frustration toward the adults in these kids' lives.

This kind of behavior isn't normal, it's *learned*. And that's what concerns me. These two kids learned to hide, which means the beating West inflicted on Trinity wasn't the first. This lazy susan has probably become a safe haven for these poor kids, and that's beyond horrific.

I reach my hand down at the girl. "It's okay, don't be scared. I'm here to help you." She can't be any older than five. I try to force a welcoming grin, but it's no use. I can tell by this kid's eyes that she's seen some morbid stuff. "You can trust me, I'm a police officer." Not that it's any comfort to her since her abusive father is an officer too.

She nods and takes my hand. I have to bite my bottom lip to remain composed in front of her. I'd like to tell her what a piece of work her dad is and that most police officers aren't like him. But I don't.

The only thing she says to me is, "Don't foh-get Tuck." I assume that's her brother situated behind her.

"I won't. Tuck is coming out next." I duck down to see the terrified little boy. "Isn't that right, buddy?"

Tuck's eyes don't have the same hardness as his sister's. And I'm thankful for that. He's obviously scared, and rightly so. I can only hope his memory won't carry the events of tonight into the rest of his life.

"What's your name?" I ask the girl.

Once she's completely crawled out, she says, "Abbi."

"Do you want to help me get your brother out of this cabinet, Abbi?"

She nods.

Apparently the dog wants to help too since she invades the space between Abbi and me with her nose.

Tuck turns his head to avoid the dog's licking. "No, Shuguh," he says as I pull him out and onto his feet.

He quickly stands behind Abbi as Sugar continues to nose at his hand for affection.

"How old are you Abbi?"

She holds up four fingers.

I drag a hand down my face. I have no words for this moment. These kids are *babies*. West has to be a special kind of prick to destroy two tiny lives with his corrupt behavior. Not to mention the way he nearly ended his wife's life.

Just as my heart ignites on fire with vengeance, Chandler and Ballard enter the home again.

They stop in their tracks when they see the kids.

"Seriously?" Ballard says as she gives me a disappointed expression while she tightens her golden ponytail.

I shake my head with the same level of disappointment. "Seriously."

She tosses her hand in the air. "Unbelievable. This kind of thing doesn't happen around here."

"It does now."

Ballard ignores my remark and squats down next to me in front of the kids. She gives them a wide grin. I know it's forced, the same way her chipper tone is forced when she says, "Hey, friends," to the kids. "Y'all okay?"

Abbi nods.

"How does a car ride sound?"

Tuck shakes his head vigorously with a fearful expression.

"Foh ice cweam?" It stings when Abbi asks this with excitement, as if she didn't just hide with her brother three feet away from where her father brutally assaulted their mother.

Ballard raises one shoulder. "Sure, we can grab some ice cream."

Tuck's expression brightens. Then he coughs in Ballard's face a couple of times.

She winces as she wipes her face with her forearm. "How about you grab a blanket and your favorite toy?" She says this with a ring to her voice. "Then we'll get you two some ice cream."

Abbi faces the dog. "What about Shu-gah?"

I rise to my feet and nod in the direction of the dog. "I'll take Sugar if you promise to call me when you get back home so I can drop her off to you." Retrieving one of my cards from my vest pocket, I write my personal number on the back of it then hand it to her. Not that she even knows how to use a phone or won't lose the card before she's back home. But she seems mature for a four-year-old, and I want to be a police officer she can trust.

Abbi nods, snatching the card from my hand. Then she takes Tuck by the arm as they hurry into their bedrooms.

Chandler gives me a knowing expression. "What happened to the pound?"

I cross my arms and raise one eyebrow at him without a response.

Ballard scratches Sugar behind the ear before she rises to her feet. "It's a little strange Martha didn't stick around for her grandkids after she gave her statement, isn't it?"

"She left?" I shouldn't be surprised at this point, but for the kids' sake I would hope there was at least one stable adult in their lives that might, I don't know, stick around to make sure they're safe after their father was taken to jail for assault and their mom was taken to the hospital.

Chandler begins to exit as he says, "I'll take West in and get ahold of a social worker."

I shake my head. "What the hell is wrong with people?"

CHAPTER THREE

Trinity

October 1997

I swivel the lower half of my body in the chair while my arms are rested on the long wooden table at the Department of Family Protective Services building. My hand is still in a cast from the broken metatarsals—of which I'm not sure how they fractured in the first place. Probably from breaking my fall when West's body tackled me with his deadweight.

Most of that night is a blur. As the days progressed and I began to heal, my mind continued to remember pieces of the night. The last thing I remember was seeing my mom reaching her hand out to me—which I know is impossible since she's dead—then suddenly she was replaced by the hardened face of a police officer. I'm sure the vision of my mom was only a sweet dream my brain gave me while it shut down as a defense mechanism to protect my nervous system from experiencing the excruciating pain I was enduring. Or maybe it was her reaching out from heaven to rescue me. Whether it was her or not, I'll hold on to that brief sight of her forever.

Sharry peeks her head into the room with a smile. "They're here." She's the social worker that's been assigned to our case. Not that I had a choice of a different social worker, since she's the only one in this town.

I stand up and run my unbroken hand against my wiry hair to make sure I look presentable. My pulse begins to accelerate with nervous excitement. "I'm ready." I haven't seen the kids in seventeen painfully long days.

I've spent most of that time in the hospital recovering. My dad stopped by for ten minutes to give me money for a motel. I wasn't surprised he didn't stay long. He's never been a man of many words. And never really gave me much of his time, or affection. He's predictable though. At the very least, I can count on that. He eats a steak with a baked potato every night for dinner, likes to drive his convertible, and helps me out any time I've been low on cash. Which I hate to admit, is going to be a lot more often now that I won't have West to rely on.

Sharry gives me a pinched smile under her pointy nose. "Grandma wanted to speak with you for a moment, if that's okay?" She's still peeking in with just the side of her narrow face revealed in the doorway. I'm not sure why she refers to Martha as *Grandma* instead of calling her by her name. Maybe she forgot it. Or maybe saying *Grandma* is some form of manipulation she's trying to use to get me to see Martha in a positive light. I'll be the first to admit there's a fat chance of that happening after Martha's enabled West for so long.

I give Sharry a quick nod. "That's fine, she's welcome to come in with the kids." Martha's not my favorite person right now, especially since she ditched the kids at the house by themselves that night. And she hasn't advocated for me at all since a social worker got involved. But I'd do almost anything to hug my children right now. Even if that means playing nice with their grandmother.

Sharry makes a noise in her throat then closes the door.

The door opens just as quickly as it closed when Abbi and Tucker rush inside.

"*Mommy!*"

I squat down as they topple me over, jumping into my arms. I hold them both tightly against me like I'll never let them go. The laughter that accompanies my heavy breathing escapes with a strange sound. I thought I might cry in this moment. My heart feels like it's crying. My mouth frowns as if I were crying. But the tears won't come out.

I'm not sure why I haven't been able to cry since my mom died. It's like my tear ducts dried up that day. Since then, I've felt pain that would induce tears, but nothing came. I've been sad and made the sorry sob noises of a broken-hearted person, but tears are never part of it. And I've been elated, like right now, where I could cry the happiest tears, yet there's nothing leaking from my face. I must have given all my tears to my mom.

"Can we go home with you today, Mommy?" Abbi says with her beaming smile.

I release my grip on them, and search Abbi's beautiful little face. *Dirty* little face; I notice now that I'm examining it. "We'll go home soon, baby girl." I also notice her clothes are dirty too.

I take her and Tucker's hands in mine and realize under their fingernails are caked with dark brown substance.

"Have they had a bath recently?" I ask Martha without trying to sound interrogating.

She's standing close to the door where Sharry left her. "Oh, you know how children like to play."

"This seems like a little dirtier than just playing outside."

She stands up straighter and pinches her mouth. "What are you insinuating?"

"Maybe give them a bath before bedtime every night?" *Maybe get on my side and give my kids back so I can bathe them myself?*

She gives me a forced—and aggressive—nod.

I face Abbi and Tucker and kiss their little cheeks one at a time. "I missed you both so much." I hug them again and hope they can't feel my heart bursting into shambles.

The social worker placed them in the care of Martha after they spent a night in foster care. Nothing makes a mother feel more shame than knowing her kids are in foster care. Not that I could really comprehend that's where they were since I was in a hospital bed in and out of consciousness. But Martha was happy to swoop in and *save the day*. Between her and Sharry's discussions, they decided it would be better if the kids didn't see me while my face was healing. I'm still not sure if I'm grateful for that or not.

Before releasing them, I say, "Here," and dig into my pants pocket, "I brought you something very, *very* important."

Their eyes light up with excitement.

I give them a playful grin. "Promise you won't lose them?" They nod.

"Abbi, you're the big sister so make sure Tuck doesn't lose his, okay?"

She smiles. "I'll make shuh."

I notice Martha shift uncomfortably. But I'm not here to make sure she's comfortable, so I don't acknowledge her. I'm here to spend time with my kids. And frankly, I want her to leave.

"Was there something you wanted to talk about?" I say without looking at Martha. I should try to be nicer since she was the one to call the police on West. But at the same time *nice* doesn't seem to fit my new strength and determination I've been conjuring up since that night.

She clears her throat and clutches her oversized tan purse with both hands in front of her. "Yes, actually."

I hand Abbi a clear zip tie and a red one to Tucker. "I'm listening." I found them next to a work truck where a guy was fixing a light pole when I was walking here. I don't consider it stealing since they were discarded on the ground.

Martha takes a step closer with her mouth parted as if she's about to speak.

"What's this, Mommy?" Abbi says.

I look at her hazel green eyes and in a quiet voice, say, "I'll tell you in a second. While you're waiting, why don't you think about what it could be?" Then I rise to my feet and face Martha with an expectant and subtly irritated expression because she's wasting precious moments I'm supposed to be spending with my children.

"Well, there's no easy way to say this," she says, averting her eyes to the floor. "So I'll just come out with it. I think you should consider staying with West." I don't understand how such a gentle voice can be so condescending.

I do nothing to hide my expression from twisting into a revolted grimace.

She keeps her gaze at her feet. "Marriage is important, Trinity. Sometimes you have to compromise to make it work. You and West made a vow when you got married. And you don't want to be a liar, do you? Only liars make vows they don't keep."

I'm not sure when my mouth fell open, but I let it hang there for a moment longer after I realize it's gaping. Just to make sure she sees from my expression how stupid and manipulative she sounds.

She lets out a small exhale when she glances up at me. "You're so good for him." As if that's a good reason to stay married. I know I'm good for him. But being good for him isn't going to keep me safe. Being good for him isn't going to change who he is at his core.

I pull my brows together in ultimate confusion. *Can she even hear herself?* Did she forget her son nearly beat me to death? Can she not see the stitches on my cheek? Or the yellowing fade of the bruises all over my face and body?

"Please, Trinity, don't look at me like that. He's my son and the father of your children. If you don't make it work for each other, then do it for them." She glances at the kids, who are trying to figure out how to close their zip ties, then back at me with a look of remorse. "*Please,* Trinity. Will you just think about it?"

I finally close my mouth when I lift my chin up in her direction. I'm done. I've given West a second chance. I've given him third, and fourth, and fifth chances. He doesn't deserve another chance. And if I could go back, I wouldn't have ever given him a second chance after the first time he punched me in the back of the head. "No, I won't think about it."

She flashes me a stunned expression as her eyes widen. I don't blame her. I've never stood up for myself before. I didn't know I could until my potential death hit me with a reality check.

"West has no idea how to love anyone but himself." I let out a quiet, exasperated scoff of disbelief. Then in a voice low enough so the kids can't hear, I continue with, "Are you still pretending like your son didn't almost kill me? Because I'm not."

She must realize she's losing this battle since her eyes shine with angry tears as she says, "He's their father, Trinity. Have a little compassion."

She whips around and storms out of the room before I can retaliate. I'm sure I just stirred the pot, which I'm not certain was in my best interest since she's the kids' primary care provider until a judge decides I'm a fit mother.

Apparently I've landed myself in a civil case and one that is primarily focused on domestic violence and the safety of the children in our home. And because West is saying I attacked him first—which I didn't—it's making this entire situation more tangled and unfair. Not to mention West has half the police department and his father on his side. And I have no one...and nothing on my side. The consequences of being a stay-at-home-mother on the outskirts of a town that I'm not sure I want to call *home*. Somehow, this town has a way of making me homesick for a place I've never been to.

But I'm not going to let any of that stop me from fighting for my kids.

Tucker hands me the zip tie. "Mommy?" He's barely two and can only say a handful of words, so this is his way of asking for help.

"Let's see," I say, flipping the zip tie around and then bending it into a circle. "It will look like this when you're ready. But don't put the ends together until it's done." I open the zip tie back up. "There, now your job is to find things you can put on here. And every time we see each other you can show me what you've added."

"Like a bwacelet?" Abbi says bending her zip tie into a circle.

I smile. "Exactly. Maybe you'll find some beads, or a fruit loop might fit on there." I give her a quick wink. "And I have one too." I pull a blue zip tie from my pocket. "See? And whoever gets the most things to fit on their zip tie will win a prize."

I watch a mischievous smile emerge between Abbi's chubby cheeks. She knows since she's older she'll be winning whatever prize I come up with. In this case she'll be lucky if she gets a stick of gum since I'm jobless, homeless, and stuck in the grip of the system.

The door opens and Sharry enters with a black folder tucked under her arm. She takes a seat at the table and says, "Sorry, I've double booked myself today." She shrugs. "I'm not too worried about needing to keep an eye on you though. This is technically a supervised visit and I'm supposed to be in here with you," she gives me a wink, "but I trust you."

I'm not sure how to take her comment.

Grabbing a pen from the table, I begin to draw on the inside of my palm. There's a subtle ache in my broken hand when I move it with the pen. To Sharry, I say, "How much longer until I can bring them home? Their grandmother isn't my first choice as a caregiver."

"Why's that?" She opens the folder across the desk.

"I don't trust her. She just asked me to stay with West and I'd rather chew on a bug than ever see him again."

She begins scribbling on a paper in her folder. "I know it's tough. But he is their dad, so if you start thinking about shared custody and trying to get along with him and his mother, then you'll have a much easier time in court." She glances at me with a grin. "And you won't have to worry about dragging out a custody battle in court if you're showing your willingness to co-parent."

Co-parenting? I was considering a restraining order, not co-parenting. But I suppose she has a point. And I don't want to take my children away from their father. Even if he is abusive to me, I can't deny the fact that he's never once laid a hand on them. I know it's important that they spend time with him, but I don't want to have to constantly worry about my safety.

"Honestly, I've been thinking about how I can protect myself."

Sharry keeps her eyes down at the paper as her hand etches across it. "You could file for an order of protection at the courthouse." She glances up at me with pointed eyes and a dismal look.

Releasing a defeated exhale, I say, "The same courthouse my father-in-law works at?" So much for that idea. I'm going to have to get creative if I want to keep myself safe from West while somehow still allowing him in our children's lives.

Tucker pulls a book from the shelf and hands it to me. But before I read it, I press the wet ink from my palm onto the top of his hand, then Abbi's hand. It leaves a faded blue ink heart on the backs of their hands. I hope when they look at it later, they think of me. And I'm also using it to see if it's washed off by the time I have a visit with them again in two days.

Abbi and Tucker crawl onto my lap while I read story after story. But my mind is elsewhere. I'm angry that they're being kept from me. I'm frustrated I'm only allowed to see them for an hour three days a week; supervised by a stranger.

I'm baffled that I have to wait weeks for a court date, where I'm going to be judged as I defend myself against my manipulative husband. The same husband that has this town wrapped around his finger. My heart sinks at that thought. Maybe I should tone it down with my newfound courage and take Sharry's advice and try to play nice with the Laurels.

There's a gentle knock on the door before the short, gray-haired lady from the front desk enters. Her voice sounds like she's smoked one too many packs of cigarettes in her life when it rattles from her throat as she says, "Your next visit is here."

I'm not sure what that means so I pretend like I don't hear her and continue reading to Abbi and Tucker.

Sharry rises and meets smoker-lady in the doorway. In a low voice, Sharry says, "He's early."

"I know, whad'ya want me to do with him?"

Sharry faces me with a troubled expression, then looks back to the smoker-lady again. "Have him do his pee test with Sam. Then we should be done here."

After Sharry sits back down, she writes something else in the folder then closes it shut and tucks it under her arm as she rises and checks her watch. "Well, it's been about an hour, so it's a good time to start saying goodbye."

As much as I don't want to, I follow her instructions and hug my children again. I don't understand how an hour can feel like brief moments. I reassure the kids that I'll see them in a couple of days. I also remind them to add items to their zip tie bracelets and that I'll do the same.

My heart breaks when Tucker cries as he finally realizes that I'm leaving. Abbi holds him in her lap, if the sight of leaving my children in a visiting room at the DFPS office isn't enough to make me cry I don't think I'll ever cry again.

It doesn't stop my heart from breaking in half though.

I decide to use the heartache as fuel to get my kids back. Instead of feeling sorry for myself, I'm consumed by anger and frustration. But another sense consumes me. It's intense determination. And I'm going to need all the determination and fight I can to leave West and win the civil dispute.

But that determination is quickly halted when I see the neatly combed, sandy colored hair on top of West's head. He's hunched over in a lobby chair, stirring a straw in his Styrofoam coffee cup. I can't pull my gaze from staring at him. And when our eyes meet, he rises from his chair with an expression full of eagerness and remorse.

My body goes cold. I'm shocked. I thought he was still in jail. Maybe if I was expecting him here, I could have rehearsed how I would respond to him. Maybe I would have held my head up high and walked by, ignoring him. Maybe I would have smacked the bottom of his coffee cup, splattering the boiling liquid into his face. But I didn't have time to prepare. I don't even have time to process what's happening now.

"Trinity," he says gently, approaching me.

I feel the hairs rise on the back of my neck and trickle down my arms and the rest of my body. My throat goes dry, and my mouth won't open to let any words out.

He wraps one arm around me.

I wince, but it's the only movement that I make. My feet are cemented to the floor. Frozen in place along with the rest of my body and mind.

He presses his face to my neck, hugging me. He breathes me in and says, "I missed you, baby." His voice is smooth and warm. His scent is familiar. It's taking everything out of me not to sink back into his arms—into his life—like I've done countless times before. I hate that I *want* to still be with him. I hate that I still love him. But no matter what my feelings want to do, my brain is continuously whispering to me. Encouraging me to leave.

My pulse is throbbing in my throat so hard the friction feels like it might light a fire inside of my body.

When he releases me, he drags his thumb down the side of my face carefully avoiding the stitches. The stitches that are there to fix the broken wound he made.

All the visions of him hitting me flash in my mind. I remind myself that the gentle touch he's giving me right now isn't real. I remind myself that that same hand has hurt me over and over again. His gentleness is fleeting.

My breath grows more intense as I conjure up the nerve to speak. "Don't touch me." When I deliver the words, they're quiet. Not on purpose, but because I can't help it.

His hand freezes just as it slips down to my neck. His pleasant expression doesn't change. Everything starting with his grin, to the lines on his forehead, stay in place.

But his eyes shift. They dim in that twisted way they do right before he would normally back hand me.

Or throw me through a door.

Or kick me to the ground.

But he's sober, and we're in a public place right now. I'm safe from his heavy hand as long as there are witnesses.

And since I'm safe enough to stand up to him—even if my voice is weak and my body has gone so cold that my teeth have begun to chatter, and my legs have begun to shake—I decide to cling to that courage and take a step backwards out of his grip.

My gesture causes him to dip his chin and dig his furious gaze into me. I can tell by the way his eyes are boring into me, from behind his furrowed brow, that it's taking every ounce of energy for him not to do or say anything regrettable to me.

I swallow hard when I hear Sharry's approaching voice from the hallway. "Loretta, I told you to make sure he was in the bathroom with Sam when she left."

Loretta's smokey voice responds with. "He didn't have to pee."

Sharry is standing between West and me before I even know what's happening. "How about I walk you out, Trinity?" Then to Loretta, she says, "Sit with the kids until I get back." She points to West with a stiff finger, then, "And *you* need to get that pee test done before you see the kids."

West ignores Sharry's comment, taking my arm in his grip. It's tight. So tight that I feel my pulse throbbing under his thumb. "I love you, Trinity." His words are mixed with warning and desperation.

I don't know what to do. Why do I feel sorry for him? Why do I feel bad for wanting to leave?

It's easy to hate him when he's not standing in front of me. It's easy to let go of our marriage when I remember all the hurtful things he's said. But not so easy when he's saying the things I want to hear. The parts of my heart that still love him are getting louder, and my mind is so quiet I can't hear the things that were making sense before I was in his presence.

Thankfully Sharry takes West's wrist in her hand, making the decision for me. "Let go of her right now." I'm stunned that a skeleton woman like Sharry has the guts not only to speak to him like that but to defend me by taking his wrist in the way she just did.

West releases my arm without looking at Sharry. It's as if he doesn't see her at all. His eyes are penetrating into me so deeply that I can't seem to look away. I've learned that when he loses his temper it's safer to hold eye contact than it is to look away. Because when I've looked away before, I'm not able to detect his next move and I usually end up with a backhand to the side of the face. Or worse.

Sharry and I continue exiting the building while I keep my eyes locked on West, but we don't make it far before he says, "I said *I love you*, Trinity!" I hate that he sounds heartbroken.

Maybe he does love me, but love isn't enough.

And his love *hurts*.

I use the last ounce of my energy to say, "I don't want your love anymore, West." I finally look away after I say this because I don't want to see the pain and anger in his face. I don't want that sight to haunt my mind either. Because I don't want to feel bad for leaving him.

I'm not sure how I got to the parking lot. But I'm standing here now with Sharry as I try to breathe normal again. My shoulders are rising with each intense inhale and fall with my quick exhale. My ears begin ringing when I decide I'll be safer sitting on the ground.

Sharry adjusts her dark blue pantsuit before pulling her legs to the side as she sits on the ground next to me. "Trinity, listen to me."

I'm trying to drag my breaths in and out to calm myself.

"You're safe."

I'm safe.

She puts her hand on my knee until my eyes meet hers. "He can't hurt you anymore."

He can't hurt me anymore.

"And the wellbeing of your children is the main focus of my job. It's my priority to do everything in my power to make sure your kids are safe and that they have a good relationship with both of their parents. Even if their parents aren't together."

I nod as my nerves begin to finally relax.

She's on my side.

"This incident will go in the file that the judge will see. And I'll make sure to schedule your visits on different days and times from now on too," she says with a regretful roll of her eyes. "I didn't think he'd show up an hour early. I thought it'd be easier on the kids if I scheduled the visits this way." She shakes her head. "Boy was I wrong about that or what?"

Her mouth curls up into a smile, but her eyes aren't convincing. I know she's trying to ease my feelings and comfort me. But I can't stop thinking about the power West still has over me. Not just the power of his strength. But the emotional power he has over me is still so strong it creates a physical reaction from me when I try to stand up to him. And that worries me.

CHAPTER FOUR

Knox

I pull my squad car around to the back of M.L.'s restaurant. Before I head inside, I restock my vest pocket with a handful of shiny golden deputy stickers from the glovebox.

Constance is standing in the open back door with the words *Employees Only* scrawled across the top.

"Took you long enough," she says, releasing the door quickly. I have to skip the steps to grip the door in time before it closes on me.

She's upset.

I follow her brisk stride. "I have a pile of paperwork I'm trying to get through on my desk. You couldn't handle this yourself today?"

She glances at me briefly before leading us through the swinging saloon style doors of the kitchen. "This is important too."

I let out a fatigued exhale. "I'm a little tired of getting this call, Constance."

She points behind Marcos, to the corner of the kitchen and says, "I'm tired of making this call." Then she exits through the swinging doors we just came through.

Marcos is tossing breaded chicken around in a bowl when I pass him. "Hey, Marcos."

"Knox." He gives me a short nod before setting the bowl down. "I'll give you two a minute."

I give him a nod of approval before he exits.

Gripping the back of my neck, I take a deep steadying breath before approaching the kid washing dishes in the corner of the kitchen.

"Aren't you getting a little old for this, Robby?" I place one hand on the edge of the sink and lean on it as I peer down at the top of Robby's curly unmanaged hair.

He continues washing the dishes. "No."

I sink a little further down. "What do you want this time?" I say with my exhale.

A grin emerges on the side of his face when he says, "You know."

I do know, but I was hoping it would change. It seems that I'm stuck in this circular pattern of thinking with him.

I can't blame him though. Robby has an intellectual disability that makes him an easy target for bullies at school. Resulting in zero friendships or connections to anyone…but me it seems. His parents fell into drugs, and he wound up tossed around between family members until he landed here with his grandma. I feel for the kid. But I know he can do better. I also know he's starved for attention. Causing minor disturbances seems to be one of the only ways he can get it.

I dig around in my pocket and hold a sticker out between my fingers for him.

He wipes the suds from his right hand onto the side of his orange flannel shirt then takes the sticker and shoves it into the back pocket of his oversized jeans.

I lean my shoulder into the wall as I peer down at him again. "What'd you do this time?"

"Cheesecake." He continues scrubbing a plate. "Dine and dash."

I fold my arms over my chest and shake my head. "You're twelve-years old. Where'd you learn to dine and dash?"

"Everyone knows what that is."

I know I'm probably off with my thought, but I ask the question circling in my mind anyway. "You're not stealing food because you're hungry, are you?"

He shakes his head.

"You've got food at home?"

His eyes stay down as he nods and reaches deep into the sudsy water for another plate.

"Well if that's the case, I think the punishment fits the crime. Finish up your dishwashing and do me a favor," I wait a moment, hoping to catch his eyes. It's tough to get direct eye contact from him. If it was any other kid, I'd demand some eye contact. But when he doesn't look at me, and since he's not any other kid, I continue with, "When you're done, go home." I splash some of the water from the sink up at him as an attempt to get his attention.

"Hey!" he says, finally looking up at me. "You're contaminating the water with your gross germs."

"You're concerned about germs?" I begin to exit the kitchen with a soundless laugh and a shake of the head. "Coming from the kid that runs off with food in his bare hands."

If he was better at communicating through facial expressions, his would be covered in frustration. "You don't want to take me to jail?" It's disheartening the way he seems thwarted by the fact that I didn't arrest him. Not that I could legally arrest a kid.

Part of me wants to explain why he can't go to jail until he's eighteen, no matter what he does. But the other part of me doesn't want to encourage worse behavior from him by making that fact known. Since it's apparent that, for whatever reason, he *wants* to experience what it's like behind bars.

Before I pass through the swinging doors I stop and double back to face him. "You have a whole life ahead of you, Robby. Get your crap together."

When I find Constance, she's delivering two plates to a couple of women in a corner booth. Albeit too old to be giggling that loud.

She spots me and makes her way over with a disgruntled flex in the corner of her mouth. "Those women have been here for hours." She glances back at the laughter coming from the women and narrows her eyes. "They better tip good."

"Doubtful, but I like your optimism."

She faces me with an unsatisfied grimace. "How'd it go with Robby?"

I instinctively scan the patrons at the tables with my brows knitting together. "I feel bad for the kid."

"Well don't." The back of her hand strikes the center of my chest with disapproval. "He's never gonna learn his lesson if you just keep givin' him stickers and telling him to *get his crap together.*"

"I don't know what else you want from me. He's in there doing dishes, paying for his crime." I soften my hardened brow. "Honestly, I wouldn't get too bent about it, it's just a piece of cheesecake."

She releases a sad exhale as her shoulders drop. "I know…"

I look down at her. "How's his grandma?"

She tosses her hand flippantly and pulls her braid over her shoulder while her eyes drift in thought. "Not good."

I nudge her arm gently with my elbow. "He's harmless. Just keep giving him stuff to do and he'll be fine."

There's a sudden cackling of laughter from the corner booth, then the giggling women raise their empty glasses while catching Constance's attention for a refill. "I hope you're right," she says maneuvering around me. "I'll make sure he gets a ride home."

I don't think I was prepared for this. When I completed the academy, I didn't realize that I was going into such a devastating line of work. I thought I'd be fighting criminals and constantly be in the line of fire. But I've quickly learned that aside from paperwork, I do an awful lot of making sure people are taken care of. And making sure kids are okay. There's a lot of broken people, family dysfunction and sadness associated with law enforcement. And nothing could have prepared me for the devastation I've seen. And endured.

When I back my squad car out of the alley, I circle around the plaza square, then through the neighborhoods. It's Thursday evening and I'm not expecting too much action, so I cruise on the outskirts of town past the school. Mostly to pass the time.

The setting sun acts as a strobe light when the carroty glow hits my eyes and then hides momentarily behind the railroad beams that are suspending the bridge up above the river. I turn to face the bright orange sky, taking in the sunset and the one good thing I appreciate about living in this town. Then, I see someone sitting at the edge of the beams.

It's probably nothing, but just in case, I decide to check it out. Whoever is up there might be enjoying a better view of the sunset, but I don't want to get a call later about a tragedy I could have prevented.

Even if it's a kid messing around, the river is too shallow to jump in from the bridge. I refrain from turning my lightbar on, so I don't alarm them. And I opt for parking at the edge of the road near the base of the hill where I won't be seen.

Whoever is up there is facing their back to me, so they probably won't notice me until they hear me approaching. That is, if they can hear me over the sound of the rushing river below.

I scale the hill quickly while assessing the urgency of the situation. As I get closer, I can see that it's a young woman with her feet dangling below her. It wouldn't take much for her to slip off and catapult down to the shallow river. So when I say, "Not afraid of heights I take it?" I make sure not to say it too loudly.

I notice her shoulders lift subtly, startled at my invasion of her privacy.

She doesn't look at me when she says, "I like the rush." That statement doesn't give me any reassurance as to why she's sitting up here.

"What do you need a rush for?" I find a place standing behind her, ready to grab her if she decides to lean forward off the edge.

She's wearing a pair of worn-out Nikes that are shifting back and forth as she swings her feet. They look as if they used to be white, but after years of dirt roads, they've been discolored into a rusting tan. With her inhale, she says, "It reminds me that I'm still alive."

I don't know what to make of her response. "There's safer ways to remind yourself that you're alive."

She scoots a little closer to the edge, and it makes my pulse accelerate. I'm deciding how far I'm going to let her get before I pull her off the beam and down to safety. Right now, she has just a couple of centimeters left.

"Can I be transparent with you?" I say, my words coming out a little quicker than I intended.

She tosses her terribly dyed, orange colored hair over her shrugging shoulder. "Sure."

"You sitting there, it's unsettling."

She reluctantly turns her head just enough to reveal the side of her face. Only when she does her depressed expression shifts into curiosity as she twists her torso to get a better look at me. And even though her mouth is parted, she doesn't say anything. She only looks at me with interest.

If I was nervous before, nothing compares to what's going on behind my chest wall now. It's as if she's just collided into me. I even take a step back I'm so shook by her expression. Because I recognize her, and from the look on her face, she recognizes me too.

With a lifted finger pointed in my direction, she says, "You're that cop."

I tilt my head, taken aback. Her statement confuses me because I thought she was someone I met before I was in law enforcement.

She's turning to face me better and flips her legs around to this side of the ledge. "Yeah," she blinks with more energy behind her voice, "I remember you from the night that…"

She lets her words trail off as she looks down at her hands and twists the ring on her finger.

"Sorry," I say, with a shake of my head. "I'm not tracking." Maybe I've mistaken her for someone else. She has a generically pretty face, even if it is hidden behind that wild, orange hair. And living all over the city metroplex, a guy tends to run into the same looking women more times than not. Especially a guy like me. With a type, and a past.

She's still for a long moment, aside from twisting the ring on her finger as she continues to side eye me. I try to place her, but I meet so many different people every day that they begin to blend together and blur in my memory.

And I'm struggling to focus, simply because she's still on the ledge. It's unnerving. So, I reach my hand out to her. "Do you mind coming down from there?"

With her head still down, she reluctantly takes my hand then hops off the ledge. Flipping around to lean her forearms against the iron tubing, she stares out at the whisps of yellowing clouds in the sky. "You don't remember me, do you?"

I try to recall her now that her feet aren't hovering in mid-air. But I can't for the life of me place her.

She brushes a strand of hair out of her face. "You were the cop that was at my house the night my husband landed himself in jail." Her eyes dart to her shoes as her voice drops, "And me in the hospital."

Suddenly it registers who she is. The flash of that horrendous scene I walked into that night fills my mind. And the disgust and outrage towards her husband returns. "Trinity?" Her name comes out of my mouth with uncertainty.

She nods. "Guilty."

I lean my hip against the ledge, facing her. "I didn't recognize you. That night you were pretty tuned up."

"To say the least," she says, with a short sarcastic laugh.

I immediately regret the delivery of that statement. "That was rude of me to say. I'm sorry."

"No, don't be sorry," she waves her hand then turns to press her back into the ledge. The glow of the setting sun illuminates the back of her hair into an even brighter orange than it already is. "It's true. My social worker wouldn't even let my kids see me because my face was so bad."

When she turns, I recognize the lush green of her eyes staring back at me. Only this time they're not accompanied by the bloodshot red, and instead the whites have returned to their natural pale color.

"How are they?" I say. "Your kids?"

Her voice is grim as she avoids looking at me by turning her face in the opposite direction. "I'd rather not talk about it."

That's enough response to let me know things aren't going well for her or the kids. It sucks. But if she keeps her head up, she'll have them in no time. No judge in their right mind would give a wife-beater his kids back.

"Do you need a ride back into town or anything?"

She shakes her head. "No," shifting as if she's readying herself to hop back up on the edge of the beam again.

I motion towards the sunset. "You're running out of daylight, and I'd feel better knowing you were home." I don't want to admit that I would rather know she was safe than out here in potential risk of running into West Laurel. I'm still baffled he spent less than twenty-four hours in that cell. What he got as punishment was a slap on the wrist. And worse than that, his freedom is a slap in the face for Trinity.

I notice my grip tensing on the beam at the thought of West roaming freely. I draw in a deep breath, relaxing my hand. "Well, if I can't give you a ride, promise you'll get home safely?"

Trinity gives me a halfhearted nod. I wait a beat, hoping she'll change her mind and let me take her home. But she doesn't. She just stares out at the darkening sky. Apparently fixated deeply on her troubled thoughts. And I know they're troubled by the way her brows are pulled so tightly together a deep line has formed between them.

As I begin to descend the hill toward my squad car, I add, "And stay off ledges and other dangerously high places for me, will you?"

She doesn't respond. I don't want to bother her too much, so I don't look back as I continue forward. I'm sure it's taking everything out of her to keep from drifting into a depression right now.

Once I'm back in my squad car, my radio blares. It's about Robby. Again.

I hit the radio button with my thumb. "I told that kid to get home after he washed the dishes."

Chandler's voice chimes in on the other side of the radio. "I'll take care of it."

Part of me wants to head back down to the restaurant and give Robby the stink eye while Chandler escorts him to his squad car. Except I'm certain Robby would be smitten by my reaction and the fact that he gets to ride in a police vehicle.

"*That kid*," I say under my breath, and to no one.

There's a small tap on my passenger's window just before I'm about to put the car into drive. It's Trinity. So I roll the window down.

"Change your mind?" I'm not trying to hide the fact that seeing her come to her senses brings a smile to my face.

She ducks her head down with her arms folded tightly over her chest. "It's scary out here once the sun goes down."

I unlock the door for her. "I don't blame you." I toss my head to the side. "Hop in."

She stands outside the door for a moment with a shifting expression before saying, "But it's also scary getting into a car with a stranger."

"I can understand that. But I'm not a complete stranger." I shift in my seat with one hand rested on the steering wheel and reaching my other hand out to her. "My name is Officer Santino. Knox Santino."

She gives me an uncertain smile. As if she's not committed to getting a ride from me. And I get it, she's been attacked and abused by a cop for who knows how long. I'm sure she's struggling to trust me for being a man and also for being a police officer. I'd be surprised if it wasn't triggering for her.

"I don't know how to convince you that I'm a good cop," I say, pressing my mouth together for a moment and making sure I catch her gaze before continuing, "But the way that I see it, is you have two options." I hold up my index finger. "You can either get in and I'll give you a ride straight home." I raise a second finger. "Or I can follow you while you walk home. And I'll light the way with my headlights for you so you're not walking blind and alone in the dark."

The wide-eyed expression she gives me makes me want to turn away because it reminds me of the way her son looked at me after I found him hiding in the cabinet. The fear West has managed to induce into his family disgusts me. No one should be so afraid of their husband or father that it makes them leery of every other man they encounter.

But I don't look away. And instead, I shrug. "It's your choice, Trinity. But I'm on duty. And, as a police officer, it's my job to make sure you're safe. So, pick one."

There's a distant screech of an animal that makes the choice for her. Without hesitation, Trinity jumps into the passenger's seat and fastens her seatbelt.

I find myself quietly laughing at her response. It's cute. But my laughter quickly ends when I realize how flighty she is and what's caused that innate fight or flight reaction in her.

"Alright," I say. "Let's get you home."

When I begin to drive in the direction of the house that I found her nearly beaten to death in, she shakes her head and points out her window. "This way."

I pause.

With a frown, she continues, "I live in town now."

I flip the car around and head towards town. It's probably better she's not living there anymore. Safer too.

But the place she instructs me to drop her off at doesn't seem like a home at all. It makes sense why her response was accompanied with a frown. And I can't help but fill my voice with disapproval when I say, "You're staying at the motel?"

CHAPTER FIVE

Trinity

November 1997

I gather the dollar bills from the table and fold them into my pocket. I've already spent most of the money my dad gave me on the cost of living. And I'd hate to call him again just to tap into his account. But staying at the motel has proven to be more expensive than I thought. I wish I could crash at a friend's house. But divorce papers have a way of forcing people to choose sides. And I don't have anyone on mine.

I realized I was alone in this situation (the situation I've gotten myself into by being *brave*) every time I've run into his friends and acquaintances at the grocery store. People would rather hide in the adult diaper aisle than be seen conversing with me. They didn't have to say it out loud. I could see it all over their anxious expressions when I tried to talk to them.

The only people who don't see me with a scarlet letter are Sharry, who was able to get me a discount at the motel.

And Knox, who seems to have made it his personal mission to give me a ride any time he's on duty. Which has only been a couple of times. But enough to make me feel uncomfortable. I can't figure out why I don't trust him. It could be his brooding personality or the fact that he's a police officer in the same uniform as West. All I know is that I'd rather avoid his courtesy. I don't want to owe him anything.

I open the door to my motel room and lock it before proceeding across the street to M.L.'s. It's my birthday. And although I might not have any friends in this town and my kids aren't allowed to see me without a social worker in arms reach, I'm still going to celebrate. Even if that means going out for a drink by myself. I'm twenty-one today and I'm going to commemorate this day properly. Even if that means making everyone I know uncomfortable with my presence.

When I reach M.L.'s I'm greeted by the hostess who looks to be my age. Her hair and makeup are perfectly placed, along with her perfectly straight smile. Her name tag says *Candy* and I can't help but wonder if we could have been friends in an alternate universe.

The difficult part about making friends is that no one my age has kids. And the moms with children the same ages as mine are moms that are a decade older than me. It's not their fault that I got pregnant at seventeen. It's just impossible to connect with anyone. And living out of town without a job or transportation for the last five years has isolated me from any attempt I might have made at friendships.

"How many at your table tonight?" Candy says in a friendly manner.

I'm not sure how to answer her. I've only been to M.L.'s once when we were meeting West's parents for dinner. West didn't like their mashed potatoes, so we never came back.

Which eases my conscience about potentially running into him here.

That was in the beginning. When things were easy. When West would open the door for me and keep his hand at the base of my back to ensure everyone knew I was his. I used to think that was a sweet gesture of protection, but now I can only believe it was his way of claiming his possession over me.

"I'll just sit at the bar," I say, unable to admit that I'm alone.

Alone...on my birthday...

When I scan the menu, I quickly realize that I'm going to have to make that call to my dad a lot sooner than I want to. How do people afford to eat out?

"What can I get you to drink," the bartender says with a hint of an accent I'm not familiar with. She's beautiful but has a permanently annoyed expression plastered on her face. As if she has better things to do than serve alcohol to people.

"I'll just have a Blue Moon," I say, trying to sound like I know what I'm ordering.

"Draft or bottle?"

I search her face then settle for, "Bottle." Except the word comes out more as a question although I didn't intend it to.

She doesn't ask for my ID. I'm not surprised. The lack of sleep I've been getting has plagued my eyes with dark circles. And the worry line forming between my eyebrows is deeper than ever since my kids have been with Martha. Not to mention the unwanted rough look of my face since West rearranged it with his hands.

"Anyone sitting here?" The man doesn't wait for me to answer before he places himself on the swivel stool next to me.

"Looks like you are," I say with averseness, as the bartender places my drink on a coaster in front of me.

When I face him, he's giving me *the look* as he tucks his bottom lip into his mouth with his front teeth and drinks me in with his eyes.

That's one thing I didn't have to worry about when I was with West. He'd rather be accused of murder before letting another man look at me in the way this man is doing. Maybe that's why West liked to keep me home to himself. He couldn't stand the thought of another man even knowing about my existence.

The bartender tosses her braid over her shoulder and thrusts a drink in front of him, partially spilling it on his hand. "Stayin' for dinner, Danny?" Except when she says *dinner* it sounds like Fran Fine saying *dinna* from the TV show The Nanny. Although this bartender is more callous when compared to Fran.

He doesn't notice the liquid bubble down his hand. He keeps his eyes on me and licks his lower lip as he adjusts his ball cap. It sends a nauseating surge through my stomach when I catch his silent but obvious signal.

I look away and cover the side of my face with my hand.

"I might," he says to her. Then he leans over onto his crossed forearms and to me, he says, "You want some dinner, Gorgeous?"

I roll my eyes.

Pet names.

I take a drink of my beer and turning only enough to see him in my peripherals, I say, "No thanks. I'll get myself some dinner."

"How about dessert then?" The words slither from his lips.

I nearly jump from my stool when the bartender slaps a menu to the other side of the bar and says, "Move it!" to Danny.

He leans back with his hands raised in surrender. "What'd I do?"

Retrieving the menu from in front of him, she hits him over the head three times. Each thwack seeming more aggressive than the last. Then she places the menu back on the other side of the bar. "She doesn't want you botherin' her, now find a new seat or leave!"

"She can speak for herself."

The bartender flips her head to face me. "Is he botherin' you?"

I can't speak. She's terrifying. But I can tell Danny doesn't have the best intentions, which is also scary for a woman alone at the bar.

She whips her head back to face Danny. "Go," is all she says to him.

He pulls his cap off and runs his hand through his dirty-blond hair before placing the cap back on. "I'm going to Steve-O's," he says with a scowl. "Where the bartenders are nicer to me."

As he turns his back to us, the bartender says, "You mean, where the bartenders are trashier!"

Their banter makes me want to laugh, but I'm a little afraid of upsetting the bartender. So I gulp down my laughter with Blue Moon and close the menu when I realize there's only one thing I can afford.

She takes my menu when I slide it toward her. "What'd you decide on?"

"I'll just have chips and salsa."

She gives me a hard stare without so much as a twitch. Apparently she's unsatisfied with my meal choice; or lack thereof. M.L.'s must be desperate for help because I don't know how someone so impersonable was hired here in the first place.

I shrug. "I'm not that hungry." I don't know why I'm explaining myself to her. She doesn't really seem like a person that needs an explanation. Or cares for one.

She takes the menu, tucks it under her arm and makes her way to the back of the restaurant out of sight.

I try to keep my head down as the restaurant begins to fill with more people. The bartender with the long braid never returns. Instead, an older guy with a ponytail replaces her. He's all business when he hands me my chips and replaces my empty beer bottle with a new one.

I wasn't intending on drinking more than one, but since he already popped the top off and I'm going to have to pay for this, I may as well finish it. I decide that I'm going to nurse this one and make sure he knows I don't want another.

I notice the female bartender return from the back of the restaurant, but she doesn't go behind the bar. I follow her with my eyes, turning in my seat to watch as she heads for the corner of the restaurant with a tray of drinks. Then I realize she's serving a few off-duty police officers from the station. I recognize Chase Chandler with his glasses and Liv Ballard with her blonde hair hanging over her shoulders—it's usually tied back at the base of her neck; with it down she looks even prettier than normal.

There's another man at the table but the bartender serving them is standing in the way. I continue to stare at their table, wondering why West never invited them to his bowling league, or shuffleboard nights at Steve-O's, or BBQs at his parents' house. Practically the entire station showed up to those events.

Suddenly the server leaves their table, and my eyes instantly lock with Knox Santino's curious expression. A shuddered rush of embarrassment invades me. He's slouched back in their corner booth with one arm draped over the back of the seat and his other hand locked around the base of his drink on the table. Seemingly comfortable in his position, but his eyes are anything but comfortable. I'm not sure why I can't look away. Part of his expression looks as if he wants to talk to me and the other part looks as if he feels sorry for me sitting here by myself. Which makes me sort of feel sorry for myself too.

When I'm able to regain some self-control, I pull my eyes from him and take a drink; pretending that I never looked at him at all.

"Miss Trinity Laurel," I turn mid swig, and it causes me to spill some of the carbonated drink down my neck when I see Trent, West's friend. "How you doin', Hunny?" He says this with familiarity as he sits in the empty stool next to me. I'm not sure what it is about that stool, but it seems to have a magnet sewn into the cushion for lonely men.

I shake my head. I can't quite figure out how to answer him. Mostly because I'm not sure what story he's been fed from West. And by the looming expression on his face, I'm not sure it matters.

He gets the bartender's attention and points from me to him and back to me again. Apparently, this is enough information the bartender needs from Trent since the bartender sets two small glasses on the bar and begins to pour a shot for each of us.

"I'm good," I say to Trent, as I scoot the small glass toward him.

He grins and pushes it back in my direction. "Come on, Hunny, it's just one shot."

I look down at the glass of clear liquid. It's probably Vodka. West preferred beer. Or Southern Comfort, but on occasion he'd drink Captain and Coke. I try not to drink anything besides beer and that's only on occasion. The last time I drank Vodka it didn't end well, and six weeks later I took a positive pregnancy test. Nine months after that, Abbi was born.

He pushes the glass in front of me again. "Just one shot." A look of concern spreads down his face. "You look like you need it."

I reach for the glass and pick it up, contemplating on what to do next.

Just one shot. I repeat to myself. *A birthday shot.* My heart and mind are doing that thing again where they're in disagreement with each other. I don't want to regret the night, but I also want to have fun.

It's one shot, then I'll finish my chips and salsa, walk back to the motel, and pay for one more night with the rest of the cash in my pocket.

CHAPTER SIX

Knox

I've been watching Trinity since I noticed her sitting at the bar by herself. I saw Constance shoo off one guy trying to hit on Trinity earlier. But when Constance's shift ended, another man slipped right into the seat next to Trinity. If there's anything I've learned in my life and career, it's that there's nothing that invites trouble more than a woman sitting alone at the bar.

"How about you, Santino? Bringing a date to the Christmas party?" Chandler asks.

I pull my attention from Trinity's drunk laughter and the man's hand on her knee at the bar. "Am I what?"

Chandler and Ballard share a knowing look. Then Chandler says, "Ballard's bringing her husband. I'm taking Stacy. Who's your date to the party?"

I glance at Trinity again. She's stumbling out of her seat as the man braces her arms. They're both in good spirits but something about the guy makes me not trust him. "I'm not going," I say, facing Chandler again.

Ballard leans over the table in my direction. "You have to come," she says with a pleading expression. "The Christmas parties are surprisingly fun. You won't be disappointed."

"I'm good."

"Bring Constance with you." Ballard clasps her hands together like she's praying. "Please, Santino, it'll be your first party with the department."

"I'll think about it."

Chandler raises his drink. "That's what I'm talking about!"

"Don't get your hopes up," I warn. When I look back to check on Trinity, she's not there. I'm assuming she's gone to the bathroom. Then my jaw tightens when I notice the man take something from his pocket, scan the bar for onlookers, then pop a substance into Trinity's beer.

I don't hesitate abandoning Chandler and Ballard's conversation at the table.

As I shuffle around the patrons, Trinity winds the corner and finds her seat at the bar next to the cod that's leached onto her.

"Santino," Chandler says, closing in behind me. "What are you doing?" He must've noticed my shift in demeanor.

I face his concerned expression.

His eyes drift past me just as his concern fades to remorse. "Oh man, that's Laurel's wife, isn't it?"

My shoulders tense at the mention of his name.

"Looks like she's pretty wasted too." He shakes his head as his brows drop to the sides of his face. "Santino, you gotta leave this alone. You don't want to get mixed up in all," he flips his hand, "that."

I turn to make my way to the bar again, ignoring his comment, but Chandler grabs ahold of my shirt.

"Santino…" he says with warning.

With a low voice of urgency, I say, "He roofied her drink."

His mouth parts but nothing comes out. He looks where Trinity's seated then back to me with disgust. "If you're sure."

"I am."

That's all it takes for him to release his grip. "I'll get my cuffs," he says, readying himself to move toward the entrance.

"Call it in and get someone to pick him up."

With one nod, we separate into opposite directions.

Just as I fill the space between Trinity and the guy, she's pressing the bottle to her lips for a drink. But the shock of my presence causes her to stop; hovering the drink in front of her mouth when she sees me.

"Excuse me, Sir," the scum says with a forced grin. "We're tryin' to have a conversation here."

Ignoring him, I take the drink from Trinity's hand.

She twists her face in confused frustration. "Hey," she says, with a delayed swipe of her hand. "Give that back." Her words are drawn out as she delivers them with her hazy gaze.

"It's drugged," I say.

It takes a good five seconds for her to register this information. I'm assuming her delayed response is from intoxication. Then with a slow blink she looks at the guy. "Did you put something in my drink, Trent?"

I finally look at him. "Yeah, *Trent*. I'd love to hear your response to that question too."

At first his eyes are wide with guilt. Then in an instant he lets out a dry chuckle. "Why would I do somethin' like that?" He lifts a hand at Trinity. "Her man's my buddy. I'm just makin' sure she has a good time tonight."

"Some friend you are," I say, swirling the drink while I inspect it. "I'm an off-duty police officer, Trent." He blinks several times when I glance at him, an apparent nervous reaction to my revelation. Looking back at the fizzing pill disintegrating at the bottom of the bottle, I continue with, "Once my partner tests this for drugs, you're going to jail for possession and distribution without an individual's consent. Along with intent to commit a violent crime." I lower the bottle and look at him. "You've just begun a real-life nightmare for yourself, *Trent*."

And just as the words leave my mouth, Trent scurries out of his seat and makes a beeline for the exit. He doesn't make it very far before he's stopped by Chandler and Ballard. They get him in handcuffs before the restaurant even knows what's happening.

Trent is in the back of a squad car just as Trinity decides it's time for her to leave. Only she's having a hard time walking in a straight line.

"Need some help?" I take her arm in mine.

She pulls her arm from me which causes her to stumble. "I can walk myself."

I raise my brow, not that she's looking at me or sober enough to decipher my expression. "I know a back exit. You can save yourself from walking by Trent, and the police… while you're drunk."

She digs in her pocket and pulls out a wad of cash. "I'm not drunk."

"I'm trying to say that I'm not going to write you up, but I can't say you'd get the same treatment from the officers outside. And I don't think public intoxication would look good on a report when you're trying to get your kids back."

She lifts her head to give me a grimaced expression. Her voice is slurred when she says, "Fine. I'll take your *secret* escape after I pay my tab."

I fold my arms over my chest and watch her sway while she fingers through the money she's holding inches from her face.

After a few minutes of her squinting and recounting the bills, she looks up at me and in a soft voice she says, "Can I borrow three dollars?"

I tilt my head and fold my mouth in. Hesitant to help her. It seems enabling. But at the same time, she doesn't strike me as an alcoholic since she's concerned about paying the correct amount on her tab.

She rolls her eyes. "I'll pay you back."

I slowly dig for my wallet in my back pocket. I eye her intently as I reluctantly hand her a five-dollar bill.

"After I find a job that is," she alters, with a swipe of her hand. "I'll pay you back." Stacking her money together, which consists of crumpled ones and the five-dollar bill I just gave her, she makes sure to get Marcos' attention, then pays her bill. She even apologizes to him for skimping on the tip since she didn't have extra cash.

I give Marcos a nod before taking Trinity's elbow in my hand.

"I'm not drunk," she says again, as we round the corner toward the back of the restaurant.

"I'm sure." I open the back entrance and hold the door for her.

Anticipating her struggle down the stairs, I keep my grip on her elbow. And it's a good thing I do since she stumbles at the first step. I instinctively brace her by slipping my hand around her waist.

When she's standing solid on her two feet again—or as solid as she can in her inebriated state—she shifts her heavy gaze up to inspect me. "Maybe I'm a little drunk," she admits.

Her eyes shift down to my mouth as if she's waiting for words from me.

Instead of speaking, I take her elbow again and guide her toward the street. I'm not interested in wasting words on a drunk person who won't remember our conversation in the morning.

It takes about thirty seconds to cross the street to the motel where she's staying.

Before I get a chance to ask her which room she's in, she says, "Do you think I'm a criminal?"

Her question catches me by surprise. "No. At least not a hard-core criminal that I should be concerned about."

She nods and wipes her nose with her thumb. It seems like she's trying to be cool, but her intoxication makes the gesture more amusing than anything.

"No red flags?"

I take a step so I'm standing directly in front of her. "What are you getting at?"

She shrugs. "I may have spent the last of my money on celebrating my birthday instead of paying for my motel room."

I run my hand alongside my jaw as I drop my head back between my shoulders. Wondering how I got myself into the middle of this, but also knowing I couldn't turn a blind eye to her at the bar either.

"Are you mad at me?" Her eyes are partially closed when she says this.

I exhale through my nose. "No..." I say, dragging the word out. I turn to face the motel lobby, contemplating my next move. I could pay for her to stay another night. I quickly shake my head at my own careless thoughts. I need to maintain some sort of boundaries here. Giving her a five-dollar bill to cover her tab is one thing, but paying for her room is way passed crossing the line. "Can I give you a ride somewhere?"

She hums in thought for a moment. "The only people that like me in this town are my kids." She stumbles slightly when she says this, and I find myself instinctively steadying her by sliding my arm around her waist again. When her legs lock into place and her feet are firmly planted against the gravel, I pull my hand back, shoving it into my pocket. But then revert to letting it hang at my side, just in case her knees decide to buckle again.

"Can you call someone? Your parents or a friend nearby?" I'm going into police questioning mode. I can't help it. It's second nature at this point. Plus, I'm not sure how to handle this situation in any other way than a police officer would since I met her while I was on duty. And now that I'm off duty, I don't know if it's appropriate to help her.

"If I had friends nearby, I wouldn't have spent my twenty-first birthday alone."

That fact makes me sad, and I don't know what I'm supposed to do about it. And somehow, I feel like I should know what to do.

She begins pulling at the ring on her finger. "Officer Santino?"

"You can call me Knox." I glance across the street to M.L.'s where I see Chandler and Ballard near the squad car that picked up Trent.

Trinity laughs quietly to herself as she repeats, "Knox," under her breath. Then she inhales sharply to compose herself and looks up at me with overly exaggerated and piercing eyes. "I have to tell you something."

I lift my chin. "And what's that?"

"I'm not a criminal."

"We've established that."

She's squinting now. "Actually, I have to *ask* you something."

"Go for it." I need to remind myself how pointless it is to talk to a drunk person.

"So, since I'm not a criminal, and if I ask to borrow your metal clippers or hack saw, you don't have to worry when you loan them to me." She continues to stare up at me with childlike anticipation.

I raise my brow at her, then glance back at M.L.'s when I hear Ballard call my name.

She's walking toward the street. I feel torn between leaving Trinity standing here by herself, and meeting Ballard. I settle for taking Trinity by her elbow again and guiding her to a picnic table outside the motel.

"Hang tight for a second," I tell her. "I'll be right back." Then I jog across the street to meet Ballard.

Ballard looks concerned when she says, "What are you doing with Trinity Laurel?"

I look over my shoulder at Trinity, she's laying the side of her head on the picnic table. When I face Ballard again, I say, "I'm not sure."

She throws her thumb over her shoulder. "Trent's going to jail."

"Good to know."

She folds her arms and pops her hip out to one side as she gives me a suspicious look.

I lift my chin at her. "What? He deserves jail time."

"Don't you think it's weird that the last couple of encounters we've have with *her* have resulted in some douche-bag going to jail?"

I shrug, not wanting to get into the details of Trinity's personal life. Especially the parts that involve scheming and abusive men.

"She's trouble and has bad taste in guys." Dropping her arms at her sides, along with her voice, she says, "Come on. She's a lost cause."

I drag my breath in, realizing I'm going to have to reason with Ballard about my decision to help Trinity. "It's her birthday," I say this as if it's justification for this entire situation.

She drops her brow and narrows her gaze. Apparently not accepting my reasoning as sufficient.

It's quiet for a moment before I continue with, "And she doesn't have enough money to pay for her room tonight."

Ballard's mouth falls open as an exhale full of disbelief bursts out, filling the space between us with dense exasperation.

"She's having a bad night." I look intently into Ballard's eyes to tell her, without words, that Trinity just needs a little help. And I look at her more intently to let her know that I'm the one offering Trinity that help.

Ballard tilts her head. "You're not serious."

I begin to back away from her with the same unfazed expression I've had on my face since our conversation started. "We're police officers. Sometimes we gotta help people when they can't help themselves."

"Santino, come on. You're not even on duty." She throws her hands up when I continue leisurely retreating towards Trinity. "Fine. Don't say I didn't warn you."

I give her a wave as I backpedal to the picnic table.

"I'm not bailing you out if you end up in jail," she calls out to me when she's on the other side of the street again. But

I ignore her attempt at humor. Mostly because I know Trinity heard what she said.

When I meet Trinity at the picnic table, she lifts her head then drops it into her hand. "Liv doesn't like me."

I don't acknowledge her comment and instead move the conversation in a different direction. "Why don't I take you somewhere safe to stay and you can tell me why you need a saw."

"Or metal clippers will do."

I slip my grip around her hand and lift her to her feet. "What do you plan on doing with metal clippers anyway?"

She lifts the back of her other hand so close to my face that I feel as if I've gone cross-eyed.

"I need something to get this ring off my finger."

I don't know why that makes me smile, but it does. And I don't try to hide the emerging grin on my face as we make our way to my truck. "I know a better, more humane way to get that thing off."

"Is this your house?" Trinity says, staring at Constance's modest home that's painted the same color as a school bus. Not that anyone could tell at this time of night.

I point above the garage to where the porch light is illuminating the stairs leading up to my front door. "I live up there. But we'll have to go inside the house first to get what we need to pop that ring off your finger."

She lets out a sigh and continues to stare out her window in thought. I take this opportunity to get out of my truck, walk around to her side and open the door for her.

She follows me to the entrance and begins to say something as I open the door. But the last thing I need is for Constance to wake up right now, so I flip around and press my finger to my lips. "You have to be quiet," I say in a low voice. "She's sleeping."

Trinity nods, and in a whisper says, "Got it." Pretending to zip her lip, lock it, and toss an imaginary key behind her.

I ignore her juvenile gesture and quietly open the door. The house is silent aside from the box fan whirring in Constance's bedroom. I lift my hand, stopping Trinity from following me. "Stay right there." Then I stride into the kitchen and find the junk drawer. I sift through pens, loose change, and other odd ends as quietly as I possibly can, until I find some thread.

When I spin around to leave, the light flicks on and Constance is standing in the living room, tucking her robe around herself tightly.

Constance's mouth falls open as her brows drop down to the sides of her face in alarm. "What the hell?" She thrusts her hand in Trinity's direction, as she faces me. "I told you *not* to meet a girl at the bar, Zio."

"Zio?" Trinity repeats, looking at me for an explanation.

With my exhale, I say, "It's a nickname." Then to Constance I say, "We'll just be a minute."

Fire flares behind Constance's widening eyes. "You will not hook up with some blonde bimbo in this house, Zio. Have you lost your damn mind, or did ya have one too many drinks at the bar?"

Trinity's expression is sobering as she corrects Constance's assumption. "Whoa, we're not…doing…*that*."

I approach Constance. "It's not what you think."

"You know what?" She lifts her hands, keeping me from coming any closer. "I don't care to know what this is. Just take whatever you're *not* doing out of my house." She shakes her head and returns to her bedroom, aggressively flicking the light off and muttering something I can't make out as she disappears into her room.

I instruct Trinity to follow me as we exit the house and head up the stairs to my apartment. She seems more alert when we make our way inside. I hang my keys on the hook and lean against the counter as Trinity inspects the small space. She scans the couch facing the TV, then looks past the bathroom door. Craning her neck to see my bed on the far side of the large room. As she turns her torso to face the kitchen, her eyes meet mine.

"You've got more pillows on your bed than I do in my entire house."

I don't respond, mostly because she catches me off guard with her observation.

"Nice place though." Her statement is bent with sarcasm as she folds her hands in front of herself. "It's more stale than the motel room I'm living in. Do you not believe in decorating?"

I shrug at her comment. "It gets the job done."

I offered my couch to her on the way here and she seemed more than happy to accept. But now that we're in the apartment, there's something apprehensive about her. As if she's unsure what to do with herself. I know what to do with a woman in my apartment. I have no problem feeling comfortable in that area. But with this specific woman—with Trinity—I don't have a damn clue how to handle this.

She chews on the inside of her cheek for a moment before she finally makes eye contact and says, "You have an interesting relationship."

I cock my head to the side, confused.

"You and the bartender." She lifts her hands then clasps them together. "Friends with benefits sort of thing?"

I point to the wall in the direction of the house and raise one brow at her assumption. "Constance?"

She shrugs. "By the way you two were acting, I just assumed there's something there."

"Constance is my niece."

Her eyes narrow with confusion. "How is she your niece? She looks the same age as you." She gives me a look of anticipation.

"How old is that?"

She shakes her head. "I don't play guessing games."

I let my smile grow as I let her statement sink in, then, "She's twenty-one and I'm twenty-three."

Tipping her head to the side, she says, "How is that possible?"

I begin to unravel the thread in my hand. "We come from a big family. Lots of brothers and sisters and cousins. Growing up, our families were always together. So cousins were more like siblings. And young nieces were more like opinionated, bossy, little sisters." I glance at her. "Most Italian families are like that."

A hint of a smile hits the side of her mouth. "I guessed you were Italian."

I raise my brow with interest. "What made you think that?"

She laughs to herself and looks me up and down. "You! The way you talk, along with your neck tattoos. It screams Italian mobster."

"I'm not anything close to a mobster." The comment stings, but I shake her assumptions and circle back to our previous conversation. "Constance is my oldest sister's daughter."

"*Oldest sister's…daughter.*" She repeats, trying to make sense of the jumbled family tree.

"I was a surprise for my parents when they were nearing retirement. And Janice, my older sister, had kids when she was young."

"I can understand that." She nods. "And where did the nickname come from?"

I take a few steps away from her so I'm on the other side of the counter in the kitchen. "She didn't want to call me uncle." I take a glass and fill it with water at the sink. "She never got used to calling me Knox either." I hand her the glass. "But once she called me Zio, it sort of stuck. It's the Italian word for *uncle*."

Trinity's smiling with only her eyes as she sips at the glass of water. "*Zio* has a better ring to it than *uncle*."

I let out an airy laugh at the way she says my nickname. Then I wave her over to me. "Let me see that ring."

She takes a few steps closer to me, placing her petite hand in mine. She seems less jumpy than the last few times I've seen her. I'd like to think it's because she's comfortable, but a more accurate assumption would be that it's from the alcohol.

I lift her hand, inspecting the ring as I spin it, trying to gently loosen it by pulling it up toward the knuckle. It doesn't budge. I can't figure out how she ever got it on to begin with. It's suffocating her finger. Then I notice the inside of her palm looks as if she held her hand over a fire. The skin is disfigured and laced together tightly with strange bumps and discoloration.

I'm about to ask her what happened when she says, "I've tried everything." I turn her hand, palm down, and begin to thread the string between her finger and ring. "Dish soap…"

It takes me a minute to finally weave the string through and wrap it around the ring. When she doesn't elaborate on her lingering statement, I say, "Dish soap is *everything*?"

Her mouth falls to one side in a grin. "Well, I thought about cutting it off until you started wrapping this piece of string around my finger." Inspecting her hand, she narrows her gaze at the woven thread. "What *are* you doing?"

I gently pull on the string, making sure it's wrapped snuggly around her finger in a perfect spiral. "I learned this when I was in the academy. A lot of guys get married on a whim, then divorced within a few months. I guess not everyone is cut out for long distance relationships." I shift the ring back and forth, up to her knuckle. "Wrapping the thread like this shrinks the finger enough for the ring to slide right off." At that, I slip the ring over her thread-wrapped knuckle and the ring glides off, hitting the stone tile with a ping sound.

She leans down and picks it up. "Where's the garbage?"

I nod my head in the direction of the kitchen. "Under the sink."

She quickly finds the cupboard and tosses the ring in the trash as if it were a snake ready to strike her. When she closes the cupboard, she keeps her eyes fixed on the place where she just abandoned her ring.

"Having second thoughts?" I say, not understanding how anyone would want to stay with a guy that hurts them in the debilitating way West did to her.

"No." She glances up at me, then back to the cupboard for a moment. Pulling her mouth to one side, she says, "How much do you think I could get if I pawned it?"

With my laughter, I say, "I'll pay you whatever you want if you leave it in the garbage."

Shrugging it off, she meets me on the other side of the counter again. She's tracing her finger with her other hand, rubbing at the small dents left in her skin as the thread unravels. "Thanks for doing that." We're both watching as the thread gracefully falls to the counter. "It was the best birthday present I've got all day." And since I know what she's up against in this town, it's probably the only birthday present too.

She hasn't pulled her gaze from her finger. I can see the deep groove in her skin at the base of her finger where the ring was stuck for however many years she was married to West. I wouldn't be surprised if West bought it three sizes too small just so she wouldn't be able to get it off.

"I actually have another gift for you."

When she glances up at me, she looks hesitant as if she doesn't trust me. "I think I've done enough birthday celebrating." Her tone is serious.

I can tell she's misunderstanding me. So I smile, and motion toward the door. "Don't worry, you're going to like it. I promise."

When I open the door, she takes it from me and says, "After you." I give her a suspicious look. "I don't know where we're going."

"Fair enough." I file down the stairs, then walk toward the back of the house.

But once we're in the darkness, she grabs my arm with both her hands and stops me. "Wait." It's so dark I'm not sure what her expression is doing, but her voice sounds unnerved and slightly fearful.

I gently unclasp her hands from my upper arm. "You know you can trust me."

"Can I though?" Her statement comes out faster than I can register it.

My initial reaction to her comment is defensive. I'd like to remind her that I'm a trusted police officer. But then I remember she was married to a police officer, and he treated her so great that she just chucked the ring he gave her into my trashcan without so much as shedding a tear.

I'm going to need to slow down if I want to gain her trust. "Wait here," I say. "I'll be right back."

I can't tell if she nods, but I do notice she stays standing in place.

When I reach the backyard gate, I let out a quick whistle. Then I hear padding across the grass in the yard. I open the gate once Sugar reaches me, and she lets out an excited bark. "Come on, girl," I say, patting my leg to encourage her to follow me.

At first, when she notices Trinity standing near the garage, Sugar lets out another bark. But this one is with warning. Then almost as immediately as she lets the bark out, her behavior shifts with one sniff of the air, and she rushes to Trinity with enthusiasm.

Their embrace is unmatched.

They're a complete commotion of laughter, tail wagging, nuzzling, licking, and petting. It's the most wholesome thing I've seen in a while.

There's something about my job that makes life seem exceptionally depressing. The only time I'm contacted, is when I'm needed to fix a problem. Or rescue someone. Or detangle a disaster. This line of work can change a person's perspective of humanity. When all you see are tragedies and problems, it starts to make you lose hope in people.

But a woman reconnecting with her dog after months of separation, makes up for all the recent negativities. It's these small, positive, encounters that keep me going. And stop me from quitting.

Once Sugar finally settles enough for Trinity to stand, she says, "Thank you," to me, with a sincere expression.

I give her a subtle smile with my nod. If she can't spend her birthday with her family, this is the least I can do.

With a returned grin, she says, "Best birthday present ever."

CHAPTER SEVEN

Trinity

I roll away from the sunlight peeking in through the blinds. Only when I do, I'm met by the wet nose of Sugar and her soft whimper. It's the kind of whimper she makes when she needs let out to relieve herself.

"Alright," I say, shifting myself upright so that I'm seated on the sofa with my feet resting against the cold floor. "Ready to go outside?"

She jumps to the floor with the word *outside*. Her claws make a ticking sound as she pads over to the door, wagging her tail with excitement.

When my eyes and brain catch up with each other, I remember that I'm still in Knox's studio. I vaguely remember Knox leaving in the night. When I scan the apartment, I notice his bed is made but every one of his countless pillows are missing. I'm not sure where he stayed, but it wasn't here.

The night seems to unravel in choppy unconnected moments. Flashing in my mind like polaroids from a scrapbook. The bar. Knox and Chase arresting Trent. Knox's truck. The ring finally escaping from my finger. Sugar falling asleep at my feet. The last thing I remember was Knox handing me an Aspirin and making sure I drank a full glass of water before he tucked me in on his sofa bed.

I slip my shoes on. Taking Sugar down the steps, across the yard, and through the gate to the backyard where Knox retrieved her last night. Sugar knows exactly where she's going and seems in no hurry to leave after she's finished her business. She's found a stick and has begun running from one end of the yard to the other with it clenched between her teeth.

I notice myself with a smile on my face that feels natural and familiar, but it fades when I realize how much happier she is here without me. It reminds me that she's not the only one I've abandoned recently. I just hope Abbi and Tuck aren't as happy in their lives without me as Sugar is. And I'm not sure if that sort of thought is wrong or not.

"She's easily entertained, isn't she?" Constance leans her arms on the top of the gate, watching Sugar rush past the swing hanging from the big oak tree.

I don't bother faking a smile at her comment since she's not looking at me. "Better than becoming depressed."

When she flips her head to face me, her braid swings against her back in haste. Obviously unimpressed by my negative remark. I wait for the urban Italian accent to roll off her tongue. But there's nothing except a growing uncomfortableness inside of my stomach.

"Sorry. I didn't mean it like that," I say, averting my eyes from her troubled expression. "It's just...I thought Sugar would be more impacted by my absence, and the kids' absences. At the very least, I thought she'd miss us." I toss my hand flippantly. "But she seems happier than ever."

Constance doesn't miss a beat when she delivers her statement with a wounding stab. "You don't think she was sad?"

I swallow my thoughts down and hug my arms around myself with regret. The apparent disappointment in her voice has me rethinking my initials thoughts about Sugar.

Standing up straight, Constance grasps one hand around the metal fence intensely. "She was *devastated.*" She looks up into the clouds, lets out a sharp stunned laugh, then adds, "If you think she's happier here, think again. Because this is the happiest I've seen her since Knox brought her here. Before today, she'd sit there," she points to the corner of the yard. "And if she wasn't there, she was sitting at my back door waiting for Knox to get home and take her on a walk. Or feed her. Or play with her. And even then, she didn't get as excited as she is now." She faces me again, but this time her frustrated expression is replaced with remorse. "She *missed* you."

This doesn't make me feel better. It makes me feel worse. I didn't tell Constance that Sugar seemed happier because I was jealous, I was glad Sugar was happy. I was relieved she wasn't scared or worried about us. But now that I know she's been alone and wondering what happened to us, I feel incredibly guilty.

I look down at my dingy Nikes. "I'm sorry, I didn't mean to pawn her off on you like this."

When I glance up at her, she shakes her head slowly. I'm not sure if she's annoyed by me or my comment. Or *both.*

"I'll take her off your hands as soon as I can. But I don't have a home right now." I shrug. "Maybe my dad can take her since she's been a bother to you." A defeated breath rushes out of my throat. "I just feel like I'm stuck right now, and all my energy is focused on getting my kids back. And my husband…" I roll my eyes. "Soon-to-be ex-husband, isn't making it any easier."

It's quiet for a long moment. Constance is staring at me, but I pretend I can't see her in my peripherals. From the last two encounters I've had with her, I've gathered that she's intense and never smiles. As if she's in a permanent mood that causes her expression to be in a constant state of annoyance.

When I finally look at her, she says, "Did he do that?" She's pointing at the place where stitches recently held my face together.

Without breaking eye contact, I give her a short, but heavy, nod.

Finally, with a gentle, but still firm voice, she says, "I get it."

When I blink in place of using words, she nods at me with her chin raised in my direction.

"Sugar's welcome to stay as long as you need her to."

I exhale as my mouth falls agape. Stunned. I wasn't expecting her to *want* to keep Sugar any longer. Especially since she made it clear that Sugar misses me. And made it clear that she doesn't care for me. Not that I blame her. My first impressions haven't given her a very accurate depiction of the person I really am. Which is *not* a drunk that couch surfs until she's sober.

"Thank you," I say with appreciation. "Really."

She purses her lips with her tense expression. "Just show up and take care of her, would ya? It would help Knox out. Along with makin' sure she's taken care of. He stops by during his shift and checks in on her. It's not a burden but it's a lot for him and his schedule."

"I will," I reassure her. "And thank you for this."

She finally releases her grip from the fence and begins to walk toward her house. "Don't mention it." Then she stops and stands still for a moment before punching the side of her fist into her palm. When she turns around, she looks as if she's having a battle within herself.

When she finally figures out what to say, her voice is low and penitent. Opposite of the loud, fast paced way she was talking before. It's as if she doesn't want to own the words. "And if you need a place to stay. I've got an extra bedroom."

I blink and shake my head. As tempting as her offer is, I say, "Thank you, but I couldn't put you out like that." And I couldn't. I haven't even explored the option of staying with Martha. Or maybe West could stay with his parents while I go back to our house until we can figure out what we're doing with the custody of our kids. I'd rather have my own place. But in order to rent anything I'd have to get a job and support myself. Which I want to do, especially so I can prove I deserve my kids. It's just been difficult finding someone who will hire me since West has managed to stick a bug in the ear of every business owner in town.

Most people think what he did was self-defense because that's what he's been saying. No one would fathom that someone like West could ever hurt a woman. Most people think he's a hero because he's trying to salvage our marriage and raise our children. He's fooled everyone. And he's turned me into the villain. I'm still trying to figure out how I'm supposed to compete with his charm.

Constance nods once. She begins to say something, but her voice is drowned out by the sound of Knox's blue truck approaching.

When he backs up in front of the garage, he gives us a nodding gesture as a greeting before cutting the engine.

Chase is in the passenger's seat, which is closest to us. He throws his hand up with a wave in our direction.

I smile politely, but I don't return the wave since I'm not sure if his pleasant motion was intended for me.

Chase makes his way over, cleaning his glasses with the bottom of his shirt before greeting me, then Constance. While Knox gets to work opening the garage door to retrieve what look to be buckets of paint.

Constance crosses her arms and mimics the strength in Chase's straight stance. "When are you two going to paint my house?" she asks with cynicism.

Chase lets out a fake laugh at Constance. "I'm only doing this for Knox because he helped me build my deck."

"I helped you stain it." She's inviting him to retaliate.

"And I fed you barbecue."

"And I introduced you to Stacy."

Chase adjusts his glasses with a gentle chuckle. "And I am eternally grateful."

Tossing a shovel into the truck bed, Knox glances at Constance. "Leave him alone." Then to Chase he says, "Come on, help me load these two-by-fours so we can get back out there before it starts raining."

Constance ignores Knox and instead narrows her eyes at Chase. Leaning closer to him she says, "You owe me," before flipping around and heading inside her house.

Chase cups his hands around his mouth before calling out to her. "I do not owe you! You owe me! I fed you barbeque!" Then he looks up at the sky, mutters something about how it's not going to rain, then gives me a polite and slightly awkward smile before loading up the rest of the supplies from the garage with Knox.

I'm not sure what I'm still doing here. I should be calling my father for more financial assistance. Or calling Sharry to figure out where I can get some clothes to wear for court tomorrow. Or doing literally anything else other than standing here watching these two outcast police officers load supplies into the back of Knox's truck.

As I begin to turn around, Knox's voice hits the side of my head. "Need a ride somewhere?" Even though he and Constance grew up together, it's interesting that his accent is less apparent than hers.

His question causes Chase to stop what he's doing and watch for my response. Seemingly uncomfortable at the thought of me tagging along.

"I'm good." I toss my hand in the opposite direction of where his truck came from. "I was going to walk."

Knox rests his bent arm on his blue pickup truck and leans his hip into the tailgate. "Oh, yeah?" The t-shirt he's wearing exposes all his tattoos. I can even detect how his entire chest and torso were used as a canvas since his shirt is white. Not to mention it's nearly see-through; faintly revealing all the permanent-ink images that have been etched into his skin.

"Yep, I don't mind walking." My grin is a stiff line that's trying to hide my lie. Well, it's not necessarily a *lie*. I could walk in any direction and eventually wind up at the same place in this town. And since I don't know where I'm going, I could be heading in the direction I just motioned toward.

He dips his head and gives a small nod. "What's that way?"

I stumble over my words when I say, "There's...a...place..."

I don't know why, but my lacking statement causes the stubble on his face to shift as a smile lifts in the corner of his mouth. As if he senses I don't have a clue where I'm going. "Come on." He pushes himself from his truck and opens the door for me. "I'll give you a ride."

CHAPTER EIGHT

Knox

I bought my pickup truck last year before Constance and I packed up and moved to Mount Vernon. I wanted to start fresh with a practical vehicle. And I liked the color.

It's a single cab Ford F-150 with brand new tires. And because it's a standard with a bench seat, Trinity is sitting between me and Chandler with a leg on each side of the gear stick. And since there's no AC, and I haven't acclimated to the weather, the windows are down, and Trinity's discolored hair is blowing all over the place.

When I reach over to shift into third, she stiffens subtly. I purposely contort my arm to ensure that I don't touch her leg because I can tell she's worried I might.

She's different from last night. More quiet and uncomfortable. Like the fight-or-flight has returned to her sobered senses.

Chandler clears his throat. "Mind if we grab something to drink real quick?"

I nod and turn my blinker on before cautiously reaching over Trinity's leg again before shifting down. "Yeah, I need to fill up the tank too. Wanna pick something up at the gas station?"

"Yep, that works."

Trinity bunches her hair between her hands. Pulling it over one shoulder. Then she says, "I'm getting out at the gas station."

I glance at her. "You figure out where you were headed?"

Without looking at me she nods. "I'm getting a job," she bites at her upper lip before she adds, "at the gas station."

"Convenient." I don't press her further on her lie. It bothers me that she's lying, but I can understand why she's doing it. She's probably learned to lie for her own safety. And lying to stay alive is something no one should be judged for.

When I pull up to the gas pump, Trinity's leg begins bouncing. I don't think much of it. I'm sure it's a reaction to her awareness that she's on the outskirts of town and going to have to backtrack a mile on foot to wherever she *really* needs to go. But that's her choice.

"Want somethin' while I'm in there?" Chase says to me, leaving the door ajar for Trinity to exit.

"Grab a Pepsi for me." I look at Trinity. "You need anything?"

She shakes her head. "I'm good."

I hand Chandler a dollar and he heads inside.

I'm trying not to pay much attention to Trinity since she's still seated inside the truck. But when I notice the subtle movement of the truck rocking, I lock the lever of the gas pump in place. Letting it continue fueling as I lean my forearms against the open window to peer in at her and the unsettled state she's in.

Her shoulders jerk when I do this. Apparently startled. She glances at me, then back to her reflection in the rearview mirror as she runs her fingers under her eyes, removing the black makeup residue. "You wouldn't happen to have a brush, would you?" she says, combing her fingers through her hair.

I raise one brow. "I don't own a brush."

"It was worth a try." She drops her hands to her lap when she faces me. "I'm about to cut it off anyway."

My eyes run down the length of her long hair. I'm not sure who dyed her hair that way, but they should be fired. The bottom half is bright orange and splotchy while the top is the same color as a raven. So black that when the sun hits it right, like it's doing now, it shines blue. "You wanna get rid of the blonde, or what?"

She shrugs. "Yeah. Think I would look okay with short hair?"

Her dark roots have grown out enough she could pull it off. "Yeah, I think you'd look great."

She blinks with her smile. Then it falls. "Sorry about last night. I rarely ever drink. And when I do, I don't drink as much as I did." Her expression shifts to remorse, then she quickly pulls her gaze from mine and presses her hands down the length of her hair. Flattening it. "And thank you for making sure I didn't leave with Trent. I don't know what I was thinking going out last night."

It's interesting she looked away before admitting that. "It's fine. It was your birthday. You shouldn't have to spend your birthday alone if you don't want to." I raise one brow. "Just do me a favor and make sure you're in the midst of welcomed company next time."

Glancing at me, she pauses for a moment. Then she shifts to face me better. "Why do I feel like you're always asking for favors when I see you?"

I shift my head from side to side. "I like giving suggestions. It gives me peace of mind, especially with my job."

"It's not half bad advice." She turns to look out the windshield as a car exits the gas station. "And thanks for taking care of my dog. I'll make sure to come by and take care of her more. I don't want you to end up resenting her for pulling you away from work."

"It's no problem at all." I rub at the back of my neck. Hesitant to tell her why I took on the responsibility of keeping her dog in the first place. "I did promise your kids I'd take care of her until they were back home."

She swings her head to face me, and her mouth is parted as if she's about to speak. But the gas pump clicks off, interrupting her. I drop my arms from the window to take the nozzle and replace it at the pump.

I speak up, making sure she can hear me from where I'm standing outside the truck. "You know you can trust me," I say, feeling for my wallet in my back pocket. "I know you're dealing with a lot right now, but you don't have to do it all on your own. And you can tell me the truth, no matter what." I'm talking to her through the window again. "Listen, nothing you tell me could shock me. I've seen it all."

She's making her way out of the truck, but she pauses when her shoes meet the pavement. "Trust," is all she says. And when she does say it, it sounds like she's repulsed by the word.

"Yeah, it's what friends do. They trust each other. And right now, it kinda seems like you could use a friend that you can trust." We're talking across the cab, me through the window and her on the passenger's side with the door open.

She lets out a humored laugh, shaking her head. "Trust is a gamble."

I draw my head back and fold my arms over my chest. "How so?"

"Trust is a bet you make with a stranger before you even know them. What's the point in gambling on people if you know they're going to eventually disappoint you?"

"I disagree with that completely." I can't imagine what she's been through to make her shell herself up so tightly that she's afraid to make a friend.

She closes the passenger's side door and gives me a sincere expression as she faces me. "Thanks for the ride."

"That's what friends are for," I say with an inviting grin.

She responds by slowly shaking her head with a concealed smirk.

With a grin, I take a step backwards towards the gas station entrance. "Will you still be here when I get back?"

Her mouth shifts to the side reluctantly. "Probably not."

"You don't really have an interview at the gas station, do you?"

She shakes her head. "No. Not today anyway." She begins slowly walking backwards in the direction we came from when she lifts her arms. "Who knows, I might be behind that counter taking your money next time you need fuel or a Pepsi."

I give her a final wave before pressing through the entrance door. "See you around, Trinity."

When I'm inside, I make my way around a chip stand to where Chandler is.

Tossing a Pepsi at me, he says, "Let's go, I got it." He's motioning for us to go back out to the truck.

I twist the lid off the bottle to take a drink. "Quit doing that."

"What?" His proud grin spreads across his face. "Being a good friend?"

"I must be a terrible friend since I've never paid for your fuel."

He shrugs with his short laughter. "I'd make you pay for my fuel, but you always wanna drive your truck." Then he begins to take a drink of his Mountain Dew. But just as he's about to take a drink, he slowly brings the bottle down as his expression shifts into confusion. His eyes are squinting behind his glasses as he peers out the window behind the clerk.

I turn to see what he's looking at just as I hear a familiar engine rev.

Before he can speak, I've already knocked over the chip stand on my way out of the gas station.

I can't believe what I'm seeing.

Trinity is peeling out of the parking lot in a less than smooth manner, grinding through each gear until she gets up to speed.

CHAPTER NINE

Trinity

My hands are shaking with my thudding pulse that's made its way up into my throat, constricting my airway.

When I glance up at the rearview mirror, Knox is behind me in a full out sprint down the road. The truck jerks forward after I hit the clutch and shift gears again. Then as I continue forward, Knox gets smaller and smaller in the mirror until I can't see him at all.

I wish I could tell him I'm not a felon stealing his truck. I wish I could tell him to just wait at the gas station for five minutes. Because all I need is five minutes to hide and then I'll return his truck back to him.

I need five minutes to disappear because if I don't, West will see me.

And since I'm not certain that West didn't see me, I need to disappear before he finds me and uses whatever manipulation tactic he's conjured up on me.

There's no doubt that if I'm around him again, it will make it so much harder to go through with the divorce. And right now, I don't trust myself to be firm. To not give in again. Not because I want to be with him, but because I miss my kids, and my house, and financial security, and normalcy. Even if our normal wasn't always healthy. And I would be lying if I said any part of this process was easy.

Truthfully, this process is exhausting and overwhelming. And I would do almost anything to end it. Even if that means going back to the life I desperately left.

I drive faster, away from the gas station. Hoping West didn't follow me.

I turn down a side street until I'm heading down a gravel road where the houses are dispersed, and the trees are thick. Then I quickly take another turn. But I'm going so fast the tires begin to slide and the truck feels as if it's fishtailing across the road. I instinctively slam on the brakes, but I forget to press on the clutch, so the truck jerks several times before it comes to a complete stop and shuts off.

The dust the tires kicked up rushes past me in a whooshing gust before barreling in through the open windows. And all I can do is grip the steering wheel as I try to catch my breath.

As I sit in the stillness, the gravity of what I've just done begins to weigh on me. My thoughts race in my mind as I try to figure out how I'm going to explain that what I've done is not a crime or a big deal.

Afterall, Knox was just offering me his friendship.

Right?

And friends sometimes borrow their friend's pickup truck for emergencies.

Right?

And I would categorize this situation as an emergency. How else was I going to get away fast enough before West saw me?

RIGHT?

Or maybe I should have thought this through better. It seemed like the only option I had at the time. I couldn't even think. Like my brain was overridden by my instincts to get out of sight without pausing for a better option to unfold.

I finally start the ignition and get the truck turned around to head back to the gas station where I left Knox running after me. Or running after his *borrowed* truck.

In the time it takes me to get back, I come to the conclusion that this was a very bad idea. And when I drive up to the gas station and see Knox and Chase talking to Liv in her patrol car, I realize that this is much worse than I expected. Surely he won't send me to jail after I explain my reasoning behind taking the truck. Jail time is the last thing I need right now, and Knox knows it.

I hit the curb when I pull up to the parking space next to the police car. And all it does is make me feel even more stupid about what I've done.

"What the hell was that?" Knox is swinging the truck door open. "Have you lost your damn mind?"

I pull the key from the ignition and begin to slide out of the driver's side. "I'm sorry. I wasn't thinking."

He opens his hand, palm up, for me to drop the keys into. His hazel eyes are locked on mine with an expression full of disappointment. "Clearly," is all he says before facing the sound coming from the other side of the gas station.

Liv yells out to him from her open window. "Should I still call this one in?"

Knox lifts his hand as if telling her he's not going to press charges.

Thankfully.

But I can't even be happy about it because of the loud popping sound that makes my heart jolt up into my throat. And I'm pretty sure my soul just left my body. Because the sound is coming from a motorcycle, and one with a distinct clank to the engine that I've heard a hundred times. I thought in the matter of time I was away from the gas station that he would have left by now.

Then, the thing happens again. The thing where suddenly my body is doing something before my brain can decide if it's an acceptable option or not.

And just like that, I've climbed over the side of Knox's truck and curled myself between two buckets of primer and a stack of wooden beams.

Knox is peering down at me with bewilderment as the motorcycle nears us. He tosses his arms in the air and he's about to say something when he looks back over his shoulder at the approaching clanking sound and popping rev of the engine.

Then he faces me again.

Only this time his expression is full of apprehension, as if he's telling me that my instincts made the right choice for once and I should stay hidden.

When the engine stops, *his* voice makes my body go cold.

"Hey, Ballard," West says with interest. When I don't hear her acknowledge him, he moves on to Chase. "Chandler." There's a brief pause before he continues with, "How's the station running without me?"

"Fine," Chase says with a monotone.

"Better than fine," Knox interjects with a haphazard laugh. But it only lasts a moment before shifting to a more serious tone. "And if you're asking me, it's running so well without you that I'd never bring you back if I was Chief."

West's voice is stern. "Well you're not Chief. And no one asked you."

Liv quickly chimes in with, "Laurel, do you mind? We were in the middle of something here." She must exit her police car because I hear the door shut and her short steps approaching.

"Oh, yeah?" West says, apparently intrigued. "And what did I interrupt between the three stooges?" He's called them that before. Never to me, but I'd overheard him on the phone or in conversation with the other officers. But all those times, I didn't know who he was referring to until now.

"Nothing that concerns you," Knox says with assurance.

I can barely hear Chase when he says, "Santino, don't."

The sound of West's boot kicking the bike stand down, and crunching gravel under heavy footsteps makes me shrink. I tighten my arms around myself, knowing it won't hide me if he does decide to approach the truck and look over the side of the tailgate. But it's the only form of comfort I can give myself in this moment. That, and closing my eyes as tight as possible. Like a child pretending to disappear. Maybe if I can't see him, he won't see me either.

West's voice is low, but his words leave his mouth with an upward inflection like he's trying to conceal how irate he is. "Didn't I say, no one was asking you? Who put you in charge anyway? Ballard's the only one of us on duty and with any sort of authority right now."

"I'm telling you what I think despite being asked or not. And right now, I think you should be on your way." Knox isn't using the same low voice as West. Instead, his voice is solid and assured. "Or does your shoulder need a reminder of who's in charge?"

West cracks out a short laugh. It's one I recognize, and it's not good. He uses this kind of laugh when he's been challenged. It's happened many times before. Especially when he feels challenged by a confident man. And he *hates* when someone insults his ego, especially by belittling him. Like Knox just has.

I can tell West is gritting his jaw when he says, "I know she was driving your truck. She's never been good at driving stick. And I know she went home with you too."

I should have known Trent would tell him about last night. He probably had West bail him out of jail too. Apparently, Trent failed to mention the part of the night where he was trying to drug me.

The awareness of the fact that West knows I've been within ten feet of another man is terrifying to me. But I'm horrified that he's assuming I slept with Knox. And I can tell he thinks this by the way he delivers his statement with jealousy and pure rage.

I wish I could warn Knox. I wish I could unfreeze and do something to stop this entire situation.

Instead of diffusing the situation like he should, Knox mocks West with, "Like *I* said," there's a dangerous shift in his voice, "it doesn't concern you."

"Go to hell, Santino! She's *my* wife!"

"I don't think that's true after last night when I helped her—"

Before Knox finishes his statement, I hear what sounds like a scuffle but it lasts about two seconds before Liv has Knox pushed against his truck. And Chase must be preventing West from escalating, because I can hear him threatening West to leave before he gets sent back to jail for assaulting an off-duty officer.

There's a lot of intense breathing and throat clearing. Then West is back on his bike when he says, "You can all go to hell. And good luck keeping your jobs after today." He spits at the ground, then revs his bike with aggression. Several small pebbles hit the side of Knox's truck. A few manage to find their way inside the truck bed, hitting me too.

Chase takes a step toward Knox where I can see his reluctant expression. "Did you really need to exaggerate about last night?" He's referring to the statement Knox didn't get to finish before scrapping with West.

Knox's back is toward me. He lifts one hand, dragging it down the back his head until it rests at the base of his neck, where he begins massaging it. With the release of his discontented exhale, he says, "I was going to tell him I helped her unwedge the ring that he left stuck on her finger."

It's a good thing he didn't reveal that confession. There's no way West would have left as easily as he did if he knew I let Knox help me escape the grip that ring held around my finger and my life.

When the sound of West's bike has vanished into the distance, Liv pokes her head over the tailgate. "You okay, Trinity?"

I let out a breath of relief as the blood flows through my body again, reminding me that I'm still here and still hiding. I know Liv is just being nice to me because she's an officer and she has to be. But I still appreciate her concern—especially after she seemed less than enthused to see Knox helping me last night.

"Yeah, I'm good." When I rise to my feet, Knox reaches a hand up to help me out. I jump down and it feels effortless with his strength bracing me.

I look up at his coarse expression with gratitude, hoping I can somehow redeem myself. "Thank you." I face Liv and Chase. "And both of you too. Thank you. I know you didn't have to help me like that. But I appreciate it, and I promise it won't happen again." I *hope* it won't happen again. I nearly had a stroke from the stress I just endured.

Liv and Chase force a polite smile with their commiserations. But Knox isn't as gracious as he shakes his head with hindrance.

With a stern tone and hardened brow, he says, "This doesn't mean what you did was okay."

"I know," I say with remorse, hugging my arms around myself again. "I saw West on his motorcycle and freaked out. We have court tomorrow, I didn't want to mess things up, and I don't know how to be around him right now." I shrug. "Your keys were right there in the ignition. I just needed to get out of here. I don't know why, and it's not an excuse, but I couldn't stop myself."

He lets out a haphazard laugh that sounds more like a scoff of disapproval. "There's so many other choices you could have made." He thrusts his arm out at his side. "Would it have been so hard for you to have gone into the gas station? Even if he did see you, you would have been safe with me and Chandler. We're not afraid of him." His expression falls into disbelief. "But instead, your first instinct was grand theft auto."

I feel my guard going up as I defend myself. "And I wish I *had* chosen to come to you, but it's too late now. All I can do is apologize. And hope you'll accept that. Give me another chance, I'll show you I'm not an impulsive car thief."

Chase nudges Liv's arm. "We should…" He nods his head to the side, indicating her to follow.

Liv's eyes widen with her uneasy and stiff smile. "Yeah, let's…" They both scramble into her patrol car.

Knox keeps his deeply disappointed eyes fixed on mine. "I offered you my friendship, Trinity." He brushes past me, taking one step up into his truck. "But you blew it."

I drop my gaze to my fraying tennis shoes. "I told you *trust* was a gambling game."

He flips his head around to look at me again. "Not to me it isn't. It's serious. And so is breaking trust. Which is what you did by taking my truck without so much as a warning."

I understand that he's upset, but I also feel a little frustrated he won't even try to recognize that I didn't know what I was doing. "It's not like I didn't warn you." I drag the toe of my shoe in the gravel. "Offering up your trust as a bet to a stranger, you're bound to get burned."

"You only say that because you can't even trust yourself to make the right choice." He delivers his harsh (and accurate) words gently. As if he's saddened by the fact that I broke his trust as quickly as he offered it to me.

I hesitate, biting at my bottom lip before asking the question that's hovering between us. "Does this mean we're not friends anymore?"

Before he answers, the sky seems to grow grey with heavy rain clouds. He looks up and the expression on his face says he's frustrated not only with me, but by his accurate assumptions of the weather.

He lets out a sigh as he drops his gaze to mine again. "Bye, Trinity." He doesn't seem torn at all by his decision. I would probably do the same if our roles were reversed. But I can't deny that it was nice having a friend. Even if it was only for a single minute of my life.

"We wouldn't have gotten along anyway. I could never trust a cop." I don't mean for my statement to sound punitive, but it sort of does.

He seems subtly disheartened by my statement, as if I've wounded him. "I'll make sure to stay out of your way then."

And just like that, our friendship has died. Before it even had a chance to begin. Because of my own thoughtless decision.

A drop of rain hits my cheek as the sky rumbles from above. It's the closest thing to a tear, and I hate that it's landed there for a situation with someone I barely know. Where was this substitute for a tear when my kids were taken from me?

When he shuts his truck door, I catch a glimpse of myself in his side mirror. I quickly avert my eyes because, right now, I don't even want to be friends with my reflection.

CHAPTER TEN

Knox

March 1998

I hold a sticker out my patrol car window. "Now, go home. And do me a favor? Tell your grandma she's a saint and you appreciate her."

Robby takes the sticker with a smirk on his face. "I will." Then he flips around to trek down the sidewalk. I'd offer him a ride, but he lives close by and I have a feeling he still needs to burn off some energy in a more constructive way.

"And be helpful. Make her some dinner for a change!"

He doesn't acknowledge my last command.

He's on a weird kick lately. He's graduated from dine-and-dash to hanging around after school throwing rocks at the streetlights, trying to break them. It's petty, and minor enough that I haven't done much more about it than correct him, give him a sticker, and send him home.

So far, he's been unsuccessful at breaking any lights, but it's also making him late to get home after school. His tardiness has been worrisome for his grandma. So when I'm working, I wait around for him to blow off some steam before sending him on his way.

Pulling around the bus loop, I head back towards town. And on the way, I notice someone walking in the ditch near the road.

Upon closer inspection I can tell they're wearing a McDonald's uniform. And when she takes her hat off, I recognize Trinity's bronze hair as it falls against her back.

I'm still not happy she took off with my truck. Even though I've had plenty of time to get over it in the last four months. But I get it. She's still stuck in fight-or-flight mode. And for her, she's flighty and runs without even thinking about the consequences of her actions.

Part of me wants to see if she needs a ride. Especially because of where she's working. If she's walking to the nearest McDonald's, she'll have to trek along the highway to the next town. I know it's dangerous, but I also can't offer her help when she's made it clear she doesn't want it from me.

I watch her for a moment longer, wrestling with the idea of whether to help her or not, when she runs to the road and holds her thumb out. A semi passes her with its break lights shining, then he pulls to a stop on the side of the road a few yards ahead of her.

When she runs to the passenger's side and hops in without missing a beat, I shrug it off. If anything, I gotta hand it to her that she's resourceful. And she probably would have turned down a ride if I had offered her one anyway. Especially since she told me she doesn't trust cops.

I know she said that because of the way she feels about West, but if for whatever reason she truly doesn't want to be friends with a police officer, I'm not going to be the cop to push her.

When I pull into town, I park at the pavilion and plan to walk over to M.L.'s to pick up the meal I called in earlier. The parking lot is full, so I have to drive to the opposite side of the pavilion to find an open spot.

"Hey, Officer Santino," Kimmy says with a flirtatious ring to her voice as I exit my patrol car.

"Hi, Kimmy." I give her a friendly wave. "Looks like it's going to be a busy night." I motion toward the people walking around the pavilion.

She blinks her eyes playfully with her smacking gum. "That just means my tip jar's gonna be real full." She grins mischievously as she bends forward, leaning against her forearms on the trunk of her car. "How come you never come eat at Steve-O's? You know we have the best selection of whiskey in town." With her wink she says, "And the service isn't half bad either."

I smile at her politely. "I don't drink. Plus, I like the way Marcos makes the steak bites at M.L.'s."

She rises, adjusting the waistband on her snug jeans. "Well, when you get tired of those salty steak bites, you come on over to Steve-O's and we'll make you something real nice. Alright?"

I give her a firm smile and make my way around my vehicle. "Take care, Kimmy."

"See you around, *Officer Santino*." She may be using the flirtiest voice and mannerisms to converse with me, but Kimmy's harmless and uses the same flirtation with every man in town. I think it's one of the reasons Constance hates Steve-O's and made me promise not to ever eat there.

When I walk into M.L.'s, Constance is clapping her hands with no effort to the beat of the song the servers perform for kids on their birthdays. I laugh at the sight of her standing with the other servers. She's not trying to hide the fact that she hates it.

I make my way to the register that's on the far side of the restaurant. My food is already in a container waiting for me. As I begin counting out some cash to pay for my meal, Constance meets me at the register.

"I hate birthdays," she says with gravel in the back of her throat. "Who celebrates their fifth birthday at M.L.'s anyway? It's a sports bar for crying out loud."

I laugh briefly at her intensity. "Apparently," I flip around and nod to the table she just came from, "that kid does." Only when I scan the party goers at the table and land my eyes on a familiar face, my chest sinks. Because the kid celebrating their fifth birthday at M.L.'s, is Abbi.

And the worst part is that I just watched Abbi's mom hitchhike to work in a different town because no one would hire her in this one.

Constance must notice my demeanor shift since she says, "Zio? You okay?"

I face her, shaking my head with regret. "That's Trinity's daughter."

Her voice drops. "Oh, no." She glances at the table then looks at me with sorrow. "Really?"

I nod. "Yeah. And I don't know which is worse. That her dad isn't here celebrating with her, or that her mom couldn't be here because she was hitchhiking to work with a trucker to Mount Pleasant."

"That's twenty minutes away. Why doesn't she get a job here?"

I look at her point blank. "No one wants to hire the woman that attacked the mayor's son."

She tilts her head. "I thought that was a rumor."

I hand her my money and take the bag of food. "It is, but that's never stopped people from believing them, has it?"

She places the money into the register and glances back at the table again. "I'll make sure the birthday girl gets some extra dessert or something."

"Thanks, Kid."

On my way out, I take another glance at the party table. Abbi's wearing a hula skirt and has a yellow plastic lei around her neck. She's standing on the booth bench and directing her friends on how to properly color the pictures on the backs of their kids' menus. Tuck is sitting on Martha's lap. He's shoveling fries into his mouth without chewing or swallowing them.

In passing, it seems like a normal party with untraumatized children. Everyone's having a good time. There's conversation going on that leads to laughter. No one would ever think for a second that those kids have witnessed some of the most horrific events take place in their own home. A place where they should feel safe.

Part of me wants to say hi, but the part of me that knows there's a broken side to them wants to scoop the kids up and drive them to McDonald's twenty minutes away just so their mom can hug them. Just so the broken parts of their hearts can heal a little bit, and just so the memory of this day won't be one that Abbi looks back on as a day without her mom. And just so Trinity won't have to remember Abbi's only fifth birthday as a day where she was taking orders from strangers and making happy meals for other peoples' kids.

CHAPTER ELEVEN

Trinity

I t was Abbi's birthday yesterday. She turned five and I didn't get the invite until last minute.

When I asked my boss if I could miss work for the party, he told me if I didn't show up for my shift that I shouldn't bother coming back to work at all because he'd hire someone to replace me by morning. I thought working would help take my mind off missing Abbi's party.

But it didn't.

How is a mother supposed to forget that her daughter is celebrating her birthday without her?

I stopped by Martha's after work. But she sent me away since Abbi was already in bed. I brought a gift for her. I just hope Martha actually gives it to her.

I bought her a shirt from the thrift store down the road from McDonald's. It says, *Big Sis.* I thought it was perfect since she's such a good big sister to Tuck. You'd never be able to tell that they are half siblings. When Tuck was a baby, I worried that being half siblings might hinder their bond. But it doesn't at all.

I also bought a dollhouse tea set I found while I was at the thrift store. The tea pot is missing a lid, but Abbi won't mind. I've always promised her we would buy one of those dollhouses that come in a big box that you assemble from scratch and paint yourself. I thought having the tea set would be a good start to gathering the items we'll need to furnish the dollhouse after it's built. I hope she likes it and remembers that I promised we'd build her a dollhouse together.

After the last court appointment, I'm supposed to have visits whenever it works with the kids' schedules. But every time I can see them, the kids have something else going on.

I can't help but think that Martha has enrolled them in every activity known to man just so I can't see them.

Each time I give her my work schedule, she seems to find a dance class in Rockwall, or a story time in Commerce to take them to. I don't understand why she needs to drive forty-five minutes when there's a library in Mount Vernon that has story time where I would be able to join them.

She's even enrolled them in private preschools thirty minutes away.

I've offered to spend my mornings getting the kids ready. I'd be happy to take them to preschool in Mount Vernon so Martha doesn't have to drive them so far, or spend money on a fancy preschool. But Martha didn't feel comfortable with the idea since West and I aren't on good terms. Which is the same reason she refused to let me stay with her.

Since the incident at the gas station, West has been hellbent on trying to get Knox fired. And he makes sure to bring up my infidelity in front of his parents every time I get to see the kids. The *fake* infidelity that I haven't given up correcting him on. Even though it seems useless at this point to convince him or anyone else otherwise. He's poisoned the entire town with his charming lies.

I still don't understand how anyone can see him as the victim in this situation. But he's managed to successfully become just that. Even my own father was leery towards my truth after he heard from Martha that I'd turned into a lush and a jezebel overnight. I'm still not convinced that he believes me.

"You do have a history of making regrettable decisions when you drink." He said when I told him about the night I stayed with Knox. On his couch. Alone in his apartment. Because I couldn't afford a motel. Knox wasn't even there so I'm not sure how I could have slept with him.

But no one wants the boring truth. The truth which happens to be my side of the story.

That's the thing about living in a small town, the people undoubtedly feed off gossip. And when you're not from their tiny town, they'll turn their back on you in the blink of an eye. Which is the main reason I've been pushed out of the town and work twenty minutes away.

Suddenly, there's a squeal then something shoots out of the slide. I adjust my McDonald's visor before bending down to retrieve whatever flew out of the yellow tube. It's a little blue truck with flames across the sides. The happy meal toy this month. And I notice that it's the same dark blue as Knox's truck.

I zoom the Hot-Wheels car across the floor to a little boy when he pops out of the end of the slide. He doesn't pay much attention to me when he picks up the toy and climbs back up into the play maze.

I wish I could bring Abbi and Tuck here to play. And I wish Martha would show up here to surprise me with the kids some time. But sadly, that's not the relationship we have.

I finish sweeping under the tables in the play area then make my way into the women's bathroom to clean the toilets.

We're supposed to alternate the custodial duties between employees, but for whatever reason I always wind up doing them. I don't mind much. It's easier to take my time with cleaning than it is to take orders from the drive-thru where customer's muffled voices are accompanied by screaming children and crying babies in my headset. Not that I mind the children and babies, it just makes it harder to get the order correct.

"Trinity," the manager says from the bathroom entrance. "Are you in here?"

"Yep!" I'm bent over with a toilet scrubber in my hand when I kick the stall door open to reveal where I'm at. "You can come in. I'm the only one in here."

He approaches me with a blank expression. "I gotta let you go."

I stop scrubbing the toilet bowl and face him. "I sort of needed to work the entire shift today." It's true. I've calculated the exact amount of hours I need to work to support myself, while still scavenging for time with my kids.

He shakes his head. "No, I mean. I gotta let you go for good."

I tilt my head. "But, I need this job." It's the only job that gives me the type of freedom I need with my schedule to visit the kids around their outings.

Every time Martha fills up the kids' schedules for the morning, I switch my shift so I can see them in the afternoon. Or I work the opposite shift when she gets used to my schedule. It's exhausting and I'm constantly changing the hours I'm available, but it's the only way I can see my kids.

"Sorry. Your availability is unreliable." He hands me my paycheck and exits the bathroom.

Some days I can find a ride back to Mount Vernon. But other days, I guess people would rather not have their car smell like dirty shoes and old french fries. Which is why it took me the rest of the day to walk back to Mount Vernon after I was fired.

By the time I get back to the motel, it's already after 9 o'clock. I wanted to visit the kids before bedtime. It's too late now to stop by Martha's. Plus, she doesn't like when I come over unannounced. Which makes things more difficult since I have to make sure she'll be home when I call.

I open the drawer of the nightstand next to my bed and pull out a piece of paper with an ongoing equation scrawled down the center.

I subtract $3 for the last meal I had, and then subtract $275, which is what I owe the motel owner for the agreed upon monthly payment. Then I'm left with $28 and no chance of any sort of incoming funds.

Unless I call my father. But I'm supposed to be proving I can provide for my children. But right now, I can't even support myself.

CHAPTER TWELVE

Knox

I toss a stick in the yard, encouraging Sugar to chase after it but she only lays her head back down between her paws.

"Come on, Sugar." I pat my leg to encourage her to follow me. Instead, she continues laying in her sad position on the cement slab in the backyard.

She's been less energetic as Trinity's absence grows longer each day. Although I can usually get her to muster up enough excitement to play fetch for a few minutes. But her extreme lethargy has been going on for almost a week now and I'm beginning to worry.

"You want to go on a walk, girl?"

Nothing.

"Want a treat?"

Nothing.

"Inside? Wanna go inside?"

"She's not allowed inside the house," Constance says from the open kitchen window.

I toss my hands up and turn to head into the house. "I don't know what's wrong with her."

Constance is standing by the microwave waiting for her frozen dinner to heat up. "Can't you see that she's depressed?"

"I think she might be sick."

"She's not sick."

I open the freezer and take out one of the frozen microwave dinners. "She's probably tired from old age."

"I *know* it's not that," she says with certainty.

I retrieve a knife and stab a few holes into the plastic wrap covering the frozen Saulsberry steak and mashed potatoes. I also don't strike back in this conversation because I don't want to acknowledge where it's going.

I maneuver around the counter until I'm next to Constance, who is glaring at me. I pull my gaze to her food, waiting for her to take it out of the microwave that just beeped.

"You need help getting that?" I say, when she continues to stand in front of the microwave without removing her food.

When she doesn't speak, I place my hand around the handle to open the microwave door, but she quickly pushes it closed again, as her glaring eyes narrow.

"What are you doing, Kid?"

She places her hands on her hips in haste, then with her exhale she says, "That poor dog misses Trinity." Her pointed finger hits the center of my sternum. "And you know it."

I open the microwave again, and this time she doesn't stop me when I take her food out and slide it across the counter. I take this opportunity to place my tray of food in the microwave before she tries closing the door again. "How long do I cook this for?" I spin around to dig in the trash for the box with the instructions. Avoiding all conversations that will lead to a discussion about how Sugar misses Trinity.

Constance takes the box from my hands and throws it into the living room. "*Zio!*" When she says this, she sounds just like my mom used to when I'd get in trouble as a kid. And it makes my chest sink for a moment.

Ignoring her, and my aching heart, I face the microwave and decide that two minutes should be long enough.

When I still don't acknowledge her for the entire time my food is being nuked in the microwave, she finally pulls her macaroni dinner toward herself and begins shifting the noodles around. "Fine." She shrugs and keeps her gaze on her food. "Don't tell her owner that she's depressed. See if I care." Then she turns around to find a place on the couch and flips the TV on.

I know I should tell Trinity about Sugar. But I don't *want* to. Not because I'm indifferent about her or her dog. But because Trinity's life is heavy and messy, and she made it clear she didn't want me in the middle of it.

I sit next to Constance and turn the TV off.

She takes the remote from me and turns it back on with an unreactive expression.

"I want to say something to you, Kid."

She forks a bite of mac into her mouth as she keeps her eyes on the TV with disinterest in me. "You don't have to turn my show off to talk to me."

I exhale slowly, preparing my confession. "I know Sugar misses Trinity, alright?"

She chews on her food with her attention on the TV, acting like she can't hear what I'm saying. But I know she's listening to me, so I continue.

"And I'll let her know her dog is miserable without her."

Constance shrugs. I know she's only pretending not to care. She does this sometimes, as if reverse psychology is going to make me do what she wants. I'm not sure why she's being stubborn about it since I've already given her the answer she's looking for.

We continue to eat in silence until a commercial break. Then Constance sets her tray on the coffee table and wipes her face with her hands before saying, "She promised she'd come by to take care of Sugar." She finally looks at me with interest. "Why do you think she broke her promise?"

I exhale with regret. Knowing I could have done more to salvage a friendship with Trinity, but also not wanting to get in the way of her life. She's trying to juggle more than any one person should have to juggle in a lifetime, and she's doing it alone. I didn't want to add another component to her juggling act by invading the situation she's in.

Yeah, I was upset when she took my truck. But I got over it. I'm just not sure she's gotten over the fact that I might be just another jerk cop in her life though.

"It was something I said." I slouch, dropping my head against the back of the sofa.

She adjusts herself on the couch to face me better. Then she lets out a short laugh with her growing smirk. "You know when you brought her here that night? I wasn't happy about that because when I served her at M.L.'s, I didn't like her. With her ugly dyed hair and uncertainty when she was looking at the menu. And I liked her less when you two were creeping around in my house together doing God knows what."

"Looking for string."

"I'm sure." She rolls her eyes as her mouth shifts to one side and her tone gentles. "But then she told me about her ex. And she took care of her dog. And her dog was happy to see her. And when I finally looked at her, like really looked at her, do you know who I saw?"

I lean forward with my elbows on my knees and shake my head gently with concern.

She drops her brows to the sides of her face. "I saw *me*." She thrusts her hand up and it makes a slapping sound when it drops against her leg. "I saw who I used to be, Zio."

I know exactly what she's talking about. And I didn't want to acknowledge it before, but I saw Constance in Trinity too. I think that's probably why I was drawn to helping her. And I know that's why I wanted to be a friend to her.

The host begins speaking again, as the commercials end and the show returns. Constance shifts again on the couch until she's facing the TV screen completely. Then, without looking at me, she drops her voice to a solemn tone. "I don't want to be disappointed in you."

Her lingering statement punctures my ego, but also causes another sensation to emerge in my core. Something between motivation and inspiration expands through me.

I take the empty microwave dinner containers, and the box Constance tossed in the living room earlier and place them in the trash.

I regret not handling things better with Trinity now. I've been caught up in my own unwillingness to open up to people, that I chose the easy way when Trinity gave me an out.

It's easy to walk away from someone that's messy and broken and avoiding you. It's harder to show up when you know that they need you and you can do something to make their bad situation better.

When I begin putting my tennis shoes on, Constance says, "Heading up there?" Referring to my apartment.

"Nope," I say with a grin.

She gives me a confused expression.

I retrieve the leash that's on the window ledge near the entrance. "I'm going to make sure I don't disappoint you."

CHAPTER THIRTEEN

Trinity

I swing the garbage sack next to my leg while I walk. It's the sack that's holding my belongings. And it's pathetically empty since most of my clothes and necessities are still back at West's house where a court order made it clear I'm not allowed to enter. The same court order that gave him full custody of our children. And the same house I used to call home, not even six months ago.

I'm carrying my things because I need to ask Martha *again* if she'll consider letting me stay with her.

I've run out of money.

I can't get ahold of my father.

I have no friends in this town.

And I can't get a job with my lacking rapport.

This is my only option. I won't go back to West. As easy as it would be, I won't do it. I'd rather not live with Martha either since I know West will come around. But I don't plan on staying with Martha for long. And I'm beyond desperate at this point.

I climb the steps up to the beautiful porch deck of Martha's white painted colonial home. It's picturesque and screams *plantation farmers*.

There's seven bedrooms. More than enough space for us to share. Although at this point, I'd live in a van if it meant I could be with my kids.

I give two firm knocks and clear my throat before the front door swings open.

Martha looks stunned to see me. "Trinity." Her bright, blue eyes are wide, and I can tell she's fervently searching her mind for an excuse as to why I can't come in. Or why I can't see my children. Although, this time she might have a good excuse since West was granted full custody of the kids at the last court appointment and I was given weekend visits when it's convenient for him.

"Can I come in?" I'm being bold and forward. Mostly because taking Sharry's advice and *playing nice* got me nowhere.

Martha looks over her shoulder then steps outside onto the deck, closing the door behind herself. "It's not a good time."

I shift my weight to one side. "It's never a good time, is it?"

She blinks and her eyes widen more with her dumbfounded expression. "Excuse me?"

Regretting my careless statement, I change the subject before she decides to send me away. "Are the kids here?"

She folds her mouth in, as if she's locking the truth behind her thin lips. "How about tomorrow? We'll meet you at the pavilion under the gazebo in town."

I exhale with regret. I don't understand why she's keeping them from me. And frankly, I'm getting tired of playing this dancing game with her. Where I'm constantly shifting my life around for her illogical scheduling.

"You were there," I say. "You heard the judge. He said that I get to see the kids on the weekends. And it's Friday evening."

My eyes shift upward as young laughter comes from an upstairs room behind her. I know it's Tuck. His laughter is contagious, and I even smile when I hear it because I feel a giggle in my stomach that I can't refuse—despite how depressing my life is.

"I remember," she says with a regrettable exhale. "But Matthew is watching the tube and he's on the phone making transactions. Tomorrow is better. Is there a time that works for you?" I know she's minimizing her husband's gambling by calling it a *transaction*. He loves watching horse races from his brown leather La Z Boy recliner while making phone calls to his bookie. And if horses aren't racing, he'll settle for dog races or sporting events. Anything to throw money at.

I wish he'd throw some at me.

I give her a look of remorse when I begin to say, "Actually my schedule is completely free. I'm not working at McDonald's anymore."

"Oh," is all she says, as if I've just given her the worst possible news.

"And, Martha?" I look up at the window where I know the kids are playing. "I was hoping you would reconsider letting me stay with you."

Her expression is horrified when I say this. I wish she wasn't so extreme with her facial expressions. It's making this conversation ridiculous.

I continue, "It would only be until I'm able to support myself. I promise. I've already applied for jobs all over, and once I get a job and make enough to get my own place, I'll be out of your hair."

She's shaking her head *no*, delivering her response without words.

But it doesn't stop me from arguing my case. "I wouldn't be a bother. I'd help with getting the kids ready in the morning, I'd do chores and whatever else you need." There's a scream of anxiety in my voice. "Or maybe me and the kids could move back into the house and West could stay here with you? Can we please just talk about this? *Please?*"

Suddenly the door swings open and Matthew is standing behind Martha. "What are you standin' out here for?" When he notices me he says, "Oh, Trinity, I didn't know you were comin' by tonight."

Martha fumbles for words.

Before I lose my momentum, I say, "We were trying to line some things out. And I was hoping I could stay here for a little while. Just until I can support myself."

The laugh that erupts from Matthew is not just a blow to my pride, but it's embarrassing. Once he's regained his composure to speak, he says, "You know that's not gonna happen with how things are goin' between you and West, don't you?"

I exhale with defeat but keep my pleading eyes focused on him, showing how desperate I am without having to say it out loud.

He shakes his head with his ingenuine grin. "And especially not after the divorce papers that showed up for him." His grin shifts into a firm line. "He was tryin' to salvage y'all's marriage. But I don't think you're the young lady we thought you were, Trinity. You haven't been real honest with us at all. And if you had been, we woulda been happy to help you."

I tilt my head in confusion. "Help me?" What's stopping them from helping me now? What's stopping them from letting me stay here where my children are?

He nods slowly, dropping his chin to his neck as he places his hand on Martha's shoulder. "With your alcoholism, Hunny."

My mouth parts with surprise. In this moment, I realize why they've been reluctant to have me around the kids. They think I'm the one that's been getting drunk. They *believe* I attacked West. They *believe* I cheated on him. They believe all his lies, and I probably don't even know what half of them are. And in this moment, I also realize that they've given up on me.

When I decide it would be pointless to beg or defend myself from West's lies, I accept defeat and settle for pleading, "Can I just see my kids?"

Matthew looks down as he rubs the back of his neck in thought. "You know, that'd be alright with me as long as Martha sits with y'all."

Martha lifts her face to whisper to him. "I'd prefer if we were outside for no longer than a minute. It's almost the kids' bedtime."

He gives her a nod, then to me he says, "I'll send the kids outside to see you," he shoots a pointed look with his finger in my direction, "for a *minute*. It's almost their bedtime." As if I didn't hear what Martha just said.

Martha follows Matthew inside, and I can hear her lock the door after she shuts it. It makes me wonder what West could have possibly said that would make his mother so afraid of me.

Stepping off the porch steps, I twist the garbage sack in my hands as I walk in a circle of anticipation.

Then, I hear Abbi's voice yelling *Mommy* from the other side of the door before I hear the lock unlatch and see her burst through it, straight into my arms.

My heart is heavy when I hug her. She's so excited and I already know this visit won't be long enough for either of us, which makes my heart ache.

Martha finally makes her way outside with Tuck. I can't help but notice how he seems timid as he approaches me. I kneel down and wait for him to hug me, but he seems unsure. And the worst part is that his hesitancy just caused my heart to fall out of my chest onto the dirt between us.

But Abbi's full of excitement. I keep my hand reaching out towards Tuck as Abbi begins to tell me all about the different things she's been doing. Ballet with Miss Ramoine. Swimming lessons with Mr. Jake. Story Time with Mrs. Goodridge. Baking with Nana. Riding the tractor with Papa. Lunch at Papa's office with Nana at City Hall.

Once Tuck sees how excited Abbi is, how easy it is for her to talk to me and how naturally she twists my hair between her fingers, he decides to sit on my lap. I hold him as my heart searches for its way back up into my chest again.

The back of his head smells like a mixture of shampoo and sweat. It saddens me that it's not the same shampoo I use to use and makes him smell different. But I'm happy Martha obliged my previous request to bathe the kids before bedtime. I keep my gripping arms around him until I'm certain my heart has fully crawled back into my body and begun to beat again.

"And sometimes, I get to go to the movies." Abbi hasn't stopped talking about their endless adventures since the first hug I gave her. "But that's only when Daddy can take me since Tuck is too little foh the movies."

This causes me to perk up, since it's the first mention of West she's made thus far. I wish I could ask her more about West's involvement in their lives. But I know Martha would interject if I tried, since she's sitting on the porch pretending to be preoccupied with the squirrels running up and down the trees.

Instead of prying about their father's connection to them, I decide to change the subject.

"Have you and Tuck been keeping up with your special bracelets?" I force a grin, even though my heart hurts from my lacking involvement in their activities.

Abbi nods. "I'll go get my bwacelet and show you! Don't leave, Mommy."

"I won't," I say, nuzzling my face against the top of Tuck's head again. "Me and Tuck will wait right here for you." I kiss the side of Tuck's plump face. "Won't we, Tuck?"

But instead of giggling like he used to when I'd kiss his face, he nervously squirms free from my arms and says something to Abbi that I can't quite make out.

"You don't want to stay with me?" I say, with my arms stretched out to him as he begins to climb the porch steps.

He shakes his head and repeats the unfamiliar phrase before following Abbi inside.

I look to Martha for clarity, and she has an expression full of pain when she says, "He said he wanted to go with Abbi." She looks away and dabs her fingertip at the edge of her eye, as if she's keeping a saddened tear from falling free. Because she knows that if she does let that tear out, it might just force her to acknowledge how messed up this entire situation is. And if she does that, then she'll have to change how she's been treating me and face the fact that her son is a selfish jerk. Which she'll never do.

And then, just like that, my heart drops down into an unrecognizable and unformed pile in the base of my torso. Heavy in my stomach with grief. Because the realization that I haven't spent enough time with my own child to understand his jumbled toddler speech causes me to feel not only guilt and shame, but it erupts a new sense of gut-wrenching bereavement in me.

And I don't bother trying to shift my heart back into place. Instead, I put on a smile when I hear Abbi and Tuck barreling down the stairs inside the house. Because I have to be strong for them on the outside, no matter how deformed and battered my insides are.

When Abbi and Tuck reach the porch, they're both excited to show me their zip tie bracelets.

Abbi takes Tuck's bracelet from his grip, handing it to me. "Look what Papa put on Tuck's." I let Tuck take the locked zip tie from my hand, as I see several beer bottle caps with holes through their center laced onto his zip tie.

It had crossed my mind that Matthew or Martha would find the zip ties and toss them in the garbage as trash or a hazard. But I smile when I realize that, even though it's beer caps, at least Matthew was helping. Making it a fun experience for Tuck.

Abbi lifts her zip tie, that's also been looped into a circle, and shows me everything she's added to it. "I found this one fuh-st." It's a small acorn cupule that looks like a miniature woodland hat for a fairy. There's a hole that's punctured through the cupule, similar to the holes in the beer caps from Tuck's zip tie. I can't help but think Matthew probably helped with that too.

"This is incredible," I say to Abbi.

"And this one," she continues with her eyes glued to the items snuggly wrapped around the zip tie, "is fwom a flow-uh in Nana's kitchen." She tilts her head and speaks from the side of her mouth. "It kind of fell apawt."

"That's okay." I kiss the side of her head. "It's perfect."

She continues uncovering each item. Metal can tabs. Plastic bread clips. Leaves. Cardboard cutouts of various characters from cereal boxes.

But one item catches my attention.

"What's this?" I ask, while holding the rectangular cardstock.

The phone rings, then Matthew calls for Martha from inside the house.

Martha gives me a worried look, so, I say, "It's fine. We'll be right here when you're done with the call."

She nods with uncertainty but goes inside the house anyway.

Abbi begins telling me about an old skeleton key on the zip tie that she found in Martha's jewelry box when I touch the card again. "Tell me more about this one," I say with curiosity.

She smiles and says, "That one is fwum Office-uh Santino. He told me to call when we went back home so he could bwing Shu-guh back to us."

My heart skips a beat when she says his name, knowing they had an interaction while I was unconscious, and one where he gave this card with his phone number to her. The saddest part is that they were both anticipating that Sugar would be back home with our family by now. But it's been six months since their conversation. And I feel incredibly guilty that I haven't stopped by to take care of Sugar like I said I would.

I give Abbi a forced smile. "That was really nice of Officer Santino to take care of Sugar for us, wasn't it?"

Abbi nods as her smile shifts into a frown. "How come you, and me, and Shu-guh, and Tuck, and Daddy don't live at the house anymow?"

I set her zip tie bracelet on my lap and pull her in for a hug. "I don't know, baby girl," I say this against her dark brown hair. "But I'm sorry it's taking so long for us to be together again." I refrain from mentioning that her dad and I will never live in the same house ever again.

Tuck begins digging in my garbage sack and Abbi is quick to shift her attention to him. "Tuck, no! That's Mommy's. Don't touch."

"It's okay, Abbi," I say with a heavy heart, noticing how her feelings about our broken family seem to be seeping through into her behavior as she takes her emotions out on Tuck's innocent curiosity.

Tuck quickly pulls something out of the sack and runs to attach himself to my body, hiding from Abbi. I know I'm not his first choice of comfort, and that he'd probably prefer hiding behind Martha if she were out here. But I take this moment as an opportunity to remind him of who I am.

"What'd you find in there, Tuck?" I gently rub my hand between his shoulder blades. "Can you show me? Can Mommy see?"

He lifts my disappointing zip tie. There's a few pieces of garbage shoved on there from a McDonald's meal I brought back to the motel one night after my shift. It's sad and pathetic. But when all my thoughts and energy go toward trying to find time to be with my children, nothing else seems to matter. Not even silly made-up zip tie games.

"I think you lost, Mommy. You only have…" she begins counting the pieces of garbage. "One, two, thwee, foh. Foh, things."

"I think you're right. I definitely lost." I give her a peck on the cheek. "I guess you and Tuck get to split the prize."

Abbi's eyes light up with her smile. "What's the pwize?"

I hand her two mints I took from a bowl in the motel lobby. I'm beginning to instruct her on sharing one with Tuck when he says, "Donald's," noticing the logo on the trash bracelet.

Martha emerges from the house as Tuck yells, "*Donald's,*" again.

Martha reaches down to pick Tuck up and he goes to her without hesitation. Which stings, as if my heart muscle has been pinched by fingernail clippers.

Who am I kidding? It hurts like hell that my son prefers his grandmother over me.

"No McDonald's tonight," she says to Tuck.

This makes him drop his head on her shoulder and begin to quietly whimper. And somehow, I feel like it's my fault that he's upset.

Martha rubs his back, comforting him. I'm thankful she's being good to them, and her gestures seem sincere. But part of me steams because I'm the one who should be holding Tuck.

My shoulder is the one his head should be pressed to.

I should be the one giving him the comfort he needs.

I'm his mother. I deserve to be doing those things for him.

When Martha faces me, I can tell she's going to ask me to leave, so I quickly say, "Would it be okay if I used your phone?"

She lets out an exhale through her nose, as if she's reluctant to let me in the house. As if I'm some criminal that's burned her in the past. Which I haven't. The only thing that has changed is that she believes the lies her son fed her about me.

"Let's get you inside, Abbi," she says, turning her back to me. And ignoring my question.

Abbi begins to skip up the steps, then she looks back at me and says, "Come on, Mommy."

I have to look at my shoes to keep myself from verbally tossing blame at her grandmother for not allowing me inside. And I keep my head down to bury the throbbing pain that each passing moment continues to create in my heart. It's not the rejection of West's parents so much as it is the fact that this situation is hurting my children. And it's so wrong that none of the adults with authority in their lives are doing anything to prevent that kind of confusing and torturous pain for them.

Martha says, "Mommy has to go. It's time for you two to get ready for bedtime."

Abbi stomps her foot. "I don't wanna go to bed. I want Mommy!"

Tuck's whimpers begin to turn into cries as Abbi protests Martha.

When Martha continues to head inside without an answer for me, I say, "Martha, please."

She faces me, then over the cries of my children, she says, "You can use the phone, *briefly*. Then I think it would be a good idea for you to go." She directs her attention to Tuck and Abbi again. "Say bye to Mommy."

"What about tomorrow?" Martha's not looking at me when I say this. "Can I still see them at the pavilion?"

She gives a short nod. "Does two o'clock work for you?"

"Two is good, thank you." I finally approach Martha and lean over to give Tuck a kiss on the back of his head while he's still held in her arms. Then Abbi gives me a shuddered hug, and follows Martha into the house with tears streaming down her face and over her pouting lip.

I wish I could scoop them up and take them with me. I wish I could give them chunks of my heart to fill the broken places of their little hearts.

The part that I can't seem to accept is that they don't have to suffer. If West's parents would only accept me. If they would only let me be part of my children's lives again. If they only listened to me. None of this pain would be happening. My children wouldn't be walking away from me right now. They wouldn't be suffering.

I hate every part of this.

Waiting a moment, I make sure the kids are upstairs before heading inside. Far be it from me to make things more painful by lingering around in the house when it's their bedtime.

When I enter the home and walk toward the kitchen, Matthew notices me from his chair placed in front of the TV. So I give him a wave and say, "Martha said it was okay for me to use the phone."

He gives me a nod then faces the TV again.

When I'm in the kitchen, I lean a shoulder into the wall where the phone is placed, to call my father.

He doesn't answer.

So, I try again.

And again.

But after it's clear he's not home, I hang the phone back onto the receiver and turn to exit the home in defeat.

I haven't been able to contact my father in a month. He doesn't have an answering machine either so there's no way of leaving a message for him. I suppose I could send a postcard to him. But it would be pointless since I don't have any way for him to contact me back.

I push open the door as I begin to leave the house, when I remember Abbi's zip tie bracelet. I backtrack to the kitchen again, holding onto the very last speck of hope I have.

I quickly rummage through the plastic sack where I find the bracelet. And still attached to it is the card with Knox's phone number.

When I place the phone between my shoulder and ear, my heart begins to accelerate.

The last time I spoke to Knox he was angry that I took his truck without asking. I've had time to reflect on that and realize that I could have handled it differently. And I know I jumped to conclusions assuming our friendship had to end over something that a gentle apology and some time to cool off could have fixed. I just haven't had the opportunity to tell him that yet.

If I wasn't so desperate, I might reconsider what I'm doing, which is pressing the buttons on the phone to dial Knox's number.

The miserable truth is that I am desperate. I *need* help and I'm not about to give up on asking for it. Because fighting the uphill battle to be with my kids is worth burdening every person I know for help. And I won't give up until I've exhausted every option I have.

"Hello?" Knox's voice moves past my eardrum and down into my core, filling the most concerned places of my being.

I swallow hard, trying to formulate a tone that sounds strong and steady like his voice. "Hi, Knox." He's my very last option, and coincidentally, also my only option at this point. And I don't know how he's going to react to my cold call.

"Who is this?" He sounds equal parts confused and concerned.

"It's Trinity Laurel." I can't wait to have my maiden name back.

There's a pause before he says, "How'd you get my number?"

I'm not sure how to tell him I stole it from my daughter's garbage bracelet. So I decide to avoid telling him, and instead say, "I'm sorry to call you like this, but I could really use a friend right now."

I can hear in the way he drags in his inhale, then slowly releases his exhale, that he's contemplating the best way to let me down.

I sort of wish he'd just hang up and make it apparent that he doesn't want anything to do with me. It's easier when people let you down with a clean break rather than drag it out only to disappoint you later.

I hear the jingle of his keys before he says, "Where are you? I'm coming to get you."

His direct response startles me so much that I audibly gasp. And I can see Matthew lift himself from his chair enough to turn around and glance at me, before facing the TV again.

I thought Knox would demand an apology. Or remind me, again, how I broke his trust. I thought I'd have to, at the very least, grovel.

I turn so my back is facing Matthew when I quietly say, "I'm at West's parents' house." Then I give him the address and let him know I'll wait for him outside.

He doesn't ask any more questions. All he says is, "I'll be right there." Then the line goes dead.

As I hang up the receiver, I don't feel like what I've done was a mistake.

Until I hear the sound of West's motorcycle approaching in the distance.

My throat feels as if it's being choked shut. My blood rushes out of my veins and retreats into hiding inside of my heart as I wait for him to pull up to the house and cut the engine.

I'm not sure what the best way to go about this is, so I continue to stand still in the kitchen. Peering through the edge of the window, watching as West makes his way up the steps. I don't know what I'm going to do if he sees me, mostly because I don't know what *he* is going to do if he sees me.

Once he's in the house, he greets his father and makes his way to the living room. I take this opportunity to slip out the front door as quickly and as quietly as I can.

I nearly jump off the porch, skipping all four steps, and keep my feet moving under me as I head down the dirt road. There's only one road to Matthew and Martha's house, so I know I'll meet Knox along the way. But I need to hurry and get out of West's sight first.

"Trinity, stop!"

Too late.

I stop. Only because I know how much West loves to chase me when I don't listen to him. And being chased by West never ends well.

I flip around to face him. He's comfortably jogging toward me. I hate the black V-neck he's wearing. I also hate the way his thighs are flexing behind his jeans with each stride he makes. And more than anything I hate his sandy windblown hair and his eager expression.

But the truth is that I don't hate any part of his appearance right now. And I'm so disappointed in myself for being weak to something as insignificant as his attractiveness.

Lately, the only time I've been in his presence is when he berates me from a distance with insults and interrogation.

Or when we're on opposite sides of the courtroom. Where he's wearing a suit and refusing eye contact. I understand wearing nice clothes for court, but a suit is overreaching in a town as small as Mount Vernon. Even the judge is underdressed. I know this because I saw the pajama pants and suede slippers he was wearing under his black robe.

This is the first time I've been in close contact with West in months.

So when he's standing in front of me with the very clothing that first drew me to him when I was seventeen, I feel all the familiarity of his presence. I only wish I could convince myself to genuinely hate it.

He gives me a sweet grin. "Where you headed off to so quickly?"

I can tell he's sober, which is a good sign. He's not so aggressive when he's sober.

"Work." I lie.

He's looking at me sweetly too, with his consuming blue eyes. "Come back inside for a little bit." He swings his head in the direction of the house. "I'd really like to talk to you."

I tuck my bottom lip into my mouth and hold it there with my teeth. This would have been a lot easier if he had been angry when he saw me, instead of looking at me with that yearning expression.

He lifts his hand up next to my face, which makes me wince as I press my eyes closed. When I open them again, he looks hurt. Then his eyes shift to my hairline, as he gently runs a finger along my forehead and tucks a strand of hair behind my ear with his grief-stricken expression.

"Your roots have grown out," he says, shifting his gaze from my darkening hair to my uncertain eyes. "Can we please talk?"

I shake my head slowly. "I really need to get to work." *And I need to get out of here before my strength runs thin.*

He reaches for my hand, but I move it away and clasp it around my plastic sack of belongings.

His voice is spread with quiet concern when he says, "Why did you send me divorce papers?" Brushing his hands down the backs of my arms he adds, "I know you still love me. I can *feel* it."

I look away by turning my face toward my shoulder when he begins to close in on me. I know what he's doing. He knows how weak I am when he's kind. He knows one kiss from his mouth is like a lasso around me.

My reluctance to give in to his physical gesture causes him to exhale a frustrated breath. "Trinity...look at me please."

I face him again and press my mouth together, a silent indication to inform him he's not going to get what he wants from me.

He drops his head back with a subtle eye roll, when he says, "I know we've got our issues. But it's nothing we can't work on, is it? I love you," his voice shifts down as if he's in pain, "and I *miss* you." He clenches his teeth with his tightening jaw. "I miss you *so* much."

I look down for a moment, unable to stare into his ocean eyes. Because I'm an empathetic human and I can't stand to see his shining eyes reveal the brokenness of his heart.

"Sometimes...," I say, with my regretful inhale, "I miss you too." Which is true. More than anything I miss having someone in my life that I can count on. Someone that understands me. Someone that wants to laugh with me about the silly things our children do. *Someone*, so I'm not lonely anymore.

A smile grows at the corner of his mouth. "I've changed." He slips his hands around my waist, and I feel my body tense as my heart shrinks. "I'm sorry your feelings got hurt by what happened. I was under a lot of stress when the new sergeant position opened for me. It was like I had a microscope at my back all the time. But it's different now. I don't drink anymore and I'm not going to drink anymore." He gently grazes his index finger against my cheek. "And after everything that's happened between us, I still want to be with you."

I finally look up at him. And my chest feels as if it's being stirred up and mixed with tar. Thick like molasses and unforgiving. Especially because he's dismissing the fact that he nearly ended my life with his hands.

"Let's go back to the way things were." He pulls me close to him, so our torsos are touching. "We can light those divorce papers on fire. Get you moved back into the house. You can stay home with the kids again." He leans the side of his face down on the top of my head. And I don't have a clue how someone that's hurt me so much can still comfort me with the same hands that nearly killed me.

My voice is soft when I say, "West..." Wanting him to stop being nice to me. Wanting him to stop making enticing promises. Wanting him to go back to hating me because I'm too weak to hate him when he's kind and loving.

But I know his words have no weight. I know he's making empty promises. I know he might treat me well for a month or two, then the cycle will continue.

And I can't keep doing this. I don't trust him, and I have to be strong. I can't let him push me around and dictate my life anymore.

He kisses the top of my head. "Why don't you come inside? We'll see what Mama made for dinner. We can eat together and talk through all of this. Just like we use to."

He's wrapping his arm around my shoulders.

"We'll forget all about the last six months."

He's leading us back to the house.

"I meant to tell you." He clicks his tongue. "I bought a new truck."

My feet are following in step with his.

"You're gonna love it. I'll take you for a drive later. I know you like it when I drive you around."

What am I doing?

"West, I can't," I say, making sure my voice is pleasant and gentle. "I have to go." My heart begins to drum nervously on the other side of my chest wall.

He chuckles softly. "Baby, you don't need to worry about going to work anymore. I'll take care of you."

Don't give in. It's just manipulation. Don't give in. They're empty words. Don't give in. He's a liar. Don't. Give. In.

Somehow, I stop walking.

And when I do, West drags his arm off my shoulders, down my arm, past my wrist, and lands at my hand. He stops walking to face me. Only when he inspects my hand, his smug grin slowly falls with his gaze as he looks down at my finger.

My mouth parts and I begin to speak but he interrupts me with, "Where's your ring?"

I'm waiting for him to look at me, but he's staring at my hand that's beginning to tremble in his thick grip.

"I can't wear it at work." I lie. It's a horrible lie too. And one so terrible that West sees right through it.

His jaw cracks when he opens his mouth with a scoff. Then he finally lifts his gaze to meet mine. And when he does, a cold chill rushes through my body starting in my stomach and courses through my limbs.

He turns back to look at the house as his breathing intensifies. Then he faces me with a frenzied expression. "If you ever want to see the kids again, you better march your ass inside that house and explain to me what the hell is going on."

CHAPTER FOURTEEN

Knox

Before the phone call, I had taken Sugar down to the motel where Trinity's been staying. I thought it might help the both of them to see each other. And I needed a reason to reach out to Trinity again. But when I talked to the manager, I found out that she lost her job and couldn't afford to stay at the motel any longer. I had just made it back to my apartment when the phone rang, giving me the reason I needed to see her.

After my conversation with Constance, I realized, I want to be someone Trinity can count on in this town. Nobody in her situation should be alone. Or homeless.

Sugar's head is bobbing with the bumps in the road. I brought her along because I thought that being around Trinity would make her happy again. And also, so she might become a buffer between me and Trinity if necessary.

I'm not driving very fast when I round the bend that leads me down a tree covered path to the mayor's large house.

And it doesn't take but two seconds for me to see West and Trinity outside the home.

I speed up and quickly park next to them. I don't bother turning my truck off before I jump out and make a beeline toward them.

West's boring into Trinity with his contorted expression when he places one hand on his hip and thrusts the other hand out towards me. "If nothing happened between the two of you, then why's *he* here?"

"What'd he do to you?" I say, approaching Trinity.

West shoots me a contemptuous expression. "I didn't touch her."

I avoid acknowledging West since he's a pathological liar. But more-so because I'd rather not cause any unnecessary problems.

When I received the phone call from Trinity, I wasn't expecting to deal with West. But since he's here and causing the fear to erupt inside of her, I figure she could use some assistance. So I clasp my hand around her's and say, "Let's get out of here."

She keeps her head down as she closes in behind me, her grip tight in my hand.

I focus on getting her to the truck, ignoring West's *loud* lingering comments behind us.

Before we make it to the truck, West's taken her other hand and ripped her from my grip as if he's a child claiming ownership over a toy.

"West, *please*," Trinity begs. "Just stop."

He tightens his grip around her wrist. "We're married, Trinity. Whatever he's done to brainwash you into thinking otherwise isn't going to keep you away from me any longer. I'm your husband."

His manipulation is disgusting. "The only brainwashing she's experienced is from *you*."

Trinity gives me a wide-eyed look of bewilderment. As if she's astonished that I would stand up for her. And stand up to him.

West drops his grip from her and approaches me with haste. Apparently outraged by my comment.

I take a step between him and Trinity, blocking him from trying anything foolish. We're roughly the same size and build, so I'm not worried about him physically overpowering me. And he must pick up on my lack of fear since he puffs up his chest like a rooster until he's pushed up against me.

Then, as a signal for Trinity, I nod my head to the side. "Get in the truck."

Trinity stands motionless as West tries to rush through me, realizing I'm her escape plan.

"Get in the truck!" I repeat to Trinity, with more demanding urgency this time.

West is irate and his emotions have somehow given him Hulk strength since I struggle to twist his arm around his back to stop him.

"Get off of me," he says, yanking his arm free. "I'll have you arrested for trespassing on private property." An empty threat.

I manage to get a handful of the back of his shirt in my grip. Which seems to only fuel the fire since he thrusts his body around trying to jerk himself free. And in doing so, the neckline of his shirt rips down the front of his torso.

"You don't want to do this, West." I let go of the remnants of his shirt and use my momentum to tackle him to the ground. Giving Trinity enough time to rush inside the truck.

I look over to make sure she's safe before releasing West from my grip. Only my lack of attention to him leaves a moment of vulnerability where he thrusts an elbow, landing it just above my eyebrow. It's not enough to knock me out but it dazes me for a second, forcing me to stand still and recover from the blow. Which gives enough time for West to rip at the door handle of my truck. "Open the door, Trinity." Thankfully she's locked it.

Sugar begins barking in the truck, which makes matters worse.

West slowly turns around to face me, with a look that can only be described as pure rage, before clenching his fists at his sides. "You took my dog." His statement is filled with revulsion. Instead of directing his anger at me, he flips his head around, facing Trinity inside the truck and yells, "*He took my dog*!" Leaving a trace of saliva splattered against the window.

Once I'm back on my feet, I shift my weight forward, gathering enough moment to barrel into West as he's trying to bust the passenger window with his forearm.

"West!" A man's voice emerges from behind us just as we tumble to the ground again. "Knock it off. Get in the house. *Now!*" It's West's father, the mayor. And he's briskly approaching with his arms pumping at his sides and an unsettled frown masking his face.

I scramble to my feet again, walking to the other side of my truck as soon as I realize that West's father is diffusing the situation.

"Sorry for the disturbance. I was only here to give Trinity a ride," I say to West's father. I want to promise it won't happen again, but I don't like making promises I can't keep. And since

West is unpredictable and impulsive, I wouldn't put it past him to cause a scene in the future.

The mayor is gripping one hand on West's shoulder when he glances at me. "Why don't you go on. I don't want this to turn into a serious situation for y'all."

I nod. And follow his directions to leave the premises, getting into my truck swiftly.

But West is reluctant to follow his father's instructions. He slaps his hand on the truck window and screams Trinity's name with roaring fury.

I put the truck into gear, and roll forward before turning around in front of their house to leave down the dirt road that led me here.

West begins jogging next to my window, his father is yelling at him again when I pass by. But West ignores his demands to stop, and instead rips off the rest of his shirt in a fit of rage. Then tosses it at my windshield.

I can't help but exhale with annoyance as I turn my windshield wipers on to remove what's left of the shredded black cloth that used to be West's shirt.

At first, I ignore his tantrum, but once he starts smacking the side of his fist against my window, I face him.

His voice is straining when he yells, "Don't forget that every time you stick your tongue down her throat I've already been there," he shoots his middle finger up as if it's a loaded gun that he's trying to use as intimidation, "with more than just my tongue!"

I cringe at his outrageous statement and step on the gas until we're moving fast enough to leave West in a cloud of dust behind us.

The first thing I notice when we're around the bend, is the Shania Twain song, *You're Still the One*, playing on the radio.

Sweet irony.

I turn the music down and glance at Trinity. "Are you hurt?"

She shakes her head. "He can't hurt me anymore."

I guess that's a good mindset to have.

"Sorry about him," she says, glancing at me briefly before looking out her window again.

I'm assuming she's referring to West's repulsive comment and unreasonable outburst. "You don't need to apologize for him."

"I mean, sorry he was there." She drops her head back against the seat and releases a breath through her nose. "He wasn't there when I called. He usually plays shuffleboard with his friends on Friday nights. I had no idea he was going to show up when he did."

"It doesn't bother me that he was there." What does bother me is that he's prioritizing shuffleboard over spending time with his kids.

It's quiet for a moment, then she slaps her palm to her forehead and mutters, "I hope the kids didn't see any of that."

Even though I think she was talking to herself, I reassure her with, "I'm sure they didn't." I release a long exhale. "Have you thought about getting a hold of a social worker again? You could use the extra set of eyes for situations like tonight."

She runs both hands through her stiff and unmanaged hair. "We were supposed to be trying to work this out ourselves. Like *adults.* It doesn't seem like we're doing a good job though, does it?" Her voice drops with defeat. "Maybe I'll call Sharry on Monday."

If only she hadn't married a narcissist, she wouldn't be fighting for her kids like this. "That's not a half bad idea. Sharry's a decent social worker and makes sure kids go to the safest home possible."

When she turns to face me, she gasps when I look over at her. Then shooting me an expression full of horror, she draws her hand up to cover her mouth.

When she pulls her hand away from her mouth momentarily, she says, "You're bleeding." Then returns it back to where it was.

I run my hand against the place on my head where West elbowed me. When I pull it down to look at it, sure enough, it's glazed with blood. "I'll be fine," I say, wiping the blood on my shirt.

She's searching around the truck, as if trying to find something to cover the wound. "Are you sure? Do you need me to drive or anything?"

"I'm good. Besides," I raise my brow in her direction when she looks at me again, "I've seen your driving."

She lets out a puff of air with her short laugh. Then, her demeanor shifts, and her voice grows serious again. "And I'm sorry about that too. I should have never taken your truck. It was irresponsible and reckless of me."

For some reason, her apology doesn't make me feel better. I'm not mad. Instead, I feel sorry for her. She seems to keep finding herself in sucky situations she needs to flee from.

"You know what?" I shift the gear stick down, slowing before I turn onto the county road toward town. "I should have listened to you better." Shifting gears again, I avoid her probing gaze. "You were doing what seemed like the only option for you in that moment." I finally glance at her, finding a worried expression on her face. "All I'm trying to say is, I get it."

"You do?"

I raise an eyebrow in her direction again. "More than you know." I'd like to elaborate, but it doesn't feel like my place to talk about what happened to Constance. My statement seems to satisfy Trinity, nonetheless.

She tilts her head when she looks at me. "Whatever makes you *get it*, I'm glad." She rubs her temples gently. "I don't know what I would have done if you didn't answer when I called."

"You still haven't told me how you got my number."

She lets out a quiet exhale of humor through her nose, rummaging in the grocery sack at her feet with a curling grin in the corner of her mouth. When she sits back against her seat, she hands me what looks to be a mixture of garbage, acorn hats, and leaves fused together in a circular fashion.

I take it and examine it by bracing it between my hands on the top of the steering wheel, careful not to get too distracted while driving. "What is this?"

She leans over Sugar, just enough to reach her hand between mine to reveal the card that I gave to Abbi the night I found her and Tuck hiding in the lazy susan. I don't bother telling Trinity about the encounter, mostly because I don't know how'd she feel about me bringing up that night. Plus, she seems content petting Sugar and looking out her window until we pull up to the house.

Sugar has been laying her head on Trinity's lap the entire trip. Her tail is heavily slapping against the seat. But she doesn't seem to have the same energy she did the first time she was reunited with Trinity. And when Trinity opens her door, hops out and motions for Sugar to follow, Sugar stays on the truck bench.

"What's the matter, girl?" Trinity pats her palms against the tops of her thighs encouraging her to follow. "Come on, Sugar."

I walk around to the other side of the truck where Trinity has begun to pull on Sugar's collar to coax her out.

Trinity looks up at me with a hint of worry. "What's wrong with her?"

I move between Trinity and Sugar, then gently lift Sugar from the seat in my arms. "I'm not sure, but I'm beginning to think it's more than just missing you."

CHAPTER FIFTEEN

Trinity

"Band-aid? Or gauze and tape?" I ask, holding one of
each respectively in my hands.

Knox rises from the sofa and says, "Neither,"
as he tussles his hair to the side. Failing to cover the gooey-
Neosporin-covered gash on his head.

I place the bandages back into the first-aid kit and follow
Knox into the kitchen to return the small red box to its cabinet.

The blood from his head was beginning to drip down
the side of his face when we brought Sugar inside. I couldn't
take the sight any longer, and insisted he let me clean him up
before tending to Sugar and her lethargy.

I was surprised it didn't take more coercing.

Constance emerges from her bedroom with a towel
fixed above her head as if she has just taken a shower. With
narrowing eyes fixed on Knox, her accented voice fills the
room. "What happened to you?"

Knox keeps his focus on her. "I had a little…altercation
earlier."

She makes a subtle noise in her throat as a response to his answer, or lack thereof.

When she catches my eyes, I give her a polite smile with a halfhearted wave that consists of me barely lifting my hand up.

The quick, but stiff, grin she flashes at me isn't very comforting. Her gaze narrows past me to Sugar laying on the couch. Almost as immediately as she notices Sugar, she flips her head toward Knox, approaching him with a finger pointed at Sugar. "What'd I say about the dog in the house?"

When I realize what she's upset about, I say, "That's my fault. I didn't know she wasn't allowed inside." I awkwardly move around Constance and Knox standing in the tiny kitchen to make my way over to the couch. "I'll put her outside now."

As I begin to retrieve Sugar's weary body from the couch, Constance says, "*Wait.*" She's holding her hand up in my direction when she closes her eyes to calm herself with an inhale. "What's wrong with the dog?" She faces Knox. "Why is the dog still acting like that?"

Before Knox can answer, I say, "She just needs her water bowl."

Knox motions for the back door as he retrieves her water dish and fills it with fresh water from the sink before handing it to me. "She hasn't been eating or drinking much the last couple of days."

I slide my arms under Sugar's body to lift her, moving her from the couch to the floor. "Do you have any sugar?" I ask, adjusting myself more comfortably on the floor next to Sugar.

When I take the water dish from Knox, I notice he and Constance are sharing a confused expression. Understandably so. I'd think my request for a dog bowl and sugar was strange too.

I carefully place the bowl next to me on the carpet, then look up to face them. "She's hypoglycemic." I swallow hard. "I don't have her medication." I purposely fail to explain that it's at West's house. "But putting sugar in her water will help until I can get her some medication. It's strange, but the sugar works." I know this because I've done it before when West put her medication money towards a losing golf bet with his friends on the course.

I continue, avoiding their eyes because of the shame that's creeping inside my stomach, "She hasn't had problems with her glucose in years. I thought the first few times were a fluke, or that maybe she'd grown out of it. I should have mentioned it sooner. But I honestly forgot about it." Not to mention with everything going on with my kids…I guess I haven't been the best dog owner.

"It's alright," Knox says. "Nothing a little sugar won't fix." He gives me a reassuring smile before retreating to the kitchen and digging through the cupboards. Somehow that smile is packed with enough power that it wipes away the shame I was feeling too.

"I don't have sugar," Constance says, with her arms folded over her chest. I can't tell if she's irritated, but I'm starting to get the sense that she's naturally firm when she's talking.

Knox closes the cupboard and raises his brow. "You're joking."

In return, she raises her brow at him with a challenging expression. The cadence of her voice is quick and rhythmic when she says, "What do I look like? Julia Child? Martha Stewart?" She tosses her hand flippantly. "Didn't think so. If I want cookies, I buy them with the sugar already baked into them from the store." Then she mumbles something about the time it takes to bake cookies and how hot the stove makes the house, but I don't think she's saying this to get a response from either of us.

Knox rolls his head to the side before passing through the living room. "I think I have some upstairs," is all he says before closing the door.

Constance finds a seat on the coffee table near Sugar and me. It makes me nervous that it's just me and her. Especially because I promised I'd come take care of Sugar and then never showed. And she seems like a person that would say something about it.

As if she can read my mind, Constance says, "She's lucky you decided to stop by when you did. There's no way we would have figured out what was wrong with her. She probably would've died."

Forward. Blunt. And terrifying. Was I being too optimistic hoping Constance would meet me with a gentle response?

I glide my hand against Sugar's spine. "I know I haven't been very responsible for her. I should have come by like I said I would. I should have called to check on her. I should have done a lot of things differently."

"Yeah." There's a lilt to Constance's voice when she says this. "You should have."

Her words sting. But there's nothing subtle about Constance. And I don't know why, but I appreciate that about her. At least I can count on her to always tell me the truth. Even if it comes out abrasive and slightly offensive.

She clears her throat. "Where'd Knox find you?"

Tilting my head, I give her a curious look. "*Find* me?"

"He left hours ago with Sugar." She adjusts the towel on her head. "Said he was gonna find you."

He was trying to find me? I'm realizing that before I called him, he was already out looking for me. My awareness of this fact makes my senses perk up as if my body is on alert. I'm not sure why I'm having such a strong visceral response to this realization. And I'm not sure if I'm supposed to feel this good about it.

She continues. "I hope you see his character in his actions." She looks at me pointedly. "And I won't assume *your* character from your lack of dog care."

Before I can further elaborate on my disappearance, Knox barrels through the door with a bottle of maple syrup and another bottle of honey in one hand, and an unopened bag of sugar in the other.

He places the variety on the coffee table next to Constance. "I wasn't sure how much you needed."

I smile and drag my finger across the top of the bag of sugar, opening it. "This is fine. Thanks."

I pull my legs underneath me, so I'm seated on my heels with better stability when I pour a little bit of sugar into the bowl.

The room is quiet while both Knox and Constance watch as I gently swirl the sugar in the water bowl with my finger. After the sugar is mostly dissolved, I rub the mixture on the inside of Sugar's cheek a few times until she begins to show interest in her bowl and laps up the water for herself.

Constance digs her elbow into her knee and braces her chin in her palm. "I can't believe that worked." It's the first time I've heard any sort of indication of happiness in her voice, albeit it's only *hinting* in her tone.

I shrug. "The medication is better for her, but regular sugar is easier to find and works in emergencies."

With her face still smashed in her palm, Constance says, "I guess Sugar really is a fitting name for her."

This makes me smile.

Ignoring her comment, Knox sits on the couch with his feet on the other side of Sugar. Then leaning forward, he begins to pet her gently. "Where do you get the medication?"

I keep my eyes on his hand brushing against Sugar's back, careful not to show how nice it makes me feel that he cares so much for my dog. "The vet."

He nods. "How much does it cost?"

"More than I have," I say with a short laugh. Then I get brave, and look up at him.

His hazel eyes hold on to mine for a long moment, then, "How much do you have?"

I shrug, pretending that his eyes aren't affecting me. "Eight dollars."

Then my anxious petting on the back of Sugar's coat runs into Knox's resting hand. A gentle gasp escapes up into my throat as I pull my hand away, acting like I don't notice what just happened by rising to my feet. Then quickly busying myself, I put the bag of sugar in the kitchen.

Constance gives me a look of disapproval. "And how do you expect to care for your dog with eight dollars and no medication?"

I shrug with a shake of my head. "I always manage."

Knox interjects with, "If you need some cash—"

I cut him off, "I already owe you for covering my bill on my birthday." I return to the couch but change my mind about sitting next to Knox and decide to stand where my hands can't run into his again.

Constance rises from where she was seated on the coffee table. "I'm no veterinarian, but I do know that it can't be good to keep givin' her sugar." Constance approaches me so she's only a few inches from my face. I can smell the damp scent of her freshly clean hair under her towel. In a low voice she says, "Woman to woman…what's goin' on with you?"

I glance at Knox. And I'm not sure why I do this. But it causes Constance to look at him briefly before looking back at me with narrowing eyes.

Then she tilts her head toward Knox. She points one finger in his direction with her raised voice. "You. Out!"

Knox points to himself with a confused expression.

Constance nods and points to Sugar. "Take her with you."

Knox begins to say something with his disgruntled expression. But then he must change his mind since he closes his mouth, picks up Sugar, and exits the house without saying anything. I have a feeling that she's the only one that he allows to speak to him like that.

When the door closes, Constance brings her gaze back to mine. It's weird looking down at someone her size that possesses so much strength. She can't be much taller than five feet since I'm just under five six and I'm craning my neck to look at her. She's still just a few inches from my face which makes me hyperaware of how badly I might smell. The odor I'm permeating is a damp mixture of sweaty emotions and Texas heat that I've succumbed to today.

"Now," she says, in the only tone she seems to use, which is *firm*. "I'm gonna need you to be straight with me if you're gonna stay here."

"Oh, no," I say politely. "I wasn't going to stay here."

She blinks with disapproval. "It's nighttime. Where'd you plan on stayin'?"

"I was going to—"

She tips her forehead toward me with raised eyebrows. "Be. Straight. With. Me."

I release a dissatisfied exhale because I know that what I'm about to *be straight* about is going to be humiliating. "I've been trying to get ahold of my dad, but he hasn't been home." I shake my head. "I got fired from McDonald's and ran out of cash for my motel room. And I just—"

But she stops me with certainty in her voice. "You're stayin' here."

I contemplate on arguing for a moment, but ultimately decide to agree with her. Mostly because it's my only option for a safe place to rest tonight. And, partly because I'm a little afraid to argue with her.

"I know what it's like," she says with penitence. Which strikes me silent since I've only ever heard her speak in a demanding way.

I search her brown eyes and hard expression, trying to make sense of what she's saying.

She tugs the collar of her robe to one side, revealing a jagged scar along her collarbone that looks as if the bone had broken through the skin at one point. "My ex was a jerk too."

And with that, I feel my guard shrinking down for the first time since my mom died.

CHAPTER SIXTEEN

Knox

"Here." Constance hands me a wad of small bills.

"What's this?"

She snaps her wallet closed, placing it back into her oversized black leather purse. It's decorated with a red dragon etched across the front. "The medication."

I give her a perplexed expression as I pull my brows together.

She tosses one hand into the air and rolls her eyes. "For the dog."

"I know what medication you're talking about."

She furrows her brow. "Then why are you lookin' at me like that?"

I lean my shoulder into the doorframe of my apartment so I can stand more comfortably. "I don't understand why you're doing this for her."

Adjusting the purse strap, she gives me a smirk. "Just tryin' to be the help I wished I had," is all she says before retreating down the stairs. And I know, from her gesture, not to press her about it.

As her foot hits the last step, I call out to her. "Did you make any coffee?"

She's approaching her car as she looks back up to me and yells, "No. I'll get some at M.L.'s. I'm working a double."

I nod slowly, realizing I'll have to go into the house where Trinity is. "My water's not working again," I confess. "Mind if I...?"

She lets out a menacing laugh.

I drag my hand down my face. "Kid..."

"Zio..." She's teasing me. And not making this easy.

Opening the door to her car, she finally says, "She was still sleeping when I left. We were up 'till midnight. So if you hurry, you'll probably get a shower and a cup of coffee before she wakes."

With my nod I give her a wave and say, "Thanks, Kid."

I quickly retreat inside my apartment and gather my uniform and thermos. It's six in the morning, and I'm assuming Trinity's sleeping in, especially after their late night. So when I approach the front door to Constance's home, I make sure to be as quiet as I possibly can when I enter.

But when the aroma of freshly brewed coffee infuses my nostrils, I decide there's no point in muting the sound of the front door as I toss it closed.

I hear Trinity gasp when the door slams before I see her.

"I didn't know you were coming down," she says with wide eyes when she pokes her head from behind the open fridge door. She places a carton of eggs on the counter. "Hungry?"

That's when I notice it. She and Constance must have done more than stay up talking last night since the bronze ends of her hair have been chopped off.

"Nah." I raise my handful of items. "My water's not working, and I need a shower. I'll just be a minute." I place my empty thermos on the counter and head for the bathroom.

A small wave of guilt begins to trickle over me. No matter how cold I make the shower, it doesn't seem to wash away the feeling. I'm not sure if I feel this way because I wasn't more protective of Trinity before yesterday. Or because waking up to her making coffee in the kitchen is making my chest heave.

If I could only get this shower colder.

When I finish getting ready, I head back into the kitchen to fill my thermos. Only it's already full of coffee and there's a bagel with a fried egg and cheese next to it that's snugly placed in a ziplock.

Trinity's tossing a stick for Sugar to fetch in the backyard. So I open the sliding glass door and call out to her in the middle of the yard. "Hey!" I hold the ziplocked bagel above my head. "This is unnecessary."

She's facing me with her hands on her hips. "You're welcome," she says, making her way over to me.

I press my back against the cupboard and edge of the counter to make space for her to enter the kitchen. Only when I move to close the sliding glass door behind her, my arm grazes her left shoulder. I don't think anything of it until she grips her upper arm with her other hand and winces.

I slide the door closed and crease my brow in confusion. "Sorry." At first, I think she's joking, but the expression on her face continues to twist for a moment. I approach her. "I didn't mean to—"

"It's not that," she says, dropping her head back and blinking up at the ceiling as if she's trying to get through the wave of pain. "Yesterday, West pulled on my arm. My shoulder's been sore ever since."

Her statement sends a flame down my sternum. And the guilt I was feeling before grows as the deep rage I have against West expands even more intensely.

I hate to ask, but West is three times her size and could do a lot of damage to her. So to ease my own concern, I say, "How hard did he pull on your arm?" My pulse begins to accelerate with anger as I wait for her response.

She blinks up at me with a worried expression. "It was pretty hard." She shakes her head and looks down as she gently squeezes her shoulder. "But considering what he's done before, it was nothing."

I press my mouth into a firm line, exhaling to contain my frustration and regain my composure. I can't wait to fill out a report for this when I get to the station. With a sharp inhale I say, "Can I?" Motioning toward her arm.

She nods, releasing her grip to pull her t-shirt sleeve up. Revealing her bare shoulder. There's no bruising, so that's a good sign.

I take her arm in my grip and gently move it from left to right. "Does that hurt?"

She shakes her head no.

I lift it up and down. "Any pain there?"

She shakes her head again.

But when I flip her palm and raise her hand, she winces and sucks in a sharp rush of air before gripping my wrist with her other hand to stop me.

"That," she says. "That's painful."

"Do you wanna get checked out at the hospital?"

Her eyes widen and drive into me with concern. "Do you think I need to see a doctor?"

"Maybe?" I pull my gaze from hers and look down at her hand still clasped around mine. I focus on the tendons stretching in her hand. Because I need to distract myself. I can't look at her when she looks like that without wanting to get physical justice. I'd like to injure West by doing things to him that would get me banned from police work.

With my attention still on the anatomy of her hand, I say, "If it hurts, it's probably a torn tendon. But you won't know for sure unless you get checked out."

She squeezes my hand and turns with her step toward me. I'm not sure if she does this so I have to look at her again, but it gets my attention. "I don't have health insurance. And I can't afford a doctor." She finally releases my hand and leans her hip into the counter. She's staring into the living room when she says, "What do you do for a torn tendon?" Her voice sounds hopeful.

I shrug and dig into a drawer where the ziplocks are. "You could try icing it." I open the freezer and fill the ziplock with a handful of ice cubes. "And rest. Try not to use the arm for a week or two? I mean," I press my fingers across the top of the ziplock, closing it before I hand it to her, "I'm no doctor. So if you want a professional's opinion, I can give you a ride to the doctor and spot you some cash."

"*I need a job*," she mumbles under her breath. Then she shakes her head with a short grin. "It'll be fine. Ice and rest it is for now." She takes the ice pack and presses it against her shoulder. "If it still hurts next week I'll go in. I've recovered from worse without seeing a doctor." Her comment doesn't bring me any comfort.

"Alright…" I say with hesitation. I drag my thermos and bagel from the counter and dip my chin. Forcing a smile over my frustration with West's unreasonable abuse. "Thanks for this."

She looks down with her emerging smile. "Sure thing."

I motion toward the door to leave when I say, "Don't make it a habit though."

"Just trying to pay you back."

"You don't need to do that."

"It's the least I can do for the help you and Constance have given me. I don't want to be a burden."

I tilt my head with sincerity and give her arm a gentle squeeze of reassurance. "Trust me, you're not a burden."

Biting at her bottom lip, she stifles a smile. I'm certain she's happy to hear that her presence is welcomed.

She scrunches her nose like she wants to tell me something uncomfortable.

"What?"

She circles her thumb against her shoulder. "Could you *not* report that stuff you saw last night?"

I raise my brow. Concerned that she wants to protect West from the punishment he deserves.

She drags her hand against her eyebrow. "I just don't want to make things worse with West. You know, because of the custody with the kids and everything."

I hate it, but I get it. "This time." The words feel wrong as soon as they come out. But I understand she has a target on her back. And with every report she makes, somehow, West is able to fabricate a story against Trinity that makes her look so much worse than him. It still shocks me the people in this town believe any of it.

She looks up at me with widened eyes, stunned it was so easy to get me to agree.

"This time I won't report it, but if I see him so much as look at you wrong…" I let my statement linger, allowing her to fill in the blanks with her imagination.

With her nod, she smiles and says, "I don't plan on seeing him again without Sharry as my witness."

"Good idea."

We stand in silence for a moment. Looking at each other. Waiting for the other one to say something and refusing to acknowledge the ease between us. And the growing familiarity.

"I should probably go," I finally say. I turn to leave, then turn back to her for a moment. "I like your haircut, by the way."

She touches her hair that's chopped just above her shoulders and stifles a laugh when she looks down at the floor.

Opening the door to exit, I say, "See you later, Trinity."

She waves before spinning around toward the back door again.

When I'm in my patrol vehicle I notice there's a grin on my face. I shake it away and start the car. I can't feel this way about her.

Friends. Sure.

I can show up when she needs a friend.

But I can't linger in the moments we share in Constance's kitchen with a grin on my face. With a lightness in my soul. And an eagerness to be around her again. It'll only turn into torture. We're living two completely different lives.

And my unwillingness to be happy might be the saddest part of mine.

Constance hands me a takeout container that smells like a patty melt I can't wait to eat. "Busy morning?" she asks in a monotone.

I hold the container in both of my hands when I raise my brow. "Not really. Why?"

She presses the back door to M.L.'s open a little more. She crosses her arms firmly, positioning herself on the slab of cement at the tops of the short steps that lead into the restaurant. "You're two hours late." She nods at the styrofoam container in my hands. "Foods probably soggy and cold by now."

I don't know why, but an uncontainable smile widens across my face. Much like the one I encountered in my squad car earlier, after I spent the remainder of my morning in the kitchen with Trinity.

Constance narrows her eyes curiously as a similar expression emerges on her face. Then her mouth falls open. "Why are you smiling like that?" Her tone is filled with fluty interrogation.

"I wasn't hungry until now."

She tosses her braid over her shoulder. "Uh huh." She knows there's more to the grin.

I roll my lips in, pressing my mouth together to stifle my growing smile.

"Was Trinity awake this morning?"

I roll my head back, looking up at the sky to avoid her peering eyes. "She made breakfast." I say this as generally as I possibly can, so it doesn't seem like Trinity took the time to cook an egg and place it between a bagel with a delicious slab of cheese. Just for me. "It's crazy what a difference breakfast makes." I'm not doing a good job of playing this off as a simple gesture.

She raises one eyebrow. "You sure *breakfast* is what made such a big difference in your morning?" is all she says before retreating back inside.

I head back down the alley to my squad car, taking a bite of the patty melt before pulling out of the alleyway. I quickly notice that the bagel from this morning tasted a lot better than the patty melt. No disrespect to Marcos, but it's true.

I make my way around the pavilion downtown when I notice Trinity running at a full sprint into the entrance of M.L.'s. This morning, we didn't discuss her plans, so I'm not sure what she's been up to all day. But something about the broken expression on her face isn't sitting well with me.

I pull into a parking spot in front of M.L.'s and quickly head inside.

Trinity is vigorously slapping her hand on the bar counter. With a demanding tone I didn't know was in her, she says, "Tell me where the phone is! *Now!*"

The waitress looks terrified, she's holding her hands up and shaking her head. "Please, ma'am. Calm down."

"I need to call the police!" The words erupt out of her with a gritty sound of urgency.

Constance rounds the corner from the back and tries diffusing the intensity with a steady tone. "Candy, take my section," she says to the waitress. "I'll deal with this."

I motion past the greeter with, "I'm here for that." I nod in the direction of Trinity's loud fixation of the phone's whereabouts.

She nods with a fearful expression.

As I'm approaching, Trinity catches my uneasy expression with her determined eyes. "Knox." She grips the front of my uniform in her hands. She doesn't even wince at the shoulder pain I know she's experiencing with her lifted arm. And her breathing intensifies when she says, "West took the kids. He *kidnapped* them."

CHAPTER SEVENTEEN

Trinity

"How do you know they were kidnapped?" Knox asks with a rasp to his voice when he says *kidnapped*.

Suddenly, my shoulder throbs. Like instinct, my other hand grips the painful area, waiting for the throb to end.

Knox places his hand over my good shoulder and cranes his neck down so his eyes are right in front of my face. "Kidnapping is serious, Trinity. You need to be certain about this. So I'm going to ask you again. How do you know your kids were kidnapped?"

I clench my teeth together, trying to keep them from chattering just as my body goes cold and my hands begin to tremble. "I was supposed to meet them at the gazebo in the pavilion today. They're late. And after what happened yesterday evening…" I swallow hard. "I can just feel it. I know he took them."

He nods as his eyes soften. "I don't doubt it." He glances at Constance then back to me. "But we should try to get in contact with him or his parents before making any accusations." His voice quiets when he says, "I'm going to find your kids." His eyes widen with sincerity. "I promise." Then he turns around and begins talking into his radio as he heads out to his car.

"This way," Constance says, placing her hand between my shoulder blades to coax me forward. "There's a phone in the kitchen you can use."

I walk with her to the back of the restaurant where she passes through swinging saloon doors into the kitchen. I follow and notice the guy with a low ponytail—the same guy that was working the bar the night of my birthday—he's grilling burgers next to a grease basket full of french fries.

Ponytail guy keeps his head down but adjusts his eyes from Constance to me, then back to Constance as he straightens his posture, standing upright with expectancy.

"She's gotta use the phone," Constance says, tossing her thumb in my direction. "It's an emergency."

Ponytail guy nods and goes back to grilling.

There's a phone on the wall above a small paper covered desk without a chair. Constance hands me the receiver and says, "Take your time," before leaving me on the opposite side of the kitchen from ponytail guy. Who seems as if he could care less that I'm in here at all.

I turn my back to him as I dial Martha's number. I twist the phone cord around my finger, impatiently waiting for her to answer. After several rings, she finally picks up.

"Martha," I say with my inhale. "I thought we were meeting at the pavilion today?"

Martha hesitates before responding with, "West insisted on bringing the kids."

After last night? She thought it would be okay if West and I were alone with the kids? I was hoping I was wrong. I was hoping that West had no idea that I was visiting the kids today. And I never thought Martha was so stupid until this moment. And if I'm wrong, if she's not stupid, then she must be as manipulative as her son to put him in charge of the visitation.

"He didn't show," I say with irritation.

Her voice becomes weak when she says, "Oh…" She sounds confused. As if she thought my call was to complain that West brought the kids for the visit. But now that she knows he didn't show, she seems lost for words.

Still, I can tell she knows something.

I can *feel* something is off. As if with each passing moment I can *feel* the distance growing between me and my children. And it's not just emotional distance anymore. I can *feel* the physical distance growing too. As if the tether is stretched so far between us that it's about to snap.

"Martha," my voice is a hard whisper, "where are they?"

She clears her throat, and I can hear Matthew ask who she's talking to. In a muffled voice, as if she's covering the receiver with her palm, she responds to him with, "*It's Trinity.*" It's quiet for a few seconds, then, "*West didn't show up for the visit today.*"

Matthew's heavy voice hits my eardrum. "Trinity, it's Matthew." His voice rises when he says, "West was plannin' on meetin' you in town before takin' the kids with him to Arizona for the week. He was gonna relay the info when he saw you."

"*Arizona?*" My voice spikes with the twisting of my stomach. "What's in Arizona?" I don't even care that West skipped the visit at this point. I'm more concerned that he's been planning a trip a thousand miles away with my children and no one thought to tell me about it beforehand.

Matthew lets out a quiet groan with his exhale. "He thought the kids needed a vacation after what they've been through."

"You didn't think to tell me about this before now? You didn't think they might miss their mom while they're away?" I don't care that I sound defensive. I'm surprised I got the words out at all with the throbbing my heart is doing behind my chest wall.

"It's not forever. They'll be back in a week or so," his tone shifts down, "Bye now."

There's a click on his end. Terminating the phone call so instantaneously that I don't have a moment to digest the information I've just been tossed.

I struggle to place the phone on the receiver because my hands are trembling severely. If that wasn't bad enough, I seem to be unable to catch my breath too.

I'm angry.

I'm frustrated.

I'm *broken*.

And I feel the worst betrayal I've ever felt by West.

I'd take being pummeled to unconsciousness over him taking my kids any day.

When I turn around to find Knox so I can report the information I've gathered from this brutally short conversation, I nearly trip. On nothing. It's as if my legs forgot how to walk.

I brace one hand against the wall. I can't even ask ponytail guy for help, since he's not in here anymore. I try to steady my racing breath along with my pounding pulse so I can call out for help.

Luckily, I don't have to since Knox rushes into the kitchen when he sees me straining for air.

The saloon doors are still swinging when he reaches me. His arms slip under mine, pulling me to his chest.

I wasn't expecting Knox to hug me. I wasn't expecting anyone to hug me. Instead of trying to figure out what I should do, I hold my eyes closed with my cheek pressed into him. And for the first time in a severely long time, I *relax*.

There's an overwhelming comfort being enveloped in his arms. More comforting than I've ever felt in anyone else's arms.

We stay like this for a long moment. My thudding pulse slows. My breathing slows.

"He took the kids to Arizona," I finally say in a hushed voiced.

"I know," his tone is gentle. "Marcos just told me."

"Ponytail guy?" He must have overheard my side of the conversation despite how discrete I was trying to be.

Knox pulls his head back to look down at me but when I don't reciprocate the eye contact he's looking for, he says, "Yeah, ponytail guy." He gives my arm a gentle squeeze. "Are you okay? I mean, I know you're not, but are you okay enough to walk out of here?"

More relief washes over me with his understanding words. "I think so."

I can feel him trying to end the hug. So I pull away from him.

"Astonishing," he says with a curious expression, as his grip slides from my back to clasp his gear belt.

I take another step backwards. "What?"

He rubs the side of his jaw, inspecting me with his gaze. "If this had happened to anyone else, they'd be in tears."

My eyes dart between his. "I don't cry," I say flatly.

His perplexed expression twists into uncertainty. "You won't cry?"

"I said I *don't* cry." I lift my arms to cross them, but when I do my shoulder aches. So I resort to holding onto my shoulder with my hand. He's still looking at me like he wants an explanation. So I give him the best answer I feel comfortable with. "I feel sad inside of my body. But even if I tried, I can't cry. It's just something that doesn't happen for me."

Now he's narrowing his eyes with his creasing forehead. Apparently still confused.

"I haven't cried since my mom died."

This direct statement causes his expression to shift into remorse. He's probably going to say he's sorry for my loss. I hate telling people about it because they never know what to do or say. I'd rather just avoid it all together. In fact, I'm sort of wishing I hadn't told him.

With a soft voice, he says, "I bet she would be really proud of the mom you've turned into."

My mouth parts but nothing comes out. This is the first response anyone has given that made any sense. And made me feel good. But I don't know how to say that to Knox. I'm not sure what *is* appropriate to say considering our second chance at friendship and close corridor living arrangement. I'm not even sure if it was appropriate for him to hug me. And it's certainly not appropriate for me to have any sort of feelings for him that entice more than a friendship.

My children are somewhere between here and Arizona and I'm struggling to contain my feelings for a man I'm only barely friends with. It's ridiculous.

He continues, "Without a doubt, you are one of the strongest people I've ever met. It's incredibly admirable." Just as I was looking at him to make sure he understood that I can't cry, his eyes shift between mine. Ensuring that his statement sinks into the very depth of who I am.

It does. But only for a moment, because I don't believe that I'm as strong as he's saying I am.

He nods his head to the side. "Come on, I'll give you a ride to the house."

When we're in his squad car, I release a heavy exhale with the realization that I'm stuck in the wrong place of a custody battle and a hundred steps in the opposite direction from getting my kids. "What do I do now?" I'm saying this more to myself. Sometimes speaking my thoughts out loud helps me process everything better.

Knox seems to have a response, nonetheless. "This entire situation sucks, Trinity. And I'm sorry for that." His grip tightens on the steering wheel briefly before he shifts the car around so we're on the street, heading in the direction of the house. He glances at me as his voice shifts down, "I hate to say it, but there's nothing we can legally do."

"You're joking." My voice is harsh and filled with disbelief.

"West is the legal father, and he has sole custody over the kids. Only a judge can change that."

I stare at him for a moment longer. Hoping he'll come up with a better answer than that. Hoping somewhere in his brain he'll remember some stupid clause or something about jurisdiction that will help me get my kids back. Or better yet, send West to prison for kidnapping!

Instead, he gives me a look of regret that shakes my sternum as if I've just been stabbed in the heart. "Without a change of custody, there's nothing I can do."

I hate it.

I don't accept it.

But sitting here with the urgency to do something isn't going to change the fact that I have no idea where West and the kids are in Arizona. I don't even know how to get ahold of them.

So, I make a plan to contact Sharry on Monday. And I'll call West's parents to get the number for the hotel he's staying at. So I can at least talk to the kids.

Knox hangs up the phone and looks at me. "They're good with you working in the kitchen. Marcos said he needs help in the morning until after the lunch rush. And since your schedule has suddenly opened," he says with a hint of humor, "I told him you could start tomorrow."

I nod and swallow the grief trying to ball up in my throat. "Thanks for doing that." I fake my happiness with a smile. Happiness is the appropriate feeling I should have since I've been desperate to get a job in this town. But I feel the opposite of happiness. At least I can hide my true feelings by faking a smile on my face.

"He had to hire you after I told him the breakfast bagel you made me was better than anything I've eaten at M.L.'s," his tone is teasing.

But I don't feel like reciprocating the humor after the day I've had.

"Can I use the phone?" I want to try contacting my father again. He still doesn't have a clue what's going on. And I don't have a clue where he is. Which makes my stomach turn.

Knox moves out of the way, revealing the phone for me. "Sure. And you don't have to ask. As long as you're staying here, the phone is yours now too."

I give him a short smile. "Thanks." Taking the phone, I dial my father's number, trying not to imagine the worst. Knox looks as if he's about to leave so I pull the receiver against my chest and say, "Would you mind staying?"

He turns slowly. "Yeah, I can stay." His words come out with uncertainty. Maybe he wants me to elaborate on why I'd like him to stay. I'm honestly not sure, but I do know that I don't want to be alone right now. Especially with my mind plaguing me with the worst-case scenario.

Knox faces me completely as he leans his back against the counter with his arms crossed over his chest.

I mouth a *thank you* to him just as the call is answered on the other side of the line.

"Hello?"

"*Dad!*" Hearing his voice floods me with a wave of relief. "Where have you been? I've been calling and I was beginning to think something might've happened to you."

"I'm sorry, Trinity."

"It's been over a month."

"Yeah," he lets out a soft chuckle. "I was in Cape Cod. Didn't think I'd be there as long as I was."

"Why didn't you tell me?"

"I didn't know how to get ahold of you. And I didn't know I needed to check in with you before traveling."

"Dad—" Glancing up at Knox, I notice he's smiling at me, and somehow it shifts my strong feelings towards my father's absence into a calmness. I release an exhale, and with my newfound smile, say, "Well, now you have a number to reach me at for next time."

He chuckles again. Which is odd. My father *never* chuckles. Or laughs. Or smiles. Frankly, he walks around with a dreary cloud over his head most of the time.

"If it makes you feel any better, I..uh…I wasn't alone."

"You weren't?" He hasn't done anything with anyone in over a decade. Not even with me. And besides the short visit with me at the hospital six months ago, I don't know the last time he left the house to go anywhere besides the grocery store or work.

Then his chuckle turns into giddy laughter, and I'm certain I just heard someone's voice in the background too.

"Trinity, I've met someone."

My mouth falls open. I'm not sure if I'm happy for him. I know my mother was the love of his life and the light in this world to him. And although he raised me and provided for me long past the time I needed him to, he never dated anyone. And even though it's been over a decade since her passing, it still stings knowing he's sharing moments with someone else that were meant to be spent with my mom.

"Her name is Anastasia."

But who am I to take away his happiness? "That's great, Dad." I force the words out, and they sound as meaningful as I hoped they would.

"We're planning to move to Cape Cod together. She has a lovely beach house with an incredible view." His voice rises when he says, "You're more than welcome to visit whenever you'd like."

I'm struggling to process all the information he's throwing at me.

And in my silent struggle he continues with, "I'd be happy to get you and the kids plane tickets."

I crease my brow. Hearing him say things like *lovely beach house* and *incredible view* and *I'd be happy to,* are boggling my brain receptors. He's never spoken like that. Not since I've known him anyway.

Before my mom died, I only have snippets of memories with them. The two of them were always happy and smiling. Maybe he used to be more poetic in his spoken language. Maybe for him, being in love ignites that person inside of him that's been curled up in the fetal position under an endless rainstorm. Maybe this *Anastasia* lady understands the dreary parts of my father. Maybe they're perfect for each other.

"A visit to Cape Cod sounds nice. I'd like that a lot," I finally say. "And I can't wait to meet her."

"How *are* the kids doing? Didn't sound like Martha was being very cordial with letting you visit them last we spoke."

He's even remembering details of my life like he never has before. I like this new side to my father with his pleasant vocabulary and thoughtful concern for my life. "It's worse now. West's run off with the kids to Arizona."

"Arizona? For how long?"

I rub at my eyebrows and glance at Knox who's not smiling at me anymore, but instead has a stern expression on his face. He's probably thinking about punching West in the face. Which is fine by me. "I'm not sure. Matthew said West would be back in a week or so. But that doesn't sound promising. And knowing West…well, you know West."

"What about his job?"

"He's not working yet. Sabbatical leave until the department decides what to do with him."

"Well," my dad says with a scratch in his voice, "the devil loves to shake an idle hand."

"You think he was bored? That's why he took off with the kids?"

"Maybe that. But what I meant is that I don't think it's healthy for a man to live without a purpose. And typically, a job that provides for our families gives us men a sense of purpose." He clears out the scratching in his throat. "It seems to me that since West isn't providing for you, his new purpose has turned into obsessing over you. Even if that means using the kids to get my attention."

"How do you figure?"

"Sometimes a man gets desperate. Love can make a man crazy. Just don't confuse his craziness for love. After what I realized he's capable of doing, I hope you stay as far away from him as you can."

A soft laugh escapes my mouth. "Don't worry. He'll never fool me into going back to him. I filed for divorce, and I've been waiting for him to sign the papers. It hasn't stopped him from trying to use his old tactics to get me back though."

"You know what they say about the devil?"

"He likes to shake an idle hand?"

"The devil is a gentleman in the worst disguise."

This makes me smile and roll my eyes. "Tell me what you really think of West, Dad."

"You know I've never been a fan," he lets out a gentle sigh. "I *am* glad you're finally seeing that for yourself."

I glance at Knox who's grinning at me again. "Well with all the information you've given me I've come to the conclusion that, apparently West is the devil."

My dad lets out a burst of gut laughter that's so loud I almost feel a dampness in my eyes. As if happy tears are trying to work their way out. But as soon as I blink, they vanish. It's baffling knowing the joy filled man on the other side of this phone call is my father.

Once he's not laughing anymore, he says, "You know what I don't understand?"

"Hmm?"

"How is it that West has legal rights to take Abbi with him anywhere?" My stomach drops with his question. Suddenly, I'm starting to miss the dad that didn't remember the details of my life and just showed up for me briefly when I wanted him to.

With a shuddered inhale I say, "I never told him."

It's quiet for a moment.

When I glance at Knox he's staring at the floor in thought with his chin braced against his fist. And my face flushes with the realization that he might be able to hear this entire conversation from where he's standing.

My dad makes a humming sound in his throat before he says, "He didn't think it was odd when he wasn't on her birth certificate?"

"He didn't think anything, because I put his name on her birth certificate."

My dad's voice is quiet when he says, "Oh, Trinity. For Abbi's sake, you might want to fix that."

I know now that I shouldn't have done that. But at the time, I thought we were going to be together forever. I thought I could trust the man that I called my husband. I thought I was doing the right thing for all of us.

The rest of the conversation is pleasant. I give him Constance's phone number so he can contact me with any future travel updates. And her address so he can send some money. Even though Constance insisted I stay for free, I want to make sure I'm contributing wherever I can by paying rent and making meals.

After the phone call, I meet Knox in the living room. At some point, while I was on the phone with my dad, Knox left the kitchen and found a spot on the couch to continue his deep staring at the floor.

Only when I sit next to him, he rises to his feet with a look of disturbance plastered to his face. As if he's figuring out how to put the circulating thoughts of his mind into words. And I'm not sure I like the way those thoughts are making him look at me.

The sweet grin my dad's conversation left on my face slowly drops into a firm line. "You heard." It's not a question. It's a regretful statement.

His stance is wide and strong as he lifts his chin. Turning his gaze away from me to stare out the window, he begins to speak with bewilderment straining his voice. "What I don't understand is that you're allowing him to take Abbi, and he's not even her real dad."

"I know it's confusing." I clasp my hands together firmly on my lap. "But when I met West, he wanted to be a dad so badly. And when I finally mustered up the courage to tell him I was pregnant, I decided not to tell him the part about how he wasn't the biological father."

Knox's jaw is cocked to the side as he shakes his head. He's still not making eye contact when he says, "You're lying to both of them."

I don't see how this is any of his business, but for his sake, I want him to know why I kept it a secret. "It's painfully simple." If anything, telling him might restore the peace between us. "He wanted to be a dad. And Abbi needed a father."

"So you chose the biggest prick to fill that position?"

My tone shifts down defensively when I say, "He wasn't always like how he is now." I'm not trying to defend West. I'm trying to defend myself and my immature decisions.

Knox runs his hands through his hair. When he drops his arms to his sides, he finally looks at me with disbelief. "I'm sorry, I'm not trying to tell you what to do. But with the information you know, you have to see that you could at least get Abbi back by telling him the truth."

"His name is on her birth certificate. You said it yourself, he's her legal father. Which means he has all the rights that her biological father would have." I shake my head slowly as my expression fills with remorse. Because I know what I'm about to say isn't going to make any sense to Knox. "Having West as a father is better than growing up without a father at all. And West believing he's Abbi's father, is so much better for her than if West knew she wasn't his."

Knox is shaking his head. As if he won't even allow the information to enter his brain. "Help me understand how West existing at all is good for anyone." His brow drops with his tone. "Especially for a child."

I hold my hands in a steeple and press the tips of my fingers against my mouth. I wait until I can find a reasonable voice to speak to him in before I respond. Then I rise to my feet and approach him so I'm standing directly in front of him. My words come out with slow dictation. "I'm going to say this once, so please listen carefully."

His stern expression is replaced by a softness as his brows fall to the sides of his face when he sees how serious I'm being and how hard this is for me to say.

I continue, "I was drunk when I got pregnant with Abbi. It was a one-night stand. I don't even know who her father is.

But as horrible as West is to me, he's a good enough dad that I know he wouldn't hurt the kids." I swallow hard. "Unless he knew Abbi wasn't his. If he knew the truth, he'd have no problem treating her the way he treats me. And since he has all the rights that a biological father has…"

Knox's hazel eyes widen as his face falls firm. As if he's just had an epiphany about this real-life nightmare I know as *my life*.

His throat rolls before he says, "I get what you're saying." Then he rubs at the back of his neck, his eyes searching the walls before they lock on mine again. "But I don't like it." He pulls his hand from his neck and places it on my shoulder. "And I *truly* believe there's a way around it. And a better way to get to the truth."

CHAPTER EIGHTEEN

Knox

April 1998

She's closing in on three weeks since she's seen her kids. Her life is like a string that's been tied in knots. Tangled in the worst way. And after carefully looking into her situation with West, I found *nothing*.

There's *nothing* she can legally do to get her kids back right now. West has every right to take the kids as long as he wants. As far away as he wants. Because he has full custody.

And I hate that for her. I hate that a piece of paper holds so much authority over her life.

When I leave my apartment, I notice her in the backyard, sitting on the swing with her back to me. And it's in this moment, where she's barely swinging, with her gaze fixed at the bare dirt in front of her, that I realize how painful this is for her.

I'm not sure if she wants to be left in her thoughts or if she wants some company. If it were me, and I had been working as many hours as she has been working at M.L.'s, I'd want some solace too. At the same time, if my kids had been ripped out of my life, I'd want to work as many hours as I could to distract myself from reality. But more than any of that, I'd want someone by my side to go through the struggles of my life with me.

I decide to leave her to her thoughts and load up my tools in my truck before I head out. Constance is leaving the house just as I toss a bundle of shingles into the back of my truck.

"Working on the house again?" She's braiding the end of her hair while lifting her shoulder to keep her purse from falling down her arm.

I close the tailgate, lean my hip into the truck, and face her. "Yeah. You headed to work already?"

She glances in the direction of where Trinity is sitting outside. "I don't have the heart to stick around until my shift starts." She ties the end of her braid with a hair tie and looks at me again. "She's been out there since before the sunrise. No coffee. No breakfast. I don't think she's showered in days." She lowers her voice and leans in toward me, nearly closing the space between us. "And she screams in her sleep."

I draw my head back. "*Screams* in her sleep?"

"From the nightmares."

"How do you know it's nightmares?"

She pats my shoulder. "Because I'm the one that wakes her up from them."

I've been so consumed with figuring out a way for Trinity to get her kids back, that I've forgotten about the years of abuse she went through with West. Who wouldn't suffer from nightmares with her past?

Constance leaves me standing in my bewilderment as she gets into her car. I give her a short wave as she drives off. My hand drops along with my smile. Because I didn't realize just a few feet away from where I've been resting soundly at night, Constance and Trinity have been fighting for a good night's sleep.

I abandon my truck and retreat to the backyard. Sugar looks up when she hears the gate latch. When she realizes it's me, she comes over to receive a scratch behind the ear. I keep my eyes on Trinity though, waiting for her to turn around.

When she doesn't, I approach her until I'm holding the scratchy weathered rope of the swing in my hands.

She still doesn't acknowledge me.

I shift my face around the swing, still holding the rope in my hands, to peer down at her. "Did you fall asleep?" I'm trying to lighten her downcast mood.

Her shoulders rise as she lifts her hands from her lap to grasp the rope below my grip. "I wish I could sleep that easily." Her voice is solemn when she delivers her quiet statement.

I pull the swing back gently then release it. "Constance mentioned you're having trouble sleeping."

She lifts her feet up as I continue to push the swing gently. "I think all the worrying I should be doing during the day plagues me at night. I wish I knew how to sleep without dreaming."

"Pillows."

She turns slightly to face me, then facing forward again she says, "Doesn't everyone use pillows?"

"I mean, *more* pillows." I gently give her back a push when she swings toward me. "You can make a barricade around yourself. Or hold the pillows for comfort." I hope she doesn't read too much into my advice, or she might ask me to elaborate and I'm not ready to do that. "I can loan you some extra pillows if you need some help falling asleep." I have more than enough.

"It's not the falling asleep part that I need help with, it's the nightmare part."

I give her another gentle push and her hair flutters with the breeze. "If I knew the antidote for nightmares, I'd tell you. But, trust me, pillows are a good start."

She drags her feet against the ground until she slows to a stop.

When she doesn't say anything, I drop my hand down on the rope to cover hers, as a form of comfort. Her back rises with her deep inhale. She seems distant. Not purposely distancing herself from me, but distant in her thoughts.

With my hand still gripped around hers, I shift around the swing so that I'm in front of her. I drop my hand down so I'm holding the base of the rope, close to the long piece of wood she's seated on, when I squat down in front of her. "You okay?" I know she's not *okay* but I don't know what else to say to her right now when she's apparently not in her body, and instead, has drifted entirely into her thoughts.

She blinks and sits up a little straighter, but she's still mostly slouching. When her eyes catch mine, her pupils shift and I can tell she's back in her body again. "No one tells you how isolating divorce is." She bites at her cheek for a moment, then, "No one talks about how lonely it is. Or how much you'll miss just having someone there." Her voice shifts down with a hint of sarcasm, "Even if that someone caused you more pain than comfort."

I search her face. Trying to understand what she's saying without letting my chest tighten with anger toward West and what he's done to her life. Trying to keep my breath easy and just *listen* to her.

She takes advantage of my silence and continues, "He was the temple that turned into my own personal tomb, burying what was left of me after my mom died."

That guy's a real pissant.

"I'm sorry. Losing your parents is tough. Especially your mom," I say gently, and with full understanding. "When did it happen?"

With her fatigued exhale, her shoulders drop. "When I was ten." She shrugs one shoulder with the smallest movement. "Bone cancer," is all she says, knowing that no further explanation is needed after that short but painfully heavy statement.

When she first told me that her mom had passed, I thought it was more recent. I thought she was older. But losing a mom as a child, it's unfathomable. And my chest feels sore just thinking about how she had to continue her life without her mom. She had to go to school with the other kids and pretend like she wasn't dying inside. She had to cry herself to sleep, because her mom's absence was the most painful at bedtime. She couldn't talk about how she felt, because no one understood. And I know she suffered in this way, because I did too.

When I say, "My mom died when I was eighteen," her mouth parts as her eyes come alive with empathy.

She continues to look at me as if waiting for me to explain. But I can't do that right now. And I don't want to. Right now, is about her sadness. I don't want to invade that space and make it about my own torment.

"How'd your dad handle it?" I say, diverting the conversation toward her again.

She tilts her head, thinking. "My dad was heartbroken and kind of shut down. I don't blame him. But he wasn't present for me at all. And I hated being home. It felt like I was living in the fading memory of my mom while the dust collected on her nightstand and pictures of her in our house. He kept the drapes closed because that's how they were when she died. He left her chair scooted out at the kitchen table. He kept her toothbrush in the bathroom. He left her entire wardrobe in their closet. He didn't want to let go of what was left of her. He even left her voice on the answering machine for years until I finally convinced him to buy a new phone. And even after he got a new phone, he didn't bother setting up the answering machine."

"Sounds like he really loved her."

"He did." She drops her head back, looking up at the rope secured around an above tree limb, as her thoughts expand. "And I wanted someone to love me as much as he loved her. And since my dad's ability to love died with my mom, I went out looking for that kind of love in the wrong places."

I'm not sure I want to know, but I ask anyway. "Where was that?"

Her mouth shifts to the side as she regards me silently for a moment. I have an idea of what she might say knowing that she got pregnant from a drunken one-night stand. But I want to hear it from her instead of making my own assumptions, so I continue to wait until she's ready to answer.

She drops her gaze, unable to confess while looking me in the eyes. "I did a lot of dumb stuff to feel something."

"Like sitting on the wrong side of a railroad bridge?" I jokingly remind her of our second encounter.

Glancing up at me, she reveals a small grin. "Yeah...risky stuff like that." She drops her hand from the rope and it gently grazes my grip as she slides both of her hands onto her lap. "I didn't care how dangerous the people were that I was hanging out with. I would still get blackout drunk. I'd do anything to forget the hole my mom's death left in our lives. It's a miracle I didn't get pregnant sooner."

That confession makes me sad for her.

"I don't remember half the nights I was a teenager because I was so out of it. And when I met West at an alumni party in Abilene," she closes her eyes tightly, "he consumed me." She sounds as if she regrets allowing him to *consume* her. A better word she could have used to describe what he did would be *destroy*.

I tilt my head, intrigued by a minor detail in her story. "Alumni party in Abilene?"

She glances at me. "Yeah, he graduated there."

I'm perplexed by this information. "An alumni party with the police academy in Abilene?"

Her brows drop with a bewildered nod at my questioning. "I grew up in Abilene."

My eyes are darting between hers with curiosity. "I graduated from the police academy in Abilene."

Her mouth parts momentarily before she says, "You did? When?"

Jogging back in my memory, I say, "I joined when I was eighteen. Graduated two years after. So that puts graduation at three years ago."

"That's funny you both went to the same academy."

"Strange I never saw him."

"You wouldn't have. He graduated a while ago." She squints at me. "He's much older than you. Which made him more comfortable with me. And a wandering seventeen-year-old that lived a block away from the police academy was an easy target." She rolls her eyes. "He worked hard to get my attention and made sure no one else did. He was confident instead of sounding stupid like the guys my age. He took me for a ride on his Harley which made me feel the rush of death and inadvertently created that feeling of being alive I so desperately wanted. Within a week he told me he loved me. Shortly after that he told me that he wanted to be a dad, and I told him I was pregnant. He married me on the spot. Somehow, he always knew exactly what to say to get to my heart. Even if it was, sometimes, fabricated to manipulate me."

She shakes her head and her face twists with regret. "I married a warm body. I hate to admit it. But I just wanted *someone* to want me and want my baby. Someone that wanted more than a night of fun. And West was the first guy to show any lasting interest in me. So I jumped at the opportunity."

There's a sudden sinking in my chest at her confession. And I finally understand why she stayed with West for so long. She didn't think she had a choice. She didn't think she could do any better. And she was in a hurry to find someone. She was alone. And I'm certain being a lonely, pregnant, teenager was more terrifying than jumping into a relationship with someone she barely knew.

I take her hands in mine. "You were young and afraid and didn't know what kind of jackass West was."

"Yes. That's exactly right." She gives me a heavy expression, as if she's being understood for the first time. "For years, it's felt like the saddest song has been playing on repeat. But up until now, I was the only one that could hear it."

"You were making decisions that most adults don't have to deal with. And you were still a kid."

Her eyes drop when I say this. Like she's saddened by the reality that she was just a kid forced into an adult world.

I tuck my hand under her chin and gently lift her face until she looks at me. "You didn't even have a mom to help you through any of it. And from the sounds of it your father was checked out in his own suffering. But you were brave anyway. Not because you had to be, but because you wanted to be brave."

Her eyes are ticking back and forth between mine, as if she's in disbelief that I'm able to see that part of her.

My voice is almost a whisper when I say, "Fear is a reaction, Trinity. And courage is a decision, and you made the hardest choice by choosing courage." I smile. "You were seventeen and reacted to your fear of being alone. But then you charged forward through your fear. You *chose* courage. And every day since, you've been choosing to be courageous. That deserves some credit."

Her chest is rising with her intensified breathing.

I continue to look into her green eyes, trying to figure out if I'm the one creating this reaction in her or if it's something else only she sees in her mind. Her eyes have shifted from the heavy haze I saw when I first walked into the backyard, to an alert version of the eyes I've come to recognize as our conversation has progressed.

And now, her eyes are bright; almost shining, as if she might…cry.

Folding my mouth in, I'm at a loss for words. It's apparent that some kind of emotions want to burst out of her, but she's trying with all her might to hold it in. And I'm not even sure she knows she's doing it.

I can't take the sight much longer without one of us saying something. So, instead of talking, I rise to my feet, pull her from the swing, and hold her in my arms. I hug her against my chest, one arm wrapped against her ribs, and the other clasped around her head. And I give her space to move through the feelings. I *hope* she feels safe enough to move through them.

Her heavy breathing continues. I can hear her grinding her teeth she's clenching her jaw so tightly. And I don't do anything to stop it, because I know the heartache she's endured has fueled her to be brave for years. I know she's had to be tougher than anyone she knows. She's had to keep going even when the struggle was unbearable. And I know it's not going to take one hug from a man she barely knows to open the festering wound she's desperately kept closed with a cheap bandage.

Despite my best efforts to get her to *feel* the agonizing depth of her painful life, she doesn't cry. Not that I want her to cry. But crying might help. Especially since it seems like she refuses to cry even when it's acceptable. And expected.

I can feel by how tense she's become in my arms that she's not going to let it out. At least not today.

Placing my hands on her shoulders, I pull her from me to look at her. She's still looking at me intensely. But her breathing has gone back to its normal pace.

When I open my mouth to speak, I hear a sharp smack. The sound causes not only me and Trinity to face the noise, but Sugar looks up too. And in an instant, she jumps up and rushes toward the fence on alert.

The sound happens again, and again. It's almost a popping sound. Like a Blackcat exploding. Or…

CHAPTER NINETEEN

Trinity

Sugar barks a deep warning bark as another pop echoes above our heads.

The strange gloom that was circling in my core shifts to a feeling of urgency at the popping sound. I flip around to face Knox with concern. "What was that?"

Without responding, he releases me from his grip and rushes through the gate. I follow, securing the gate behind us, when we're met by the sight of a kid in a flannel throwing eggs at his truck.

When the kid sees us, he narrows his eyes at Knox before pulling his gaze toward the truck. Then he cocks his arm back, ready to fire another egg.

"Robby!" Knox is jogging over to the kid to stop him. "Do not throw that at my—"

The egg hits the back window with a crack, and the yolk is sliding down the glass before Knox can complete his statement.

Without hesitation, Robby is in a full-blown sprint down the street.

Knox's voice is low, he doesn't bother looking at me when he says, "Get in the truck."

I follow his orders and get in the truck, mostly because I'm intrigued to see what happens next. And the exhilaration of the last fifteen seconds is making me feel alive for the first time in weeks. The kind of *alive* I used to feel on the back of West's motorcycle, or when I was stealing Knox's truck to avoid West.

Knox is backing out of the driveway and blazing down the street before I've even buckled my seatbelt.

"You know that kid?" I ask, wondering what sort of prank this is between them.

He's turning down a road toward the school. "Robby..." He drags a hand through his hair. "He's always doing stuff like this. He's harmless, but he's troubled. Parents are heavy into drugs, and he's being raised by his decrepit grandmother."

I don't know why, but that makes me smile. "At least he's not following in his parents' footsteps and getting into drugs."

"Yeah, well, if he had any friends he probably would be."

That makes me stop smiling. Poor kid. Egging Knox's truck seems more personal than a prank now that I know he's doing it by himself. "What's his riff with you?"

"This is the first time he's targeted me directly with his stunts." He shifts the gear stick aggressively. "And since he's suddenly targeting me, I'm going to find out why he thought it was a good idea to get my attention by egging my truck instead of talking to me like a normal person."

He turns down a street where the houses are outdated, and the lawns are either full of weeds, garbage, or overgrown with grass.

I brace myself by placing one hand on the dash when he hits the brake and puts the truck into park.

He's out of the truck before I know what's happening. I'm already invested and need to know where this is going. It's intriguing seeing Knox being a police officer, even if he's in a t-shirt and jeans instead of a uniform. I can tell he's in police mode by the change in his demeanor as well as the intensity behind his actions.

I jump out of the truck, nearly running to keep up with his stride across the lawn. He rushes up the steps of a small, salmon colored house with a broken screen door. It's so broken that when Knox swings it open, it falls off the hinges. With one hand, he sets it against the house.

"Mrs. Alinksy!" He bangs on the door and calls out in his police officer voice. "Mrs. Alinsky! I need to speak with you about Robby!"

This lasts for an entire minute before the doorknob turns and the door gently opens, revealing an elderly woman that is no less than a hundred years old.

The home is so dark behind her that I can't make out anything inside. She's squinting, probably from the first sunlight she's encountered in ages. Shading her hand above her eyes, she says, "What can I do for you, Officer Santino?"

Knox places one arm on the doorframe. He looks *huge* in comparison to this matted, white-haired woman in front of us. Nodding in the direction of his truck, he says, "Robby egged my truck. I followed him here. I'd like to speak with him for a minute, if that's alright with you?"

"What on God's earth was he doin' that for?" Her words are mumbled, and her hand is trembling above her brow. I've never been this close to someone so old, so I'm not exactly sure if her trembling is normal for her age.

"It's a personal matter."

Shifting in the doorway, she calls out into the darkness of her home. "Robby!" The rough strain in her voice causes her to let out a phlegmy cough. Then, "Robby! Officer Santino is here to see you."

It's quiet for a moment then the teenager from Knox's yard emerges from the dark. He's wearing a Bulls basketball jersey and black basketball shorts, which is a change from the jeans and blue flannel he was wearing just minutes ago. He's breathing hard, as if he just ran a race. Which he did when he outran Knox in his truck.

He lifts his chin up to Knox in a friendly manner, but his expression is bland. "What's up, Santino?"

"*Officer* Santino," Knox corrects, with his jaw set in place.

Robby runs his hands through his hair. It sort of stays sticking straight up when he does this because of the sweat on his scalp that emerged from the sprinting he was just doing. "Sorry." Opening his mouth and running his tongue against his back molars, he continues with, "What's up, *Officer...*" There's a long pause, before he finishes his statement with, "...Santino."

I can't tell if he's being weird or sarcastic. But there's something off about the kid.

Knox throws his thumb over his shoulder. "What's your deal? Why'd you throw eggs at my truck and then run off."

"I didn't do that." Robby shakes his head aggressively back and forth, causing his sweaty, curly, red, hair to fall into his eyes again.

Knox straightens his posture and crosses his arms over his chest. "Oh yeah?"

"Yeah," Robby's nodding aggressively now and his hair is flipping all over the place. "I was...uh..." his eyes drift behind

Knox, "…mowing the lawn." He lifts his arm in unison with his statement. Which is obviously a lie since I saw him with my own eyes tossing eggs at Knox's truck.

Knox twists his torso without moving his feet, looking out at the lawn where one line of grass has been mowed before the lawn mower died. Or whoever was mowing the lawn quit and left the mower there. In this case, it must've been Robby.

When he twists back around to face Robby, he says, "And that's why you're so out of breath."

Robby nods. "Yeah, and also why I'm wearing different clothes than the egger."

Knox must know he's lying now.

Mrs. Alinsky is standing behind Robby. Her eyes are a little more open now and adjusted to the sunlight. She's looking back and forth between Robby and Knox. She opens her mouth but only another phlegmy cough comes out.

Knox rubs the back of his neck with one hand and places the other one against the doorframe again. "It's weird, I could've sworn the kid that egged my truck ran right… down…your…street. And straight to your house." He pauses between the words. I'm not sure why since we all know it was Robby that egged his truck. He was less than twenty feet away from Knox. If I were asked, I could instantly point him out in a lineup at the station.

"That is weird," is all Robby says, with the same careless expression he's been wearing since he emerged in the doorway.

Knox stares at Robby for an uncomfortably long moment. Robby never looks back at him though. He looks at the cement porch steps. He looks up at the sky. He watches a couple kids ride by on their bikes. He even glances at me. But he never looks at Knox.

"I guess your alibi checks out," Knox says, pushing himself from the doorframe and down the steps. He waves at Mrs. Alinsky. "Sorry for the mistake."

Mrs. Alinsky waves her arthritic hand before slinking back into the darkness of her home again.

"I'll get that screen door fixed and then I'll be out of your hair," Knox says, walking backward to his truck. I'm not sure if Mrs. Alinsky even heard him since she's disappeared into the depths of her home.

Knox retrieves his tools from the truck bed, then heads back to the entrance of the home with a pleasant grin on his face.

Robby is still standing in the doorway, watching Knox's every move.

Funny how now that he's not in trouble he doesn't have a problem looking at Knox.

"Hold this," Knox says, placing the door into position for Robby.

I'm still standing at the bottom of the steps, observing this interesting encounter.

Robby holds the screen door in place and watches Knox screw the loose hinges back into the frame. I'm trying my best to focus on Knox's kindness for helping them, but my eyes betray me and stare at the muscles tensing in his forearms as he grips the buzzing power tool in his hands. I roll my eyes at my own ridiculousness. And coincidentally it forces my gaze to fall on every other part of the house that needs fixing. Poor Mrs. Alinsky, too bad her son is consumed with drugs and her grandson doesn't have enough stamina to finish mowing the lawn.

It takes less than a minute for them to fix the door, and by Robby's expression, he's impressed. "Wow," he says. "That was kinda fun."

As Knox is picking up his tool bag, he says, "Get your shoes on and you can help me fix some other things."

Without a word, Robby grabs a pair of shoes and is out the door heading over to Knox's truck.

"Where are we going?" I ask Knox.

With a grin that causes my heart to spring, he says, "My house."

"Your apartment?" I'm confused why that would require a grin like the one he's giving me.

He waves me toward the truck. "Come on."

"Knox," I say, causing him to turn his neck just enough to catch my eyes. "What are we doing?"

"I told you." He lets out a small laugh that's filled with clandestineness. "I'm taking you to *my* house."

CHAPTER TWENTY

Knox

"Here," I say handing Robby the hammer. "Your turn."

He takes it from me. "If I knew we were gonna be sitting on your roof fixing shingles all day I would've worn pants. Check out my knees." He shoves his leg in my direction. "Looks like burnt toast."

I laugh at his accurate depiction of his discolored knee. Then I pull the last shingle from the pack into place. We'll need to get several more done if we're going to finish this project today. Which I've already decided we're going to do.

"I'm gonna grab another pack," I say, motioning toward the ladder. "Think you can handle that last shingle on your own?"

He doesn't acknowledge me, and instead pulls the last shingle, centers a nail, and begins unloading the hammer into it.

When I reach my truck, I notice Trinity standing under one of the trees at the side of the house. Her expression is covered with concern as she gazes up at the branches.

I abandon the shingles to open the cooler and pull out three Cokes instead. When I pass by Robby, sitting on the roof with his feet perched on the gutter, I toss one of the Cokes up to him. "Take a break and find some shade."

He catches the Coke and then gives me a salute.

I point to his feet as I pass around the corner of the house. "And get your shoes off my gutter before you break it."

When Trinity sees me coming, she gives me a short wave by lifting one hand from her crossed arms. Pointing up to the tree, she says, "You know this is dead, right?"

I hand her a Coke, opening mine to take a quick swig before saying, "No, it's just hurt. It'll come back with some love."

She gently nudges me with the Coke I just handed her, scoffing at my dismissive remark. "This is a dying forty-foot sassafras tree that's going to land on your newly renovated house." Shaking her head she adds, "Also…" She pops the top of the Coke open. "How is it that we've been friends this long and I've never once heard about your house before today?"

I raise one brow. "How is it that you never told me you knew so much about trees?" I don't mention that this is the first time she's outright called us friends. I'm still hesitant with her, making sure I don't do anything to scare her off.

She scrunches her nose. "Answer my question first."

I didn't think telling her about my house was so important. "It never came up. Your turn."

"That's a terrible answer."

"It's the only one you're getting."

"Fine." She rolls her eyes. "I don't know a lot about trees. But I do know a sassafras tree when I see one because we had a sassafras tree in our backyard. I remember my mom trying to save it. She and my dad were constantly on the phone with professors from the agriculture department at any university that would take their call." Her eyes soften with remorse. "They ended up figuring out it was diseased. My mom still did everything she could to salvage it. After it died, my dad never cut it down. Even when a windstorm broke several of the branches. It just sat out there, falling to pieces." She looks down at her Coke briefly, then back to me. "He's going to get himself hurt."

I tilt my head with confusion. "Your father?"

Shaking her head, she points past me toward the house. "No. I mean, Robby."

Without missing a beat, I drop my can of Coke and rush to the house where Robby is dangling from the roof.

"Do not let go of that roof!" I call up to him when I'm just below his dangling legs.

His hands are gripped on either side of the ridge where the roof is at its highest point. Because of the vaulted ceilings, it's a good twenty-foot drop and a possible broken bone or two if he decides to let go.

With his short laughter, he says, "Catch me, Knox."

"*No!*" I instinctually lift my arms at his request. I can only hope he doesn't drop at this point. "Listen, Robby, you need to pull yourself back up onto the roof again."

He twists his head slightly as he looks down over his shoulder. "I can't!" His body shifts, swinging back and forth as he adjusts his grip. "I'm not strong enough."

"Stay right there." I'm already on the other side of the house and climbing the ladder as I release this demand with a groan.

Scaling the roof, I straddle the ridge as I lean forward to grasp Robby's forearms. I hadn't considered how sweaty he would be, but since he's on the scrawnier side it doesn't take much to hoist him back up onto the rooftop.

When I free my grip from him, he begins to laugh.

"What are you laughing about?" My brows knit together with frustration. "You could have gotten seriously hurt."

With his laughter, he says, "Think it would have sent me to jail?"

"No," I say pointedly. "Probably the hospital, but not jail." I thrust my arm at my side with impatience. "And stop doing crap that's going to get you in trouble, Robby."

He stops laughing and begins inspecting his hands. I'm sure they're stinging right about now. There's nothing pleasant about gripping shingles when the sun's shining like it is today.

"Are you boys going to be okay?" Trinity calls out from below us.

"For now," I say, taking a step back with my eyes narrowed at Robby. And I have every intention of making the rest of his day *safely* miserable.

Only when I step back my boot slides on the handle of the hammer and I lose my balance. My arms begin circling as I try and regain my footing, but I'm already tripping over my own feet as my body gains momentum from the steep angle of the roof. Before I detect the next move, I'm tumbling and then midair as my gaze fixes on Robby's horrified expression for a split second. I know I'm going to hit the ground when I lose sight of him and hear Trinity screaming out my name in terror.

CHAPTER TWENTY-ONE

Trinity

After Robby and I, somehow, managed to load Knox into his truck, I drove Knox to the hospital where they did an X-ray and found three fractured ribs.

Knox is supposed to rest, ice the area, and go back to work in a week with minimal activity to ensure his ribs heal properly in the next six weeks.

I've made him a bowl of soup today. I know the broth will aid in his recovery. But I'm reluctant to go up to his apartment since I'm not sure how he handles this sort of thing. Some men like to be waited on, hand and foot, when they're healing. And others would rather be left alone. Like a wounded animal burrowed in its den; more vicious when they feel threatened. I'm not certain which of those categories Knox falls under.

I stir the vegetables and noodles once more, before scooping some into a tupperware.

Despite my uncertainty of Knox's demeanor, I've decided that I'm going to be brave and take the soup up to his apartment.

As I exit the house, treading across the lawn, I hear a loud thud, followed by a heavy, explicative, groan.

I don't hesitate to rush up the steps to his apartment. Bursting through the door, I find Knox grimacing in his bed as he holds the side of his torso. His expression quickly shifts into confusion when he sees me advancing toward him.

I set the tupperware on the counter and approach him with concern. "Are you okay?"

Gently adjusting himself so he's sitting upright while still holding onto his torso, he says, "Are *you* okay?"

I tilt my head with misunderstanding.

"You're the one that came bursting into my apartment." His eyebrow kicks upward. "Without knocking."

I suddenly feel as if I'm intruding. "I was on my way over," I say, twisting my body to gesture below us to where the lawn separates his apartment from Constance's house. "I heard a thud. Then you yelled. I thought maybe you fell and needed help."

He lifts the side of his jaw toward me as his eyes gentle and a small grin spreads across his face. "Understandable. In that case, yeah, I'm okay." He nods his head toward the floor. "I stretched a little too far when I was trying to reach for my water. Ended up spilling the entire thing, along with my gear belt."

That explains the heavy thud I heard. I take a step closer to investigate the empty glass on the floor and the water covered gear belt. When I look at him again, he's still smiling. "Hang on a second," I say turning toward the kitchen.

When I return, finding a place to sit on the bed next to where his legs are tucked under the blanket, I offer him the tupperware bowl of soup.

Taking the bowl in one hand, he says, "What's this?"

"Chicken noodle," I say with a ring to my voice. "I thought you might be hungry."

"Homemade noodles too." Scooping a spoonful and bringing it to his mouth, he closes his eyes and makes a moaning sound as he chews on the contents behind his lips. Then, "This is really good." He eats another spoonful and pretends to cry with pleasure. "This is *amazing*. How did you make it?"

"With love."

His smile falls, and his eyes hit mine with curiosity.

I immediately wish I could put the words back in my mouth. I didn't mean to let them slip but I've grown to say that as automatically as someone says they're *good* when asked how they're doing.

"I didn't mean to say that." I shake my head and feel my face reddening. I have to look away to ensure the embarrassment won't grow any further. "I guess I got used to saying that every time West would ask me how I cooked something so good. I'd jokingly tell him I made it with love."

Knox gently nods, then scoops another spoonful of soup into his mouth.

"I didn't mean that I…made it…with love…because…I love…y—"

"Hey," he smiles, "I know what you meant. And I know what you didn't mean. You don't have to justify or explain yourself."

I glance at him and fold my mouth in, as if that might keep my face from turning red again.

"But I'm sure there's a little love in here since I can tell you love to cook." He winks as he cools the spoonful of soup with his breath.

So much for not turning red again.

I don't know why I do it, but I drop my eyes down to scan his bare tattooed torso. My curious gaze could be considered normal since his ribs are broken and I might be thinking about where they're at in the healing process. But I don't look because I'm curious about his fractured ribs, I look because I'm curious about him. And his body.

Even when I notice what I'm doing, I can't look away. I know by now Knox has caught my gaze and sees exactly what my vision is hypnotized by. Which causes my throat to tighten and my pulse to accelerate.

Knox clears his throat, probably uncomfortable by my ridiculous response to his muscled body.

I force my eyes to look around the bed, and say, "So many pillows," to try and bury how mortified I feel by changing the subject.

"Didn't we already talk about this?"

I glance at him and he seems amused by something. Probably my flushed expression. "I don't think so," I say, making sure my eyes don't drop below his chin again.

"Remember, the night you stayed on my couch? Or when I told you pillows help with sleeping?"

I vaguely remember the details he's explaining. Then, I let out a short laugh. "You need six pillows to fall asleep?"

"I need six pillows to feel…secure." The last word comes out more as a question, almost as if he's not sure he wanted to admit that to me. Or maybe it's the first time he's put a word to the feeling.

I regard him silently for a moment. Chewing on the information without looking into it too much. But part of me wants to know why a man, as tough and brave as he is, needs to feel secure when he's alone in his bed at night.

The spoon makes a clanking sound as he drops it into the empty bowl. "Thank you for bringing this over."

I nod, taking the bowl and setting it in my lap. "There's more if you're still hungry."

He takes one of the pillows and pulls it to his torso. "I'm good. Thanks though. And thanks for checking in on me too." He's probably trying to hide himself from my prying eyes.

What am I doing? He's my friend. If I keep slobbering over him, it's going to completely change the dynamic between us. And I'm not even divorced yet. He probably thinks I'm ridiculous. I'm certain he's not looking to get involved with a mother of two who has a sociopath for an ex-husband. Well, soon-to-be ex.

Get it together, Trinity. Do not sabotage this friendship with your lonely hormones.

When I look at him and smile, he adjusts the pillow by hugging his thick arms around it. This is when I notice the woman's face on his upper deltoid. She's beautiful, and I wonder who she is. But I can't stop to ask, because my eyes continue to drag down the length of his arm. Scaling down the tattoos, that reveal tree branches, a small fetus tucked sleepily inside a womb, a dark eye looking behind a broken wall, a large house with flames in the windows, the Statue of Liberty, several handprints in various sizes that sprinkle down to the base of his wrist where a man is pulling at his face and screaming in torment. At first glance, the content of the tattoos seems completely irrelevant to each other, but somehow the artist connected them like a story.

There's a physical desire I have to reach out and touch the tattoos, as if to provide some sort of comfort to the man on Knox's wrist.

Instead, I pull myself from the bed to place the bowl on the kitchen counter and retrieve a hand towel draped near the sink. When I return, kneeling near Knox's nightstand to begin cleaning the spilled water, I don't say anything.

It's as if the tattoos unraveled an emotion I know so well, yet I don't have a clue at all what it means to Knox. And since he had a difficult time talking about his six pillows, I'm certain he wouldn't say anything about the pain associated with those tattoos.

"I can get that," he says. "You don't have to clean up my mess."

With my eyes fixed on the floor, I place the glass on the nightstand. Then begin wiping off the water from his gear belt with the hand towel. "I don't mind." I place the gear belt on the bed and continue soaking up the water from the floor. "I know you'd do the same for me."

"I wish I could do a better job at helping you with your messes."

My body tenses at his statement.

My throat tightens.

The blood in my hands freezes as my fingertips grow cold.

I can even hear my heartbeat thudding in my ears.

"Knox…" I say in a whisper. Hoping that he'll fill in the unknown between us with some words. Because I sure can't do that right now. If I said what's inside of my head, I'm not sure how he would receive it. Since what's inside my head are thoughts that revolve around my physical desires, and my need to run my hand down his muscled arm, and chest, and abs, until I…

Am I so shallow that I would give into my physical attraction toward him? Am I feeling this way because I'm lonely? He shouldn't have made a big deal about the soup. Telling me I'm a good cook is the quickest route to pull at my heartstrings.

"Trinity…" he says my name in the same hushed way I just said his.

When I look up at him, his eyes are bouncing between mine rhythmically. Then he smiles. But something about the way his grin is stretched to one side of his face while his eyes shift into half-moons, is painfully familiar. Familiar in a way that it feels like I already know him. And painful in a way that I wish he'd never look at me like that again, so I don't have to experience this shockwave of emotion.

An aggressive knock pulls my attention to the door.

Knox begins to pull himself out of bed, but I rise to my feet and press his shoulders back down.

He lets out a quiet groan, wincing at the pressure.

"I'm sorry," I say. "But you shouldn't be moving around so much. The doctor said you need *rest*. So, rest and I'll get the door."

As I walk from where I'm standing near the bed to the door, I hear hurried footsteps shooting down the stairs. I glance back at Knox in confusion and, since he heard it too, his expression is similarly confused. I face the door again, twisting the knob to thrust the door open.

"No one is here," I say, poking my head out further to see if I can spot whoever just fled from his doorstep. Then, when I step out onto the small deck, something crunches under my shoe.

"Odd," he says. Then his voice grows deeper, as if he's speaking from the bottom of his lungs when he says, "Come back inside." He sounds more fearful than demanding. Like he's concerned for my safety.

But no one is out here. And I need to tell him about what I've just stepped on. "Knox," I say, bending down to inspect the crunchy matter below me. "Whoever it was, left some sort of...bugs here for you."

This causes Knox to abandon all advice from the doctor to rest in bed for a week. He's thrusting the comforter off himself and stomping across the length of his apartment to meet me in the doorway before I can protest.

"What the hell?" He's bent down beside me now. I can smell his piney deodorant mixed with his body's scent when he reaches his arm out to retrieve one of the intact bugs from the pile I just stepped on. And it takes everything out of me not to close my eyes and inhale his pheromones like a pre-teen girl with a wild crush.

Thankfully I don't have to restrain myself much longer since Knox kills my thoughts by shifting the dead bugs in his hand right in front of me. "It's cicada exoskeletons."

CHAPTER TWENTY-TWO

Knox

May 1998

"Again?" Constance says, from where she's standing at the base of the stairs below my apartment.

I finish picking up the last pebble, placing it in my palm as I descend the stairs to meet her. "Yep," I say, tossing the pebbles into the dumpster. "At least it wasn't worms again."

She shakes her head. "Who do you think would do somethin' like this? They're obviously targeting you and know you well enough to know where you live."

I shrug. "It doesn't matter. As long as they're not breaking any laws, I don't mind too much." And if I'm being honest, I have an idea who it might be. And if it's who I think it is, I'd rather him leave bugs and rocks at my doorstep than cause havoc around town.

She lets out a quiet huff and hands me a thermos full of coffee. "Speak for yourself. If they start leavin' dead bugs at my doorstep, you better believe I'm gonna have a problem with it." I don't correct her that the culprit has never left anything dead on my doorstep. The closest they've come to dead bugs were the cicada exoskeletons they left a month ago.

I gently tip the thermos back and forth. "Did you make this?"

"Nah." She raises one brow with interest. "She did."

The door to her house makes a sound when it snaps closed. I turn to see Trinity making her way over to us.

Constance leans in closer to me, and in a quiet clipped voice, she says, "That one's been unbearable the last few nights with her screamin' nightmares."

"Again?"

Constance nods and takes a step away from me. "Maybe you could hurry up and finish remodeling your house so she can move into the apartment," with a low voice she adds, "and out of my house."

"Sorry about the wait," Trinity says, meeting us in the driveway. "I thought that phone call with Sharry was going to be a lot quicker."

"Everything okay with that?" I say, hoping to catch her gaze.

Without looking at me she nods. "Yeah, as okay as it can be I guess."

I'm not sure what happened between us, but ever since she brought soup up to my apartment after I fractured my ribs, she's been intent on avoiding me.

She swings her torso to face Constance. "Ready to go?"

Constance gives her a nod and they begin walking toward her car, not before Constance tosses her head in my direction and gives me a look of displeasure.

I pull my brows together and shake my head at her. Disappointed that she's annoyed by Trinity's inability to sleep. It's not Trinity's fault that trauma plagues her dreams.

I give them a wave as they pull away.

Constance decided to make their work schedules the same so they could carpool together. I know Constance prefers to do things by herself, so I'm proud of her for thinking of Trinity. But I wish she'd remember how hard it was for her to sleep after what happened. Maybe that would help her empathize with Trinity better.

Sadly, all Constance's trauma did was grow a layer of thick skin over her emotions and lock a cage around her heart. I hope the same doesn't happen to Trinity.

At the station, I find Chandler swiveling in his chair as I place my thermos on the desk in front of him.

Glancing up at me, he says, "Thanks, man." Then twisting the lid off the thermos, he pours some of the contents into his coffee mug. "I've missed this." He hands it back to me when he's done, inhaling the aroma from his cup before taking a sip. "She really does make a nice cup of joe." He shrugs one shoulder. "Maybe you could get her to teach Stacy how to make coffee."

"Not a fan of Stacy's coffee?"

"I mean…" He sips at his mug again. "It's fine. But *this*," he dramatically slurps the dark liquid, "this is incredible."

I inhale then release my exhale slowly, thinking back to the first time she made me coffee and breakfast. "She's a great cook too." I take my thermos and plop down into my chair behind him.

"Sounds like wife material."

I twist around in my seat. "She's still someone else's wife. I can't even entertain that idea." Although I'd like to.

At first I thought maybe I was just infatuated by her beauty and ability to make the *best* food I've ever had. Then I thought her strength drew me to her. I even liked the way I made her blush by just looking at her. But now that she's taken a huge step away from me and made it clear she doesn't want me to look at her in a way that makes her cheeks turn pink, I feel like it's not my place to push something she's not into.

No matter how inspiring I think she is.

So I've done my best to turn those feelings off.

And the more time I've spent watching her at a distance, and comparing her life with Constance's, I'm almost sure I'm drawn to her because I'm trying to redeem myself after what happened to Constance.

After what happened to *me*.

"Born November 2nd, 1976," Chandler says this with a chime to his voice. "To her mother, Clearwater Ann Tóth." He chuckles quietly to himself without turning around to face me. "Clearwater, I like that name. It's unique and interesting." Clearing his throat he continues, "Father, Bridges Dean Lovell. Another interesting name. She was born at First Presbyterian Hospital in Abilene, Texas." He turns away from his computer screen to glance at me with a smirk on his face.

I know what he's doing, and I don't like it. "Chase Chandler," I swivel my chair around to face my own desk, "born a moron."

"Come on," he says. "You know you're curious."

"No." Facing him again, I fold my arms over my chest. "I'm not curious at all. And you shouldn't be digging into her records like that. This information would be a lot easier to get with a simple conversation with Trinity."

He adjusts his glasses and shrugs one shoulder. "I can't help it."

I exhale with annoyance. "Why don't you make yourself useful and give me a ride to pick up my cruiser." While I was healing from my rib fractures the Chief thought it would be an opportune time to take my squad car into the shop for maintenance.

"Tóth, what do you think that is?" He hits my shoulder with the back of his hand. "Sounds like it could be Hispanic, or maybe Italian, like *Santino*."

"It's not Italian." I rise from my chair and give the side of his seat a kick. "Come on, I need a ride to the repair shop to get my car."

Chandler groans. "Fine."

"I'm hurt, Chandler. You're acting like snooping around on women's personal information is more fun than hanging out with me."

"I'm not acting." He finally rises from his chair, following me toward the station entrance. "Snooping on your not-girlfriend-roommate is the most exciting thing I've done in months. So, thanks for entertaining me."

I grip his shoulder, heeding him out the door. "Leave well enough alone, Chandler." But he's right. Small towns don't come with a lot of crime. Or people. Which is exactly the reason Constance and I moved here.

CHAPTER TWENTY-THREE

Trinity

"Which one is the cheeseburger with pepperjack and no pickles?" Candy asks, examining the two plates I just finished garnishing with a side of steak fries.

I look up from the ribeye I've been pounding with the meat hammer. "Uh," my eyes flash between the two plates, "the one on the left is pepperjack."

"The one on the left. Thanks." She swipes the plates, spinning out of the kitchen.

Marcos pulls a pan of baked potatoes wrapped in aluminum foil from the oven and slaps them on the counter. "I'm gonna head out back for a smoke," he says, squeezing one of the potatoes to ensure it's cooked through. "You got this?"

I nod. "Yep. Take your time."

I'm being more polite than serious about encouraging him to take his time. The restaurant is packed today. In fact, business has been so busy there's typically a wait time for seating during the lunch and dinner rushes. I don't mind too much since I'm spending my time being productive doing one of my favorite things, which is cooking.

Plus, it keeps my mind preoccupied on something besides the safety and wellbeing of my children. Sharry's gotten more involved with my case. There's not much she can do besides enforce West to report his and the kids' whereabouts. Other than that, West can do pretty much whatever he wants. Including random road trips and vacations across the southwestern part of the United States. But Sharry ensured that, from what she's gathered, the children are safe.

The fact that West has full custody of our children makes me feel like someone has bound my arms behind my back, taped my mouth shut, and tossed me into the ocean with a boulder tied to my ankle.

And I hate everything about that.

"Where's Marcos?" Constance rushes into the kitchen, balancing four plates on a tray.

"Smoke break," I say.

She nods and flips around to exit.

"Oh, wait," I say, scurrying around the stove toward her with a *very* hot baked potato in my hands. "Can't forget this."

She does this weird thing with her mouth, then, "Thanks." I'm not certain, but I think that was her best attempt at a smile.

I begin rubbing a mixture of salt and pepper with some other spices on each side of the steak I'm about to sear, when Candy pops her head over the saloon doors. "Hey, Trinity." Her ponytail is still swaying from the rushed momentum of her brisk walking. "When you get a sec, there's a couple sitting at table five that wanted to see you."

I give her a quizzical expression, revealing I haven't learned the table numbers since I'm typically in the kitchen and don't need to learn them. "Is that on the left side?"

She gives me a polite smile. "No, it's the table for two by the window on the right." Her smile grows wider as her eyebrows lift upward. "I think they want to thank the chef."

Her comment makes me smile too. "Thanks, Candy. I'll be right out."

I take my time with the steak and Constance enters the kitchen.

When I catch her gaze, I say, "I've gotta say hi to a couple of patrons real quick. Can you cover for me until Marcos gets back?" I rinse my hands quickly in the sink. "Don't worry about those street tacos, I'll get them when I get back. This should just take a second."

She gives me a short, reluctant, "Sure."

Since I've been working here, I have yet to be thanked personally by a customer. A wave of nervous excitement pulses down my body and into my stomach. Circling around like a marry-go-round. I wonder if anyone ever thanked Marcos for his kitchen skills?

I meet Candy on my way into the restaurant. Voices are overlapping above the sound of the TV screens at the bar. "Candy, was that table on my right?"

She nods with her grin. "Yep, on your right. Near the window."

"What'd they order?"

"Cheeseburgers." She passes me to head into the kitchen. "One swiss, one pepperjack with no pickles."

I nod, remembering the order, then head for the couple seated near the window.

The rush of nervous excitement flips in my stomach. Then retorts when I find the table, almost immediately shifting into dread.

The woman at the table sees me first and smiles as she leans over the table to speak to the man seated across from her. "Is that her?"

I don't have to hear his answer to know that I'm *her*.

Of course I'm *her*.

And I hate that I'm *her*.

I stop before I completely reach their table. I'm hoping my body will do that thing, where it takes over, making a choice without first consulting with my brain. But nothing happens, except for my heart continuing to pound against my sternum.

"Well, I've gotta hand it to you, Trinity, you haven't forgotten how to make a cheeseburger," he says when he faces me.

I should have known it was West asking for me. I mean, how many people get a pepperjack cheeseburger without pickles? He's the only person I know that eats his burger that way.

"I don't know how I'm gonna live up to your cooking skills," the woman says. She has a terrible perm, and I can tell she just used the cheapest box of blonde hair dye to color her hair too. Probably the same cheap box that West used to buy for me.

Because West likes blondes.

How many grown women have naturally blonde hair? I used to think he cared more about me looking like a blonde barbie doll than he cared about what I wanted. Which makes me so much happier that Constance insisted on cutting off every strand that was discolored by the bleach he used to force me to put into my dark hair.

The woman puts her hand out in front of me. "I'm Kimmy, I don't think we've met."

I shake her hand. "Trinity."

"I know," she says with a grin full of teeth. "I work at Steve-O's. West told me all about you."

I wonder which version of me he told her about. The one where I'm a drunk. The one where I'm an angry lunatic. Or the one where I'm a harlot. Because I know it wasn't the one where I was the survivor of his abuse.

I try to force a smile, but nothing happens because I feel like I'm going to puke. "Nice to meet you."

West tosses a fry into his mouth. "Mmm!" He smacks his lips as he finishes chewing. "I have missed havin' a good meal made by your sweet little hands." He locks his eyes on mine with a fear inducing drop to his voice. "Mama can cook, but you know I've always preferred your cookin'."

Kimmy shoots him a look that's full of hurt. I can tell she thinks she's his girlfriend. It's too bad. And I feel a little sorry for her. Some girls think sleeping with another man makes them his girlfriend. That should probably make me feel hurt too since he's moved on without signing those damn divorce papers. But I've become so resentful of him, that I only have one concern.

"Where are the kids?" I say, challenging him with my own unyielding expression. My insides might be twisting into knots, but I refuse to show him any emotion other than indifference right now. "Are they with your parents?"

He lets out a short laugh as he sags down in his seat, contentedly, and places a toothpick in his mouth. "I bet you'd like to know where they are." His voice contorts with his coiled expression. "And I'll let you see them."

I can't help it when my daring expression grows into a hopeful wide-eyed look. And I can't help but let the words leave my mouth when I speak with trepidation. "When? Please, let me see them today. It's been months, West."

I don't mean to sound so desperate. But I don't know how to fake my concern for my children. I *have* to see them. And I am desperate.

I know I've just made a dire mistake when the corner of his mouth curls into a satisfied grin. "Are you done playing this game, Trinity?"

If anyone is playing games, it's him. There's an empty glass with several ice cubes near his plate and I can't help but wonder if its contents used to be Captain and Coke. Which would explain his overconfident behavior.

Leaning forward, he takes my hand in his and rubs the side of my wrist. "Ready to come back home yet?"

When Kimmy flips her head to face him, her tight little curls bounce with her scoff. "*West!* I thought we—"

"Shhh…" He hushes her. Then, his eyes drift from her protruding breasts spilling out of her v-neck t-shirt, over to my waist and up my body until they stop at my mouth. That's when he drags his tongue from one corner of his mouth to the other. As if this direct gesture is enough to entice me.

Instead, it causes a heavy nauseating sense to crash into my stomach. Like a wave of disgust. No, it's more than that. Like a horse trough full of reeking vomit tossed down my throat.

Rubbing my hand, he continues. "Babyyy…" His heavy gaze finally rises from my mouth to meet my eyes. "Come home."

At this, Kimmy kicks back in her chair and pulls her purse over her shoulder. "I must've been blind to let you bring me here. I don't even like red meat." She pulls her undersized jeans up over her stomach. "And I thought you said she was blonde." She makes her way past me with a quiet, "Excuse me," before she faces West once more. "I can't believe I ruined my hair for you." Then she trots out of the restaurant, making her way across the street to the other side of the pavilion where Steve-O's is located.

I'm glad she came to her senses before West had a chance to twist his charm around her. I only wish I had been as brave as Kimmy to walk away at the first signs of his narcissism.

Gently tugging my hand so I have to step closer to him, he says, "What do you say? Ready to go and see little Tuck and Abbi? They miss you, you know? Always asking about where you are, and when they'll see you again."

I close my eyes at the mention of their names. He knows just where to hold the knife in my back to get me to do what he wants. It's not fair. But with the screwed up system, I'm starting to feel like I have no other choice but to do what he wants in order to see my kids.

I open my eyes, and notice he's biting his lower lip as he stares down at the lower half of me, as if I'm some object for his pleasure.

My entire body is revolted by him. It's easy to be disgusted by someone when they're inebriated and acting like a complete fool. But it's also easier to get what I want from him when he's been drinking. I know if I go with him right now, he'll take me straight to the kids. He'll give me exactly what I want.

All I have to do, is give him *exactly* what he wants. He's just playing another game with me.

Well, I can play a game too. And at this point, a few minutes of numbing myself while West does whatever he wants to me seems worth the torture. If it means I can spend an entire evening with my children, I'd do almost anything at this point.

Two arms wrap around my waist. Only they're coming from behind me, so they can't be West's arms. I'm whisked off my feet and lifted from standing in front of West, to standing in front of Knox.

He drops his piercing hazel eyes down to mine with a hardened brow. "Go wait for me in the kitchen."

"But…my kids." I dart my eyes between his, trying to read his expression. "He's going to take me to my kids, I just have to…" I can't even finish the statement. Because I realize the regret of what I was about to agree to. And the tremendous error in judgement I was making.

What I was considering doing with West, is so wrong. And desperate.

And, now, with Knox in front of me, I know I wouldn't be able to live with myself if I slunk back to West for one night. Even though it means giving up time with my kids.

But the truth is, I'm *so* desperate to see them.

"What's the problem here, Sir?" West says, staggering to his feet. He was always good at hiding his inebriation until he had to stand or walk.

I can already tell this isn't going to end well. West is more drunk than I initially detected.

I take a step back when Knox straightens himself in front of West. "Why don't you tell me what the problem is."

It takes several seconds before West focuses on Knox's face and recognizes him. Once he does, his relaxed expression shifts into annoyance. "Oh, man, not *you*."

Before I can decide whether I should warn Knox of who West turns into when he's drunk, I'm being pulled by one arm toward the kitchen.

I look down at the small hand grasped around my arm and then the person who is attached to it. "Constance," I say. "Please, I need Knox to know that West is a different person when he's drunk. He's so much worse than when he's sober."

She continues pulling me through the saloon doors into the kitchen. "Knox can handle himself." Once we're on the far side of the kitchen where the desk is located, she turns me around to face her and grips my shoulders. "Are *you* okay?"

I nod. "I'm okay."

She releases a sharp exhale along with her grip on my shoulders. Placing her hands firmly against the desk, she shakes her head, and says, "I knew he was the guy."

I narrow my gaze at her curiously. "How did you know?"

She blinks at me.

"How did you know it was him?" I say slower, in a low voice.

Her jaw pops open to the side as she regards me silently for a moment. "I could just tell."

Then, before I can get a more acceptable answer from her, there's shouting and the sound of glass breaking.

Constance and I share a look, then rush toward the saloon doors to peer down the hallway toward the dining area.

I don't even have to look to know it's West who's shouting. But still, for whatever reason, I look. And sure enough, he's throwing his hands up in a tantrum.

"I'm leaving!" he roars.

His voice at that level sends a tremor through my spine that tightens every muscle on its way down my back.

Chase Chandler is nearing the exit to open the entrance door and ensure West leaves. While Knox is taking cautious steps behind West, gesturing toward the exit.

West flips around as if he's going to say something to Knox, but in doing so, he catches my gaze. His angered expression shifts upward into hopeful urgency.

"*Trinity!*" My name reverberates up out of his throat and hits me like a train. "Trinity, please don't do this to me! What'd I do? Please, just talk to me." I know he's putting on a show for the bystanders in the restaurant. And by the way they are reacting to his statement, I realize how convincing he can be to people that don't know him like I do.

This causes Knox to take West's arm and escort him out of the restaurant in haste. The last thing I see is Knox striding briskly behind West before they disappear past the window, to the side of the building where I can't see them anymore.

I don't know why I do it, but I hurry out of the restaurant to meet them on the sidewalk near the building.

West sees me before Knox does and says, "I didn't mean it, baby. Listen, I'm all sorts of confused since you left." His voice is breaking. "Please, just don't leave me."

His manipulation makes me sick. My stomach is twisting in knots and I'm beginning to regret running out here. And even more so after Knox turns to face me.

His expression is hardened, and he seems to be frustrated that I'm out here at all. "Go back inside, Trinity. You're only making things worse."

His words hurt. I'm not sure if he's right or not. All I can focus on is that West is right here, and he knows where our children are. And if I can just convince him to let me see them…

"*Please*," West begs. He hits the back of his head against the brick building and lets out a whimper. Part of me thinks maybe he did this so he'd feel enough pain to muster up some tears to cry. The other part of me thinks that the emotional pain he's feeling is what made him hit his head against the building. Because for him, physical pain is more bearable than heartache.

Knox pulls him from the wall and West crumbles near Knox's feet. It's pitiful. "Pull yourself together, man." Knox tries to pull West up by his arm, but West refuses, slinking back down the side of the building. "Get up, Laurel, I don't wanna hurt your shoulder again."

West's an emotional mess. His hands are covering his face. "Please don't leave me." When he looks up, his reddened eyes meet mine. "Don't hate me anymore, Trinity. I'm so tired of you hating me."

My chest sinks at his assumption. "I don't *hate* you." I'm astonished he would say that, and it's apparent in the shift of my aching tone. "I never *hated* you." I clench my teeth together with my furrowed brow. "I *loved* you!" My voice begins to rise. "And what does that say about me for loving someone that treated me the way you did? I deserve so much better than you."

He's rising to his feet, and somehow the tears have vanished and the sneering expression he had inside the restaurant has returned. "Is that what you think?" He flicks his tongue at the corner of his mouth. "You think you can do better than me? No one is ever gonna love you the way I did."

"That's not true," my voice is firm and full of determination. "Because *I'm* going to love me better than you ever did!"

He lunges at me, thrusting his arms out in my direction. But somewhere between his reaching hands and the step I take away from him, Knox and Chase take one of West's arms each and pull him away before he touches me. It's instantaneous.

At this point, I notice Matthew emerging from City Hall, which is on the other side of the street next to M.L.'s. He probably heard West yelling from his office. The entire town probably heard his cries. I'm certain Matthew's going to bail West out of this predicament like he's done a hundred times before. And I realize I need to get out of sight. I don't want this encounter to be used against me somehow.

I back up, then turn around to go inside the building. I keep my gaze down at my Nikes, but it doesn't stop my peripherals from seeing every head turn to watch me. The restaurant is quiet, aside from hushed conversations and the sports announcers on the TVs, as I walk past the tables until I disappear into the kitchen.

Constance is waiting for me with the same hardened expression Knox was giving me outside. If she wasn't flipping burger patties, she'd probably have her arms crossed over her chest.

"I thought I could convince him to let me see the kids," I say, in my defense. Even though she didn't ask me to elaborate on anything. But she didn't have to. Her expression was full of questions.

She drops her dissatisfied gaze to the burgers. "How'd that go?"

"We didn't get that far in our conversation."

Knox bursts through the saloon doors in haste. Everything he seems to be doing is in a rush. "What were you thinking?" he says, with one hand outstretched at his side.

I open my mouth to speak but nothing comes out. Mostly because he doesn't have any authority over me. Which means he has no right to talk to me like that.

He paces for a moment, locking his hands on top of his head briefly, before finding a place to plant his feet in front of me. Tossing his arm out at his side again, he says, "Do you *want* your kids back?"

I pull my brows down in frustration at his stupid question. "Of course I do."

"Then stay away from him. What good has ever come from you being near West Laurel?"

I don't have a response to that.

His neck muscles tighten. "What do you think would have happened if Constance hadn't called?"

I look at Constance. She gives me a haphazard shrug. I'm not surprised she called him. And I'm not mad she did either. Because, honestly, I don't know what would have happened if Knox hadn't shown up. I don't know that I wouldn't have walked out of here with West if he had suggested we see the kids. Is it so unbelievable that a mother would give up her morals just to be able to hold her children in her arms for one short moment?

Knox is rubbing at his brow now, like all I am is one giant headache to him.

"It's my life," I finally say.

This causes him to drop his hand, slightly lifting his bereaved gaze up at me.

I swallow the lump in my throat before continuing. Because I know that my hostility is unwarranted by Knox. "Why do you care so much about what I do with my life anyway?"

He regards me silently for a moment, tilting his head with his thoughts. Then taking several steps toward me, closing the space between us so our faces are almost touching, he speaks in a low voice, "Because it's my life too. And as a police officer, it's my *job* to protect and serve my community." He takes a short step backward, but keeps his eyes locked on mine. "And that means keeping you safe, even if I have to save you from yourself."

The back entrance slams shut. Marcos enters through the saloon doors where nothing but the sizzling sound of grease is audible. He tosses his thumb over his shoulder. "I was out on a smoke break." He looks from Knox, to Constance, to me, then back to Knox before he walks toward the sink to wash his hands. "So," he says, breaking the silence once more, "what'd I miss?"

CHAPTER TWENTY-FOUR

Knox

June 1998

"When will you be back?" I say, leaning my shoulder into Constance's bedroom doorway.

She zips up her duffle bag, releasing a sigh. "I have work next Friday." She tosses her braid over her shoulder before hoisting the bag off the bed. "So I'll be back before then."

"That's ten days away." I don't mean to, but I sound concerned.

She draws her brows together in confusion. "Yeah? What's your problem with that? *Dad?*"

"Don't call me that."

"You sound just like him."

"Don't do things to make me sound like him."

She rolls her eyes. "Then, are you gonna tell me what the problem is with my trip duration?"

I don't want to admit that she's been the buffer between Trinity and me. Or that she's the one that wakes Trinity up, saving her from her nightmares. So instead, I say, "I don't have a problem." Things haven't been the same between Trinity and me since I stopped West from going berserk on her at M.L.'s. And I can't shake the image of her letting that *man* touch her. Even if it was just her hand.

"Good." She presses through the door, running her bag into me before I can move out of the way.

"Excuse you," I say, taking a step back. "What's in there? A body?"

She flashes me a glare. "Don't joke about that."

"Too soon?"

Her eyes darken.

In defense, I say, "It's been six years."

"No matter what line of work you're in, it will never be acceptable to say stuff like that to me." She heads for the entrance, so I hurry in front of her so I can open the door. "Thanks," she says with a downward inflection, as if I've inconvenienced her.

"You sure you don't want me to go with you, Kid?" I can tell she's afraid to go. That's why she's being so hostile toward me. And also why she's in such a negative mood. More negative than usual.

She sidesteps out of the door. "No, I'm good." Once she's fully outside of the house she gives me a short grin from the side of her face. "I'll call you when I get there." But it's her eyes that tell me she's scared.

"It's not too late to change your mind," I say, hoping she decides to stay or decides to ask me to go along with her. Either one of those options would make me feel a lot better.

"Thanks, Zio," she adjusts the overfilled duffle bag to the other shoulder, "but this is somethin' I gotta do on my own, you know?"

"I know." I nod with a reluctant grin attached to the side of my face. "I'll be expecting a phone call in less than forty-eight hours. That should give you more than enough time to get there."

"I'll call from every gas station on my way."

And with that, she loads her bag into her car and pulls out of the driveway.

I hear the back door slide open, then shut again. Trinity walks through the kitchen with a craning neck and eager expression, almost like a concerned child worried their parent just left without saying goodbye. She shifts her head back and forth, then when she sees me standing near the entrance with the door still open, she says, "Did Constance just leave?"

I tilt my head curiously. "Didn't she tell you?"

She shakes her head no. "Where's she going?"

I close the door and exhale, realizing Constance probably doesn't want anyone to know where she's going since it would drift up her past. "Road trip."

"A road trip?" She says this with astonishment. "Alone?"

I shrug, then pass her into the kitchen. "It's summer, nothing wrong with wanting to take a little vacation."

"For how long?"

"Ten days or so."

"Oh," is all she says. And it tortures me, since I can tell she sounds worried. But I don't know what else to say since things have felt heavy between us, despite the concern I've developed for her.

I don't know exactly when it happened. Sure, I've cared about her wellbeing and empathized with her sucky situation.

I've even acknowledged her natural beauty—which has nothing to do with my concern for her. But something shifted when I saw her at M.L.'s, holding West's hand. Looking at him as if she was debating on going back to him.

Something about that day made me *want* to protect her at all costs. Something made me feel responsibility for her life in a way that I've never felt for another woman. Not even Constance. Something tethered me to her and no matter how hard I try to ignore it, I can't deny that I care for her more than a friend. That I'm attracted to her more than a friend. That I want her more than a friend.

But she's not even divorced yet, so how do I feel all these feelings that are more than friendship if I can't do anything about it?

That's why I continue to go back to my first instinct. Which is to *ignore* them. And inadvertently I end up ignoring her too.

When I pull a frozen dinner from the freezer and toss it on the counter, she says, "Please don't eat that."

I lift my chin in her direction when I face her. "It's this or a trip to the pavilion." I lift the small frozen dinner and shake it gently. "And I'm hungry right now and already paid for this. So, I'm gonna eat it."

She approaches me and tries to take the frozen tray from my hand, but I lift it up out of her reach.

Dropping her head to the side, she says, "Have dinner with me. I was just about to put some chicken on the grill."

How am I supposed to ignore my feelings if I'm eating dinner with the person that's causing those feelings?

I lower the tray and let her snatch it from my grasp this time. "You sure?" Far be it from me to decline a meal.

"Yes, I'm sure." She tosses it back in the freezer and then opens the fridge to retrieve a ziplock of marinating chicken. "I thought Constance would be here for dinner. But since she left, there's extra for you."

"Glad I'm your second choice," I tease.

She faces me with a serious expression.

Apparently, no one but me is enjoying my humor tonight. The humor I'm trying to cling to so I don't portray what I'm really feeling.

"Can we stop being like this with each other?"

I'm taken aback by her forward remark. "Stop what?"

She drops her shoulders with her exhale. "It just feels like there's this awkwardness between us or something." She lets out a short, exasperated laugh of disbelief. "I mean, I thought we were friends. But lately, it feels like you've been avoiding me."

"I've been respecting the space you've created. I would never try to do something I felt might make you uncomfortable. And maybe that was perceived by you in a way I didn't intend it to. But I'm not avoiding you." *Maybe I was a little bit.*

She narrows her eyes at me with her growing smile. "You sure?"

I close the space between us by taking a few steps closer to her. Then placing my hand on her shoulder, I say, "I'm positive. Now let's get this chicken on the grill, before I starve."

After dinner, I stay for a little longer to watch a rerun of Maury. We just learned that Jason is not the father of Alexa's baby when I point the remote at the TV screen, turning it off.

"What's on after Maury?" Trinity says with a tired voice. She's curled up on the opposite side of the couch with a throw blanket, even though the temperature in the house doesn't permit for one.

"Probably another rerun. I didn't check." I rise to my feet, my arms outstretched up over my head with my yawn. "But I better get to bed." I give her lower leg a gentle pat. "I'll see you tomorrow."

She perks up, adjusting herself upright on the couch as she looks at me with desperation. "It's only nine o'clock. There's still time to watch another show."

I rub the back of my neck with hesitancy. "I don't know…"

She flashes me a desperate smile. "Your choice. Any show. *Please.*"

And with the way she says that last word, I realize where her desperation is coming from. She's terrified to be by herself. I don't know why I haven't thought about how Constance's absence would affect her until now. "I'll tell you what, how about I grab some things from my apartment, and I'll stay in Constance's room until she gets back so you're not alone in the house."

She blinks. "You would do that?" She sounds relieved.

I hope this isn't crossing a boundary. "Yeah, that way you won't be alone, and I don't have to stay up any later watching reruns until you fall asleep."

Her eyebrows drop to the sides of her face with reassurance. So, I leave the house for my apartment. But once I get to the door, there's a mason jar on the top step. I pick it up and bring it inside with me. And when I flick my kitchen light on, I see several moths flying around in the jar.

With my exhale, I place the jar back on the top step outside of my apartment, unscrew the lid, and then place the lid back on the jar once all the moths are freed.

I'm ninety-nine percent sure Robby is doing this, but I don't have a clue why. And since I haven't had a negative encounter with him in months, I'm not going to stop him to ask about it.

I change my clothes and gather a few things from the apartment then head back down to the house where only the throw blanket greets me from the place where Trinity had been laying on the couch.

"Do you prefer chamomile or lavender?" Trinity says from the dark kitchen.

I walk across the living room to Constance's room and toss my things on her bed. "Chamomile or lavender? What are we talking about?" I'm finishing my question as I enter the kitchen where Trinity twists the knob on the stove to heat a kettle of water.

"Tea," she says, with her back to me. "Do you drink chamomile or lavender?"

I lean my hip into the counter and see that she's already placed two mugs near the stove where the tea kettle is heating. I feel like I can't turn her down despite how tired I am. "Which do you like better?"

I can see her smiling as she turns her face slightly to reach up and open the cupboard. She retrieves a small cardboard box with a sleeping bear and the word *Chamomile* scrolled across the side. "I like to switch it up. But I'm feeling chamomile tonight."

"Chamomile it is." I don't have the heart to tell her I'm exhausted and ready for bed. Hopefully she'll feel more relaxed after the tea. And hopefully it doesn't take too long to make since I'm ready to crash.

She turns around and faces me. "I feel a little ridiculous."

"Why's that?" There's something cute, almost innocent, about her when she confesses this.

Pressing her palm into her forehead she laughs quietly, then, "I'm an adult. I shouldn't be afraid to sleep alone. But I've never spent a night by myself in my entire life."

"That's not true. You stayed at the motel by yourself."

She shifts her weight to one hip and folds her arms. "That doesn't count. I was literally sharing walls with people around me and above me. We were all in the same building together."

"You've really never spent a night by yourself?"

She shakes her head and folds her mouth in, stifling her grin. "Never."

"How is that possible?"

"I lived with my dad until I was seventeen and then immediately moved in with West. If West wasn't home, I still had the kids with me. There were people all around the motel, albeit most of them were shady, but not enough to warrant any distrust. And now, I have Constance right across from me in her room. There's always been *someone* else around."

"Well, I'm happy to fill in for Constance until she gets back."

The kettle begins to sputter a few quiet whistles, and Trinity pours the steaming water into the mugs before turning the burner off. "Do you like cream or honey in your tea?"

"No," I say, taking the warm mug from her. "This is fine. Thank you."

She takes a small sip from her mug and lifts her eyes to watch me, making sure I'm drinking mine.

I force the floral infused liquid down. "Why are we drinking tea before bed?"

She takes another sip. "It's supposed to help you relax."

"If I relax anymore, I might fall asleep standing here."

She laughs, then holds her mug between her hands and gives me a curious look.

I gulp down another drink. I'm not sure if she's looking for a compliment, so just to satisfy her uncertainty, I say, "You're right, the tea is very relaxing."

She's watching me, now. Not my expression or the way I continue to drink the tea, but her somber face is scanning the length of me. I'm not sure what to make of it, or if there is anything to make of her alluring expression. It's making me smile, but she doesn't notice since she's not looking at my face. After a quiet moment of her staring me up and down, she finally says, "What do all your tattoos mean?"

My smile fades when I look down at my ink covered arms. Sometimes I forget they're there. They've become such a part of me that I don't notice them anymore. And since I don't notice them, I forget to remember why I got them in the first place.

"It's a long story," I say, trying to hide the hint of remorse in my voice with a forced smile.

"I like bedtime stories," she says, sipping at her mug.

I shake my head. "I wouldn't call it a bedtime story."

"What kind of story is it?"

"*A nightmare.*"

I lift my regretful gaze up to meet hers. I'm expecting to see eagerness in her expression since that's how her voice sounded before I looked at her. But now that I'm looking at her, I can see that her expression is covered in the same sort of tortured pain I'm feeling remembering the events that inspired my tattoos.

"Whatever happened," she says, "It won't change our friendship." Touching my shoulder she adds, "Or the way I feel about you." I don't have a clue how she knows the story etched down my arm is personal to me.

I search her expression, but she keeps her eyes fixed on my arm. So I lift my t-shirt sleeve, revealing the top portion of the tattoo. "This," I smile at the black and gray ink that's created the masterpiece over my shoulder, "is my mom."

She glances up at me with a small grin. Then her eyes fall back down to my shoulder. "She's beautiful."

"She really was." I point to the burning house behind the tree branches just below my mother's neck. "She died in a house fire."

Trinity's mouth parts when she faces me, but no words come out. They don't need to. Because I can see the deep empathy she's enduring for me.

Touching the inside of my bicep, I continue with, "We lived in Manhattan, north of the Statue of Liberty."

I'm not sure when Trinity began gliding her hand across my arm, but she slides her finger down from the image of the Statue of Liberty to the handprints scaling down the inside of my upper arm.

"There were others in the fire too," I say with a heaviness in my voice.

"Who else?"

I wait for her to look at me. Then swallowing the knot in my throat, I let the confession out. "My dad, my grandparents, my cousins, my aunts and uncles, my sister, and my nieces and nephews." And somehow, sharing the saddest parts of me makes me feel better. As if she's taking part of the painful burden, and carrying it with me.

The understanding in her eyes is full of something I've never seen in any expression on any human before now. And it helps me not feel so alone.

Before she can say anything, I twist my arm, revealing the only place of color, where a coral-colored fetus is sleeping soundly in the womb. "My cousin was pregnant and lost her baby in the fire. She survived, at first. But her burns were so extensive she ended up...she didn't make it." I swallow back the sharp lump in my chest before continuing. "We all lived in the same apartment complex together. And everyone died together."

"Except for you and Constance."

I nod. "Except for me and Constance." Although it's felt like we've been dead since the fire. Only because we haven't been fully living our lives. Not by choice, but because we can't.

She turns my wrist, revealing the screaming tattoo of a man at the base of my arm. "Is this you?" her voice is gentle and concerned.

I nod. "It's the pain that was inside of me until I let it out."

She looks at me. "How'd you get it out?"

Clenching my jaw, I look down at her as my brows pull together with shame. Wanting her to take back that question. Wanting her to focus on the story I've just told her and not on what I did after that story happened.

"What'd you do?" she asks intently.

I think the main reason I don't want to tell her, is because I'm worried it might change her perspective of me, even though she promised it wouldn't. But I say it anyway, because the only thing I want more than being her friend is for her to trust that every word that comes out of my mouth is the truth.

"I got revenge for the fire that killed my family." Telling her any more than this could derail everything Constance and I have worked for. So I hope Trinity doesn't press for more of an explanation.

She studies my hardened expression for a moment, then she drops her gaze back down to my arm. Running her hands over the artwork. "How'd you survive all this?"

I let out a long, heavy exhale before answering. "One day at a time."

When she looks up at me again, she seems torn. As if she's feeling shattered devastation. And at the same time, maybe for the first time since her kids were taken from her, she's found some semblance of hope. Realizing that a person can come out on the other side of a catastrophe.

Without a word, she slips her arms around my torso, pressing her head against my chest. Hugging me.

I wrap my arms around her.

And she holds me closer.

And I let her.

Because after the few times I've given her hugs when she's needed them, I know she's hugging me now because I need it.

And it feels like the first time I've been able to remember that story without my soul filling with rage.

CHAPTER TWENTY-FIVE

Trinity

"Why can't you keep the house?" I ask my dad, switching the phone to the other ear and holding it there with my shoulder. "I mean, you own it. You could rent it out instead of sell it. Or just keep it and have two houses."

"It's unnecessary, Trinity." My dad's voice spills from the receiver into my ear. "It all comes down to the fact that we don't need two homes. It makes more sense for me to sell this house and move to Cape Cod with Anastasia."

"What about all our stuff."

"It's just stuff, sweetie. I'll take what I need, but I'm old. I don't need all that stuff anymore."

I release a frustrated, and slightly defeated, exhale. "When do you close on the house?"

"Next week."

I nearly drop the receiver when he says this. "That soon?"

"Listen, Trinity. If you'd like to come down to Abilene to pack up whatever you want to keep, you're more than welcome to do that. I'll even meet you there and we can go through Mom's things."

Going through Mom's things together would have been nice to do eleven years ago when I was grieving the loss of her. But there are a few things I'd like from my room.

"What do you say?" he asks.

"I'll see if I can get work off and then I'll give you a call back." What I'm concerned about isn't taking work off, I know that won't be a problem. But getting a ride to Abilene is.

After our conversation, Sugar scratches at the back door so I open it, meet her outside and toss one of her toys so she can retrieve it. I do this for several minutes as I try to come up with another plan to get down to Abilene. I haven't been to the house since I left when I was seventeen. All I took was a bag of clothes. I always expected my things to stay in my room forever. And I expected my dad to live there for the rest of his life.

My dad and that house have been the only consistent things in my chaotic life. And now they're changing. And that fills me with a mixture of anxiety and sadness.

Sugar finally stops to take a drink from her water bowl before she finds a shady place under the oak tree. I should probably refill her water bowl before Knox stops by to give me a ride to work. Only when I pick up her bowl, I find a butterfly sprawled out with its wings open. Drowning.

"Oh no," I say, gently scooping the butterfly out of the bowl, careful not to bend its wings.

I find a sunny place on the far side of the yard and sit in the grass. Ensuring the butterfly won't get too much sunlight and burn.

"I know what it's like to feel like you're drowning," I whisper to the butterfly in my hand.

"Hey," I look up to see Knox in his uniform, standing in the doorway with a grin. "What are you doing out here? You're gonna be late for work."

I look back down at the butterfly as it begins flapping its wings, regaining its strength as it dries. "And I know what it's like to need a little help when you pick yourself back up after drowning," I say this to the butterfly and hope Knox doesn't think I'm out of my mind for talking to an insect.

He's approaching now. "You *are* supposed to go to work today, right?"

I smile up at him when he stands in front of the sun, shading my eyes from the brightness. "I am." I look back down at my hand just as the butterfly flutters its wings and lifts itself up into the sky.

Knox points to where the butterfly just left my hand. "Were you holding a butterfly?"

I only smile at him.

His pointing finger shifts toward my face. "You're not the one putting bugs in front of my apartment are you?"

This makes me laugh. "Help me up," I say, reaching for him.

He grasps my hands in his and pulls me to my feet. "Seriously, are you?"

We're walking back inside the house now. "You know it's not me leaving you presents at her doorstep. I was only helping that butterfly regain its strength after it was drowning in Sugar's water bowl."

"Okay," he says this with relief, "good." As if he was really considering that I've been leaving insects at his apartment.

I head into my bedroom to get ready for work, cracking the door and raising my voice so he can hear me. "I spoke with my dad earlier. He said he's moving to Cape Cod and wanted me to come down to get some of my stuff before he sells his house."

"The house in Abilene?" he says, from the living room.

"Yeah." I pull a clean shirt over my head. "He wants me to come down before next week though."

"That soon?"

"Well, yeah." I brush my hair quickly before pulling it into a ponytail at the base of my neck. "He's already sold the house and needs it cleaned out. But I don't know how much stuff I'll take with me. Or how I'll get it back here. I'm sure if I made it down to Abilene, my dad would give me a ride back. But he's probably going to be packing too."

Knox doesn't respond to this.

I open the door to exit my bedroom, and nearly run into Knox's chest.

He's smiling down at me. "Are you trying to ask me to take you down to Abilene?"

I smile back at him. "I think I am trying to ask you for a ride to Abilene."

His smile twists suspiciously. "Nothing sounds more interesting than seeing the house you grew up in."

My smile fades. "I'm not so sure I want you to drive me there anymore."

"Come on," he says, with a genuinely amused expression. "You're going to be late for work."

CHAPTER TWENTY-SIX

Knox

Trinity is asleep with her head against the truck door. And the sight of her sleeping is incredibly distracting to me, which doesn't combo well with the fact that I need to pay attention to the road.

We left just after seven this morning, which makes our arrival time around eleven. Trinity was quiet all morning and fell asleep almost as soon as we got in the truck.

I pass by a sign indicating that Abilene is just twelve miles away.

"Hey," I say, gently rubbing my hand up and down Trinity's arm. "I'm going to need directions to your father's house soon."

She blinks a few times before stretching her arms and legs out in front of her. Her voice is still sleepy when she says, "Just drive to the police academy. I wasn't joking when I told you I lived right by there."

She nestles herself against the window and begins to close her eyes as if trying to fall asleep again.

"Trinity…" I say. "We'll be in Abilene in less than ten minutes. I need a co-pilot. I haven't been to Abilene in years. I don't know my way around like you do."

She rubs her eyes and yawns, stretching her arms out again. "Fine. I'm awake." She points out the windshield. "Keep on this road until you see a Tractor Supply."

"Alright, what's after the Tractor Supply?"

"You don't remember?"

I glance at her then back to the road. "I told you, I don't know my way around Abilene very well."

"East Lake Road is after Tractor Supply. Turn left, then take a right and my house is there. If you keep going straight after the first left, you'll end up at the police academy." Her directions come out as more of an irritated demand.

"Someone didn't get enough sleep last night, did they?"

"Sorry." She rubs her eyes and sits up straighter in her seat. "I had trouble falling asleep."

I take her hand in mine and give it a gentle shake. "You know, I heard that chamomile tea is supposed to help you fall asleep."

"Apparently six pillows does the trick too."

That makes me laugh so hard my side begins to ache. But the thing that really makes me ache in the worst way, is that she hasn't released her grip from mine. And I can feel the heat between our palms burning like a flare. I have to shake my head vigorously to focus on the directions again.

When we finally arrive in front of Trinity's house, I sense a familiarity in the area. She was right, and she lives directly down the road from the police academy. I'm sure I passed by this neighborhood a million times when I was at the academy.

I follow Trinity to the front door. When she turns the knob, it's locked.

"The convertible's gone too. My dad must've went out for a lunchbreak or something," she says. "Come on, I know how to get in through the back door without a key." She motions for me to follow her.

"It's weird how familiar this place feels now that I'm here. I think I may have partied in this neighborhood when I was at the academy too."

"Do you have a credit card I could borrow?" she says, ignoring my statement.

I raise my eyebrow at her with suspicion.

"I'm not going shopping if that's what you're worried about." She pops her hand out in front of me. "I need it to open the door."

"That's not what I'm worried about."

"What is it then?"

I lower my brow. "I don't want you to break it."

She shakes her hand, palm up. And I notice the string of scars laced across her palm. "I won't break it." She smiles. "I promise."

Pulling my eyes from her palm, I take my wallet out of my back pocket and hand her my card.

She drags it down between the doorframe and the door. It snags on something, then she twists the doorknob and presses her hip into the door. The lock clicks and the door swings open.

"See," she says with a proud grin, handing my card back. "Just needed it to get inside."

"You sure this is your house?" I tease. Looking around at the backyard, I notice it's well kept and looks recently mowed. The garden beds are aesthetically managed. Even the hedges are perfectly shaped and rounded. The only thing out of place is the dead sassafras tree looming over the yard with its decaying and cracked branches.

She nods, motioning for me to follow her into the kitchen. "I'm pretty sure I was able to break in because I knew that card trick would work. And I knew it would work on this particular door, because I've done it a hundred times before this."

"Or you could be breaking and entering."

Her smile falls. "Funny." She rolls her eyes playfully. "The house you need to worry about is that one. Which is probably the house you partied at." *She was listening to me earlier.* She points to a rooftop peaking over the fence that's kiddy-corner to her backyard. "Come on, I'll show you around."

As she gives me the grand tour, I notice several family photos on the walls. The only person that seems to age in the photos is Trinity. Aside from her father's subtly balding head and her mother's change in haircuts, you wouldn't tell that a decade of time passed between the framed pictures. Only the last photo, where Trinity is about ten years old, does her mom seem to age with the bitter deterioration that a cancerous body goes through.

The home is small, but bigger than Constance's house. And it also looks as if it's been stuck in time. I notice several things needing updated. Not to mention the electrical work throughout looks as if it hasn't been replaced since the sixties. There are heavy floral drapes covering the windows in the living room. And the orange shag carpet from the lower portion of the home decorates the stairs we walk up, not stopping until it reaches the hardwood flooring outside the bedrooms.

"You look a lot like your mom," I say, following Trinity into a bedroom with matching mahogany furniture. There's a black bedspread with neon patterned shapes perfectly draped over the bed.

"That's what everyone says." She begins rummaging through her closet at what I assume are nostalgic memories.

"You don't look much like your dad at all though."

"Yeah, everyone says that too." She's pulling shoe boxes full of photos from her closet.

I pick up a small porcelain figurine from the dresser. It's a lady with one of those long, frilly, red dresses the women in Spain used to wear. "How'd your parents meet?" I set the glass figurine back in her place and scan the magazine cut outs taped to the walls.

"I think they met at work."

"Were they from here?"

"Dad grew up outside of Abilene. And my mom moved all over." She smiles when she looks up at me. "She used to call herself a lost gypsy when I was little."

I smile at that statement. I like that she can talk about her mom without even a hint of sadness. She continues looking through old photos and begins telling me about the people in them and the stories behind each picture.

I listen intently, learning about her past. But I'm also watching her. Taking in the most comfortable person I've ever seen her be. I can tell that, although it's apparent she spent a lot of time personalizing her room, her memories were attached to the people around her when she lived here. And that box of photos will have more memories for her to look back on than this house will.

The front door slams and Trinity perks up. "Dad?" She holds her posture still, listening for his reply. "We're in my room!"

There are slow footsteps across the hardwood floor, then the gentleman from the photos appears in the bedroom. Only he looks to have aged several decades, despite not that much time passing since the last living room photo was taken. I guess that shows how much being stuck in grief can age a person. He doesn't seem to notice me and has his back to me so he's facing Trinity.

Trinity hops up from her place and greets her father. She gives him a stiff side hug, and he seems even less affectionate about it than she is. I don't know why I'm surprised. She did say they didn't have the closest relationship for the last eleven years since her mom died.

"How'd you get inside? I thought I locked the front door."

Trinity shoots him a stiff grin. "Yeah, you locked the back door too."

He snorts. "That card trick still works, huh?"

"You're the one that taught it to me."

He snorts again. Then he looks around at the boxes on the floor for a long moment. "Finding your old trinkets?"

"Yeah," she says, finding her place on the floor near her closet again. "I mostly came back for my old pictures. Feel free to get rid of the rest of my stuff."

He nods and stuffs his hands into his pockets as if he doesn't know what else to do with them. It's quiet again for a moment. I'm not sure if I should take this opportunity to finally announce myself. But I'm interested in the strange silent dynamic between Trinity and her father. So, I just keep watching them curiously.

He begins shifting back and forth on his feet. "Well, I brought some lunch." The shifting intensifies. "I thought we might eat at the table together one last time."

She glances up at him and nods. "That sounds nice." Then she must remember I'm still sitting in her room, since her eyes shift past her father and catch my gawking expression. "Knox, I'm so sorry." She looks at her dad as he turns around to see what she's talking about. "Dad, this is my friend Knox." She gestures toward me. "Knox, this is my dad."

He pulls his hand from his pocket and reaches it out toward me as he walks closer to where I'm seated. "Nice to meet you, Knox."

I rise to my feet and grip his hand in mine. "It's great to meet you, Bridges. I've heard a lot about you. I know how important it was for Trinity to get down here to Abilene and see you and the house again." I might be exaggerating a little bit, but I'm mostly doing it for Trinity's sake.

His grip tightens and freezes in place mid-shaking of my hand. "What was that?" He tilts his head to the side in confusion.

I pull my hand from his grip and fan my palm open toward Trinity. "I was saying how excited Trinity was to get back down here to see you."

His drooping eyes are shifting back and forth between mine, and suddenly I feel like I've said the wrong thing.

"You know," I continue, eager to change the subject. "I actually went to the police academy just down the road from here."

Now Trinity is giving me a dumbfounded expression.

I rub my hands together. "I'm sorry, but I've got the feeling I may have misspoke earlier." Maybe they both know I'm overexaggerating about the fact that Trinity was eager to get here. The truth is that she was underwhelmed by the venture. So much so that she slept the entire four hours it took to get here. But no father wants to hear that.

Both Trinity and her father share a look that causes Trinity's confused expression to shift into uneasy laughter.

"That's alright," her father says, dropping his eyes to the rug at our feet. "Honest mistake."

"My father's name is, Ed," Trinity says, with an inviting grin. "Which makes it weird that you called him Bridges. Ed and Bridges don't even sound the same at all. They don't even start with the same letter."

At the mention of the name Bridges again, I can't help but notice the way Ed's expression fills with dread.

Trinity continues, "I don't remember ever telling you my father's name, now that I think about it." She frowns at me. "Where did you come up with the name Bridges?"

I can't tell her that my best friend was snooping at vital records out of boredom. I mean, I'm going to tell her that's where I got that name from, but definitely not in front of her father. Could it be possible that Chandler misread the document? Maybe I heard wrong, and he did say Ed, or Eddy, or even Edward—and somehow my brain mixed that name up with Bridges.

And just as quickly as I come up with an excuse, Ed speaks before I can, with, "He probably figured it out."

No, I definitely remember the name correctly.

Trinity tilts her head at her father. "Figured what out?"

The dread on his face shifts to remorse. "I wasn't prepared to talk about this today, but…" He shoves his hand back into his pocket, turning to look down at Trinity, who is still sitting on the floor. "Maybe it will help you own some things you've been keeping secret too."

"Dad?" Trinity says his name as if it's a warning. "What're you talking about?"

I sit back down on the bed and watch as my misspoken words turn into a life changing event for Trinity, when her father says, "Your biological father's name is Bridges. Bridges Dean Lovell."

CHAPTER TWENTY-SEVEN

Trinity

It's a good thing I'm already seated on the floor since the room begins spinning.

"My *biological* father?" I press my hands to the sides of my head, trying to shift my thoughts, along with my brain, into a place where this phrase makes sense. "Dad?" I drop my hands at my sides, begging him with my expression to tell me what he's saying isn't true. "What do you mean, *biological father?*"

My dad won't look at me. "Sweetie," his voice is a whisper.

"I don't understand," I'm shaking my head, "you're not my father?"

When he shifts his eyes up to mine, they're welling with tears. And I *hate* the sight of him like this. Because the last time I saw him look at me in this way, the last time he whispered *sweetie* to me with that broken scratch in his voice, he was telling me my mother died.

"Dad, *please,*" I drop my tone to the same quiet place he's speaking at. "Am I your daughter?"

He nods with assurance. "Yes." His eyebrows fall to the sides of his face with certainty and comfort. "Of course you're my daughter. I raised you. I love you." Dragging his hand down his face, he exhales slowly with regret. "But we don't share DNA."

"But your name is on my birth certificate." I've seen it for myself.

The look of remorse on his face deepens as the lines crease on his forehead. "When I adopted you. Your mother and I had it changed."

I bite my lower lip. I haven't stopped shaking my head, as if I can stop this from being true just as long as I reject it as the truth. All I have to do is keep shaking my head. *Right?*

"Your mother would have been so much better at this," he says more quietly as he presses his thumb and index finger to his temples with one hand. He said the same thing when I was going through puberty and had outrageous mood swings. He said it again when I confessed that I was a pregnant teen. I didn't like it when he said it those times, and I don't like it now.

He stays in this position for a long moment. I'm too afraid to speak so I just watch him. Waiting. Waiting for an explanation. Waiting for him to give me a hug and make this all better.

When he drops his hand to his side he continues with, "I need a moment." Then he turns and exits the room. So much for a comforting hug from my father.

I'm astonished.

Shocked.

Dumbfounded.

Betrayed.

There's even a small part of me that feels humiliated. Like somehow this is my fault. Like I should have figured it out. The clues were there. We look nothing alike. We don't act anything alike. And he's never been comfortable around me in the way I imagine a father should be.

Suddenly I feel the warmth of Knox's hand on my shoulder.

I can't look at him. He's probably going to say sorry for causing this entire fiasco. Not that I blame him or think it's his fault at all. I'd like to know how he found out my biological father's name before I did. But I'm not bothered that he knew. Especially since he seems just as surprised as I am.

I can't look at him because I know he's going to say something to try and make this situation better. And that will only make me feel worse. Because there's nothing that can fix this. Honestly, I'm still hoping my dad walks into the room and takes it all back.

Knox squats down beside me, keeping his hand placed on my shoulder. I don't mind the comfort. I actually wish he'd hug me.

And just as that thought enters my mind, Knox wraps his other arm around me and tugs me closer to him. *Hugging* me.

"This really sucks," he says against the top of my head. "Sometimes things happen outside of our control. Sometimes we're surprised in the worst possible way, and it feels like everything is wrong. Sometimes we get blindsided and there's nothing we could have done to prevent it."

I wrap my arms around his torso. I get a feeling. One that I get when I'm sad or upset. It's strong enough to permit tears for the average person. But for me, nothing happens. No tears. Only feelings stuffed inside and swirling around my body with nowhere to go. As if my heart is trapped in a see-through box, being tormented with agonizing feelings that make me bleed. Everyone looking in can see what's happening, but no one can get close enough to do something about it.

After a long, quiet moment passes, he says, "I know this doesn't make any sense right now, but dammit you don't have to be so strong all the time."

I sink into him. Because he seems to be the only one willing to give any comfort to me. And more so, because I was wrong. His words didn't make me feel worse. They made me feel *better*.

His arms gently tighten around me.

"How did you know?" is all I say.

"I didn't know." When he shoots out a heavy exhale, my hair waves with his breath. "Chandler looked up your records. He didn't look into it much, but now I'm realizing he found your sealed birth certificate on file and not the amended one. The original document said your father's name was Bridges. I honestly thought I was going to get on your dad's good side by already knowing his name." He draws back to look at me. "But that didn't work out in my favor at all, did it?"

The tiniest hint of a smile curls in the corner of my mouth. "No, it didn't." I tilt my head to look at him better. "I kind of feel like throwing up."

"Is that better or worse than crying?"

"I don't cry."

He lets out a breathy laugh. "I remember."

I pull away from his arms and he releases me from his grip but keeps one hand on my back between my shoulders.

"I just don't understand why they waited so long to tell me. And if my dad waited this long, why couldn't he keep it to himself for the rest of his life? Why did I ever need to know?"

"You would rather not have known?"

"I don't know. What if my biological father is…bad?"

"Bad?"

"Yeah, what if he's a lowlife? Or a drug dealer? Or has another family and I'm some love child?" The question I'm more concerned about is why he didn't want me? And I don't want to know the answer, because it might hurt more than finding out my dad isn't my dad.

There's a sound near the doorway and I look up to see my father standing there with a floral decorated envelope in one hand.

"I'll let you two have a minute," Knox says, as he begins to rise to his feet.

Gripping a handful of his shirtsleeve I stop him with, "Don't go."

He seems surprised by my reaction.

I release his shirt from my grip. "I mean, I'd like it if you stayed." As of right now, he's the only honest person in my life.

He nods assuredly.

My father looks from me to Knox, then to me again. He rubs the top of his head with his hand then drags it down his face. In his same familiar hushed voice, he says, "We were going to tell you together when we thought you were old enough to understand."

He's getting right into it.

He continues, "But your mother got sick when you were five. Then the doctor visits became endless. Her health was our number one priority. Remission came and left before we had a chance to celebrate recovery." His eyes glisten when he says, "And you remember how the last few years of her life were." He wipes his eyes with the back of his hand. "She suffered a lot in the end. It was horrible for her, and it wasn't easy on me or you. Then after we lost her…"

His sentence lingers for a long moment as he looks at the dark rug on my floor. Something he does when he's uncomfortable. "And I d-didn't know how to express that… *grief*…with you." His droopy eyes meet mine. "I'm so sorry I wasn't there for you. I didn't know how to deal with it and be available for you too. I knew you would want to talk about her, but I couldn't utter her name without breaking down. It's still difficult for me, Trinity. You have her strength, and I'm proud of you for finding it."

I lift my hands and press them against my chest. Making sure my heart doesn't fail and fall out of my body. Because even though I wished he'd been more affectionate in my life, for the first time I understand he *couldn't*. He was home every night, he made dinner, he put a roof over my head, he made sure I went to the doctor and got my homework done. But he never really connected with me in the way I saw other fathers connect with their daughters. Because he always knew the truth.

He was preoccupied with my mother's deteriorated health from the moment I was old enough for him to connect with me. Our time together was always with my mother between us. She was the glue that held us together. When she was alive, he left all the hugs and kisses and warmth for my mother to give me. And the entire time he raised me after her death, he knew he wasn't my father. But he still chose to keep me.

"It's okay," I say gently. "Like you said, nothing changes the fact that you're my dad and I'm your daughter." If anything, I could have had a worse father raise me. My father may not have been a protective lion like I wanted, but he took care of me knowing he didn't have to.

"After she died," he swallows hard. "She…uh…" He shakes his head gently. "I'm sorry, I'm not sure why I'm having such a hard time getting these words out."

I take a few steps toward him and touch his shoulder. "It's okay, Dad. I don't care who this Bridges guy is. You're my dad. And always will be."

He smiles at me through the grief-stricken expression on his face. A silent thank you.

Clearing his throat, he looks down at the floral envelope and says, "She made me promise to give this to you when you were eighteen. But you were already living an adult life on your own by then. And after Abbi was born and you'd gone off to live with West, it just never seemed like the right time to give it to you."

I take the envelope when he hands it to me. "What is this?"

"Your mother wrote…" He presses his palms at his eyes then blinks several times. "She wrote that for you before she…" He can't finish his sentence, and instead continues with, "It explains everything." He takes a step back and turns around to exit my bedroom. Before he's completely gone, he places his hand against the doorframe. Dropping his head with his back still to me he says, "I'll be in the kitchen when you're done."

I'm staring at the envelope when he walks away. It's stuffed so full that it feels as if ten pages are folded up inside. I flip it around and my name is scrawled across the back in swirly cursive letters. My mother's handwriting. Which makes my soul sting with a bittersweet sensation.

Knox hasn't said a word. Instead, he's stood by my side through the entire discussion with my father. He's provided a comfort I didn't realize was missing in my life. Just by standing near me, I feel as if I have the strong protection of a soldier ready for combat mixed with the steady affection and loyalty of a wolf to his pack. As if I've discovered a feeling that I had no idea I had been searching for my entire life.

"I don't know what to do now," I say, stepping closer to Knox until he's wrapped one arm around my shoulders and pulled me close to him so that the sides of our bodies are touching.

His voice is thick with empathy when he says, "Would it help if I opened it for you?"

I shake my head. "I don't know." I look up at him. "Maybe?" My throat is tight and not because we're so close to each other, but because I'm terrified of what we're going to find inside the envelope.

He gives me a simple nod and removes his arm from my shoulders as he takes the envelope from me. He shifts his torso to the side and looks at my bed, then shifts back to me. "Should we sit for this?"

I nod. Holding myself in my arms to keep from shaking.

He sits at the edge of my bed, and I find a spot next to him.

Searching for a place at the corner of the envelope, he slips his finger underneath the sealed part of the paper then begins to slide it across, tearing the envelope open.

My heart begins to accelerate. "Hang on."

He stops and faces me.

"I'm not sure I want to know."

His posture drops along with the envelope when he sets it in his lap. "Wanna know what I would do?"

I hesitate before nodding.

He raises his eyebrows and looks out my bedroom window in thought for a moment. "I'd open it."

"Why? Whatever is in there, I'm afraid it's going to hurt my dad."

Or it might hurt me.

"But your dad already knows what's in here." He lifts the opened envelope between us.

"He also knows that I *don't* know what's in there. And as long as I don't know what my mom wrote, I can't hurt my father."

Or myself.

"He wouldn't have given it to you if he didn't want you to know."

I bite at my bottom lip for a moment as my knee begins to bounce up and down. "I don't know, Knox. This feels insane."

With his smile he says, "Trinity, this *is* insane." He places his hand on my bouncing knee until I press my foot flat against the floor and the bouncing stops. "But I'm right here with you and I'm not going anywhere."

I nod. "Okay." But I'm not fully convinced. I also know I'll read it at some point, so what's waiting going to do besides prolong the inevitable.

He's pulled the papers out of the envelope and the stationary is decorated with the same flowers as the envelope. For the life of me, I can't remember her having this floral stationary. I remember her garden in the backyard. I remember the potted plants decorating the porch. I remember her herbs in the windowsill of the kitchen. But I can't remember the floral stationary.

"I don't remember that stationary," I say.

Knox lets out a quiet laugh. "You're about to read a letter written by your mother, and all you can think about is that you can't remember the paper she used?"

I drop my face into my hands and mumble, "I can't do this."

I feel him shift from sitting beside me, to kneeling in front of me. "Trinity," his voice is gentle and full of spirit, "this is massive. It's okay to feel overwhelmed. Hell, I feel overwhelmed, and this has nothing to do with me." He gently pulls my hands from my face, forcing me to look at him. "But I can't think of anywhere else I'd rather be right now, than doing this with you."

Now my throat is tightening, and my pulse is accelerating because of how close he is to me.

"I see this going one of two ways," he says, taking the papers he set next to me and holding them in his hands again. "Either I read the letters out loud to you, so you're forced to hear what your mother wanted to tell you." Glancing at me he adds, "I can't promise I won't make any mistakes reading out loud to you." He looks back down at the papers. "Or you can read them in your head, and I'll sit right here." He pats the empty place on the bed next to where I'm sitting. "And I won't go anywhere until you're ready to leave."

I chew on the options he's given me for a moment. Imagining which option will be less of a blow to my father's pride, *and mine*. Then I take the letters from his hands, put on my bravest face, and before I begin reading, I say, "You promised you were going to sit next to me."

Dear Trinity, my stubborn darling daughter full of spirit and sass,

This is one of the toughest things I've ever done.

Right now, you're playing outside near the decaying sassafras tree that I refuse to stop trying to bring back from the dead. Maybe one day the scientists and professors at the universities and laboratories will find a cure for diseased sassafras trees. And maybe they'll even find a cure for diseased bones in cancerous women like me.

Until then, I hope that you find joy in everyday things.

I hope losing me doesn't make you bitter.

I hope you still find moths to save from spiderwebs. And I hope you always stop to play with your shadow at the end of the day when the sun is low and barely peeking over the horizon.

I hope you grow to be as gentle and kind as you are now.

I hope you never lose your taste for delicious home cooking. And I hope you continue to hone in on your baking skills and create the best birthday cakes that put my desserts to shame.

And most importantly, I hope you never forget who you are.

I hope you remember how much I love you. And I hope you know that I'll never stop loving you.

I hope one day you find a man that loves you more than your daddy does. And I hope that man cherishes every dark hair on your beautiful head. I hope that you have a wedding better than any wedding ever had. And I hope the both of you have the most wonderfully loved children together. Because motherhood is the greatest gift.

And I hope you find peace in life when things don't go your way—I know I've had my share of things not going my way. And I hope that when you do make mistakes (because trust me you will) that you forgive yourself, learn from your mistakes, and move on.

My sassy girl, when you read this, you'll be a young woman with the world at your fingertips. You'll have just graduated high school (Congratulations!) and you'll be taking on the biggest adventure of your life. Figuring out where the person you are fits into this big round ball of matter we call home.

And with your newest adventure, I have one last story for you.

Don't tell me you're too old for stories!

Remember the gypsy traveler? Of course you do. I've told you the stories of my childhood every night before those long eyelashes brushed against your little cheeks as you finally fell asleep. Now, I have one last story to add to the gypsy traveler saga.

Make sure you're sitting, because this one is a doozy.

Once upon a true time in reality, young gypsy Clearwater (that's me in case you've forgotten), was dancing, as she often did, while her parents and older sisters played and sang their gypsy tunes for a crowd of onlookers. Her bracelets jingled against her wrist as her boots kicked at the dirt, knocking a dust cloud into the air.

Gypsy Clearwater was just a seventeen-year-old girl at the time, but when she twirled in her layered gypsy skirt and kicked her leg up over her head, she had the poise and stability of a professional dancer.

One day, as Gypsy Clearwater gathered the earnings from the crowd, she noticed a yellow van parked just a hundred yards down the vacant backroad. As she looked closer, she noticed several boys running up the tree trunks until they were upside down and doing backflips in the air, then landed perfectly on their feet. A woman was washing clothes in a barrel behind the van. An older man was juggling three machetes. Closer to the dense tree line were a couple of young men, one pretending to be a bull and the other pretending to be a matador, flicking his t-shirt while his bare chest glistened with sweat in the summer heat.

Gypsy Clearwater finished gathering the earnings from the Hungarian songs her family had just played, while ever so subtly glancing toward the acrobats and jugglers in the distance. Her curiosity got the best of her, and she took her sister by the arm and begged her to walk down to the van where the young men were.

Just as soon as Gypsy Clearwater and her sister, Gypsy Selah, were tittering down the road, the young men who were pretending to be a bull and matador jumped down from a tree above, startling the girls.

"What's your name?" the older of the two boys asked.

"Clearwater," Gypsy Clearwater said. "What's yours?"

"Bridges." He smiled at her. And when he turned to face the other boy, she noticed an earring in his earlobe as he said, "This is my brother…"

But Gypsy Clearwater didn't pay attention when Bridges introduced his brother. Or when he shook her sister's hand. She didn't pay attention when Selah suggested they leave. She didn't listen when her father instructed her to return to their RV. And she didn't hear her mother calling for her after dark.

Instead, Gypsy Clearwater spent the next few days with Bridges.

They stayed up while the crickets chirped, and the fireflies lit up the sky. Gypsy Clearwater fell asleep in Bridges arms under the early morning sunrise when the birds began to sing. They talked about their families. They shared the same gypsy lifestyle. They loved performing. They even began to talk about their future when they held hands and walked down by the river.

When Gypsy Clearwater's family played Hungarian songs, Bridges family began to perform their acrobatics and juggling acts.

The families united their skillsets and traveled on the road together. Becoming one big gypsy family.

Two years passed and Gypsy Clearwater couldn't have been happier. She was loved by Bridges. She was pregnant with his child. Which made dancing slower, and her kicks lower. But she knew she'd have a baby that lived the same fruitful gypsy life with her delightful gypsy parents.

The crowds loved the show. Entertainment was the gypsy lifestyle after all.

But not all people are meant for gypsy entertainment.

Gypsy Clearwater went into early labor. It was two weeks before the due date, but early enough that Bridges felt concern for both Gypsy Clearwater and the baby.

The families were preparing for one of their biggest Hungarian shows. Gypsy Clearwater begged Bridges to go to the hospital with her, but his mother insisted he stay for the show and perform while she take Gypsy Clearwater to the hospital.

Later that night, after Gypsy Clearwater had given birth to a healthy (slightly premature) little girl named Trinity, Bridges's mother went back to give Bridges a ride to the hospital.

But they never made it.

That same night, a group of men that didn't believe in the gypsy lifestyle brutally murdered the gypsy families. Which included hanging Bridges and his brother from a tree. The massacre left Gypsy Clearwater in a dazed nightmare.

She was left alone in her grief with her new baby.

She was thrown into the fast-paced life of the American Dream.

She learned to dress like the rest of the country.

She learned to speak like the rest of the women around her.

She took her nose ring out and stopped wearing jewels on her face.

She cut her hair and got rid of her boots.

She learned to type and gave herself manicures.

And then she became a receptionist for a company she had never heard of, nor knew anything about. Nor did she care to find out. Her job was simply to provide for her and her daughter. The faster she finished her work, the quicker she'd get home to Trinity.

But while she worked, she met a blond-haired man with a quiet disposition. A man that asked her out for dinner. A man that opened doors for her and was kind when he met her daughter. A man with gentle blue eyes and a cautious smile.

And when that man asked Gypsy Clearwater to marry him. She said yes. And she began to go by her middle name, Ann, so that the neighbors would feel more comfortable.

When people commented on the way that her daughter looked nothing like her new husband, Ann never corrected them. She only said things like, "I must have strong genes."

"But where did she get her green eyes from?" They'd ask.

She never had an answer for them. Because answering them would only lead to pain.

Sometimes she would see a glimpse of Bridges in Trinity's eyes, but she never spoke of him again. Because it only hurt to remember his jet-black hair, and emerald-green eyes. It stung when Trinity's smile resembled his. And it was torture when she went to bed, because she'd dream of Bridges every night. Only to wake up next to a man that was safe but would never be him.

When Ann stopped being a gypsy. She stopped remembering the gypsy life. And she let Bridges die along with those memories. It was the only way she could live her new life without pain.

So after that, the only times she danced to the Hungarian sounds in her head, were when she was in her backyard, tending to her garden with her little gypsy daughter. Rescuing butterflies and spinning in circles to the silent sound of her ancestors.

The End.

My sweet and sassy, Trinity.

Never forget that you came from a place of love.

Never forget that the man you know as your father treated us well and loved us like no one else. He stood by me while I was sick. And he gave us a comfortable life I never thought I'd have.

Remember where you've been and where you came from. And never forget who you are, Trinity. Never forget you're the granddaughter of a Hungarian gypsy, and the child of love. And you wouldn't be where you are today if it wasn't for the balanced mixture of tragedies and blessings that ebb and flow within our lifetimes.

Please don't be angry that we waited to tell you. We didn't think you'd understand until you were older. And for me, it was too painful to dig up those forgotten memories. Until now.

There's something about writing down the truth that has given me so much peace.

Always remember, be true to yourself and others. Respect yourself and others. And you'll always have peace.

You're a brave girl, Trinity. Whatever you do in this life, be determined and be brave. Never give up, even if it kills you.

I know you'll do great things in this world. I know you'll be a better woman than I ever dreamt of being. And I know when you find love, you'll fall for someone as strong and handsome as Bridges, and as genuine and honest as Ed.

Lucky you, you got to have two fathers in this lifetime.

I love you to pieces my stubborn girl.

Until we're dancing in a garden together again,

Love,

Mom

CHAPTER TWENTY-EIGHT

Knox

Her chest is expanding and deflating at a rate I'm sure would explode a blood pressure machine if she were hooked up to one. I'm not sure if I was allowed to, but I've been reading over her shoulder the entire time. So I'm certain the sudden onset of hyperventilation is because of everything she's just learned about her family.

And it's *a lot*.

It was a lot even for me and I experienced one of the most horrendous massacres that Bowery and Canal Street ever saw.

In a flash, Trinity has gone from learning she has a father different from the father that raised her, to learning that that father was murdered for his unorthodox lifestyle. No one should be murdered for their beliefs.

That's a lot to take in in such a short amount of time.

I'm cradling her in my arms. I don't know when it happened, but she's positioned in my arms like a child. Unable to catch her breath. And part of me just wishes she would go ahead and let the floodgates open. *Couldn't her mom have written in that letter that it's healthy to cry?*

"You're safe," I say. I'm not exactly sure why I say it. But it reminds me of the night I met her on the floor of her home. Brutally beaten and disfigured. And *terrified*. Just like she's terrified now. Understandably so, the world as she knew it was just flipped upside down.

"I-I..." she chokes on her words, and I still can't believe she's not in tears.

"Shh, it's okay," I say, rocking her in my arms, "take your time to feel your feelings. You're gonna be okay." I'm letting her know she can take a moment to catch her breath before she speaks.

She swallows and I hear the gulping of air before she lets out a tearless sob when she says, "I miss her so much."

I continue to hold her. To rock her. To comfort her the best I can. *The best I know how to.* As she cracks out a few more dry sobs until she catches her breath. And I understand those choking sobs that accompany the heartache of missing a mother.

I hate that this moment reminds me of holding Constance back when she tried to run inside our home. The memory flashes in my mind. I held her in a bear-hugged grip so tight that, even when she was kicking my shins with her heels and scratching my forearms, I wouldn't let her go. Because I knew if I let her see inside that burning building, she'd never be able to unsee it.

Trinity finally breathes in a shuttered inhale and releases it slowly through her mouth. Her body relaxes when she does this, and she pulls her face up from where it was buried against my shoulder.

I adjust her so that she's seated next to me and prepare to wipe her face, but there's no sign of even the smallest shed tear. So instead, I lift her chin up so that she pulls her gaze from the letter in her hands to look at me.

"Your mom was right about you," I say.

She tilts her head and narrows her eyes curiously.

"You're the bravest person I know, Trinity. And so stubborn." I give her a small grin. "But you're stubborn in the best way. You never give up on what you know is right and you never let go of what you believe in."

She releases another long steadying exhale through her mouth.

I brush her hair out of her eyes. "And I know your mom would have been so proud of who you are, despite the misfortunes of your life."

When she smiles, her mouth is still pulling her wavering lips into a frown, but she's trying her hardest to feel normal again. If that's even possible after what her heart's just been through.

CHAPTER TWENTY-NINE

Trinity

My mom was right, finding out the truth provided a sense of peace for me.

The only things I brought back with me from my dad's house were my boxes of old pictures, a family photo from the living room, and a few scrap books. Nothing in the house held any sort of value. Except the pictures. The memories attached to them are priceless. Which is why I've been staring at the stack on the floor in my room since we got back to Constance's house hours ago. Trying to organize them has shown to be harder than I thought, especially since I continue to get distracted.

I hear the front door open and then close gently.

I'm sure it's Knox. I rise to meet him in the living room.

He's setting two glowing jars on the coffee table. "You won't believe what I found on my doorstep tonight."

It takes just a quick glance to know what's in the jars. "Fireflies." The flashing lights inside the jars are mesmerizing in the dimly lit living room. I squat down until I'm nearly eye level with the jars. "We should let them go."

"We will," he says, squatting down beside me. "I thought you'd like to see them first. With your insect infatuation and all."

I push his arm playfully until he falls to his side, bracing himself with his hand on the floor.

He laughs. "It was only a suspicion until your mom confirmed it in her letter."

"Who said you were allowed to read my letter?" I'm still being playful with him.

He's sitting on the floor now with his elbows perched on his spread knees. "When I see words, I have to read them."

"I wish I would have known that before I told you to sit by me."

He doesn't respond but continues to smile at me.

A long moment passes while I watch the fireflies swirling around in the jar as their bodies light up and then dim again. When I look at Knox, he's looking at me with a gentle expression. It's an unfamiliar expression. But a pleasant one. Sort of like the one he was giving me when we were in his apartment after his rib fractures.

Only this time, he seems to be guarding his thoughts by keeping his mouth closed.

"What?" I say with my growing smile. I can't help that my smile is growing. The way he's looking at me is creating an automatic smile on my face, I almost want to start laughing.

His mouth parts slightly for a moment, but still no words come out. I want to ask him what's going on. But part of me is nervous to know. Afraid that it might disrupt the playful dynamic between us.

I rise to my feet and hold the jars, handing one to him. "Ready?"

He doesn't take his eyes off me when he stands up and takes one of the jars from me. "No…" His voice is a deep rasp when he says this.

My smile fades and my eyes grow wide with the heavy sensations he's creating behind my chest.

He continues, "I like what the light does to your face. It's like candlelight."

I like that he's thinking about my face, and candlelight. I like that he likes my face in candlelight…or firefly light. I also like that he manages to make me feel *calm*. It's the opposite of what I felt with West. Even in the beginning, West made me feel nervous and uneasy. I thought I was supposed to feel butterflies that made me want to throw up. I thought that's what it felt like to love someone. But Knox is making me rethink all of that with his steadiness.

He's looking at my eyes, as if he's captivated and can't look away. And for some reason I'm letting my eyes captivate him, and *invite* him.

When he looks down at my mouth then back to my eyes, he inhales so heavily his chest expands and he moves closer to me but only to take a step back.

No! Don't move away. Move closer to me!

Am I a harlot for wanting him when I'm still technically married?

"Alright." He's motioning toward the front door now and waves me over. "Come on, we gotta free these guys before they run out of oxygen."

And just like that, I stuff away the feelings he's creating inside me and resort to being platonic.

I follow him out the door without putting my shoes on. The grass in the front yard is thick and strong. Opposite of the soft grass in the backyard. I wonder if the previous owners of the house did that on purpose. Planting painfully dense grass in the front lawn and luscious grass in the back for little feet to run on when they rushed out to the swing.

We continue walking toward the side of the house where the porch lights can't reach, and the darkness becomes tenebrous. I can't even see my own hand when I lift it out in front of me. We're both relying on the glow from the jar to provide enough light to see.

"Ready?" Knox is holding his jar out like it's a roman candle about to burst into flames.

I laugh. "They don't bite."

"I know that." He pulls the jar closer to his torso as if my statement disarmed the beetles.

We twist the lids off and it takes a few seconds before the fireflies realize they're free and begin flying out of the jars.

I set my jar down and a couple of the fireflies begin to crawl up my arm.

Knox inhales sharply through his nose when he notices the small lights flashing. "They're on your arm."

"I told you they don't bite. They're very docile and don't have any sort of defense mechanisms."

"Then how do they eat slugs?"

I look at him, although I can barely see his expression. "And I thought I was the bug guru."

This makes him laugh.

And I like it. And I wish he'd laugh again. I wish he'd close the space between us like he did when we were inside, only this time I wish he wouldn't stop. Maybe the crawling fireflies are making him stop.

"You know, they flash their lights to communicate when they're trying to find a mate?" I nudge the last bug with my finger, trying to coax it off my arm so Knox might want to stand closer to me.

"I can't believe you're an actual bug lady." He lets out a quiet laugh this time. "But no, I didn't know that," he says, looking across the grass at the pulsating glow of the freed fireflies.

I look at him for a long moment until a firefly catches my attention by flying in front of my face. Then I become entranced by the small neon glow in the yard.

We watch them for a long time as the sound of the cicadas rises and falls through the night. When only a handful of fireflies disperse around the yard, Knox faces me again. It's even darker out and I can barely see his silhouette now.

I'm not sure what his expression is doing or if he can see mine, but I smile anyway. "Well that was fun." I begin walking toward the house, wanting to be in the light again where I can see his expression.

I hear Knox following behind me as his boots crunch against the stiff grass. "That might be my favorite porch gift so far."

I throw my head back when I laugh, but then I instantly rip my head forward and curl into myself with excruciating pain.

I'm on all fours on the ground when Knox bends down near me. "What happened?" His voice is full of concern.

"I don't know," I say. "I stepped on something sharp."

"Probably a piece of glass or a sharp rock." He swiftly maneuvers me from the ground and positions me in his arms. "We'll check it out inside. You don't want to walk on it and wedge it deeper into your foot."

That imagery makes me cringe with discomfort.

Once we're inside he maneuvers me so I'm sitting on the kitchen counter. Then he turns the light on to inspect my foot.

"Is it deep?" I ask, too afraid to look at the damage.

He glances up at me. "Oh yeah," then with his grin he pinches something from the bottom of my foot, "real deep." He doesn't seem to be concerned anymore.

He reveals a small spiky plant in his palm.

"What is that?"

He seems much more relaxed than when he first set me on the counter. "Burweed." He tosses it into the garbage and begins rummaging in the cupboard for the first aid kit.

I grab my foot and bend my knee until my foot is resting on my other thigh. There's barely a drop of blood on the bottom of my foot. "It felt like I stepped on barbed wire." Now I know why the concern evaded him so quickly. I'm slightly embarrassed he carried me inside because I stepped on a thorn.

"Good thing you don't need a tetanus shot for burweed." He's smiling with amusement when he swipes away the tiniest drop of blood with an alcohol wipe and presses a band-aid over the area. "I think you'll live."

I can tell he thinks I'm being dramatic about this. But stepping on a dried weed with thorns in the dark of the night is startling. And painful.

"I'm not trying to minimize your pain. I've helped a few kids in the neighborhood get them out of their hands and feet before." He holds my waist and helps me down from the counter.

"Kids?"

"Yeah," he holds his gaze on mine, "kids are the only ones running around outside with no shoes on. And burweed is all over the neighborhood."

I let out a short laugh. Even though he's filling me with a lot more feelings than humor. "Thank you," I say, looking up at him as I put equal pressure on my feet. My not so painful feet, now that I know what I stepped on. "For helping me."

His gaze softens and he squeezes my shoulder. "Anytime."

I wish he'd close the space between us like he did earlier in the living room. I wish he'd kiss me and tell me all the thoughts he's keeping from pouring out of his mouth and into my ears.

Then, as if he can read my mind, he steps closer to me.

His throat rolls as he brushes my hair over my shoulder. Then he slowly slips his hand behind my neck.

I'm caving to his touch. Giving in to him and surrendering to the ache his presence has placed on my lips.

Then, "Trinity, it's after midnight."

No.

"I have to go in early tomorrow."

No, not your job.

"There's a blood drive at the library and the chief said he'd give us an extra day of paid vacation if we help out and donate."

No, why are you so responsible?

"I don't mean to be so abrupt." He takes my hand in his for a moment. "How are you doing?"

I shrug.

Aching for you.

"I'm okay." I lift my foot and wiggle it. "Like you said, I'll live."

He smiles. "No, I meant," his smile disappears and is replaced by a full expression of remorse. "You had a long day. Going back home. Finding out about your dads. Reading the letter from your mom. That's a lot to process."

It is a lot to process. But at the same time, it feels more like relief. If anything, it provided the answers I needed that explained why my dad was the way he was with me. Why he was always so distant. Why he struggled to connect with me. Why he never told me the truth to begin with.

It doesn't make it okay that he was emotionally unavailable or that he didn't protect me better. But in one single letter from my mom, she was able to answer all those questions I've had about him and provide a sense of belonging for me for the first time.

I know where I came from. I know my story. And that, somehow, provided exactly what I needed.

"I feel good about today."

And I really, honestly do.

CHAPTER THIRTY

Knox

I almost kissed her. I *wanted* to more than anything.

But then I was stopped by the concern I felt for her. And stopped by my own morals. And stopped by the fact that she had the most intense day of revelations. It would have been selfish to kiss her.

Even though I'm almost certain she wanted me to. But not completely sure. And because of that uncertainty, I didn't want to add another layer of confusion to her life.

I toss from my left side to my right side.

I'm not going to miss sleeping in Constance's bed at all when she gets back. My bed is so much more comfortable.

I jostle the thoughts around in my mind from the events that played out today, only to toss again to my other side because I can't fall asleep.

It's two in the morning when I look at the clock. I'll be lucky to get four hours of sleep before I have to get ready for work.

Trinity went to bed over an hour ago. She doesn't have to work until the afternoon tomorrow, so she has time to sleep in.

I wonder if she's tossing and turning thinking about the kiss that almost happened between us too.

Then, it happens.

It.

The thing I've been so relieved that I haven't endured.

The thing Constance warned me about.

The thing that causes me to recoil in this bed before tossing the covers off myself and retreating toward Trinity's bedroom.

The thing that has Trinity contorted in her bed when I fling the door open and flick her light on.

It's still happening.

It.

And although Constance warned me about this, she forgot to mention what I should do if it happens.

So I'm left to my own devices.

I grasp Trinity's flailing arms and hush her gently before the neighbors hear her and think she's being attacked.

She continues screaming and shifting her body back and forth as if she really is being attacked. Her arms are unintentionally hitting herself in the face and I'm worried she's going to accidentally injure herself.

Hushing her isn't working, so I hold both her hands in one of mine and use my other hand to shake her shoulder. "Trinity, you're okay. Shh... You're safe." I'm using a calm tone, but loud enough that I hope it wakes her from her night terror.

She continues flailing around so violently, her hands slip out of my grip.

I can't just watch this happen.

I follow my instincts and wrap myself around her. I'm lying on my side next to her, holding her arms against her body in a bear hug. My legs are intertwined with hers to keep them from kicking me, and herself. And I press my forehead to the side of her head and continue to gently hush her with my mouth close to her ear. Hoping she'll wake up soon.

The screaming quiets just as her body jerks still. Then her eyes flutter open.

She leans her head away from mine, searching my face in confusion. I'm sure it's strange and startling to see me next to her in her bed when she was just asleep.

I need to justify why I'm holding her in her bed. And quickly. "You had a nightmare." I pull my arm free by sliding it out from underneath her. Then I release my grip from her arms and begin to brush away the strands of hair stuck to her damp forehead. "You were screaming. I came in here to make sure you were okay."

She nods. But her expression is still adjusting to what happened.

She's looking at me and then around her room as if she's separating whatever was in her nightmare from reality.

She blinks several times. "What else happened?"

I shake my head and take one of her hands in mine. "Nothing. You were screaming and I tried to get you to stop. I was afraid you'd hurt yourself, so I held onto your arms and legs until you woke up."

She blinks at me again.

"I'm sorry. But I didn't know what else to do to get you to stop."

"It's okay." She nods in understanding. "I'm sorry I woke you." Her brows draw together as she pinches her eyes closed and shakes her head briefly. "I haven't done that in a while."

"You don't have to apologize." I don't have the heart to tell her I wasn't sleeping because I was thinking about kissing her. Especially since it seems like such a trivial thing compared to the terror she was just experiencing.

I release her from my grip and begin to move out of her bed.

"Knox," she says.

I look back at her as she grips my wrist.

"Could you stay?" She lifts the covers and scoots over.

I nod and climb in next to her.

She shifts her back to me, then pulls my arms back around her, and I don't stop her. She seems incredibly comfortable with me, which provides a silent invitation for me to let my own guard down with her. Not to mention holding her in my arms feels a lot better than my pillows.

"Sometimes when I'm stressed or don't get to bed on time," she pauses to release a long breath before finishing her sentence, "it happens…"

I don't need her to elaborate on what *it* is. I know she's talking about the night terrors. I know sometimes people relive their trauma in their sleep. I know, because it's happened to me.

Her voice is less scratchy when she says, "Do you want to know what I was dreaming about?"

Something tells me whatever it is, is going to keep me from falling asleep. But if it makes her feel better, then I'll welcome the sleep deprivation. "If you want to tell me."

She scoots up on her elbows and then rolls to her side so she's facing me. "Sugar was pregnant. And she was barking at West. I don't know why. She knew not to get too close to him. But it didn't matter, because when he straightened his leg out his boot hit her right in the stomach. He kicked her, over and over and over. I was screaming at him to stop. But no matter how hard I tried, I couldn't grab him. Every time I reached for him, he'd just slide from my grip. And when I tried to hit him, it didn't hurt him at all. Like I'd lost all my strength. Suddenly I was in the house and Sugar had given birth to lifeless puppies. West scooped them up into a garbage bag before I could check on them. Then he tossed the bag into the dumpster. I ran after him to get the puppies, to see if any of them were still alive. I thought maybe I could revive them. But when I opened the garbage sack, Abbi and Tuck were in there. And they…"

"That's awful, Trinity." She doesn't have to finish her dream for me to know what she saw. Even if it wasn't real. I know what it's like to have a bad dream that feels real. "I'm sorry you had that nightmare."

She gives me a look of remorse and her voice is grim. "It wasn't just a nightmare."

My pulse grows heavy with distress. "What do you mean?" I ask, hoping she doesn't say what I think she's about to say.

Her brows draw together, and she winces as if she's experiencing the pain of whatever's in her mind. "Sugar really did have puppies." She looks at me and swallows hard. Her mouth parts, but then it clamps shut when she turns and looks up at the ceiling. As if she's looking into her mind and seeing the real life horror unfold before her again.

The rage coursing through me is causing my heart to ram against my chest wall so hard I can feel it beating in my neck. Because I'm realizing my fear was right. That the first part of her nightmare wasn't just a dream, but a horribly traumatic memory of something West did to Sugar and her puppies. And if he's capable of doing something as horrific as that and going on with his life as if it meant nothing, then he's certainly capable of doing something far worse.

Pricks like that always push a little further. They always dig a little deeper. Needing to cause more pain to their victims to feel in control.

I don't say anything. Instead, I scoot closer to her, covering her in my arms. I grip her cold hands and pull her backside so close to my chest that I feel her trembling subside as her breathing calms.

With her relaxed inhale, she says, "This feels a lot safer than when Constance does it."

I'm glad she says that because I was wondering if I was crossing a line by holding her in her bed. Her words help relax my own thudding heartbeat. "You let Constance hold you?"

"Not like this." She tucks the backs of her legs in, pressing them against the front of mine. "She sits next to me and holds my hands. It's silent until she yawns a few times and then asks if I'm going to be okay by myself."

That makes me smile. Because that's exactly what Constance would do. I don't know how, but Constance doesn't struggle with nightmares. Not even after what happened. But I do, and I've struggled with them since day one.

"Sometimes I have nightmares about the fire."

Her body tenses briefly. "The one your family…"

"Yeah," I press the side of my face against the back of her head. "It was six years ago when it happened. Six years ago today, actually. Close to this time of night too."

She faces me briefly, eyeing me with suspicion before facing the other direction again. "You're lying." I know she's not meaning to cause discomfort, but those words make me flinch.

"I would never lie to you."

"How did it happen?" She grasps my hand and laces her fingers between mine.

"The phone rang," I begin, refusing to acknowledge the way her deformed skin feels against my palm. Not that the texture of her scarred palm bothers me. "It was after midnight, so everyone was asleep. I had just turned eighteen and still lived with my parents." I let out a frustrated breath remembering the night. "When I answered the phone, immediately I knew Constance was heavily intoxicated. She snuck out with her boyfriend to go to the clubs all the time. Even though it was the middle of the week, she was out getting drunk. She also got into fights with her boyfriend, and this night was no different."

"I can't imagine Constance drunk."

"Back then, it seemed to be the only thing she was good at." With a sharp inhale I continue, "She was all the way in the city. So it took a long time for me to get to the club she was at. And just as long to get back to the apartment building. Where we lived was more like a boarding house than an apartment complex. But because of that, it made it easy to block the only two entrances to get inside. The windows were barred because of the neighborhood we lived in. Which made escaping the fire impossible.

"The entire building was in flames when I pulled up. I remember feeling so helpless. My only concern was making sure Constance didn't run into that building and get herself killed. I held her back as she kicked and scratched. She was determined to save our family, while I was determined to save her. They all burned to death that night while Constance and I were tortured by their painful cries.

"And in that moment, I made a vow to Constance that I would protect her at all costs. And after the investigation proved the fire was an act of malice, I was bound and determined to get revenge."

Trinity turns around to face me. She presses one hand to the side of my face and her eyes are begging. "What do you mean?"

I fold my mouth together for a moment. Trying to figure out how I can deliver this statement without causing her to flee from me. "Constance's boyfriend was part of a violent gang. They were notorious for setting places on fire. With the help of our inheritance and the insurance money, we were able to hire someone to help track them down."

"What'd you do?"

I twist my wrist to reveal the back of my hand. "My knuckles are still swollen from what I did to her boyfriend's face before he went to prison."

She exhales with relief. "I thought you were going to say you killed him."

This causes a short, exasperated laugh to escape my mouth. "I'm not a murderer, Trinity. And because of that entire incident I decided to become a police officer. Constance and I wanted to move far away and start over. I have no desire to set foot in New York ever again. But despite the way I feel about Manhattan, Constance takes a trip back to where we grew up in Little Italy every year."

"What does she do?"

"I don't know what she does. I don't ask. And she doesn't tell me." I shrug. "I go on with my life like it's any other day because I don't want to remember that the last time I was near my family they were burning to death. I want to remember my mom's laughter and Italian cooking. I want to remember my father's gentle criticisms that were always followed up by him telling me how proud I made him. I want to remember my cousins bickering. My aunt's sequence dresses. My sister's outdated blowout. My grandma's crucifix and dependence on prayer. My nephew taking my wallet from my back pocket every chance he got. And my niece's smile. I want to remember the good times. So I acknowledge that they're gone and remember the day they were taken. But I don't take a trip to spend ten days to do it." I point to the side of my head. "Besides they still live here, in my memory."

She's biting at her bottom lip. Then, "I'm sorry that happened to you. And to Constance. Was it the same boyfriend that broke her collar bone?"

I'm not sure how she knows that. Constance doesn't talk about that with anyone. Not even me. "No," is all I say.

I take her hand from my cheek and press it to my lips for a moment. Then I lift it so I can inspect her palm.

She must notice what I'm doing because she says, "I forgot to turn my curling iron off. He held my hand around it until my skin melted. He wouldn't let me go to the hospital and instead he poured rubbing alcohol over it to combat an infection."

My throbbing pulse returns. Too bad we don't have any inheritance money left, or I'd hire a private investigator that would surely put West behind bars.

When I wait to catch her gaze, I notice her eyes are closed. She's ready to fall back asleep. And I hate that she revealed how her palm was burned so casually, as if she was telling me about what she ate for lunch.

I pull her even closer and tuck her head under my chin. It's the only thing that seems to keep me from walking out of this house and swelling my knuckles against the side of West's face. "He'll get what he deserves," I say. "Sometimes it takes a little patience, but officers that think they're above the law eventually trap themselves in their own web of lies."

Despite his dad being the mayor, he's not invincible or invisible to the people that are keeping a close eye on him. Guys like West always end up behind bars. And I don't mind helping move that process along, any way I can.

CHAPTER THIRTY-ONE

Trinity

Last night was a nightmare that turned into a dream. Even after I woke up, I stayed there in Knox's arms feeling his breath against my shoulder while he was still asleep.

I can't explain the security I felt with him near me.

I can't explain how comfortable it was when he quietly pressed his mouth to the back of my head when he thought I was still sleeping.

I can't explain the way things are changing between us.

I trust him, without being scared of him hurting me.

And I can't help but want that comfort and trust.

I'm sweeping the kitchen when the phone rings. I'd like to make sure the house is cleaner than it was when Constance left since she'll be home tonight.

I lean the broom against the back door. "Hello?"

"Hello, this is Sharry from DFPS. May I speak with Trinity?"

"Hi, Sharry, it's me."

"Trinity, I have some good news for you," there's a lilt to the way she says my name. "West signed the divorce papers. The judge needed an updated address to mail you the information for the court date. I've got a pen and paper here whenever you're ready."

I don't know what to say.

I know the address to Constance's home. But for whatever reason it's not coming out of my mouth. Because what I really want to talk about is what sort of scheming West is doing by signing those papers. Every part of me doesn't trust him. Especially when he's doing what I want.

"Trinity? Are you still there?"

"Y-yes." I switch the phone to the other ear. "Are you certain it was West?"

"He dropped the papers off himself." She clears her throat as her voice grows low. "I'm sure this is shocking, but it's happening, Trinity. After court, you're free."

"What about my kids? What about the custody agreement?"

"It'll all be settled in custody court. For now, it's one step at a time and finalizing the divorce is step one."

I'm two miles out of town and more than halfway to Matthew and Martha's house. I tried calling to save myself a trip. But they've either gotten caller ID and ignored the call because it was me, or no one is home. Which seems to be the case every time I call. I hope it's the former so I'm not wasting my time walking this far out of town for nothing.

I'm still in disbelief from the phone call I had with Sharry this morning. Which is why I'm going to speak with Martha. And if I time this chat right, maybe I'll get to see the kids for a minute too.

I can't wrap my head around how suddenly West changed his mind. He's been adamant about getting back together with me. Maybe something clicked when I stood up for myself outside of M.L.'s. Maybe he finally realized I'm not budging on this. And since he changed his mind about signing the divorce papers, maybe he'll change his mind about splitting custody with me too.

When I reach the house, I'm relieved to see that only Martha's Volkswagen is parked outside the house. Meaning Matthew isn't home to talk for Martha. And West isn't here to cause any potential problems.

I knock on the front door and wait for the pattering sound of children's running footsteps. But I don't hear anything until the door swings open, revealing Martha on the other side of the screen door.

"Oh, Trinity." She seems stunned to see me.

I begin to open the screen door but then stop myself from seeming like I'm intruding. "Could we talk for a second?"

She turns to look toward the kitchen then back to me. "I've got a pie in the oven."

"It'll only be a minute." I take a step back. "I won't even come inside."

She looks toward the kitchen then back to me again.

I beg her with my expression. "Please?"

She lets out a short breath and reluctantly pushes the screen door open. I can feel the air conditioner from inside the home seeping through the screen door when she walks out to the porch.

She probably thinks I'm here to see the kids. Who are obviously not here right now and are probably with West or at some swimming lesson I'm not invited to. So I decide not to bother her with questions about them, and instead say, "West signed the divorce papers."

She looks surprised and begins to lift her hand up to her mouth before realizing what she's doing, then stops herself by clasping her hands together in front of her chest. "I didn't know."

Just as I feared. If he hasn't mentioned it to his own mother, he's probably scheming. And the worst part is I have no idea what he's up to. "I guess he dropped the papers off this morning."

She looks sad. "He took the kids to the fair in Sulphur Springs this morning. He must've stopped by the office on his way out of town."

"I was sort of hoping he talked about it with you." I wipe the sweat beading on my forehead with the back of my hand. "But I guess there's not much to talk about since you didn't know he was going to sign the papers."

"No," she says, looking down. "I suppose not."

It's quiet for a moment. Nothing but the heavy whir of the cicadas is between us.

I'm about to tell her goodbye when the buzzer on her kitchen timer goes off.

She holds up her index finger. "That's my pie." Then she flips around and disappears into her cold air-conditioned house. Only someone with a small fortune could afford to bake a pie in the middle of summer.

I take her absence as my opportunity to leave. It was pointless to walk here. She apparently has as much information as I do. Which is none.

I'm already a few yards from the porch when I hear the screen door slap closed. "Trinity!"

I turn around.

"I'm out of cream and need to run to the grocery store." She waves me over with a jingle of her car keys. "I'll give you a ride into town."

I don't know where her friendliness is coming from. But since I'm probably on the verge of a heat stroke, I decide to accept her offer.

The radio is playing old country when I get into the car, and even though her air is on full blast, it feels more like a heater is blowing in my face.

"Thanks," I say, keeping my eyes forward. "For the ride."

"No one should be walking in this heat at this time of day."

I don't tell her that I tried to call first. I don't want her to feel bad, just in case my assumptions about her ignoring my call are correct. That would just make this car ride even more awkward than it already is.

"I know this has been difficult," she says. "Not seeing the kids and all. And sobering up is no easy task, but I can tell you're trying to get better."

I gently close my eyes. Mustering up the strength to be as calm as I possibly can while I deliver my next statement. "I don't know exactly what you've heard." I'm trying to keep from throwing the blame on her son. "But I don't struggle with drinking. I don't even like alcohol."

She keeps both hands gripped at the top of the steering wheel as she folds her mouth in. She's probably trying to keep her thoughts from exploding out of her mouth. After a long pause, she settles for, "I just don't know who to believe anymore, Trinity."

Me! Believe me!

I tilt my head in confusion. I don't know how to ask her to elaborate on that offensive statement. So I just sit in my confusion until she decides to speak again.

"I'd love it if the two of you could reconsider this divorce and reconcile. I'd love it for both of you, I'd love it for the kids, and I'd even love it for myself. It'd make everything a lot easier."

That's not going to happen.

"But I understand that you're both adults. And you need to make your own decisions."

I can't believe she's finally accepting this. It took her son signing divorce papers and dropping them off himself for her to accept it. But at least she's finally acknowledging that we're not getting back together. "Thank you for understanding that."

She pulls into an empty space on the east side of the pavilion and puts the car in park. Without facing me she speaks in a slow, quiet voice. "I don't...I don't know how to help you while supporting my son." I can tell that was a difficult thing for her to say. And as much as I don't like it, I'm also able to see that her confession is understandable. Anyone in her position would probably struggle. Especially one who was being fed lies by their own son.

I shift in my seat. "I'm not asking you to do anything besides prioritize the kids. All I want is to split custody. And I know that you know children need their dad *and* their mom."

"He's my son." She blinks at the tears forming in her eyes. "What would you do for your son?"

Just when I thought maybe she and I were making some progress, she completely sides with him. Again. There's no use in trying to change her mind now. I open the door and get out of the car. But before I close the door I say, "What would you do if you weren't allowed to see your son?"

When she blinks a tear rolls down her cheek. She seems too stunned to wipe it away. And instead, she puts her car into gear as I shut the passenger door.

She doesn't look at me the entire time she backs out and drives in the direction we just came from. She's probably too upset to get the cream she needed from the store. Or maybe she never needed any cream to begin with.

I wish I had thanked her for the ride. I wish I had done a lot of things. I wish I had prioritized my relationship with her better. I wish I had reached out to her for more. I wish I had asked for more than just babysitting to go out with her son. Her son, who liked to use me as a punching bag. I wish I had confided in her when West first started getting drunk. I wish I had gone to her for help the first time he back handed me. I wish I had brought the kids over to see her more often, without West there dominating the conversations. I wish I had opened up about my life when she first asked.

Because maybe if I had let her in instead of walling her off, maybe then she wouldn't feel so torn about telling the truth about her son.

CHAPTER THIRTY-TWO

Knox

The most exciting part of the blood drive was when the principal of the elementary school passed out at the sight of a needle.

But because my entire day was uneventful, it left a lot of time for doing things like thinking about Trinity. And looking forward to my shift ending so I could go home and see her again. And wondering if she really felt as safe as she said she did when she fell asleep in my arms.

When I pull into the driveway, Constance's car is parked in her spot. I don't bother going up to my apartment to shower first. Instead, I head straight inside the house.

I can hear someone in one of the bedrooms when I enter the house.

"Hey, I'm back here," Constance says.

"Is Trinity here?" I immediately feel self-conscious asking that before even greeting Constance when she's been gone for the last ten days.

"Nope, just me."

"How'd it go?" I ask, uncinching my gear belt.

Constance emerges from her bedroom with a disposable camera in one hand. "I gotta picture with that dancer you used to flirt with."

I'm untying my boots when I say, "I did not ever flirt with that guy. I just treated him like a human being every time I waited at the bus stop."

"You must be pretty unforgettable because that's not what he thinks." She sits on the couch and shifts the camera in her hands. "Anyway, he's still dancing in his underwear on the corner of Holloway."

I plop down next to her. "That guy had the craziest stories."

"Yeah, well," she nudges my shoulder, "you should come with me next time so you can talk to him yourself."

Without moving anything but my eyes, I glance at her. "Maybe." And I'm not sure if it's the recent change of heart from talking with Trinity last night, or if it's because I'm sleep deprived, but I mean it when I say this to her.

She nods once, then flips the camera in the air and catches it. "You're not allowed to change your mind after I get these developed though." She lifts her arm dramatically. "I'm pretty proud of the pictures I captured. A sweaty man in his underwear dancing on the corner. Views from the top of the Empire State Building. Penniless musicians in the subway."

"You don't have to show them to me, I used to live there."

"Yeah, but I like to torture you sometimes." She sets the camera on the coffee table then rests her elbow on her knee, cupping her chin in her hand when she looks at me. "So, what'd I miss while I was away?"

A burst of air shoots out of my mouth. "Where do I start?"

We spend the next hour talking about everything that happened with Trinity and her dad in Abilene. She tells me about the things that have changed and all the things that are the same in Manhattan. We both avoid talking about the fire or the new building that's replaced the apartment we grew up in. She tells me about all the jars of food she bought from the food stands along the highway on her way back through Arkansas and Texas. And I tell her about Trinity's night terrors last night.

"Sounds like you handled it, Zio." She pats my shoulder. "You always know what to do in a crisis."

"Don't say that's what makes me such a good cop."

She rolls her eyes. "I wouldn't dare compliment you anymore than I just did."

"Thanks, Kid," I laugh. "Means a lot you keep me so humble."

She rises from the couch, but turns to face me with a curious expression.

After a moment, I say, "What're you looking at me like that for?"

She's holding the camera again and pressing it under her chin while she chews on the side of her cheek. "Would it be so bad if she knew?"

I scoot forward on the edge of the couch and brace my elbows on my knees as I clasp my hands together. I know what she's getting at. But it wouldn't do any good telling Trinity. Especially after I told her I would never lie to her.

"This is who I am now." I shrug. "It wouldn't make any difference if I told her."

"I think it would."

I roll my head back and groan. "Remember Chicago?"

She blows raspberries. Which means I've hit a sensitive spot. "Chicago was a learning curve. This is different. You can't deny that you're in love with a traumatized girl."

"I didn't say I was in love with her."

She turns around. "You didn't have to."

I leave Constance to her packing and head for the backyard to make sure Sugar has water, especially since it's been a scorcher of a day.

After I fill Sugar's bowl, I stay outside to make sure I don't need to refill the water again. But my attention is quickly pulled away from Sugar's hydration levels to the sound of glass shattering.

I rush across the yard, making my way through the gate when I see someone sprinting down the road. I immediately begin inspecting where the shattered glass came from when I notice the window to my apartment has a gaping hole in it.

There's only one person brave enough to shatter my window and then run straight home. So I'm in no hurry to find him.

Constance flings her front door open. "Did you hear that?"

I'm walking up my apartment steps when I point to my window.

"What the hell?" She shades her hand over her eyes as she inspects my window.

"I'm pretty sure it was Robby," I say. "I'm going to check out the damage before I talk to him."

"Talk to him?" She's following me up the stairs now. "Do you see how well talkin' to that kid has worked out for you? He needs a hard kick in the ass if you ask me."

I'd like to defend him. But I can't. Not this time. And not because I'm upset that Robby broke my window. But because I'm upset by what he left on my doorstep.

"Eww! Sick!" Constance covers the bottom half of her face with her hand when she looks down into the box at my doorstep. "Is that a dead turtle?"

"Robby!" I'm pounding on the door of his grandmother's house with the side of my fist.

When the doorknob turns, I'm expecting to see his grandmother, but instead I see Robby.

And he looks pissed.

I'm taken aback by it. I've honestly never seen any sort of expression on his face other than curious or solemn.

"What do you want?" His words are clipped.

I throw my hand out to the side. "What you did, Robby." I shake my head and pull my brows together in disappointment. "That kind of behavior is uncalled for. And frankly, it's not going unpunished." I nod my head toward my patrol vehicle. "Get in the car."

He doesn't hesitate to push past me and slam the door behind himself.

I grip his hands and put them behind his back as I cuff him. "If you want to act like a criminal, you're going to get treated like one." I open the door to my patrol car. "Watch your head."

He doesn't resist.

He doesn't say a word on the way to the station.

He doesn't argue when I place him in a cell.

And he doesn't look at me when I tell him he's in a load of trouble.

I'm pacing in front of his cell. I'm irate. And disappointed. I can't help it. I don't understand how this kid is capable of tormenting an animal. Granted it was a turtle and they get run over by cars and die every day. But what he did. Killing a living creature and then leaving it on my doorstep as some message. That's cruel. And troubling. And makes me wonder what else this kid might do. First it's animals…then what? People?

Chandler walks by the end of the hallway and gives me a nod.

I return a firm nod and continue pacing.

After a moment, Chandler doubles back.

He walks toward me, cleaning his glasses with a small cloth before shoving the cloth into his vest pocket and returning his glasses to his face. He's inspecting the cell when he says, "I don't think we're permitted to hold juveniles."

I stop pacing and face him. I look back at Robby, who still has a grimace on his face. Then I turn my back to him and lean toward Chandler's shoulder so only he can hear me. "It's just to scare him."

Chandler blinks at me.

"I have a good reason," I say, defending my motives.

Chandler shakes his head. "You have about ten minutes before you find yourself written up." Then he flips around and guards the end of the hallway to ensure the sergeant or any of the higher-ranking officers don't come this way.

I open the cell and stand in front of where Robby is sitting. He has no problems furrowing his brow at me while he continues the silent treatment.

I get right to it. "Why'd you break my window?"

He doesn't respond.

"And why'd you kill that turtle?"

This causes his glaring expression to shift. "*You* killed the turtle by leaving it out in the sun all day."

I killed the turtle?

I didn't know it was there, how could I have killed it?

Unless…

I release a long exhale. Realizing I've made an error in judgement. And thankful that Robby's not turning into a monster like I'd thought. "I wasn't at the apartment. I've been staying at the house all week. And I didn't see the turtle until about fifteen minutes ago when you threw a rock through my window."

The anger evades his face as he sits up straighter with the familiar expressionless appearance that normally masks his face. "You weren't at your apartment?"

I shake my head slowly.

"What about the fireflies?"

"I happened to run up to my apartment for just a minute last night and found them."

He drops his gaze and nods in understanding. "I threw the rock because I thought you stopped caring about the stuff I left you. I'm sorry I broke your window."

I approach him and place a gentle grip on his shoulder until he looks up at me. "I owe you an apology for jumping to conclusions. I should have asked you about it before handcuffing you. I wasn't being a very good police officer."

"Yeah, I know. You didn't even read me my Miranda Rights."

I let out a short laugh. "You don't deserve to be treated like a criminal. In fact," I exit the cell and motion for him to follow me out, "You deserve to be treated with some ice cream."

On our way out, I notice Chandler's smug grin. Instead of justifying myself, I give him a pat on the back as a thank you.

After I take Robby out for some ice cream, he decides to walk home and promises not to leave anymore living *gifts* at my doorstep.

As I return to my patrol vehicle, I notice Trinity getting out of a parked car at the pavilion. I don't know why, but a certain kind of jealousy trickles through my core. It burns imagining her settling into someone else's passenger's seat.

The car she was in backs out and then drives away toward the edge of town.

I quickly get into my car and drive over to where Trinity is. She's walking toward the gazebo with her back to me. So, I open my door and stand with one arm on the hood of my car and the other arm draped over the door.

"Where you headed?"

She hesitates before flipping around. She looks frustrated when she faces me, but it quickly shifts into a smile. Realizing it's me, she places her hand on her hip and shades her eyes with the other. "Home."

I nod my head toward my passenger's side. "Hop in. I was just headed that way."

She walks over and joins me in the car.

When I pull out of my parking spot, I can't help but let curiosity get the best of me. "Who were you with earlier?"

"Just now?"

I nod.

Her shoulders drop with her exhale. "I went to talk to Martha. She insisted on driving me back to town since it's so hot out today."

My entire body relaxes, realizing she wasn't with anyone I need to be jealous of.

"West finally signed the divorce papers."

I nearly run a stop sign when she says this. The sudden announcement causes me to hit the break more suddenly than I intended, which forces us forward before we slam back against our seats.

She lets out a short laugh. "Forget how to drive?"

"Trinity," I'm facing her with disbelief.

She gathers her hair, pulling it to one side. "Yes?" she says curiously.

"He signed the divorce papers?"

She nods with a smile.

"Does that mean…?"

She bites her bottom lip, stifling her grin. Then she nods. "I'm free."

I put the car in park and unbuckle my seatbelt. "Then I don't have to feel guilty about doing this." I lean over my computer and other equipment that's between us, and gently take her face in my hands.

Her chest is rising and falling heavily as her eyes dart between mine.

"Is this okay?" My voice is quiet and raspy.

She nods rapidly as her eyes fixate on my mouth.

Then, as if it's the most natural thing, I pull her close and press my mouth to hers. The exhale through her nose is deep, as if she's relaxing for the first time in years. With our mouths pressed together, her lips part, inviting me. I devour the taste of her. She's sweeter than the vanilla ice cream and caramel topping I just indulged in. Although if I had known this was going to happen, I would have saved my appetite for her.

There's a loud honk that forces us to separate.

I place one arm around her headrest and shift in my seat to see who's honking at us.

"Chandler…" I mutter. And he's grinning from ear to ear.

CHAPTER THIRTY-THREE

Trinity

How long was one document keeping me from experiencing something I didn't know was possible to experience? Maybe I would have filed for divorce years ago if I'd known what I was missing out on.

I've been reliving that kiss in my mind since Knox pulled into the driveway and dropped me off. I wanted him to kiss me again. But instead, he went to his apartment, changed clothes, and then left to buy a new window to replace the broken one in his living room.

And I've been laying in my bed, replaying the feeling of his hand slipping around the back of my neck to pull me deeper into the kiss he initiated. The kiss that tasted like the caramel parts of a sour apple lollipop. The kiss that was packed full of heavy passion and delicate consideration. Until it was abruptly ended.

I don't know what we are, but I can safely say we're not friends. We're *more*.

And I couldn't be happier about that.

Although, I don't understand how he could kiss me like that and then just go back to his normal life without so much as a conversation. Not that we didn't talk more in the car about the divorce and what that entails. But he seemed overly concerned about getting the window fixed as soon as we got to the house. He's been in and out of his apartment all evening.

I hear the sound of Knox's truck before the headlights creep through the blinds and dance across my bedroom wall when he pulls into the driveway. My pulse skips and I feel a sudden giddiness in my stomach. I toss the covers off myself and scoot out of bed. If he's not going to talk about us, I will.

I swing the front door open and nearly run into Knox's torso on my way out the door.

"You're in a hurry," he says with a smile. Then looking down at my bare feet, he adds, "And without shoes…" he drags his eyes up my body until they land on my eyes, "…again."

I can't seem to breathe steadily. I don't know if it's his heavy gaze holding me in place. Or if it's because of all the unsaid things hanging between us.

"I wanted to see you."

His grin grows on one side before he folds his mouth in and looks toward the street when I say this. He lets out a short laugh then grabs my hand. "Come on." He leads me out of the house but just as my feet meet the grass he stops.

After a moment, I say, "What is it?"

"The last time you walked across this grass without shoes, you got a weed stuck in your foot."

I shrug, taking a step in front of him.

He's still holding my hand and pulls me toward him. "Hop on," he says, guiding my hand around his back shoulder. "I'll give you a piggyback ride."

I laugh when I place my hands on his shoulder and wait for him to hunch down so I can jump onto his back.

He continues to carry me even after we've crossed the lawn. Scaling the steps, it doesn't take long before we're inside his apartment.

I begin to release my hold on him to slide off his back but he grips my legs. "Hang on a sec." He shifts to the side and turns the light on revealing the broken glass that's still scattered on the floor under the window he replaced this evening. "I haven't had a chance to clean up yet."

I squirm. "Let me down and I'll help you."

He doesn't release me, instead he walks toward his bed. Right before he meets the mattress, he spins around and gently lowers me until I'm seated at the edge of his bed. He turns back around to face me, and reaches his hand out to push my hair over my shoulder.

I smile up at him.

"I wanted to see you too," he says with intensity in his eyes.

I narrow my gaze and tilt my head to the side. Confused by his statement.

"I was just about to walk inside the house when you opened the door. Then you told me that you wanted to see me." He tucks his index finger under my chin and lifts it gently before lowering his face just inches from mine. "I was coming over because I wanted to see you too."

Then, he meets my lips with his. He kisses me, and I kiss him back, lacing my grip around his forearms, making sure he knows that I want this.

His grip at the sides of my face, pulling me closer—feels good and right. His breath against my mouth—feels good and right. The warmth from the sides of our legs touching—feels good and right. Everything about him feels good, and *right*.

When he pulls away, he's smiling as he finds a spot next to me on the bed. "The last time we kissed, it felt cut short."

I slip my hand around his neck. "I was thinking the same thing." I begin to lean toward him again, picking up where we just left off.

But he gently draws back and takes my hand in his. He's still smiling when he looks down at our hands, now resting in his lap. "Before I kiss you again," his serious gaze shifts up to mine, "I want to know what this is."

What this is? I don't know exactly how to answer that question. I don't want to scare him off by being forward and telling him I'm falling for him. He's made me feel comfortable and safe more times in the last year than West did during our entire marriage. He's shown me respect that I didn't know was possible. I mean, he waited for my divorce before he even kissed me.

Yet, here I've been suppressing romantic thoughts about him for months, and with one (no, scratch that), *two* kisses from the guy and I'm so far gone that I'm spinning and don't even mind the blurred vision. I'm just hesitant to tell him that.

He lets out a slow exhale through his mouth before folding his lips together. I can tell he's waiting for me to say something. But I can't.

I'm terrified.

He's been increasingly supportive throughout my separation with West. He's showed up. He's comforted me. He's been everything and more than I could have dreamt of. But I thought the same thing about West, and here I am celebrating the fact that he signed the divorce papers, by kissing my roommate's uncle.

"Butterflies," I finally say.

Knox nods slowly, as if he's trying to indicate he's listening and ready for an explanation that I'm not sure I can fully provide.

"Before, I'd get butterflies. And I was looking for love in every stranger that gave me butterflies."

He rolls his tongue between the front of his teeth and the back of his lip, concentrating on my words.

I continue, "But love isn't butterflies. Love is safe, and steady, and comfortable, and *right*. And I feel all of that with you." I swallow hard, nervous to admit the next part of my statement. "I'm falling in love with you, and it scares the crap out of me."

His mouth shifts to one side before a grin sneaks out. "You should be afraid to fall in love."

I pull my brows together with concern. Not the response I was expecting, especially since he's smiling at me like that.

He shifts his body so he's facing me better, still holding my hand in his grip. "But I'm not afraid, because I'm not falling in love with you."

My pulse halts as my lungs deflate. I begin to pull my hand from his, but he hangs on to it with both hands before lifting it to his mouth to kiss the disfigured skin along the inside of my palm. It makes me want to scream and push him away, but the logical parts of my mind tell me to stay and listen to him because he's shown me nothing but kindness and respect. And he must have a reasonable explanation for what he's just said.

He gives me a look of endearment. "I'm *growing* in love with you, Trinity. I don't want to fall in love. Because everything that falls, breaks. And I don't want either of us to break and fall out of love. I want to walk in love with you. I want our love to move through the ebbs and flows of life. I want our love to grow. *Together.*" He releases my hand and holds my face, looking at me deeper than anyone ever has. And I can't help but notice the way he used the same words to describe love and life as my mom did in her letter.

He traces my collarbone in thought. Then dragging his fingertips down my arm until they slip around my waist, he leans forward guiding me to my back. There's only mere inches between our mouths. "Be afraid to fall in love, Trinity, but don't be afraid to grow in love with me."

My eyes are shifting between his. There's a familiarness in his hazel gaze that hits my heart in a place that seems as if it was waiting for him all my life. "I'm growing in love with you too."

I lock my hands around his forearms and in the same way lock my mouth on his. Kissing him with a desperate passion that begs him to consume me.

He's circling his finger around the back of my shoulder as my cheek rests against his tattoo covered chest.

"Do all your tattoos have a story?" I ask.

He presses his cheek into the top of my head. "Most of them."

"What's this one about?" I trace a dead lion sprawled across an altar. It takes me a moment to notice that the lion's mane is chopped short, as if it were cut off.

He lifts up to look at his chest, then lays back against his pillow. "Ever read *The Lion, the Witch, and the Wardrobe?*"

"No."

"You should."

"Does a lion die?"

He shrugs.

"Who cut off his mane?"

"I'd hate to spoil it for you."

I turn to face him, resting my chin on my folded arms against his chest. "Cutting off a lion's mane seems pretty humiliating."

He nods in agreement as he draws his hand in circles against my back.

"Why'd you get it tattooed on your body?"

His chest, and me, rise with his deep inhale and then lower with his exhale. "It's a reminder. We face obstacles in life. And challenges. Sometimes we're stripped of everything, but it only makes us stronger when we get to the other side."

"The other side?"

He leans forward and kisses me on the lips before sitting up against his headboard. "This is the other side. The good stuff. The parts of life that make you smile." He's talking about losing his family and getting to a place in life where things are good. Like right now, with his job, and his life, and us.

That makes me smile. But then my smile fades because I remember that even though this might be the other side for Knox, I still have parts of my life that haven't reached the other side yet. Like having my kids in my daily life.

I sit up and pull myself against the headboard next to him. "Is this everything you ever wanted in life?"

"I'm happy, if that's what you're asking."

I shake my head. "What about your dreams?"

He shrugs.

I press my top teeth into my bottom lip and face him.

He picks something from my cheek and then with his thumb and finger pressed together he says, "Dreams are like making a wish." He looks at me then back down to his hand. "Pick a finger."

I touch his thumb.

He opens it, and the eyelash from my cheek is pressed to his thumb. "Make a wish."

Instead, I flick the eyelash away. "Wishes are fleeting."

"So are dreams!"

I shake my head.

He smiles and wraps his arm around me. Pulling me toward him, he kisses the side of my face. "Okay, what are your dreams?"

"First, I want my kids back."

"I want that for you too."

"Then I want to get an education. When I dropped out of high school, I wasn't thinking about the future. But now that I don't have my diploma, it seems to be the one thing that keeps me from moving forward." I bite the inside of my cheek. "And I feel so embarrassed every time I fill out an application and I have to write that I'm a 21-year-old without a high school education."

"Those goals are more than attainable."

"You think so?"

He nods. "You're going to get your kids back. I'll even back you up in court if you need a witness." That makes my heart grow three times in size. "And you can get your GED, easy."

I'm beaming. "I think I want to do something like what Sharry does when I grow up. That's my other dream."

He laughs. "When you grow up?"

"Yeah." I shift to my side so I'm looking at him. "I'd do a better job than Sharry too."

"I'm sure you will. Any more dreams?"

I want to talk about the parts of me that see him in my future. But even though he told me falling in love was the only thing I should be afraid of, I can't help feeling a little bit of doubt that he might disappoint me too.

"That's all." *For now.* "What are your dreams?"

"I don't have any." His mouth is curled into a small grin on one side.

"Everyone has dreams."

"Not me." His smile falls into a firm line as his gaze drifts toward the moonlight beaming in through his window. "Dreams always come at a cost."

CHAPTER THIRTY-FOUR

Knox

August 1998

I'm in love with everything from her Hungarian features to her sensitive soul. I even love the way she gets nervous when I kiss her in public and call her my girlfriend out loud.

I know it's only a matter of time before West catches wind of our relationship. But I don't care. There's absolutely nothing he can do about it. They're divorced.

He didn't even show up to court, but that didn't stop the judge from finalizing the divorce anyway. The only thing left to do is figure out the custody agreement for the kids.

"I'll pick you up after your shift," I say, with my arm extended so I can reach her hand. It's uncomfortable for my shoulder when I hold her hand in my car like I'm doing now. But I'd break my arm if it meant I could be closer to her.

When I pull into a parking spot in front of M.L.'s she releases my hand, and I hate that we're not touching anymore. She leans over and kisses the side of my mouth with a short peck. "I can get a ride with Constance. We're on the same shift tonight."

I put the car in park and shift in my seat so I can look at her better. And feel her again by placing my hand on her thigh. "I'll pick you up after your shift," I repeat.

She laughs and closes the space between us. I meet her mouth, and this time, I kiss her, releasing a heavy exhale through my nose. Wishing I could keep kissing her, but knowing she has to get to work.

My radio blares, but I ignore it. Making sure Trinity has all my attention.

Chandler and Ballard are working today too. One of them can take the call.

Trinity is the one to pull away first, but I can tell it's killing her almost as much as it's killing me to leave her at work for eight hours. "I'll see you tonight," she says, exiting the car.

But just before she closes the door, the radio blares again. "*Five-year-old girl. Unresponsive.*"

Chandler acknowledges dispatch asking for the address.

And when dispatch comes back with, "*Sixty-Four Richards Road. Right off Lane Ten and a half,*" my chest sinks, because I know exactly where that is.

Why did it have to be that address?

Trinity's mouth falls open with her eyes fixed on my radio. "Sixty-four Richards is..." She doesn't finish her statement because she doesn't have to. We both know where the address is. And there's no way in hell I'm going to let Chandler or Ballard take that call.

"Shut the door, Trinity."

Her widened gaze shifts from the radio to me. "*Abbi...*" Her voice is a painful whisper.

She's standing in the worst place, right between the door and the vehicle. I put my cruiser in reverse but keep my foot on the brake. Because if I reverse with her standing where she's at, I'm going to injure her. "Close the door."

She's shaking her head now. And I can tell by the way she looks down at the passenger's seat with urgency, that she's about to invite herself along on this ride.

"Please," I say, desperate for her to listen. "Move out of the way."

Just as she pulls the door open wider, I shift my car into drive and hit the gas. Making sure no pedestrians are in the way before I drive onto the sidewalk and turn my car around. I flip my lights and sirens on just as I glance in my side mirror and see Trinity sprinting as fast as she can after me.

I'm so sorry, Trinity.

I hate what I'm doing. But I know if I brought her, it would only devastate her. I don't know why Abbi's unresponsive. I don't know what happened. What I do know is that whatever the situation is, Trinity doesn't need to see it.

My adrenaline is coursing through my body faster and heavier than I've ever felt it. So much so that my breathing has intensified. I'm not normally worked up like this, but something about the fact that it's Abbi has me feeling anxious to get to her.

I kill the sirens as the wheels of my car slide against the curve in the dirt road, just as I see the Laurel's two-story house.

I'm out of my patrol car and in the house searching for Abbi before I've announced myself. "Sheriff's department!" I'm also the first one on the scene.

A woman's sob gives me direction, and I scale the stairs three at a time before finding a child's playroom where Martha is desperately clinging to Tuck while Abbi's blue, lifeless body is sprawled on the floor.

Pain. It's as if I've been punched in the gut. The pain is deep, hitting a part of my being that I thought was unreachable after losing my family in the fire. This is too personal for me. This is Trinity's daughter. But I'm the first on the scene. Abbi needs me at my best, not crippling at the very sight of her.

I can't feel this. I can't let my emotions take over. So I do what I do best in a crisis, and I try to fix it.

I radio in for medics and pray Chandler hauls ass while I drop to my knees and begin chest compressions.

"What happened?"

Martha's in hysterics.

Abbi's sternum gives way to my palm like she's made of plastic.

"*Martha*! What happened?"

She's screaming when she says, "I don't know! She was fine. I went to help Tuck in the bathroom for just a minute. And when I came back. She was seizing." Tuck begins to cry as Martha's sobs grow louder.

I jog my mind to figure out what to do for a kid that's unconscious from a seizure. "How long has she been out?"

"A few minutes. I called immediately."

I stop compressions and tilt Abbi's head back to open her mouth so I can provide her rescue breaths. But in doing so, I notice a bulge in her throat.

She's choking.

I immediately pull her up under her arms and raise my leg up so I can drape her body over my knee. "Come on, Abbi. Don't give up." Then I begin pounding my open palm against her back. "Stay with me. Come on, Abbi. *Breathe*." Heat wraps around my throat in a chokehold, and I know I'm getting emotionally involved because this situation is too personal. And it has everything to do with Trinity.

"What are you doing to her?" Martha's screaming doesn't faze me. The world could be falling apart right now, and I wouldn't stop trying to save this girl's life.

Suddenly the front door bursts open and Ballard announces her presence.

"Up here!" I call out from the bedroom.

Ballard's instantly at my side while Martha continues screaming over Tuck's crying.

I continue firmly hitting Abbi's back. "She had a seizure then went unconscious. But I think she's got something lodged in her throat."

Ballard nods. "What can I do?"

Martha screams and shakes my shoulder trying to stop me. "You're hurting her! Stop it!"

I nudge my head to the side. "Get her outta here."

Without hesitating, Ballard guides Martha down the stairs and outside when I hear the ambulance arrive.

Two paramedics rush upstairs and kneel at my side, and I tell them what happened. I'm beginning to worry about how long she's been without oxygen which makes my spine tense.

She cannot die.

She will not die in my arms.

She *will* be okay.

One of the medics lifts Abbi's head, opens her mouth, and holds her face in place. The medic looks up, then gives me a nod to go ahead and hit Abbi's back between her shoulder blades again. And this time, when the strike of my palm meets her back, a neon green bouncy ball shoots out of her throat and hits the floor.

A deep rush of air inflates Abbi's lungs as her body expands with her gasping inhale.

I release a heavy breath of relief and begin to rub my hand in circles against Abbi's back. "Good job, Abbi." Even though her body is limp, her lungs are working again.

The paramedics quickly assess her, before heading outside to retrieve a gurney.

She's still unconscious, but when I sit back and rest the back of her head against my chest, I can't help but give her a small hug. "You're okay, Abbi. Keep breathing." The blue color of her skin disappears and the pink color of life rushes back to her. And I've never been more relieved to see life return to a body.

When the paramedics strap her to the gurney, I radio in to let dispatch know Abbi's on her way. Following them out the door I watch as they roll her into the back of the ambulance. "Her name's Abbi," I tell the female paramedic that's closing the back door of the ambulance truck.

She nods. "Thanks, we'll make sure she's taken care of."

"Do me a favor?"

She looks at me with anticipation.

"Keep your sirens off." I rub the back of my neck. "Don't wanna draw extra attention to this with the gossip in this town. Since she's a kid and all."

"Sure thing." Then she closes the door and sets off down the dirt road.

I'm not sure when Chandler got here, but he's holding Tuck in one arm and clicking his flashlight on and off to distract Tuck with his other hand.

I approach Ballard, who's taking Martha's statement. Ballard glances up at me and says, "Go ahead, we've got this."

Chandler looks at me, nodding his head toward my patrol vehicle.

They've got this.

As fast as I can, without sliding off the road, I drive down the dirt path until my tires meet the pavement of the county road. I'm nearing town and about to take a shortcut through a neighborhood to get to the hospital, when I see someone running along the side of the road. When I see *Trinity* pumping her arms at her sides as her hair swings back and forth with her stride.

I drag my hand down my face, heading in her direction. She doesn't stop running when I stop my car and tell her to get in. Which forces me to have to U-turn and slow down next to her.

I roll my passenger window down as I keep my speed at her running pace. "Get in, I'll take you to…"

I can't finish my statement. At this point, the less she knows the better. Especially since she's obviously upset with me for leaving her behind.

There's another car coming in this direction, so I pull up ahead of Trinity then park on the side of the road to let the car by. When I get out of my vehicle, Trinity continues past me without even glancing in my direction. Her cheeks are flushed and she's sweating. Running at this time of day, this time of year, will give anyone heatstroke. Not to mention that her adrenaline is at an all-time high.

I place my hands on my hips and walk in the direction she's running. "You're going to pass out before you get there at that pace."

"Good." That one word is enough to make my heart sink. Less than twenty minutes ago she was in love with me. Now, she's so hurt that she's pushing me away. All because I wouldn't take her to her daughter. In my defense, it was for her own good. It would have killed her to see Abbi like that. Then again, maybe Trinity is exactly who Abbi needed to wake up to.

I drop my head back between my shoulders. "She's at the hospital."

She stops in her tracks and waits a moment before flipping around.

I begin walking to meet her, she's a good ten yards away from me and my cruiser. "Come on, I'll take you there."

This is enough to change her mind and get her to walk towards me again. Only her arms are swinging at her sides in haste. "The ambulance that passed me. Was that her?"

I nod. "Yeah, that was her."

Her intense stride doesn't stop when she barrels into me, hitting my shoulders with the sides of her fists. I grab her arms and maneuver her around until I'm cradling her arms against her chest with her back pressed to my torso, so she can't hit me again. Not that she was trying to hurt me, or that her blows were painful. I know she's worried about her daughter. I know her response is a reaction no mother in her position would be able to control.

She's heaving and I know it's not because she was sprinting down the road.

"Easy," I say with the side of my face pressed against her head. Trying to calm her with my voice. "It's going to be okay. Just relax."

She kicks her feet on the pavement. "Why is she at the hospital?" Her voice is strained in a way I've never heard before. Panicked. "Ambulance only drive with their lights off when they have no reason to be in a hurry." She's gasping. "And the only reason they wouldn't be in a hurry, is if she…"

Her body goes limp in my arms. "Hey, hey, hey, take a breath for me." She's misunderstanding the situation.

I can see and feel the life leaving her just as the darkness of depression prematurely begins to seep in.

I hoist her up and carry her to my passenger side and set her down in the seat. Squatting in front of her, I flip the AC in her direction so the cold air can cool her off and dry the perspiration drenching her body. "Listen to me," I say, gently shifting her face in my direction with my palm.

She won't look at me. Her eyes are downcast and she's deep inside her own thoughts.

I kiss her, desperate to get her to listen. She doesn't seem to respond, so I cup her face in my hands and say, "She's alive."

Her eyes flick up to mine.

I have to get her back in the right mindset before she sees Abbi. "Don't you give up, Trinity. She needs your strength. Don't you dare give up on her, and don't you dare give up on yourself."

CHAPTER THIRTY-FIVE

Trinity

How do you breathe when the thing that gives you life is ripped away from you?

How do you breathe when that same thing that makes your heart have a beat is nearly torn out of this world?

How do you breathe?

"Hey, come here." Knox takes my hand, pulling me closer, to hug me before we enter the hospital. "I'm gonna get an update before I head back to the station. I've gotta fill out a report." He draws his head back to look at me. "Or...I can stay here with you."

I shake my head. "No, I'll be okay. You should go." I bite at my bottom lip with a shrug of my shoulder. "I'm trying to be strong." I don't sound at all convincing.

"You are strong." Kissing my forehead, he adds, "And brave."

I don't feel brave. My insides are swirling with the most intense fear I've ever felt. But I try to remind myself that sometimes, I have to do things while I'm scared. And not knowing what condition I'm going to find Abbi in, has me terrified.

I walk with him inside the hospital where he gets the attention of a nurse. "I'd like to get an update on a little girl, Abbi Laurel. She was just brought in with the ambulance." He motions toward me. "This is Abbi's mother."

The nurse points Knox in the direction of a woman behind a small window. "She can help you with an update."

Knox thanks her and squeezes my hand. "I'll be back as soon as I can to check on you and Abbi."

Then the nurse takes my arm, comforting me and guiding me at the same time. "If you want to follow me, I'll take you to her. She'll be right through these doors here."

I follow her through a set of doors and down a short hallway. She's trying to make small talk, and I'm able to answer her with auto responses that my mouth has learned to give while my mind is preoccupied with my weighing concern for my child.

My child that I haven't seen in months.

My child that was declared *unresponsive* over the radio system.

My child that Knox informed me will be okay. Indicating that right now, she's not okay.

When the nurse opens the door to a room, I don't waste a moment stepping past her to get to Abbi as quickly as I possibly can.

There's a doctor and another nurse discussing something quietly near Abbi's bed, but I don't acknowledge them. I'm too consumed by the need to know she's alive. I need to see for myself that she's still my same child. With a heartbeat. Breathing. And alive.

I drape my arm around her as her eyes slowly blink open. But just barely enough so I can see her irises. "Mommy?"

My lungs inflate with relief, as my heart beats with life again at the sound of her scratchy voice. "Oh, my sweet girl. I'm so glad that you're okay."

I hug one arm around her little body. "Ow." Her small voice causes me to pull my arm away.

"I'm sorry, baby girl."

I look up at the doctor for some sort of direction since I'm not certain, aside from choking on a bouncy ball, what happened to her. But the doctor is looking at the nurse in the doorway that led me to the room. "Is this…"

The nurse nods. "That's Mom."

He gives her a polite smile, then he looks at me. "Mrs. Laurel?"

"It's Trinity," I say.

"Nice to meet you, Trinity. I'm Dr. Steinburg." He looks down at his notes. Flipping through the papers. "It seems Abilene had—"

"My name is Abbi," Abbi interjects in the same tone I just used to correct him with my name. How ridiculous am I for thinking I was being creative naming her after my hometown? I guess that's why seventeen-year-olds aren't meant to be parents in charge of giving a child a name that will stay with them for the rest of their life.

Abbi gives Dr. Steinburg one of her contagious smiles. He mirrors her grin, then continues when he looks to me. "*Abbi*, had a seizure before choking on a toy and then lost consciousness for a few minutes."

My mouth falls open as I take Abbi's hand in mine, holding it against my chest. Never wanting to let her out of my sight again. "I'm sorry, did you say she had a seizure?"

He lifts his gaze from the papers on his clipboard. "We're going to run a few tests to see what's going on. I'll let you know what we find out as soon as I can." He begins to exit the room before spinning around to face me again. "Oh, and be careful with her chest. The officer at the scene started CPR before realizing she had a ball lodged in her throat. She'll be sore for a while but should make a full recovery from that." Then he leaves the room.

He said that *the officer* at the scene performed CPR. The officer was Knox. How horrible that must have been to revive a child. And not just any child, but *my* child that he knows personally.

Realizing what Knox was doing provides me with a deep appreciation for what he did. He saved my daughter and kept me from seeing that tragic scene by keeping me away. He wasn't being rude or controlling or heartless, like I assumed while I ferociously ran alongside the road in a panic. He was being thoughtful. And *loving*.

I pull my legs up on the bed and nestle next to Abbi. I run my index finger down her forehead and over her nose. "I'm sorry I wasn't there."

"I pretended the ball was a grape, Mommy."

"It's okay to pretend." I force a smile. "But, next time pretend to put it in your mouth instead of really eating it." I drag my finger down her cheek, then wrap a lock of her hair around my finger, in disbelief that she's right in front of me. "I've missed you *so* much, Abbi."

"You did?"

I nod. "Of course I did. My life is so boring without you and Tuck."

"But…" She blinks up at me. "Daddy said that you didn't want to see us anymore."

My mouth parts. Her words shatter my heart. "What? No, Abbi, that's not true." I'm heartbroken not only because West lied to her and she believed him, but because so much time has passed since the last time I saw her that she's speaking clearly without the lisp she's had since she was a toddler.

"Daddy must've been confused." I keep my voice as gentle as possible despite the fire boiling my blood. How could West say that to her? "I wanted to see you every day. I tried to see you every day." I hope my words don't come back to bite me in the butt later. But I'm trying my best not to say anything regrettable that could get back to West. And as much as I want to, I don't say anything negative about him either.

"Daddy said you left with your new family." She blinks and her long lashes graze her cheeks. "He said you didn't want us anymore."

I kiss her forehead as my heart accelerates with frustration towards West. What kind of monster lies to his own children about their mother? "Listen to me, Abbi, the only family I have is you. There's nothing I want more than to hug you and Tuck every day for the rest of my life. I want both of you. I love you both more than anything. And even when I'm not around, I will always love you and Tuck, no matter what."

She smiles. "Really?" Then she winces with her cough.

I probably shouldn't be encouraging her to talk so much. I'm sure her throat is painful after having a ball stuck there. "Yes. No matter what anyone else says. You and Tuck are my favorite two humans in this whole wide world." I roll over and dig in my purse to retrieve the thick rectangular card Knox gave her. "Do you remember how to use a phone?"

She nods.

I open her palm and tuck the card in her hand. "Call this phone number any time you want to talk to me. And if I don't answer, I promise I'll call you back okay?" I don't mention that I've tried calling to talk to her and Tuck every single day to no avail. But maybe now, with the phone number I gave her, she can sneak a phone call to me.

She frowns as if she's worried. "What about Nana?"

I tilt my head, confused. "Nana?"

"Yeah," she coughs again, "Nana and Papa said I can't talk to you on the phone until The Guy says it's okay."

I don't know who The Guy is, but I'm not happy that he's keeping me from speaking to my child. It's probably a name they're using in place of someone's real name. I wouldn't be surprised if it's West. But it could just as well be the judge. Or maybe they're using an imaginary person as an excuse not to talk to me.

Just as I thought I was making progress with the divorce too. Somehow this information makes me feel like I'm back to square one.

I cradle the side of her face with my hand. "You can pretend that you're calling your imaginary friend."

This makes her smile. "Can her name be Drastia?"

I return a smile. "Drastia is a great name." I pull the blanket up a little more to cover her, so there's a soft barrier between her bruised body and my hand. I hate that she's in the middle of this. And I hate that I'm asking her to lie.

"When will we get to play at your house?"

"Soon." *I hope.*

"Can we have S'mores?"

I nod.

"Promise?"

"Yes, I promise we'll have S'mores when you come over to my house." I don't even know exactly how that's going to work since my house is technically Constance's house.

She coughs again. "My throat hurts, Mommy."

I lean over her to retrieve her water. But it's empty. "I'll get you some ice water." I kiss her forehead before heading for the door. "I'll be right back."

I find the ice machine in the hall and begin filling her cup before I hear a commotion on the other side of the double doors that separate the lobby from the patient rooms.

The doors burst open, and I flinch so intensely that I drop the cup of ice. I scramble to clean it, refilling the cup just as I hear his familiar voice.

"Trinity." West closes the space between us, taking my hands in his to help me to my feet. "My mother called. I got here as fast as I could." He pulls me to his chest, wrapping me in his arms. Only his chest is covered in a thick vest and several uncomfortable items pinching and poking me. He releases me and with a horrified expression he says, "Is she okay?"

I'm not sure what to make of his exasperated panic. Or that he's okay comforting himself by pressing my body to his after we're clearly divorced. But it's his dysfunctional way of moving forward. I don't know how, but after so much time passes, he's able to pretend like he's not a monster.

I step away from him, because I know that no matter how much pretending he does, he's still a monster. He keeps his hands locked around my arms. My voice is weak. "The doctor has to run some tests, but she's awake and alert." It's not weak in the way it used to be weak, it's weak in an uncertain way. Like I'm unsure what I should be saying right now. Because I want to ask where he gets off touching me at all. But I can't ignore the fact that he's concerned for our daughter. I just can't shake the feeling that he's somehow using this event to try and draw me back in.

He releases a gust of air before hugging me again. He's in a police uniform but it's not the same navy-blue color as the uniform he used to wear when he worked here in Mount Vernon. It's more browns and tans, and he's wearing khaki-colored pants. And for the first time, I notice there's something dramatic and unauthentic about his mannerisms. As if they're forced.

I know our daughter was just unconscious, and normally I'd understand and accept a reaction like this. But I don't trust him. The last time I saw him he was drunk and lunging at me. Not to mention hiding our children from me as long as he possibly could. My innate visceral response is to shove him away and tell him not to touch me.

But since he signed the divorce papers. And since we just suffered an emotional trauma over our daughter's wellbeing. Maybe this is okay. Maybe he's trying to be sincere and that's why everything seems forced. Maybe this is what divorced parents do when they're child sees the face of death. Maybe?

I pull away from him and motion toward the door where Abbi is. Trying to keep calm. Trying to be mature. Trying not to let the fact that he's ruined the last year of my life affect me.

He rushes to her side and cradles her in his arms. "Baby, you scared me to death." His eyes are red and he's clenching his jaw, trying to keep his quivering mouth from revealing how terrified he was for her.

I understand that terror. I just went through it. He's a half hour behind my own emotions. And I can't figure out how I feel about it. Because I just learned that he's been spilling lies to our daughter. Yet seeing the protective way he's holding her in his arms with concern does something to me. And the fact that he's been crying, something that I'm not even able to fully express in my own body, rips at my heart.

"Knock, knock," the nurse says, filing in behind me. "Did y'all know Miss Abbi is Rh negative?"

I find a seat at the edge of the bed, handing Abbi the cup of ice water. "So am I. It was a big deal at my prenatal visits."

She nods with a polite smile. "Well, we'd love it if we could get you to donate some blood in case we need it for a transfusion during surgery."

West releases Abbi, walking around the side of the bed to approach the nurse. "Is something wrong with her? What does she need surgery for?"

The nurse raises her hands. "It's just a precaution. In case we need to do surgery. It's nice to have blood on hand, and typically parents are a good match. Especially with her negative blood type. We still don't know what caused the seizure. So having s—"

He shakes his head as his tone drops. "She didn't have a seizure."

"Well, the chart said—"

He cuts her off again, folding his arms over his chest. "Her chart said that, because my mother doesn't know what she's talking about." He twists his torso looking at Abbi, then back to the nurse. "She lost consciousness because she was choking. She didn't have a seizure."

I'm not sure why he's speaking to her with such certainty. He wasn't there. And he's obviously not a doctor. I've seen him act superior before, but never like this. Never toward someone in a completely different line of work than him.

"If we could speak with your mother—"

He cuts her off again. "I'll save you the trouble. My mother saw Abbi twitching, it wasn't a seizure. She was jumping to conclusions."

The nurse must realize this is an argument she's not going to win since she smiles politely and says, "Well, I'm going to take Abbi for a quick scan to rule out any serious concerns.

And in the meantime, if you'd like to donate some blood," she raises her hands in surrender, "just in case of course. We'd appreciate it."

I smile at the nurse. "I can donate."

She smiles at me and then looks at West for a response.

"Sure." West tosses one hand in the air before turning around to approach Abbi's bedside again. "I'll donate."

There's a small needle attached to my arm, pulling blood from my body up a tube and into a plastic bag. There's one connected to West's arm too.

"Thank you," I say to West who's sitting in the chair next to me.

He nods with a glance in my direction. "Yeah, she's my daughter. If she needs my blood, she gets it."

I smile at his fatherly instincts. "No, I meant..." I drag in a breath, hoping I won't regret what I'm about to say. "Thank you for signing the papers and going through with the divorce."

His face falls, and he looks down at the tube of blood resting against his arm. "Yeah, well." He sniffs, then turns his neck to the side until it makes a popping sound. "It seemed like you were serious."

I give him a sentimental smile. It quickly fades because I also feel bad knowing he's still in love with me. I love him too, not like I did before. I'll always care about the father of my children. But I will never subject myself to the mistreatment and disrespect he inflicted on me ever again.

I don't think anyone is innately a bad person. I think he made terrible mistakes. I forgive him for what happened. But I'll never forget that it happened. And I'll never let it happen again.

The side of his mouth curls up into a grin. "What?"

I stifle my own grin. Treading these new waters with him is confusing. How do we move forward? Are we allowed to be friends? Maybe not friends, but friendly? Is that something he's capable of? Has he really changed?

"It's nice," I say. "Me and you able to have a normal conversation."

His grin drifts into a firm line as his eyes fill with remorse. "I love you, Trinity."

I inhale a sharp breath. I wasn't meaning for my compassion to be mistaken for anything more than kindness.

He lifts his head up to look at me better. "I'll always love you. I hate to think that you're going to be the one that got away. And I hate that I'll spend the rest of my life comparing every other woman to you."

"West," I say his name with a painful drop in my voice. I'm not looking for this kind of attention from him. From this point forward, our conversations should strictly revolve around our children. That's it.

"I'm only telling you the truth. I know I'll never find someone as loving as you," he drops his head back against the chair, "and I'll be kicking myself in the ass for the rest of my life for ruining what we had."

I hate that his words are pulling at my heartstrings. But I don't want to be naïve to the potential game he might be playing. I can't pretend that the knot in my stomach isn't a big red flag.

He continues, "I *am* sorry that it didn't work out between us." He reaches his arm up, placing his hand over mine. "But if you ever need anything, just ask. I'm still here for you. Even if we're not married anymore."

My body stiffens at his comment and his hand on mine. I don't want help from him. I don't want him in my life. I just want our children to grow up with as much normalcy as we can provide for them. Navigating raising our children while we're divorced is going to be tricky, but if he continues these games I'm not going to play anymore.

"I'm serious, Trinity. Anything you need from me, let me know and I'll show up right at your doorstep."

If he only knew how close my doorstep was to Knox's.

I hold my inhale for a moment, preparing myself, before releasing my exhale with my words. "I miss the kids, West. When can I see them?"

"What do you mean?" His voice is equal parts gentle and concerned. "You're seeing Abbi right now, aren't' you?"

I fold my mouth in and nod. Unsure of the way he delivers his statement.

"And Tuck?" I say. "When will I see Tuck?"

He clicks his tongue with a soft laugh. Then his eyes flick to mine. "Anytime you want, baby."

A surge of horrifying familiarity hits my stomach. I swallow hard, trying to keep the bile from rising up out of my throat.

I begin to pull my hand away, feeling like even allowing this small touch is somehow being unfaithful to Knox. And myself. But West holds my hand a little tighter. Just firm enough to tell me that it's okay for us to touch like this. That it would even be okay if I wanted more touching from him. It's this small gesture that is enough for me to see that allowing him to barely cross this boundary with me will result in an unpredictable spiral of events that will lead me right back to where I started.

Which was begging for help through the window of our broken car with a busted lip and nowhere to go.

He's absolutely manipulating me.

How could I be so stupid? Of course he hasn't changed. And he probably never will.

But at the same time, if I don't give him the little parts of me that he wants, then I'm terrified that I won't ever see my kids again.

"You were able to get a job at the police station?" I'm changing the subject because the one we're on is too terrifying to continue.

He smiles. "Yeah, in Hopkins County. Sulphur Springs area."

"That's not far at all." I say this with a forced ring to my voice. But really, I'm petrified.

CHAPTER THIRTY-SIX

Knox

My fists are shaking as they squeeze around the front of my vest.

I came back to the hospital for another update on Abbi and to check in on Trinity.

But it seems she's made herself pretty comfortable. They both have their backs to me, Trinity and West.

The chairs are set up in a semi-circle and they're the only ones in the room. Aside from the phlebotomist keeping tabs on their bags.

I'm still in the doorway, waiting for a good opportunity to insert myself into their conversation and figure out why the hell he's touching her.

Then I notice it.

The subtle way she pulls her hand, but he doesn't release his grip.

The forced pitch to her voice, indicating she's uncomfortable.

The way her shoulders rise up closer to her ears in discomfort.

I didn't intend on eavesdropping, but it's inevitable at this point.

And nothing is twisting my insides more than what their conversation holds. She has to see through his conniving lies. It's almost like he's not even trying to convince her he's sincere anymore. He's gotten sloppy. Or maybe he always was. Anyone with a brain can see he's using disgusting tactics to sink his claws back into her.

And since Trinity is smart, I know she won't fall for it.

I *hope* she won't.

"Officer Santino." The phlebotomist, who I recognize from the blood drive, makes my presence known. "You're welcome to join us." She waves me over, moving her overgrown bangs out of her eyes with the back of her forearm.

Trinity turns in her chair and sees me. Her panicked expression shifts into relief.

The phlebotomist pats the chair next to West, indicating for me to sit. But I stand on the other side of Trinity instead. It's safer for West with me over here.

And as soon as I'm near her, she rips her hand free from his grip which gives me the perfect opportunity to take that same hand in mine. I smile at her and give her hand a gentle and reassuring squeeze.

The way she grips my hand says everything that she's not speaking out loud. With the simple way she intertwines her fingers with mine, she tells me she's okay and she's glad I'm here. And that's all I need for my own nerves to settle.

The phlebotomist begins detangling some clear tubing near me when she says, "Didn't donate enough the first time?"

I give her a polite smile. "No, I did." I look down at Trinity. "I'm just here for moral support this time."

She nods and places the tubing back on the cart. "It's funny," she says. "The only people I've ever met that are Rh negative are all in the same hospital at once."

I give her a polite smile.

Trinity's voice is quiet when she says, "Thanks for coming back."

I glance at West, then back to Trinity. "I'll always show up for you."

With that, West abruptly sits up and yanks the needle out of his arm. He doesn't bother putting pressure on his arm either. His fuming rage is apparent in the expression he gives and the way he refuses to break eye contact with me.

When the phlebotomist tries to apply a gauze pad to his arm, he shrugs her off, stands up, and walks out of the room with a dripping stream of blood following him across the linoleum floor.

I can't help but chuckle at his childish behavior.

"You really shouldn't stir things up with him," Trinity says. Her expression is soft, but her eyes are full of uncertainty and fear. And I know it's fear of West and his unpredictability.

I kiss the back of her hand before placing it on her lap. "I didn't realize I wasn't allowed to look at him."

She exhales. "You know what I mean."

The phlebotomist finishes taking care of West's unfinished donation before she slips her hand around Trinity's arm. "I think you're about finished here."

Trinity smiles at her, but her smile slowly fades along with the color in her face when the phlebotomist slides the needle out of the crease in her arm and replaces it with a cotton ball.

"You're losing her," I say, to the phlebotomist, grabbing Trinity's shoulders and holding them in place to keep her from slipping out of the chair. "Trinity? You okay?"

My tone is less concerned police officer, and more concerned boyfriend and apparently the phlebotomist notices too since she says, "She's alright. I'm gonna tip her chair back and get some ice."

She quickly returns with an ice pack and places it on Trinity's neck.

I'm not sure if Trinity passed out or just got lightheaded, but either way the fact that she's the color of paper is concerning.

"What happened?" Trinity says, with heavy eyelids.

"You had a little drop in blood pressure for a second," the phlebotomist says, handing Trinity a small juice box and a cookie. "Has that happened before when you've given blood? Needles make you uneasy?"

"No, I've never had a problem with needles or giving blood before."

The phlebotomist shrugs it off. "Sometimes it happens when people get nervous."

Trinity looks up at me with a hazy gaze, as if to tell me I'm the cause for her nerves. That makes me smile, since it's probably true after the interaction I had with West. I know it's not so much *me* that makes her nervous, but me around West and how our interactions typically end.

I don't mean to cause problems, but it's almost impossible for me to be around West without him feeling threatened somehow. I can't help that the guy is a child.

I warm Trinity's cold hand in mine. "It must've been the ugly uniform West was wearing, it made me a little nervous too." I say, trying to lighten the mood.

"He works in Sulphur Springs now," Trinity says, as she takes a bite of her cookie.

I'm about to respond when my radio blares with a call from dispatch about a concern that an equine owner is starving their pony. I look down at Trinity, hating to leave her and Abbi for a seemingly less emergent situation.

She gives me a smile and I notice the color returning to her face. "It's okay," she reaches for my hand. "Go rescue a pony in need."

I bend down to kiss her mouth and she tastes like a sugar cookie. "This will only take a minute."

She holds her grin, but I can see the disappointment in her eyes.

Even though her expression begs me not to go. And everything in me tells me to stay. I leave, ignoring the panging in my core.

CHAPTER THIRTY-SEVEN

Trinity

When I get back to Abbi's room, West is pacing in front of the window with one arm wrapped across his chest and the other bent at the elbow and his hand covering his mouth. He glances at me briefly, then faces the window and continues pacing again.

"Any news from the doctor?" I ask.

West subtly shakes his head. He's apparently upset with the realization that there's more than friendship between Knox and me.

And with that information, I'm able to focus on everything else in the room. Martha is seated at the edge of the bed next to Abbi and Tuck is pushing a chair around near the sink. When I see him, I almost die. He's grown so much that it hurts. Because his growth is only more proof that I haven't been around. And I hate that...for both of us.

"Tuck," I reach down for him, but he looks as if he's staring at a stranger.

Then I actually die. Because my son doesn't recognize me anymore. It only took months for him to forget my face. That's all. *Months*.

Martha notices the painful interaction between me and Tuck. Then she says, "It's okay, Tuck. That's Mommy."

This must interest West, since he turns around to watch the unfolding of my maternal death. My throat feels like his hand is squeezing it shut. Like his presence is suffocating.

I try to ignore the fact that everyone's eyes are on me, along with the fact that I feel like I might pass out again and not because I just gave a pint of blood.

I lock my eyes on Tuck's bright green eyes. The same bright green eyes that I have, and hope he sees himself in me enough to want to come to me. "I love you, Tuck." My words are soft, almost undetectable. I slowly step closer to him and squat down with my arms open. Needing him to fill the empty space between my arms.

He sticks his finger in his mouth, comforting his anxiety, before darting over to Martha's legs and burying his face into her lap.

Martha doesn't look at me again. I'm certain this is painful for her, but for once it would be nice if she could think about how unbearable this is for me.

When the door opens to the room, I sidestep out of the way and run into the chair that Tuck was playing with. I push it next to the wall and face the doctor who is followed by a handful of staff.

He raises his eyebrows. "Well, we've got quite the crew now, don't we?" Shifting to look at the other medical providers behind him to invite a laugh. Which he gets.

West approaches him with a stern expression. "What'd the head scan show?"

The doctor places his hands in his white coat pockets and shrugs. "Her scans were normal. We've done what we can for today, but I'm beginning to wonder if she even had a seizure."

West twists his torso to face Martha and uses a penetrating tone to tear into her. "I told you that you were being theatrical." Facing the doctor he continues, "She tends to overexaggerate and jump to conclusions."

I want to roll my eyes because she's not the only one that overexaggerates and jumps to conclusions.

Dr. Steinburg is nodding when his eyes glance to Martha. "You were there?"

She nods.

"Would you mind explaining what you saw?"

"Certainly," she says. "I took Tuck to the bathroom for no more than a minute. When I came back to the room, she was lying on the floor and her body was flailing around."

Dr. Steinburg nods. "Could it be possible she was still fighting to get the ball out of her trachea?"

It's quiet for a moment. Everyone is waiting for Martha to say something but she's not saying anything. Her mouth is gaping open, it's even moving up and down subtly as if she's trying to speak. But no sounds are coming out.

"That's right before I fell asleep," Abbi's raspy voice says.

West approaches her bedside and kneels so he's eye level with her. "What do you mean, baby?"

Abbi scratches the side of her arm gently while looking at West. "I fell asleep after Nana and Tuck came back from the bathroom." She coughs, then continues, "In pretend life, I was eating grapes. But in for real life I accidently ate the ball. But it got stuck here," she taps her throat, "and wouldn't come out."

West runs his hand over her head. "Well what were you doin' laying on the floor before Nana got there?"

She shrugs and her eyes widen with fear. "I got scared, Daddy. I laid down and tried to push the ball out with my hands like this," she scratches her nails against her neck then stops, "but it didn't work."

"And then Nana came in the room?"

She nods and looks at Martha. "Yeah, that's when Nana and Tuck came in. I was trying to tell her I ate a grape in pretend life. She looked sad. And I was waving like this," she waves both her hands in a big animated way, "but Nana walked away. Then I fell asleep."

West kisses Abbi's cheek. "Baby girl, you are so smart." His gentleness with her makes my heart ache and I can't tell if it's because of an affection I feel towards him for being such a good father to her. Or maybe it's an ache of jealousy, because I'm not the one kissing her cheek and telling her how smart she is.

Then he turns his attention to Martha. Rising to his feet, I notice his hand slowly ball into a fist before he leans down in her face. In a low voice, he says, "You're lucky nothing worse happened to her."

Martha turns her head away from him, and that's when I notice something familiar in her reaction.

She's done this before. I've never seen her do it, but I can tell she's turned in this way to protect herself before. Maybe from him. Maybe he's hit her, like he hit me.

"Well, in my opinion," Dr. Steinberg says. "I think we can rule out a seizure and chart this as an accidental choking incident."

Martha's eyes stay connected to the floor when West releases his fist and speaks to Dr. Steinburg. "So she's fine?

Aside from nearly choking to death on a toy because of my mother's neglect?"

I can't believe Martha's letting him speak like this. Although, I've allowed him to speak to me in worse ways without addressing it before. But, she's his mother. She shouldn't be afraid to stand up to her son.

Dr. Steinburg nods. "Yep, she's going to be just fine."

I instinctively rush to Abbi's bedside and hug her. There's a relief that expands through me that might be unexplainably the best feeling ever.

There's a strange lull in the room before Dr. Steinburg says, "Mrs. Laurel, may I speak with you?"

Both Martha and I turn to give him our attention.

He smiles politely then points to me. "Sorry, I meant *this* Mrs. Laurel."

West doesn't hesitate to hit me with humiliation. "Oh, she's actually not Mrs. Laurel anymore." He glances at me, "Isn't that right, Miss *Partridge*?"

I try to keep from glaring at him when I say, "Unofficially." Even though the divorce was finalized, I still have to go in and change my name.

He laughs and reaches down to pick up Tuck, just to humiliate me a little more by showing not only me but everyone else in the room that Tuck trusts him.

I follow Dr. Steinburg into the hallway. His posse is close behind. I can't help but notice how eager their expressions are.

"Is everything okay?" I ask with a slight cadence to my voice. Unsure what this is about but trying to stay optimistic.

We round the corner before he finally stops and faces me, closing the space between us and keeping his voice low. Which only invites the staff to close in around us too. "Trinity, we found some interesting results with your daughter's blood work."

My pulse beats up into my trachea. Blocking my airway as if I just swallowed a grape in pretend life.

He continues, "It's nothing to be concerned about and I've got a hunch you might be able to help us figure out this bizarre encounter."

I shake my head and pull my brows together in complete confusion. "I'm sorry, but I don't know what you're talking about."

"Here me out," he says lifting his finger. "While we were checking your blood types, we discovered that Abbi is AB negative."

I nod quickly, encouraging him to go on since I already know her blood type. I just want him to reveal whatever discovery he's made.

"You are B negative. And West is O positive." He pauses and looks at me with an expression full of anticipation. As if I'm about to reveal everything in the world to him.

But I don't know what any of this has to do with anything, so I say, "Is Abbi okay?"

"Yes, she's fine." He lets out a quick exhale then with a curious grin he says, "But it's scientifically impossible for West to be her father."

Panic infuses my insides. My heartbeat is banging against my chest wall. In fact, I'm certain Dr. Steinburg and his followers can see it about to ram through my ribcage.

His mouth officially releases across his face in a proud grin. "I wondered why West donated blood if he wasn't her biological father."

I can see they want a congratulations on their discovery. Instead in a hushed voice I say, "West doesn't know." I make sure I have their attention again by widening my eyes and stepping closer to them. "No one does." I fan a pleading gaze across each and every single one of their faces. "And I'd like to keep it that way."

Dr. Steinburg tucks his bottom lip into his mouth with a nod, then, "There's nothing to worry about. We are bound by confidentiality."

I exhale and my shoulders drop with relief. "Thank you."

Again, they reassure me that they can't say a word without losing their jobs. Then, the posse follows Dr. Steinburg further down the hall, but they don't make it very far before I hear their quiet whispers. I'm certain I hear someone brag about being the one to figure out the deepest secret I've ever kept too. I guess speaking amongst themselves is okay, I just hope the information doesn't turn into small town gossip.

That's the last thing I need right now.

When I swing around the corner to head back toward Abbi's room, I come face to face with West. He's leaning one shoulder into the wall with his arms crossed and his hip is popped to the side with his feet crossed at the ankles. He looks no different than every other overly confident time I've seen him. Really, the only thing out of the ordinary is his expression.

"Remember when we met?" he says dragging his tongue across his back molars with a slack jaw. "I was twenty-six and you," he huffs as a sly grin spreads across his face, "you were *perfect*." He tucks his bottom lip into his mouth and scans every part of me with his eyes. It's making me incredibly uneasy, and my veins are pulsating under my skin at a rapid pace.

"I remem—" I begin to say, but he presses his finger against my lips. Hushing me.

He's standing straight up now with his neck craning down in front of me. "I wasn't done," he says through clenched teeth.

Pressing his cheek into the side of my face, he speaks directly against my ear. "I gave you *everything*." He drags his nose against my hair, and I can hear him inhaling my scent.

He drags his lips against the corner of my mouth, holding my head in place so I can't turn away. "You were a fawn." He says against my mouth. "That's what drew me to you. And I knew a fawn would get picked up quick or ruined by the lifestyle you were living. So I saved you. I did that for *you*." He presses his forehead into mine and closes his eyes. "You were broken, but I knew that would make it even easier to get you. I was all in the night I met you at that alumni party. I was ready to settle down. I was ready to get married and start a family. And I was ready to do all that with you." He lets out a short laugh, but he keeps his eyes closed. "You loved my motorcycle. You loved the way I took charge and planned everything. You loved that I was a grown man. And then, you loved me." His eyes flash open as his voice grows in anger. "*Me*, Trinity. You were in love with *me*."

I drop my mouth open to speak because I can tell he's becoming irrational. But he covers my entire mouth with his hand this time.

"Shh…shh…shhhhh," he says, grazing his lips against my cheek before planting a painful kiss there. "I'm not finished yet."

My nostrils are flaring with each exhale that hits the hand that's still pressed over my mouth.

His voice is twisting when he says, "When you tell someone, you love them, you don't do the things you did." His eyes sink. "My father always told me to be careful what I wished for. I didn't know that wishing to be a father so badly was going to be my kryptonite. And I got my wish." His hand tightens around my mouth so much I can feel my lip pinching against my teeth. "But I was naïve enough to believe that I was raising my own daughter." He throws me at the floor.

I immediately scoot myself backwards, trying to get away from him before he seriously injures me.

It doesn't matter. In one stride he's back in front of me again. Gripping my arms, he pulls me back to my feet. I can feel the warmth of his breath against my face when he says, "Do you know how humiliating that is for me? You let another man's child call me *daddy*. What kind of person does that?" He lets out a ghastly laugh. "And nothing is more humiliating than the fact that you've chosen one of the three stooges over me. You want a boy after you've had a man, and that's pathetic. You're pathetic, Trinity."

"I am not pathetic." I furrow my brow at his disrespect. "And he's more of a man than you'll ever be."

I instantly regret allowing that statement to leave my mouth. Knowing it warrants a disaster.

Without warning, he throws me at the floor again. This time the heavy momentum causes my body to tumble. I extend my hand toward the railing near the wall, but it's too far out of reach. And instead of my hand grabbing the railing, my head hits the wooden bar before I can stop myself from hurling into it.

I roll against the floor and scurry up to my feet, running in the direction where I last spoke to Dr. Steinburg. But no one is there when I turn the corner. I begin to call out for help but my voice is pinched and nearly a whisper from the adrenaline closing my throat. It's as if I'm in a dream, screaming to wake up, but no sounds are coming out and no one is there to help me.

Suddenly a door opens to one of the rooms and a young nurse from Dr. Steinburg's posse files out with a polite smile. It quickly shifts to concern when she sees me frantically running towards her.

"Sorry, you can't be back here," she says with apparent concern. She raises both hands in front of her to hold my shoulders, so I don't run into her.

I can't find the words to say what's just happened.

I must look horrified since she says, "Are you alright?"

My voice finally returns, but not without shaking in its delivery. "Yes, I'm okay." I flip around so I'm standing next to her and point in the direction around the corner. "My ex-husband, he just—" I can't even confess what he's done. He found out that he's not our child's biological father and for some reason, his reaction seems justified. Even acceptable. It's my fault that he didn't know. I could have told him the truth from the beginning. I should have told him the truth.

The nurse is inspecting my forehead when I face her. "Did he…" she narrows her eyes, "…did he hit you?"

I tilt my face in confusion and touch the place on my head where her eyes are glued. "No, he didn't hit me." I look at my hand and there's traces of blood. "I fell." Immediately I feel guilty for minimizing his reaction. I can't keep defending him. I have no reason to anymore. He knows everything that I ever wanted to keep from him. And even if what I did was wrong, he shouldn't touch me the way he has. No one should ever treat another human the way he has treated me.

"He pushed me, and I fell," I say, correcting myself.

Her eyes widen. "Come with me," she says, placing her hand against my back.

"I can't, I have to get to my children. To my daughter." I look down the hall again, then back to her. "He knows. He heard everything."

She gives me a look of remorse, before she flips around. "I'm trying to help you."

I follow her to the end of the hall, and she opens a door just enough to peek her head in. "Dr. Steinburg?"

There's a man's voice followed by quiet mumbling, then the nurse opens the door further and Dr. Steinburg meets us in the hall.

The nurse gently touches my shoulder. While her focus is on Dr. Steinburg, she says, "Her husband found out."

Dr. Steinburg looks at me then back to the nurse.

She continues, "About her daughter's DNA."

A revealing look of understanding pops over his expression. "Yes, the blood type."

She leans toward him a little more, and in a quiet voice, she says, "He did that to her head too."

There's a split second of silence before Dr. Steinburg says, "Call the police." Scanning his eyes over my headwound, he says to me, "Let's get you bandaged up first. The authorities will arrive soon, and if you'd like me to explain anything to your husband, I can do that too."

"Ex-husband," I say.

He gives me a satisfied expression. "That's probably for the best."

After Dr. Steinburg bandages up the gash on my head, he leads me back down the hall, around the corner, and into Abbi's room.

Only Abbi's not in her room anymore.

No one is in her room.

The sheets on the bed are in disarray, and it seems they left so quickly they forgot Abbi's shoes next to the bed.

My heart is pounding. Pounding is an understatement. My heart is exploding in my chest. Over and over. It's shredding with each beat and falling apart into a million tattered pieces.

"He took her," I whisper.

Dr. Steinburg briskly strides across the room and picks up the phone. He's punching numbers before tucking the receiver between his shoulder and ear.

I'm not paying attention to what he's saying. Because I can't. My entire focus is on the fact that West took her. Again.

I can't think.

I can't hear.

I can't breathe.

All I know is that if I don't get to Abbi as soon as possible, I don't know what West will do to her. Or when I'll see her again.

Now that he knows she is every part of me and not one single part of him, there's no telling what he will do.

Then, the thing happens. The thing that I thought I'd gotten over. The thing that happens when I'm feeling pressure. And intensity. And rushed to make a decision.

Before I know what's happening, I'm sprinting out of the hospital.

I scan the parking lot.

And as soon as I see West with Abbi tossed over his shoulder like a sack of potatoes, I run as fast as I can.

West must hear me. Because he turns around, catching my gaze, and picks up his pace until he's at Martha's Volkswagen.

"Abbi!" I scream out her name.

When she sees me, she starts to cry, calling out to me. I don't know what kind of indication that is as to how she's been treated by West in the last few minutes. But it stirs the desperation in me to get to her faster.

I rush to the other side of the car and tap on Martha's window. "Martha, please! Let me explain."

She won't look at me. Her expression seems numb. She's only staring out the front window in a daze. Her hands gripped on the steering wheel. I'm sure West told her what he overheard Dr. Steinburg say. She's probably horrified. She's probably in shock that her granddaughter isn't biologically hers. She's probably disgusted that I kept this a secret for so many years. From so many people.

She's backing up slowly and I'm relentlessly trying to get her attention. I hear Abbi crying in the backseat, but I can't let myself look at her because I know I'll crumble into a mess on the pavement if I do.

Just before Martha puts the car in drive and begins to pull forward, she gives me a look. It's so shocking that I take a step backwards, as if she's pushed me away with nothing more than her expression. It's a deeply bereaved expression. One depleted of any fight she had in her for me. If there was any chance that she was going to help me see the kids, it's gone now.

Then, she exits the parking lot and quickly drives down the road in a blur.

I hear the car engine, and the wheels crunching against the small gravel. I think I even hear the cries of my children in the backseat of her car. Then, it's gone. It's all...gone.

Silence.

A vacancy only a mother without her children can understand.

"You stupid woman." His voice breaks through the silence, but it doesn't hit my heart or hurt me. Because I don't have a heart anymore. It detonated inside the hospital. And it will take a long time for me to find all those burnt pieces and put them back together.

I begin walking out of the parking lot with the last ounce of energy I have. Alone. Without anyone or anything. Not even my own heartbeat can accompany such desolation.

The only sound in my ears is the heaviness of West stomping behind me. "Do you know what you've done?"

I slowly turn around with a hollowness inside of my chest. "It doesn't matter what I've done. And it doesn't matter what you've done. Nothing matters."

I'm not sure how, but I feel the pain from the back of his hand hit me *after* I've fallen to the pavement. Maybe my brain told my body to feel the pain of the pavement before the pain of the slap. Maybe he hit me so hard it didn't register that he hit me at all until after I was splayed across the ground.

But the pain isn't pain at all. It's a reminder that I'm alive. I'm not so sure I want to be alive anymore though. I'm ready to light the match and toss it at my life. Burning away the last remaining parts of me.

"I didn't want to hit you," he says, approaching me as he rubs the back of his hand.

He takes my arm and tries to pull me up. But I don't move. I don't even look at him. My body's like a ragdoll.

"Fine." He tosses my arm, and it falls into my lap. "Get run over for all I care."

I hear him tell someone that I'm crazy when he returns to the hospital. I'm certain he's going back in there to explain how I tried to kidnap my children. Or tell everyone that I attacked him. He can keep lying. He can keep making up stories.

It doesn't matter anymore.

Nothing does.

CHAPTER THIRTY-EIGHT

Knox

"What do you mean you don't know where she is?" I say, placing my palms against the front desk.

The woman shrugs. "She ran out that door." She points her pen over my shoulder. "And never came back."

I give up pressing her for further information on Trinity's whereabouts.

After Ballard and I spoke with the doctor, we learned that Martha left with the kids. And West knocked Trinity around outside, then told the hospital staff that Trinity is crazy and tried to attack him.

Chandler volunteered to question West. He found him at his home outside of town. And the last I heard on the radio, West was spewing information to Chandler about the legalities behind paternity fraud.

Yes, Trinity should have told him the truth. But she wasn't using her secret to get his money, like he's insinuating she was. She made a choice as a teenager, one that she thought was the best for everyone. She never intended for anyone to get hurt by it. If West doesn't like it, he should just give Abbi back to Trinity. Not use her as a pawn.

I meet Ballard, who is speaking with a nurse in the back. "You good here? I'm gonna head back to the station."

"Yep," she says. "I'll be right behind you."

When I reach my patrol vehicle outside, I hesitate before opening the door because something shiny catches my eye. I squat down to inspect it.

Blood.

It is a hospital, so blood isn't something that's completely out of the ordinary. But the story I got from the hospital staff, and the eerie twisting I feel in my core, is telling me this blood is something to be concerned about.

I drop my head back and exhale. *Please don't be Trinity's blood.*

I follow a trail of droplets, but they seem to end where the parking lot meets the road. I should have listened to my instincts. I should have stayed at the hospital. That pony I was called away for didn't even need rescuing, she was just old. Chandler could've taken the call. But I ignored the feeling in my gut, pleading me to stay, and look what's happened because of it.

I quickly retreat back to my car and begin to radio in for a missing woman and a kidnapping on a couple of children. But then I stop myself.

Trinity isn't missing. I just don't know where she is.

Abbi and Tuck weren't kidnapped. Their father willingly allowed their grandmother to take them from the hospital after learning nothing was wrong with Abbi.

Nothing is emergent.

Nothing is out of the ordinary.

Except for my speeding heartbeat.

I spent the rest of the evening racing the setting sun as I tried to find any trace of Trinity, to no avail. So, I headed back to the station.

Without a lead, or luck, I'm never going to figure out where she is. The only person I haven't checked out is the last person to see her. Which was West. But after my last encounter with him, I think the guy needs some time to cool off before he sees me again. Not that he would be honest if I did ask him where she was.

If Trinity doesn't turn up soon, I'm going to report her missing. I've already decided that much.

Before wrapping up the last bit of paperwork at the station, Chandler collects his things at his desk then tells me goodnight.

I don't reciprocate. Which he sees as an invitation to approach me. He nudges my chair with his foot which causes my handwriting to scribble, so I face him with a stark expression.

"What's got your panties in a bundle?" he says with a laugh.

I continue looking at him with displeasure.

His smile falls to one side of his face. "Oh man, you're serious. Everything okay with the kid?"

I shake my head and run my hands through my hair in frustration. "Abbi's fine. Ballard located her at Martha's." I lean back in my chair and lift my arms over my head, clasping my hands at the base of my skull. "But Trinity's missing." I blow out an exasperated puff of air through my mouth, resisting the inevitable truth. "And I've been looking for her for hours without a trace."

Chandler's smile returns, not to his mouth but within the small sparkle of his eyes.

"What is it?"

Chandler hits my shoulder. "I saw her walking towards your house earlier."

"I already checked the apartment. She wasn't there or at Constance's."

"Not that house."

Before another moment passes, I've lunged out of my chair and left the station. Because Trinity is at my house.

CHAPTER THIRTY-NINE

Trinity

I wonder if my mother enjoys this same view at night from our backyard.

My dad had her cremated. And then we buried her ashes in the garden under the dead sassafras tree.

I wonder if ashes can see?

I wonder if she's there under the sassafras tree in our backyard, or if her soul is up there somewhere. Past the night sky and past the stars and galaxies and whatever else is up there.

It's nice she's not here to see what my life has turned into. I'm also glad she doesn't have to suffer in the deteriorating pain she was in anymore.

I remember the end was horrible for her. She was nothing more than a skeleton with clothes on. Her skin was elastic and her face was puffy from the chemo. She didn't know, but I could hear her at night, begging my dad to let her die. To end the chemo and her life.

That last year, the sole purpose of her existence was because my dad didn't want to let her go. Neither did I. And having her terminal presence sitting on the couch all day was better than not having her at all. Or at least, that's what dad and I thought. If it happened now, I wouldn't torture her again. I'd let her go before she had to beg for her agonizing life to end. I never wondered how difficult that time must have been for them until I was older.

As a kid, we think about ourselves. All I wanted was for my dad to look me in the eye, tell me he loved me, and to give me a hug.

And all I wanted from my mother was for her to stay alive.

But my dad never hugged me, and my mom died.

"Trinity?" Knox's gently concerned voice forces me to roll onto my side.

When I face him, he rushes to me. Retrieving me from the place where I've been decaying, to hug me. And I wonder, if my biological father were still alive, would his hugs be as good as Knox's are.

His arms are comfortable, but there's an intensity I don't recognize.

He pulls away and inspects my face with urgency. When he notices the bandage on my head, he pulls out his flashlight and shines it over my face.

I think the intensity in him is panic. "What the hell did he do to you?" The gentle care and concern in his tone from before evades his throat and is replaced by a heavy vengeance when he says this.

But I don't care if he's irate to the point of murder. He can do whatever he wants to West.

I don't care anymore.

Caring is exhausting. And it *hurts*.

I just want to be with my mom. Under the sassafras tree.

I lean back against the sickly tree in Knox's yard. It's the closest thing to my own childhood backyard. The one my dad sold to some stranger who probably doesn't even know that my mom's ashes are buried there.

"We put my mom's ashes in the ground," I say, seemingly out of nowhere. But it's in complete context for me.

Knox is still shining the flashlight in my face. It's forcing me to close my eyes and shield myself with one hand it's so bright. "You're covered in blood, Trinity. Did he hit you? Where are you hurt?" He gently tugs at my hand. "Let's get you checked out."

But I don't want to go. "Her ashes are still at the house. My dad sold that house along with my mother." My voice is nasally.

He shines the light at my bloody t-shirt, then at my face. "The blood on your shirt, it's from your face. I think your nose is broken."

It's as if we're having two completely different conversations.

"I wonder if my mom would be happy or disappointed to know how much the buyer spent on her remains. Can you put a price on a human life?" I sigh through my mouth since I can't breathe through my nose. "I guess that isn't applicable since she's not alive anymore." I look at him curiously. "Is it illegal to sell a house to someone without telling them there's human ashes at the base of the dead tree in their backyard?"

Knox drops his flashlight to the ground and cups my face in his hands. Even though it's dark out, I can still see his eyes bouncing between mine in distress. And in a desperate attempt to get my attention, he kisses me.

But I don't feel it.

Because I don't feel anything.

And I don't want to.

Feeling just leads to pain. Just like trust leads to disappointment.

"Trinity," his voice is a whisper. "Do. Not. Give. Up."

My gaze drops down to his chest. I notice the heaviness of his breath. Even though he's still in uniform, I can visibly see how intense his breathing is. He's concerned for me. Normally I'd love to be cared for so deeply. But when West obliterated my heart by taking the kids, it was the last hit I could bear. One person can only fight for so long before there's no fight left.

"No one tells you how lonely divorce is." I flick my eyes up to his. "But no one knows how impossible my situation is. No one knows what it's like to put up their defenses against someone like West." My voice is quiet when I add, "And he's always ten steps ahead of me. He's bigger than me. He has more resources. He has my children. He's stronger. He's better. And he's smarter."

"He is not smarter than you." Knox kisses my forehead and pulls me close. "And you have more capability in your tiny little pinky than he ever will in his entire life. Don't ever say he's better than you. Unless you're trying to make me laugh, because that statement is so outrageous it warrants laughter."

I don't think it's funny though. I think it's true. I truly believe that West is better than me. He's better at talking. He's better at manipulating people. He's better at lying. I guess he's better at things that I don't really want to be good at. Nonetheless, all of the things he's better at than me are the things that have gotten him custody of our children.

But it doesn't matter anymore.

Nothing does.

I begin to slip down out of Knox's grip, and he lets me. I press my back against the tree and slide down to a comfortable position on the ground. Then I look up into the sky again.

Knox picks up his flashlight and walks back to his truck. I wonder if he's giving up now too. I wonder if he sees there's no point in caring. I kind of want to shake my finger in his face and tell him *I told you so.* Because I'm right. I've always been right. Trust is a gamble. He should never have trusted me to give him my heart. Especially now, it's not in there. It's in pieces back at the hospital.

And I should never have trusted West from the beginning. He was supposed to hug me because my dad didn't. He was supposed to love me because no one else was. He was supposed to fix everything, but he did the opposite.

And even though Knox does all of those things, it doesn't matter. Because he's walking away now.

I look back up at the sky and try to find Ursa Major— the big dipper. My mom loved pointing out the constellations at night. And I loved learning about the stars from her. I loved everything she did. I wish Abbi was here so I could point out the constellations for her like my mom did for me.

I don't notice that Knox has returned until he's sliding down the tree next to me. Except he's not wearing his uniform top or his gear belt anymore. Without all the layers of his uniform, all that's left is a simple white t-shirt that's infused with his scent.

He wraps one arm around my shoulders and pulls me close to him, wrapping the other arm around my torso. He's looking up at the sky too. Or maybe he's inspecting the broken branches hanging above our heads.

Everything he does is comforting. Everything about him is protective and safe and everything I've always wanted. And I guess I was wrong. He didn't give up on me. He wasn't walking away from me. He was making himself more comfortable for me.

I lean my head against his shoulder. But I make sure not to like it too much, because as soon as I start to like it, I know I'll start to feel again. And if I feel again, I'll feel the good things *and the bad*. And the pain associated with the fact that I have no idea if I'll see my children after today, will be unbearable.

I refuse to let anything gather the shards of my heart and piece them back together again.

Rejecting the good, so I don't have to feel the bad.

So all that I feel, is nothing.

"Now I know why you said dreams come at a cost," I say.

He scoots a little closer, and holds me a little tighter. "Why's that?"

"My dream was for West to love me, and his love cost me everything from my dignity to my respect. My other dream was to get my kids back, but that's apparently not going to happen."

He speaks with reluctance. "I didn't mean it like that."

"How did you mean it, then? Because I don't see any other way that makes sense."

"I meant that any dream that I have would come at a cost because my dreams have an invisible ceiling stopping them from becoming too big. My dreams have restrictions. And my dreams have to go through a system with levels of paperwork before I'm ever allowed to begin them." He's talking up at the sky, as if he's revealing something only his thoughts recognize, and his voice has never known.

I don't understand what he's saying. I'm assuming he's talking about the system at the station. "West was an officer too, and that never stopped him from dreaming. He had tons of dreams. From taking me away from my hometown after we'd just met, to winning golf tournaments, to becoming sergeant.

Nothing stopped him and he never waited for anyone to give him the okay before he got started on his dreams."

"It's not because I'm an officer."

I lift myself away from him so I can see his face. His expression looks just as despondent as I feel inside of my own body. "What is it then?"

When I ask for him to elaborate, his expression shifts to remorse. As if he's about to shatter everything between us. As if he's worried he's going to disappoint me by breaking my trust. "Anzio Knoxville Gravano."

I shake my head. "Who?"

His eyes are shifting between mine, begging me not to run. It's causing the empty place where my heart used to be to feel uneasy.

"Me." He confesses.

I pull my brows together in confusion. "You? What do you mean?"

Then, something shifts inside of me and…I care. At least I think I'm starting to care a little. My senses perk and I care enough to know more about what he's eluding to. I just hope it doesn't hurt me.

His eyes fixate on my entirety with hope and a hint of nostalgia. "Anzio Knoxville Gravano, that was my name. And my kid sister's was, Esmerelda Lynn Gravano."

My chest flutters with uncertainty. "What? Why was that your name? And who is Esmerelda?" I thought he said his sister's name was Janice.

He exhales through his nose, considering me seriously for a moment before speaking. "Everything I tell you can never be repeated."

I nod, unsure about what's happening. Or even what he's confessing.

"I'm serious." His voice grows firm.

I nod reassuringly. "I am too."

His throat rolls as he regards me silently. Probably making sure I'm as serious as I'm trying to express to him, then, "Whatever I'm about to tell you is never spoken aloud. I'm only telling you because I want to be honest with you. I want you to trust me. I don't want you to question my integrity. And I'm telling you this because I don't want you to give up on your dreams like I've had to."

I nod again, but this time with eagerness and anticipation.

"What I told you about the fire. Most of it was true. Except for the missing information about how I was part of the gang Constance's boyfriend led."

I give him a blank look. Processing his confession.

"The gang didn't start out hard core. In the beginning we were just a group of teenagers that were into petty crime. But with boredom and time, we moved on from petty crime to misdemeanors. Car theft and what not. I don't know if hard criminals started joining the gang, or if the gang was growing on the wrong side of Manhattan, but when we went from just fifteen guys to two hundred, the lack of leadership corresponded with a lack of control." His shoulders tense. "And that's when things got out of hand. That's when colors on our jackets mattered. That's when we didn't leave our house unless we were in a group of five or more guys. That's when the initiation of new members started. And that's when fires became our tag symbol. It's also when drugs began to circulate, which led to fights, which led to threats, which led to enemy gangs, which ended in murder."

He's staring into the night as if he's seeing the events from his past playback in front of him. "I backed out." He shakes his head slowly as his expression grows grim. "But you don't leave a gang without repercussions." Facing me, he says, "There was going to be a trial for a murder of a cop the gang was involved in. Specifically involving Constance's boyfriend. And I was asked to testify against him. It's no coincidence that the night of the fire that killed my family was the night before the trial. The gang must've caught wind that I was a witness, they tried to take me out before I could speak. The more I think about it, the more I realize they used Constance to get me out of the house. They didn't want me dead. They wanted me to suffer. They wanted to make sure I got their message. And even though I was devastated after the fire, I still gave my statement."

With a heavy inhale, he continues with, "We went into the witness protection program. They took us into hiding while our identities were scrubbed, and new ones were created. We started going by our middle names and a new last name."

I tilt my head. "But Constance doesn't go by Lynn."

He raises one eyebrow and with a sigh, says, "That's because she blew our cover in Chicago. Before we were relocated here, she was with a guy. A real piece of work. She told him everything. Every secret that binds our lives. And to give you a quick picture, he was cut from the same cloth as West." He rests his elbow on his lifted knee and drags his hand down his face. "I came home one day to her collar bone sticking out of her skin and her jaw so broken she couldn't speak."

He pauses for a moment, covering his hand over his mouth as his mind puts the images from the past into words. With a roll of his throat, he continues, "When I found the guy and hit him, I was certain my fist wasn't going to stop until it broke against the pavement." He flexes his hand, then balls it into a fist. "It took two hospital visits and a plane ride to relocate after that one. Not to mention the paperwork and promises we made to the program."

With his exhale, he continues, "I kept going by Knox with the new last name, Santino. While Constance changed her name completely. She didn't want anyone to know that my face had a sister. We made up the story about her being my niece because she couldn't for the life of her stop calling me Zio, which was the nickname for my birth name, Anzio." He shrugs one shoulder. "It worked out that Zio is Italian for uncle."

I interject. Confused by what's the truth and what's a fabrication. "Are you really Italian?"

He nods with honesty behind his eyes.

"Why do you call Constance, Kid, instead of Constance?"

He laughs. "I'd called her Kid her whole life. As soon as I saw how much it bugged her when we were little, I couldn't stop myself. Plus, I couldn't call her Constance to her face without laughing. To me, it doesn't fit her at all. But that's exactly what she wanted the second go around. She wanted to be unrecognizable, so much so that she got a nose job. And she wanted to have nothing to do with her old self. So, she said goodbye to the city night life. And hello to a town that closes by 9 pm on weekdays and doesn't have a club in a hundred mile radius. We follow the rules and lay low. That's our life now. And believe me, if I had the freedom to live outside the rules I'm bound by, West wouldn't be walking like he is today. But because of my constraints, I can't ever do what I did to that guy in Chicago, to anyone ever again."

I have no idea how they've been able to live this way. I can't imagine what sort of rules they have to follow or how every move they make is under the scrutiny of a U.S. marshal.

His eyes fall heavy on mine along with his resonating voice. "The point I'm trying to make is that we never gave up. We never gave up hope and we never gave up on our faith. There was always a future ahead of us, we knew that. Even though we couldn't see it, we knew we had something to look forward to. Even if it was dictated by rules and regulations. We just had to decide to take the first step in that direction. And when we stumbled, we had each other to pick each other back up. I mean, look how far Constance has come. I don't even recognize her anymore, and not because of the nose job. But it's because of the confidence she's acquired from the things she's endured. She's stronger because of the obstacles. She's braver because of the struggles. And I am too. But it's because we had each other to lean on for support."

I tuck my hair around my ear. "I wish I had that luxury."

He nestles himself against me. "You have me. I'm trying to tell you that you do have support. You have me and Constance and even Sharry. Your job is to keep taking those steps in the right direction. Even when you feel like giving up, keep crawling forward. Because sometimes all you can do is crawl. But at least you're not giving up. And once you lose your faith you have nothing left to live for. And I know your kids don't want to grow up without a mom."

I sigh heavily. "They already are growing up without a mom."

"If it takes fifteen years, isn't that worth it for them to have a mom that never gave up fighting for them?"

His pained expression tells me that he hopes I'm the woman he sees. One like Constance, that's overcome adversity and let her trials make her stronger and braver. But I don't know if I'm that strong.

I pull my knees up to my chest and drop my head down. "Everything seems impossible at this point."

He rubs his hand over the back of my head. "Hey, it's going to be okay." He gently tugs on my arm. "Trinity, look at me please."

I lift my face to meet his gaze.

"Apparently you didn't hear me when I said that I'm here for you. And I'm not the only one either." He brushes my hair out of my eyes. "The hospital staff is willing to testify against West in court."

My eyes widen. "They are?"

He nods with a small grin. "You have people on your side. People that don't think West is a good person. People that don't think he should have sole custody of your kids. People that saw what he did to you. And even people that saw him hit you."

The broken shards of my heart come sliding back into my chest.

And when Knox tucks his index finger under my chin and presses a gentle kiss to my lips, I can sense that the gaps in my shattered heart are fused together by the way he cares for me. And even more by the way he believes in me.

CHAPTER FORTY

Knox

September 1998

"Would you like an arborist to come out and help you?" The gray-haired woman at the register asks with a smile.

I hand her my credit card. "I think I'll manage on my own."

I lean one arm on the counter and scan the shelves of the hardware store. It's the only store in town that has everything from tools, kitchen appliances, gardening, and various starter plants. Mostly for landscaping. But what catches my eye, is the section of toys. It's one aisle, dedicated for children under the age of ten. One side with tractors, Legos and Play-Doh for boys. The other side with Barbie dolls, and horses for girls. And one big wooden dollhouse is on display that I can't help but think Abbi would love.

She runs the card through the machine and hands it back to me. "Alright then, you're all set. I'll have Timmy meet you outside and help you load it up."

"Actually, could you add that dollhouse too?"

She glances at the shelf, then back to me. Pointing just below the dollhouse, she says, "That's the display. If you'd like to purchase one, it's in a box just there."

I approach the shelf and pick up one of the boxes she's talking about. It's heavy and about three feet tall and six inches wide. I bring it back to her so she can scan it at the register.

"You build it yourself," she says with a smile.

After I pay and thank her, I'm about to exit the store before she says, "Bring your daughter in after you've got it built and she can pick out some furniture. I'll even throw in a doll for free if you remind me." Her statement hits me in a way that sends a quiver down my sternum.

I give her a smile with my nod. Deciding not to correct her assumption.

I load everything up and head down the road toward my house. Not the apartment, but the one I renovated. And I'm still jarred by the woman's statement when I pull up to the driveway.

Trinity and I have never talked about what the future holds with us and the kids. We've been so fixated on *right now*. Because right now has so much to unpack.

Right now is more complicated than anything I can imagine in the future.

The future is simple. The future exists with me and Trinity living in my renovated home together with Abbi and Tuck. My backyard is huge. There's enough room for the four of us, Sugar, and even future children if that's something Trinity wants.

But we haven't spoken any of that out loud.

And even though we haven't spoken it aloud, it's not stopping me from planning my future with them in it.

That's why I'm unloading a box that contains pieces of a dollhouse I have to assemble myself. That's why I built a gated fence around the house, just in case the kids run outside unattended. That's why I hung a tire swing in the sycamore tree. That's why I bought a dog bed. That's why I put carpet on the stairs inside. That's why I painted one of the bedrooms yellow and the other green.

And that's why I've been learning how to revive the sassafras tree in my backyard. That's why I tested the soil. That's why I stopped and bought a new sassafras tree when I drove by and saw them for sale outside the hardware store.

Because they're in my future. That much I know.

We just have to get through *right now*.

I'm fumbling with my keys as I balance the long rectangular box in my hands, trying to find the key to unlock the front door, when I hear footsteps behind me.

I'm not expecting anyone, and the handful of people that know where I live wouldn't show up unannounced.

So when I turn around and see West charging at me with a two by four, it takes me by surprise.

But my body and my brain don't register what's happening in time.

And I'm still thinking about the chaotic look in his bulging eyes after he's swung the two by four at the side of my face like a baseball bat. I'm still wondering how he figured out where I live when everything goes black. I'm still trying to piece the events together when the ringing in my ears takes over and I *drift...off...into...*

CHAPTER FORTY-ONE

Trinity

"Don't worry," Sharry says, cupping her hand around my shoulder.

But I am worried.

The hospital staff Knox talked about testifying isn't here.

There's only so much disappointment one person can take. I never imagined I'd be here. I never thought my children would ever be taken from me. I never thought their father would ever, in a million years, have full custody of them.

I have a navy-blue pantsuit on. It's brand new. Constance took me to the J.C. Penny at the mall in Dallas. She wanted to make sure I looked professional. I feel like I should be an attorney representing someone. That's how professional this outfit is. And don't get me started on the heels I'm wearing.

"Are you ready?" Eric, my advisor, stands when the judge enters the room. I nod and follow suit. He's a court appointed advisor so I'm not sure if that's the same as a free attorney. But Sharry said he's good, if that's any consolation. And as he flips through some papers in a folder, I see several statements written by the nurses, Dr. Steinburg, and the woman at the front desk. I guess that's why they're not here, because they wrote their eyewitness accounts. I only hope that's as convincing as if they would have told their stories in person.

I get a brief glance at the judge's slippers before he sits. Somehow, that doesn't make me feel better. I think those slippers are bad luck. Especially since every other time he's worn them, he's sided with West and punished me in the harshest way. By taking my kids from me a little bit at a time.

I look to the back of the room for Knox, but he's not here. Before he left the apartment this morning, he told me he'd meet me at city hall later. It's later, and he's not here.

Court begins with several formalities, and tons of words thrown around like legal and physical custody, custodial parent, and primary care provider. And I'm doing everything I possibly can to keep from looking at West.

He broke my nose when he backhanded me at the hospital. Which explains why it was bleeding so much. And also explains why I couldn't breathe out of it until Dr. Steinburg was kind enough to reset it the following morning. Free of charge. I hate taking a handout. But I'm also in no position to deny one. So I let him reset my nose for free.

"Sharry Malkovski," the judge says, calling Sharry to the stand. It's not really a legitimate courtroom, so there's not a place for Sharry to go to.

So she stands behind me and clears her throat before proceeding. "Thank you, Your Honor. As you know. My job is to ensure the safety of the children and provide unbiased information regarding the capability of the parents."

The judge lifts his hand briefly. "Go on."

"I've been on this case for a year now. And I've seen Martha Laurel, the children's grandmother, provide care more than I have seen their father, Officer West Laurel. But the visitation times I was able to sit in on with their mother, were always a bittersweet experience. Because the times the children were with her, she was an attentive, loving mother. She made up games and never spoke badly about their father. She showed maturity for a woman as young as she is. And when those visits were over, the children cried because they didn't want her to leave."

"Objection," West says, from the opposite table as me. I can barely see him stand with his outburst in my peripherals.

The judge raises one eyebrow at him. "Son, this isn't a movie. It's a courtroom. You'll have your turn to speak in a moment." He looks back to Sharry. "Go ahead Miss Malkovski."

I don't know why, but I turn to see West's reaction to the judge's statement. I'd expect a scowl or some other form of defensive aggression. Even another outburst. But instead, West looks dismissive. As if he almost expected the judge to respond that way.

I've tuned out Sharry for the remainder of her statement because I can't figure out why West seems so comfortable, or why he didn't push harder for the judge to listen to him.

When I look at the judge, he seems to be tuning out Sharry too. As if he's already made up his mind about his decision for this entire custody battle.

And it doesn't seem his decision is in favor of me. Which is flabbergasting if he trusts someone as revolting and violent as West more than me. I mean, I'm the one with a swollen nose and two black eyes for crying out loud!

"Relax," Knox's deep voice infiltrates my ear canal causing me to close my eyes for a moment with relief. And when he places his hands on my shoulders and tells me to *breathe*, I inhale and exhale deeply, feeling the muscles in my body melt.

I'm not sure when he entered the courtroom, or how long he's been sitting behind me. But I'm certain that I feel more calm and more brave because he's here.

Until I turn to face him.

The calm that his presence helped set in to my nervous system quickly vanishes at the sight of his face.

His lip is split and swollen on his left side, and his cheek on the same side looks as if he was repeatedly slammed against a wall.

As my mouth falls agape, my eyes widen in horror.

He must sense I'm about to ask him what happened since he presses a finger to his mouth to remind me to stay quiet.

In the same moment, Eric clears his throat and nudges his yellow notepad in front of me.

When I flip around, he's looking forward at the judge, who is speaking court jargon I don't understand. Then I read the message on the notepad:

Face forward and pay attention. You look distracted.

Well, I am distracted. The man I'm in love with showed up late to my court session and looks as if he was hit by a truck. And I'm not even allowed to turn around and talk to him about it.

When it's finally my turn to speak, my mind goes blank. And my heart starts racing.

I try to remember what Eric told me to say before court, which only makes my pulse speed faster and my thoughts blur.

"Miss Partridge?" the judge says. He's using my maiden name. I finally changed it back to my old name just days ago. Only now I realize it's a name that was never really mine. It's Ed's last name. If I had more time to think about it, I probably would have changed it to Lovell, since that was my father's last name. Not Ed, but Bridges. Not that I'm ungrateful that Ed raised me, but I just want to feel like me. And maybe if my last name was Lovell, I'd feel more like me.

Eric leans toward me and whispers so quietly I can barely hear him in the silence of the small courtroom when he says, "Stand up."

I rise to my feet and as I do, my chair makes a screeching sound across the wooden floor. It's the same screeching sound my insides are making in desperation. Except I'm the only one that can hear that.

"Miss Partridge, you've been in this courtroom enough to know that I don't like to repeat myself," the judge says with a downward inflection.

I fold my hands in front of myself, nodding in understanding. "Sorry, Your Honor." I still don't know what to say about myself. How do you convince someone that you're an honest person and a good mom? How do you convince someone who's already made up their mind that you're a liar?

"There's been a lot that's been said about me today." I feel my pulse still throbbing in my throat. Not racing, just thudding heavily with my nerves.

"Please, speak up, Miss Partridge," the judge says, shifting in his chair, as if he's uncomfortably annoyed and ready for the session to end.

I remember Knox's comment when he was behind me. Reassuring me with his presence. Reminding me to relax with his voice. And calming my nerves with his comforting hands against my shoulders.

I inhale, lengthening my torso so that I'm standing straighter, then echo the words he said to me in my mind. *Relax. Breathe. Relax. Breathe. Breathe. Breathe.*

"There's a lot that's been said about me today," I repeat in a more articulated manner. "And the things Sharry said were true." I bite my bottom lip and inhale through my nose, preparing myself for combat. "But everything Mr. Laurel and his attorney have said about me, are completely false."

West's soft chuckle pulls my attention. I try not to, but I end up glancing over at him. It's just for a split second. But when I look at him, there's a new feeling that infuses my core when I see the way he's seated nonchalantly in his chair, smirking at me. The feeling growing inside of me is heated and angry. And more importantly, *motivating*. Because there's one thing that's for certain. I do not want my kids growing up with him instead of me.

I strengthen my stance, lifting my chin with confidence. "Tuck likes his back gently scratched before he falls asleep."

The judge slowly leans over his pulpit with interest.

"He also hates peas." I say. "He refuses to eat them, but he likes green beans. And he'll eat steamed carrots like it's nobody's business." I continue, "He calls his blanket *scared blanky* because it has little racoons on it. He thinks raccoons look like they're scared with their black masks."

I smile, even though there's a nervous shake to my voice. "Abbi figured that one out for me. She's always seemed to know what Tuck was thinking, even before he could talk. She'd tell me everything he said and thought when we'd have picnics on our property. She's such a good sister. And she loves being a big sister to Tuck. She's also very protective of Tuck." My voice grows in strength, even though it's still shaking. "So much so, that when West used to hit me, Abbi would take Tuck by the hand, and they'd hide in the kitchen cabinet together until it was safe for them to leave. Sometimes they'd spend the night in the cupboard, because it would take that long for me to regain consciousness and find them."

West shoots out of his seat with rage. "That's bullsh—"

The judge strikes his gavel.

West thrusts his arm in my direction while leaning his other hand against the table. "She's a terrible mother. The kids never hid in the kitchen, because none of that happened!"

"That's enough, Officer Laurel!" the judge says, with another strike of his gavel. "Sit down and hold your tongue or I'll have you kicked out of my courtroom."

West lowers to his chair, straightening his tie. His mouth is pinned together, with fury behind his eyes.

The judge lifts his chin toward me. "You may continue, Miss Partridge."

My arms are hugged around my body in protection. I don't know when I did that, but it must be a response my body's learned to do. Safeguarding myself. I drop my arms at my sides, remembering the determination I need to continue my statement.

"I'm not trying to say I was perfect." I fold my mouth in, and straighten the yellow notepad on the desk, thinking about what I can say to convince the judge that I'm the opposite of how West describes me. "I did the best I could with the knowledge I had. And with the lack of experience in parenting and marriage, I didn't have a lot to go off of. If I could do it again, there's only one thing I'd change." I face West directly. His eyes are dark in the twisted way they get when he's offended. But I'm not afraid of them anymore. There's nothing more he can strip from my life. "I wish I hadn't stayed. Instead of taking care of you when you were drunk, I wish I had taken the kids in the middle of the night and never looked back."

West's chest is rising and falling in the heaviest, most rapid way a chest can rise and fall.

"Miss Partridge," the judge says, "Please, don't address Officer Laurel directly."

I sit down in my chair. "That's all I have to say, Your Honor."

The judge lifts a few papers at his bench. He's rubbing his forehead with one hand while lifting a paper with the other. Probably the statements from the hospital staff that Eric handed him earlier. "I hate to do this, but after the information I've received today. I think we need to extend this court session by picking it back up next week. Is everyone available?"

West flips a pencil in the air and it lands on the table when he says, "I've got nothing goin' on for the next week."

I don't say anything.

My stomach sinks. There's been so much momentum today. What if the judge forgets what's happened? What if he overlooks West's outbursts and my sincerity?

Lifting his gavel, the judge says, "As long as there's no objections, then we'll resume this meeting next Monday at one thirty."

No, no, no. I have to wait an entire *week* to pick back up where we're leaving off?

Eric rises. "Actually, Your Honor."

The judge stops himself from rapping his gavel.

"If I'm correct, Miss Partridge was given visitation when it's convenient for Officer Laurel."

The judge nods, "Yes, that's correct."

"Well, Officer Laurel mentioned he's free for the next week. So I don't see why Miss Partridge can't spend an evening with the kids before Monday."

The judge glances at West, then shifts his gaze to mine before he says, "I don't see a problem with that."

My mouth falls open in astonishment.

Knox wraps his arms around me from behind.

I don't hear much of what happens after that because all I'm focused on is the fact that I get a guaranteed evening with my children before Monday.

Sharry was right. Eric is good.

CHAPTER FORTY-TWO

Knox

"I can't believe he did that," Trinity says, gently brushing her knuckle down the side of my face.

"I can't believe he did *that*," I say, glancing at the fading bruises under her eyes. She's not wearing the nose splint anymore, but surprisingly the swelling has gone down significantly.

"And I can't believe you didn't kill him for it."

I lift myself up on one arm and kiss her forehead. "My life would be a repeat of Chicago if I'd done what I wanted to do to him."

Her eyes get sad, but quickly crinkle in the corners with her smile. "You're too kind," she says, jokingly.

I was only out for a few seconds after he hit me with the two by four. It was such a short moment that I caught the tail end of West driving off on his Harley. He must've stashed it behind the bushes, since I didn't notice it when I pulled up to the house.

After I cleaned the blood off my face and saw that the injuries were minimal, I didn't bother reporting the incident. At this point, West Laurel is untouchable anyway. I've been doing my own digging on him. I even went as far as checking out his file at the station. To my surprise, it was spotless. Which doesn't make any sense, since I know I personally added half the reports to that file. If he hasn't charmed his way out of a predicament, he's used his dad's money to pay them off.

"What are your plans with the kids?" I say.

A beaming grin spreads across her face, and she sits up, hugging a pillow to her chest. "I've been so excited about spending an entire afternoon with them that I forgot I don't have much to entertain them with." She shrugs. "I'm sure they'd be happy playing with Sugar in the backyard or reading books on the couch at Constance's while I make them dinner." Sighing she adds, "I miss cooking for us."

I consider her statement for a moment. She deserves her own space, and quality time with her children before she's forced to hand them back over to West. Who will probably use the visit against her somehow. Twisting events to make her look bad.

I hate this for her. There's always a mind game when West is involved in a situation. No wonder she wanted to give up. I'm sure it's exhausting always trying to be one step ahead of a psychopath.

"Why don't you take them to my place?"

Her eyes gently widen.

"I'm serious. There's more than enough space for you, the kids, and Sugar." She's never been inside the house since I finished renovating and furnishing it.

"I don't know…" She straightens the dark pillowcase by dragging her hand across it.

I sit up, taking her hand in mine. Waiting for her to look up at me so I can hold her emerald gaze in the same manner. "I don't want you to stress about this. Would it help if we went out there so you can kid proof it? It's move in ready if that's what you're worried about."

She gives me a quizzical expression. "If it's move in ready, why aren't you staying out there?"

"Because I'm waiting for you." I'm not afraid to share the way I feel about her. Or share my plans of a future with her. We're growing in love, growing closer together, and growing in our lives. There's no rush to move in, but at the same time, I'd be ready to move her in with me right now if she wanted to.

Her mouth parts for a moment, realizing I've just subtly invited her into my future. Then a smile emerges as she takes the pillow she's hugging and tosses it at me.

I catch the pillow, tossing it in the pile of pillows on my floor before rolling off the bed. "Come on," I say, digging in my dresser for a shirt.

"Where are we going?"

"The house might be move in ready, but the cupboards are bare. We need to go grocery shopping."

I take her hand as we walk from the parking lot into the grocery store. Even though I can tell it's making her nervous that everyone seems to be gawking at us. Divorce is a taboo subject in this town. Not to mention dating after divorce.

I lean down next to her ear as I pull a grocery cart from the rack. "Let 'em stare," I say, inviting the challenge.

Even though she approves with a brave face, I can tell she's not fully bought on the idea of us out in public together. I don't blame her. She's been given a small visit with her children, one of which has nearly forgotten her. And I know she hasn't said anything, but we both know that with the way things are going, this could be the last visit with her kids she's going to get for a while.

I'm taking it upon myself to ensure that it's one for the books.

"What'll it be?" I head towards the produce. "Do the kids like burgers? I could grill some corn on the cob for you. Or did you want to do something easy? Spaghetti and garlic bread? I guess spaghetti and corn is good too."

Trinity quietly agrees with a, "Yeah," before pushing the cart to the other side of me.

"I think I just want some corn." My statement comes out with my laughter. "I hope I'm not being presumptuous in assuming I'd help you cook at the…"

She has a horrified expression on her face. It's so unwarranted that it feels like a rock has been thrust into my stomach.

"Trinity?"

I have to step closer to her to hear her say, "Everyone is staring."

I exhale, relieved she didn't say West just walked through the door. "Didn't I say let them stare? It doesn't bother me if people judge us, Trinity. It's a small grocery store, in a small town, with big gossip. If gossip is the worst thing that happens in this town, it would ease my mind as a police officer."

Placing her hand at her neck, she looks up at me as her cheeks grow pink. "They're not staring at us, Knox. They're staring at *me*."

I scan the produce section. At first, I assumed she was just being paranoid. But now that I'm intentionally looking, there does seem to be hushed conversations and uncomfortable glancing that follows. Then, I see what's causing the gawping looks from every shopper in the store.

Placing the corn in the cart, I step beside Trinity and guide her forward with my hand at the base of her back before she sees what everyone else has. "I'll grab the rest of the groceries." I pull my keys from my pocket and place them in her palm.

She flips her head up to look at me with uncertainty.

I nod my head to the side when we pass the entrance. "Wait in the truck. I'll be right out."

She's out the door in a second. And it seems she missed the flyers with her face on them.

I quickly retrieve the rest of the items and rip down every flyer on my way to the register.

The guy scanning my groceries across the conveyer belt is chewing gum with a bored expression. I place one of the flyers in front of him, "Do you know anything about this?"

He glances down at the scanner that makes a beeping sound when he drags the hamburger buns across it. "No." He slowly chews his gum on one side of his mouth. "They were hanging up when I started my shift."

"When was that?"

He glances at the large clock on the wall with disinterest. "Five minutes ago." He drags out a sigh. "That'll be eleven, seventy."

I pay for the items before gathering the bags in one hand and leaving the store. Tearing down each flyer in my line of sight.

I'm partway to my truck when an older woman waves me over. I can see Trinity in the passenger seat of my truck, looking at me with concern. As if she's begging me to get her out of here.

Reluctantly, I give my attention to the older woman.

Her purple permed hair must be fresh, because when I approach her, there's a sort of chemical smell radiating from her direction. "You're a police officer, aren't ya?"

I nod. "Yes, ma'am. I'm off duty today." I glance at Trinity, who looks as if she might try and *borrow* my truck again. "Was there something I could help you with?"

She takes my hand, that's not full of groceries, and says, "The papers with the woman."

I step closer to her, realizing what this is about.

She continues with a scowl. "It was the naughty Laurel boy. I saw him hangin' them up at the post office about an hour ago. They're all over town. He's been naughty since grade school, but this is somethin' else." She shakes her head. "He was in my kindergarten class. It's too bad he turned out to be a bad apple. His mama is such a sweet woman, and I know his daddy raised him better."

"Thank you, ma'am." I walk the rest of the way to my truck with speed in my step. Realizing that the only person that hasn't been fooled by West, is a purple-haired senior citizen that's known him his entire life.

I don't waste any time pulling out of the parking lot and driving out of town. Trying to put as much distance as possible between Trinity and the harassment.

"What was going on back there?" Trinity says.

I shake my head as I white knuckle the steering wheel.

"Do you know that woman from the parking lot?"

I fold my mouth together. "Trinity, I'm so sorry."

Her voice is wavering. "Knox, what's going on? I thought we were going to your house?"

"I'm taking you home. We'll keep the groceries at Constance's until tomorrow." I dig around in one of the grocery bags, until I retrieve a crumpled paper that was hanging in an aisle of the store.

"What's this?" she says curiously, when I hand it to her. I'm devastated by the tone of her voice. Because I know once she opens the paper, she's going to be humiliated. And all the excitement about spending tomorrow afternoon with her children is going to be drowned out by this one incident.

She doesn't say anything when she finally sees her face staring back at her from the black and white xerox photo paper. She simply scans her eyes over the image of herself seated on a Harley. She has nothing more covering her body than her own arms wrapped across her chest. Along the top of the flyer in large handwritten letters, is the word *whore*. With a sigh, she crumples the image and tosses the paper on the floorboard.

I speak with regret, "The woman in the parking lot stopped to tell me that West hung them all over town."

A short, exasperated laugh escapes her throat. "This is just what I need." Dropping her head back against the seat, she continues, "He's sabotaging me. If the judge sees that picture, he's never going to grant me custody of my kids. And the worst part of this is that West took that picture of me."

I face her with concern.

"Yeah." She tosses one hand up and lets it drop, smacking against her thigh. "It was his idea. I don't know why I gave into it. He wanted me fully nude, but I had to draw the line somewhere and I guess it was that." She kicks the balled-up piece of paper at her feet. "If anyone is paying attention, they'll see that that's his stupid Harley I'm sitting on."

Every part of me is struggling to keep myself from turning this truck around and finding West. No human should humiliate another person in such a degrading way. No husband should force his wife to pose in ways she doesn't want to. And he should never use pictures as extortion.

"Turn him in," I say. "This is a hate crime. Legally, he cannot intimidate you or humiliate you like this without repercussions."

"Have you not been paying attention? Do you not see what he does when he feels threatened? Haven't you noticed he gets what he wants? You've said it yourself, anything reported against him mysteriously goes missing." She makes a frustrated sound, then, "Ugh! I mean, look what he's done to our faces, Knox. We're in a losing battle. And I'm barely hanging by a thread in this fight. I just want my kids back." She straightens, calming herself with a deep inhale and slow exhale. "Let's just focus on the good."

"The good?" How is she capable of seeing any *good* from this situation?

She drops her head back with her exhale, in thought. Then, rolling her head to face me, she says, "I get to see my kids for one afternoon. Let's focus on that."

I give her a nod with my forced grin. While I'm glad she gets one afternoon with her kids, I can't focus on the *good* like she wants me to. Because all I can focus on is how West deserves more than a smack in the face with a two by four.

CHAPTER FORTY-THREE

Trinity

My stomach is in knots.

Not because of the flyers West distributed all over town yesterday. It's going to take a lot more to humiliate me than that.

My stomach is in knots because Matthew and Martha went to Dallas for Matthew to complete some leadership training. Which leaves West with the kids. Which means, if I still want my kids this afternoon, I'm going to have to face him.

When I called Martha this morning to coordinate, she informed me that West would be dropping the kids off and picking them back up. I called Sharry immediately after my phone call with Martha. I thought it would be a good idea to have her there for the exchange, but it's Saturday afternoon and the DFPS office is closed.

I haven't told Knox. But I have a feeling he senses something is off. He's been hovering over me while I smack my frustrations out into the ground beef. I'm forming a patty for burgers later this afternoon. The only good news is that I still have several hours to tell him.

Closing his hand around my beef covered grip, he says, "I think that one's done."

Turning around, I give him a begging look. Hoping he'll read my mind so I don't have to disclose the fact that West will be in close proximity of us. If the judge believed me, West wouldn't be allowed in close proximity of me. But when it comes to defending myself, it's always been his word against mine. And since I'm an outsider and he's lived here his entire life, his victimizing lies triumph over my truth.

"Hey," Knox tucks a strand of hair behind my ear then cradles my face in his hand as he rubs his thumb gently against my cheek. "Everything is going to be fine. This place is a paradise. You and the kids are going to have the best time. I'll make sure of it."

I nod and toss the last burger patty on a plate, then place them in the fridge for later.

Even though he can sense something is off, I can't expect him to read my mind.

He's buttering the corn with some kind of garlic spread when I finish washing my hands. I sidle up next to him and he sets the corn down mid-buttering. Twisting around to face me, he says, "You gotta get this worried look off your face before you break my heart."

I press my face against his chest and wrap my arms around him. "I have a bad feeling."

"I thought we were focusing on the good?"

I blow out a breath through my mouth, then confess, "Martha and Matthew are in Dallas, so West is dropping the kids off."

His jaw tightens momentarily before he begins caressing his arms against my back. Then, he pulls me closer until the side of my head meets his chest. With a long exhale, he says, "Everything's going to be okay." Placing his hands on my shoulders, he moves me away from him so he can look at me with sincerity. "I'll be right by your side the whole time."

"Promise?"

Kissing my forehead, his voice muffled against me, he says, "I promise." Then pulling his head back to look at me, he adds, "But for an extra precaution, I'm gonna give Chandler a call and have him stop by for the exchange."

Relief trickles down my spine. "That's a great idea."

"I'll invite Ballard over for the gathering too," he says with a wink.

"May as well give Constance a call. I wouldn't want her to think we were having a party without her."

He laughs at my teasing.

Then, I back away from him, remembering Abbi's dessert request. "S'mores."

Knox draws his head back, confused. "S'mores?"

I nod vigorously. "Yes, I need S'mores ingredients. I completely forgot about it." I begin heading out of Knox's kitchen and across the carpet of the living room to the entrance. "Can I borrow your truck? I need to run to the grocery store. I promised I'd have S'mores for Abbi. I don't want to let her down. I can't let her down any more than I already—"

"Trinity, it's okay." Knox has his hands on my shoulders and he's craning his neck to look at me. "I'll get the S'mores. You can stay and work on the garlic spread." A grin hits the side of his face. "If you don't remember, I've seen how you drive my truck. And I don't particularly like it."

I drop my mouth open, playfully offended.

He gives me a quick peck on the side of my mouth. "How about I give you a few driving lessons before you get behind the wheel of my truck by yourself again?"

I roll my eyes, and with a teasing tone I say, "Fine. But hurry back." I'm not purposely sending him away hours before the children are supposed to arrive. He'll be back before the drop off. I just need to focus on the good.

With another peck on my mouth, he's out the door and down the road before I realize I've been standing in the same spot daydreaming about a life where this is our home. A life where it's normal for Knox to rush out the door and run to the grocery store because I've forgotten an ingredient. It's as if I've been homesick for a place that I never thought could exist. But here I am, in a home that makes that homesick feeling disappear.

I look around the furnished living room, realizing for the first time that under the TV stand there are movies that no one above the age of ten would enjoy. With titles like 101 Dalmatians, Aladin and Sesame Street. I also notice that the coffee table has a slew of Bernstein Bears books covering it. There's even a bin in the corner with children's toys.

How did I spend the last hour in this home without so much as a tour?

Suddenly, I feel so selfish. Knox went through the trouble of ensuring the kids would have everything they needed for this visit, and I didn't even notice his efforts.

As soon as he returns, I'm going to thank him. But first, I need to take in the rest of the home. Especially since the only change I noticed from the last time I was here was that he put up a fence. That's where Sugar is now. But what I didn't notice then that I'm noticing now, is the doghouse.

I pull myself from the living room window and head up the carpeted stairs to further inspect Knox's attention to detail. The first two bedrooms are empty but one is painted yellow and the other green, the scent of paint still fresh in the rooms. I can't help but wonder if he's been preparing this home for us. For *our* family. And my heart doubles in size.

Next is the blue bathroom with a fish themed shower curtain and matching hand towel. Then at the end of the upstairs hallway is the master bedroom. Just as I press the door open, I find a half built wooden dollhouse in the middle of the floor. There's a few scattered tools and a small can of sky-blue paint next to it.

How did he know? I never mentioned that I was going to buy Abbi a dollhouse. I squat down to touch the stairs and wonder how long it took to craft each individual step. But before I can inspect the dollhouse any further, I hear the phone ringing.

The phone?

I didn't know there was a phone here. Or that it was set up for use. Or who would be calling.

I hurry down the stairs and listen for the ring when I'm in the kitchen. I spot the phone on the other side of the refrigerator and answer it. For all I know it could be Knox.

"Hello?"

"Trinity, good." It's Constance. "I was hoping you'd answer."

I twist the cord around my finger. "You were?"

She clears her throat. "I heard Knox's phone ringin' off the hook. So I went up to the apartment to see if it would ring again. Sure enough, a kid was lookin' for someone named Drastia. I told them they had the wrong number. But before I could even walk out of the apartment, the phone rang again. The little girl asked for Drastia again and said she'd gotten the phone number from Officer Santino. It didn't take long to put two and two together. I'm pretty sure your daughter is tryin' to get ahold of you."

"Thanks, Constance. I'll give her a call."

The knot from earlier returns to my stomach.

I hang up the receiver, wait a moment, then pick it up again. Pressing the phone to my ear until I hear the dial tone. Then I punch in the number to Matthew and Martha's home and wait for Abbi or West to pick up. But no one answers.

I call a second time.

Then a third.

There's no answer.

Abbi shouldn't be calling me right now. She should be getting ready for our visit.

The knot is twisting so hard that I feel another knot joining in on the chaos inside my stomach.

Something's not right.

I get a sudden epiphany and pick up the phone again. This time I dial the number to West's house. Our old home.

On the second ring I hear the little voice of Abbi on the other line.

I exhale with relief. "Baby girl, it's mo—," I stop myself remembering the code name she came up with for safe phone calls. "It's Drastia. Are you okay?"

"Yes, Mommy," hearing my name come out of her mouth steadies my racing heart and untangles the knots in my stomach. "I mean, Drastia. I'm okay. But I need you to come over."

I tilt my head, confused since I thought Martha had coordinated for West to drop the kids off later today. "Why's that?" The creeping of the knots is returning to my stomach.

"Because something bad happened."

CHAPTER FORTY-FOUR

Abbi

20 minutes earlier

Tuck pulls Cinderella off the bed and throws her into the hall. I don't like it when Tuck throws my toys, so I yell at him. "Tuck! No throwing! Bring me Cinderella now."

Tuck doesn't listen to me. He runs out of the room instead.

I pick up Cinderella in the hallway, then put her back to bed.

"It's okay," I say, patting Cinderella's head. Then I talk to Cinderella again, "Nana says Tuck is a toddler and he's still learning, so we have to be nice to him when he's bad." Cinderella would nod if she was alive, but since she's not, I move her head up and down for her.

I wish I was at my Nana's. I don't like when we have to stay at Daddy's house.

Sometimes Daddy is good. But sometimes Daddy is bad and throws things like Tuck does.

Maybe it's what boys do. Maybe Nana was wrong. Maybe Tuck throws things because he's a boy. That explains why Daddy throws stuff too, since he's not a toddler but he's a boy like Tuck. Just older.

Except Papa is a boy. But Papa doesn't throw things. Maybe when Daddy and Tuck are old, they won't throw things anymore.

I finish putting the rest of my dolls to bed because I have to leave them for a while, and I don't want them to miss me.

Nana said we get to eat dinner with Mommy tonight. She was sad when she told me, so I tried not to be too happy in front of her.

When Nana talks about Mommy, she always gets sad.

Sometimes I hear Nana and Daddy talking about Mommy, then Daddy gets mad and throws stuff. Sometimes when he throws stuff it hits Nana. I don't think Daddy means to hurt Nana. Just like Tuck doesn't mean to hurt Cinderella.

I wonder if I should pack my Princess Jasmine purse, just in case we get to have a sleep over with Mommy.

I miss Mommy. A lot.

Mommy did everything I liked. And even though Daddy is Daddy and Nana is nice, they don't do everything like Mommy. And they don't smell like Mommy. And they don't feel like Mommy.

I don't tell Nana and Daddy because when Tuck used to cry for Mommy at bedtime, Nana would get sad, and Daddy would get mad. And I don't want to talk about Mommy and make Nana sad and Daddy mad.

My purse is full now. I put my princess pajamas in there and there's no more room for anything else.

My princess pajamas remind me of my princess jellies. I run to my closet and find my golden glittery jelly shoes and put them on my feet. Only they shrunk.

"Daddy!" I say, trying to mash my foot into my shoes. It hurts, but I really want to wear them to show Mommy. I wonder if she remembers my princess jellies. "Daddy!" Maybe I can cut the shoes and then my feet will fit in them again. I don't know why my shoes are so small. I was four when Mommy and Daddy lived here, and now I'm five. So my shoes should still fit. "Daddy!" I'm going to find scissors and cut my shoes before we have to leave and see Mommy.

There's a loud thud and then a crashing sound in the kitchen. Then I hear Tuck crying. I leave my jelly shoes and run to the kitchen because if Tuck is crying, he needs me to help him. I'm his big sister, I know how to take care of him when he cries.

Tuck is on his back and he's crying on the kitchen floor, so I walk over to him and help him up. But something hurts my foot. I pick it out. It's a sharp white pokey thing.

There's lots of sharp things on the floor.

"Tuck, did you throw something?"

He shakes his head. I pick him up and carry him even though he's getting heavy because he's three and a half now.

"I drop it," he says.

I carry him to the living room, so he doesn't get a sharp thing stuck in his foot, like I did. I set him on the dark spot of the carpet. Sometimes when I have to stay with Daddy I like to lay on the dark spot. It reminds me of Mommy because she would always sleep on the carpet in the living room at night when Daddy would throw stuff. Sometimes Daddy would throw Mommy. But it's because he's a boy like Tuck and they throw things because they're boys.

"What did you drop?"

"I drop plate."

"How did you get a plate?"

He points to the kitchen. "I climb up."

"You can't climb on the counter, Tuck! That's dangerous." I put my hands on my hips so he knows that I'm serious. That's what Nana does when she's serious, so I'm going to do that when I'm serious.

"Ouch!" Tuck says, pointing to the broken plate on the kitchen floor.

"Yes. Don't touch. It's ouch!"

I'm yelling again. I don't want to yell at Tuck. He's still learning. I need to be nice to him.

I sit by Tuck and pat his head like I patted Cinderella's when I put her to bed.

"Stay here, okay, Tuck?" I pat his head again. "I'm going to find Daddy." Daddy will know what to do with the plate.

I look in Daddy's room but he's not there. I plug my nose because his room smells like a skunk. I look in the bathroom but he's not there either. Then I go outside.

Sometimes Daddy uses the tractor in the field. I listen for the tractor, but I don't hear it. I look out in the field, but I don't see him. Maybe he's in the shed. I run to the shed but Daddy's not in the shed. The cars and the truck are here, so I know Daddy didn't drive to Mommy's without us. Maybe I will call Mommy. Maybe Mommy knows where Daddy is. I still have the card from Officer Santino. Mommy said I could call her any time.

I go back inside to get my purse. That's where the card is.

Tuck isn't sitting on the dark spot of the carpet anymore. I get mad at him when I see him by the table. He's smiling so I know he's okay and he didn't go into the kitchen where the broken plate is. But I'm mad because he didn't listen to me.

"Tuck, I told you to sit on the floor!"

He shakes his head really fast back and forth. "No! I don't sit! I pull it!"

I put my hands on my hips again because I'm being very serious again. "You have to listen to me, I'm the big sister." I point to the carpet. "Sit. I'll be right back."

"No!"

I need to call Mommy. Mommy does everything right so she will know how to make Tuck listen to me.

I run in my room and get my purse and then run back to the living room where the phone is.

Tuck is smiling again. "I pull it!"

I don't know why he keeps saying that. "Sit down." I say pointing to the carpet.

"No!"

"Tuck, you have to listen to me."

"Shut up!" The voice is Daddy's voice, but I don't see Daddy.

Then the blankets on the couch move and I see Daddy's arm for a second before it hides under the blanket with the rest of him. I'm happy I found Daddy. I don't know why he was hiding from me though.

I leave my purse by the phone. Running over to Daddy, I shake his arm. "Daddy, Tuck broke a plate in the kitchen and he's not listening to me when I tell him to sit down."

"Deal with it, Abbi. Can't you see I'm tryin' to sleep?"

I don't like when Daddy doesn't help me. I also don't like when Daddy smells funny. When he smells funny, he throws things. And I don't like when Daddy throws things. Even if he is a boy.

I grab his arm and pull it. "Daddy, get up. Tuck won't listen to me."

"I hungry," Tuck says.

I look at Tuck and he's playing with something on the little table in front of the couch. There are too many brown bottles on the table to see what it is.

I pull Daddy's arm again. "Daddy, you have to take us to see Mommy. Remember? We get to eat dinner with Mommy tonight."

Daddy doesn't say anything this time.

"I pull it!" Tuck says.

I let go of Daddy's arm. "I'm calling Mommy."

"Look, Abbi!"

I look through my purse and find the card with the number Mommy told me to call when I need her. I leave my purse next to Daddy on the couch. Maybe he will see it and remember we have to leave.

If Daddy is too sleepy, Mommy can drive us to dinner.

I press one number at a time, but it takes too long because a lady's voice says the number I dialed is incorrect. I have to be faster the next time I press the buttons.

"Look, Abbi!"

When I look at Tuck he's smiling. That means he's happy and he's not hurt. "What is it? I'm trying to call Mommy."

"Abbi, look at it!"

I don't know what he's talking about. But I want to know what he has that's making him happy and smile. So I walk over to where he's standing by the tiny table with the brown bottles that make Daddy smell funny.

"I pull it."

"No, Tuck!" I have to stop him before he pulls it again.

"No, Abbi. Look, I pull it."

But when he pulls it this time, there's a bright light that flashes like a light turned on and off really fast in a dark room. And with the bright light, there's a loud, loud, LOUD, bang. And after the light and the loud bang, there's a ringing.

Tuck is holding his ears and crying but I can't hear him crying because of the light, and the loud bang, and the ringing.

And something is wrong with Daddy because he's still sleeping, and there's red stuff leaking down his head. And there's red stuff on my Princess Jasmine purse too. And I think Daddy's dead.

CHAPTER FORTY-FIVE

Trinity

Run. Run. Run. Faster. Faster. Faster.

I repeat this over to myself.

Over and over again.

Run.

Run.

Run.

Each time my foot strikes the ground, the only thing I allow my mind to think is *run*.

Faster.

Faster.

Faster.

Because the faster I run, the faster I will get to Abbi and Tuck. And the faster I can figure out what the hell is going on.

On the phone, Abbi said West was dead.

I know what she said, but I don't know what she means.

She wasn't crying. She probably doesn't understand what's going on.

I wonder if Knox would have chosen the house he renovated if he'd known he was living on the same County Road 228 as West.

Before I left, I called the police and Constance. I told her to find Knox at the grocery store and tell him to meet me at West's house. I didn't tell her why. Maybe I should have. Knox might think the worst. But maybe that'll get him to the house sooner. Even so, I'll reach the house before him on foot.

I'll get there before the police too. I can already see where the road curves and splits off into the dirt path that leads to West's house. So, all I need to do is keep running.

Run.

Run.

Run.

They look like little ants from here, but I can see Abbi sitting outside on the porch step with Tuck.

Faster.

Faster.

Faster.

When she sees me, she hops off the step and runs toward me.

"Mommy! Mommy!" Her arms are wide open, but her feet aren't moving very fast. And when she reaches me, I can see why she was shuffling towards me. Her shoes are too small for her feet.

I ignore the shoes and hold her as tight as I can without hurting her, while I continue to run toward the house.

I set her back down next to Tuck and I hug both of them. And Tuck doesn't even try to squirm out of my grip.

Kissing the tops of their heads, I say, "Where's Daddy?"

"On the couch." With a pouting expression Abbi lifts her purse, and I notice drying blood on her right hand. "Tuck shot Daddy and ruined my Princess Jasmine purse." She says this as if Tuck only spilled milk. But this is so much more than a broken glass of spilled milk.

There's blood on the purse and Princess Jasmine has a smile on her face despite the red smear across her torso and legs.

I didn't think my heart could beat any faster. But right now, I can feel my pulse throughout my entire body. My face is pulsating right along with my legs. Every part of me where blood is coursing is banging as if the blood is trying to burst through my veins.

Turning my back to the house, I face the road. Hoping to see a squad car. Or at the very least, hear sirens. But there's nothing.

What's taking so long?

I don't want to go inside the house. But something tells me I have to. That I need to.

"Abbi," I squat down in front of her and Tuck, "I'm going to check on Daddy, okay? And I need you to take Tuck and walk over to the tree right there."

"That one?" She points.

I nod with a smile so forced the corners of my lips are quivering. "Yes, baby girl, that one. I want you and Tuck to pick thirty pecans from that tree, okay? Can you still count to thirty?"

She nods. "I can count to one hundred!"

"Okay, well how about you find a hundred pecans together. And I'll be right back."

She holds Tuck's hand. "Come on, Tuck." As soon as their backs are to me, I open the front door and enter the home.

West is lying on the couch. Nothing seems out of the ordinary, aside from the smell of marijuana and alcohol. And the broken plate on the kitchen floor. If I didn't know any better, I'd think West was sleeping on the couch.

I step between the coffee table and the couch. His pistol is in the middle of the table pointing straight at him. There's broken glass where the bullet must have shattered several beer bottles before it hit him. And when I finally look down at him, there's a bloody hole at his temple.

I exhale with shock and cover my mouth with both hands. I want to run outside again, but my feet are planted in place. Unable to move even though my body is screaming to leave.

Then, West's upper body expands, rising with his inhale. *He's breathing.*

My own breathing intensifies as a chill scatters up my spine and down my arms. And my heart is beating into my throat like a jackhammer.

Before my throat completely closes, I say, "West?"

He groans and his arm slips off his chest and falls against the floor near my feet.

I bend down, placing two fingers against his wrist to feel for a pulse. "West, are you alive?" What am I saying? Of course he's alive. But how? He has a bullet hole in the side of his head, right along his temple against the weakest part of his skull.

When he groans again, he shifts his head this time, revealing the other side.

I'm stunned to see that the bullet went all the way through. So much so that there's a burnt hole on the couch cushion, revealing the white fluff inside. I wouldn't be surprised if there's a hole in the house too.

My pulse is throbbing through my body again.

Somehow, my feet move. But they don't go in the direction of the door. They move toward the phone on the other side of the couch. I pick it up and dial 911 again.

There's a voice, "911, what's your emergency?"

"My name is Trinity," I can barely get the words out. "I just called ten minutes ago. I'm with West Laurel in his home off County Road 228. I found him with a gunshot wound to the head."

Dispatch takes the rest of the information, then she asks me to wait on the phone with her until help arrives.

But I set the phone down, because West just said something and moved again.

"Trinity," his voice is hoarse and full of agony. "What happened?"

I move so that I'm kneeling on the floor next to him. My mouth is wide open and I'm certain my eyes might pop out of their sockets.

I must be in shock. Shock that he's speaking. Shock that he's able to move. Shock that he's coherent. There's no way the bullet missed his brain. I'm looking right at the hole on the side of his head. He shouldn't be talking, or moving, or *breathing*.

I have to be imagining this. That's the only reasonable explanation.

His arm lifts slightly from the floor in an ungraceful manner, so I take his hand and set it on his chest and hold it there. "You're alive." I say more to myself, trying to convince my disbelief into believing that what I'm seeing is really happening.

"My head." He lifts his other hand, and it flops against his forehead. "My head hurts so bad." His words are slow and heavy.

I don't know if I'm supposed to tell him what happened.

I don't know how I'm supposed to even feel in this moment.

For so long, I wished for something to happen that would take West out of my life. Not death. But I wished something would happen so that I could get my kids away from him and back into my life. I wished for all sorts of things. Like that he would leave and never look back. I wished he would fall in love with someone else and forget about me. I wished he would change. But never, in a million years, did I wish for something like this to happen.

I hear a vehicle coming down the dirt road, and relief hits me like a waterfall when I recognize the deep rumble of the truck engine.

"I can't...I can't see," he says, with a moan.

He's had his eyes closed since I walked in the door. Understandably, I'm certain he's in excruciating pain right now.

As the engine shuts off, I can hear Knox calling out my name. I stand up and pull the drapes to one side, just to make sure it's him.

His panicked expression shifts to concern when he looks up and sees me through the window. I can tell he's about to run inside the house. So I point to Abbi and Tuck under the tree. I need him to make sure they don't get caught up in the chaos about to ensue. He gives me a nod, then bolts towards the kids.

There are several police cars on their way down the path now too.

"I can't open my eyes."

I flip around to face West. He's trying to sit up. I don't know if he should be moving after a bullet just went through the side of his skull, so I gently press my hand against his chest to coax him down again.

He gives in to my gesture and lays against the couch with his palms pressed to his face. "I can't see, Trinity." His voice is growing with concern as he grips my arm tightly in his. "What happened to me? I can't see!"

"Open your eyes." I don't like his grip on me. It's returning all the horrific ways he's ever wrongly touched me.

"*I can't!*" Just as the words leave his mouth, his eyelids flutter open, then shut again. But the glimpse I get is enough information I need to understand why he can't see.

My hand closes over my open mouth instinctively.

His eye sockets are nothing more than a bloody mess of unidentifiable parts. The bullet hit lower than I thought. That's why he's not dead. The bullet never hit his brain.

But it destroyed his eyes.

Chase bursts through the front door. Once it registers what he's seeing he immediately looks at me with concern.

Does he think I shot West?

"Trinity, put your hands on your head and back up toward me until I tell you to stop." Chase is using his police officer voice, not his Knox's friend voice.

He definitely thinks I did this.

Maybe if I had made a better effort to get to know him, he wouldn't be doing this. Because he would know that I'm not capable of committing such a heinous crime as this one.

I place my hands on the top of my head when Liv enters the home, followed by Knox.

I haven't turned around or started backing up yet. So my face is the first one everyone sees when they enter the home.

"Trinity...?" West is pleading. I've never heard him sound so terrified. "Please, Trinity, don't go. Don't leave me."

Noticing that West wants me near him, Chase tilts his head and glances at Knox in confusion, then back to me. "What's happened here?" He adjusts his glasses with one hand before unclipping the latch of his gun holster.

My hands are still on my head. "It was an accident."

"Trinity, where are you?" West lifts his hand, reaching for me but only grasping at my shorts until I take a step away from him.

Knox begins to approach me, but then slowly draws his brows together as he scans West and his desperation to touch me. Then he looks around the floor until his eyes climb across the carpet, up the legs of the coffee table and halt when they meet the pistol. That's when his eyes flick up to mine with dread.

I only wish I was able to recognize what that dread means. I hope he doesn't think I did this too.

West is flailing his arm pathetically in my direction and I suddenly realize this is worse than death for him. "Trinity," his voice is close to tears, "Please, Trinity."

Chase and Liv are staring at West in utter disbelief.

But Knox is staring at me. His mouth parts, and there's even a sound erupting from the bottom of his lungs, as if he's about to speak.

That's when I drop one hand from my head, pressing my index finger to my mouth, indicating for him not to let that sound out of his throat. Begging him not to say a word.

"He's blind," I say urgently, trying to get the information out to end the confusion circulating in this room.

Everyone is looking at me now. Apparently shocked, but also needing clarification.

I lower my arms hesitantly. "He's blind, because the bullet shot his eyes out."

CHAPTER FORTY-SIX

Knox

I begin to speak again when I approach her, but this time she places her fingertips against my mouth. Her eyes are pleading, as if she's still silently asking me not to speak.

"My eyes?" West is gently touching his own face.

I look back at the pistol on the coffee table but there's no magazine. Then, I realize that the action is locked back to the rear. Meaning the gun is empty.

When I was outside with the kids, Abbi told me that Tuck had been squeezing the trigger before the gun fired.

If the gun fired without a magazine, that means West probably left his gun out thinking it was unloaded. The idiot forgot to eject the last bullet from the chamber.

That's when I realize Trinity's right. Because West's eyelids stretch open, only to reveal the darkened bloody area where his eyes used to be.

That's also when I realize that what Abbi told me under the pecan tree is true too. That Tuck really did shoot West with his own pistol. Not on purpose of course. But this entire incident was simply because of a child's natural curiosity. And an adult's carelessness.

What kind of dumbass keeps a gun in reach of a child?

Chandler questions Trinity again, but my focus drifts from Trinity's paranoid expression down to West whose flailing hand just nicked my pants. And he doesn't even know it's me.

"Trinity, what's happening? What happened to me?" he says with desperation. "My head hurts so damn bad!"

Flipping around to face Chandler, I say, "This was an accident. She didn't do it." Then just as quickly as I face Chandler, I twist my torso to reach a hand over to pull Trinity out of the house.

Because I know what's coming.

Trinity warned me twice about speaking, and I know it's because West didn't know I was here. But she knew that once he heard my voice, he wouldn't be so cooperative. Even if he did just get shot in the head.

As we rush down the porch steps and toward the tree where Abbi and Tuck are gathering pecans, I can hear West's roaring voice along with the crash of what I assume to be his body falling against the coffee table.

There's another patrol vehicle followed by an ambulance that's making their way down the dirt road now.

When we reach the tree, hand in hand, Trinity yanks on my arm until I turn around to face her. Then she thrusts herself at my torso until she's clinging to me so tightly, I worry she's going to fold in on herself.

I grip her in my arms. "Hey..." I say gently. "It's okay. You did everything right. It was an accident."

She releases the heaviest exhale against my chest before she pulls away to meet my eyes. "Is it wrong that I'm happy he's alive?"

Searching her expression, I can't figure out a response to her question. The guy has been nothing but a thorn in my side, and even worse for Trinity. I'd think she'd at least be a little disappointed he survived. I'll admit that I am.

Shaking her head she glances past me to where the kids are still by the tree. "I can't imagine what it would have done to Tuck if he'd had to grow up knowing he killed his father."

That's all it takes for me to change my mind about the situation and feel a little better that West is still alive. Plus, without his sight, how much havoc can he continue to cause?

Abbi rushes to our legs, wrapping her arms around us. "I want to hug too."

Trinity releases me to pick up Abbi. But Abbi's not done with me, once she's hoisted on Trinity's hip, she holds on to my neck with her little arm.

I feel something hit my back. I unwind Abbi's arm from my neck so I can turn around. And when I do, I see Tuck throwing pecans in my direction. "What're you doing, buddy?" I say with a smile, trying to lighten the heaviness of the last few minutes.

Abbi pulls on my neck again. "Sorry, Officer Santino. Sometimes Tuck throws things because he's a boy and he's still learning."

I look from Abbi to Trinity, then back to Abbi again. "Well, I guess I better teach him a little self-control, huh?"

Abbi faces Trinity and asks, "Mommy, what's self-control?" Just as I approach Tuck and squat down in front of him.

"Hey, Tuck," I say, picking up two pecans in my hand. "Remember me?"

To my surprise, he nods. I'm not sure if he does remember me or if he's confusing me for someone else. Either way, I'm glad he's giving me his attention.

"You know, pecans are for eating, right? Not throwing." I squeeze the pecans until they crush against each other, breaking open. "Give me your hand," I say, gently picking out the nut from its shell and placing it into his open palm.

I can tell he's had pecans before because he instantly tosses it into his mouth. Then putting his hand out for another one, he says, "Please?" before he's done chewing the one still in his mouth.

I smile, handing him a broken nut and then toss one into my mouth.

"I want one too," Abbi says, from Trinity's hip.

Trinity gives her a look then Abbi faces me and says, "Please?" with a smile.

I rise to my feet and hand her a pecan before Tuck is at my side, tugging on the edge of my shirt. When I look down at him, he lifts his arms up towards me. So I bend down to grip him under his arms, and hoist him up.

There's a sound coming from the house and West is laying against the stretcher while the medics roll him out. He seems more relaxed now and there's a white bandage around his head. But the sight is still traumatic. So I face Trinity and say, "Come on, let's get them out of here. They don't need to see this." I nod my head toward my truck and open the passenger door for them to pile in.

Hopping in, I don't waste a second getting my truck turned around.

"Shouldn't I leave a statement with Liv or Chase?" Trinity says in a rush.

I shake my head and smile at her. "Did you forget your boyfriend is a police officer?"

Abbi giggles next to Trinity. "Mommy doesn't have a boyfriend."

I know it's soon and we'll have time to explain everything to Abbi later. But I can't wait to have that conversation.

"What this?" Tuck says, grasping the knob of the gear shift between him and Abbi.

I hang on to it tightly, so he doesn't kick me out of gear, then say, "It's a gear stick. It balances the speed and torque inside the truck."

Abbi chews on her fingernail when she says, "Daddy's truck didn't have a gear stick."

"Torque," Tuck repeats with a laugh that pulls our attention away from Abbi's statement.

I shift down as I turn onto the county road. Before I get up to speed, I say, "Want to shift gears with me?"

Tuck nods with excitement and wraps both his hands around the long metal shifter.

I carefully move the gear lever as the transmission pops. Then I speed up and shift again.

Tuck is laughing. "Again!"

Abbi wiggles herself to the edge of the bench seat. "I want a turn too."

"No," Tuck says, turning sideways so his back is to her, blocking her from taking the shifter from him. "My torque."

Abbi's brow creases. "Tuck, it's a gear stick. And it's my turn."

I'm about to shift down again before turning down the road toward my house. "Alright, Tuck. This is your last turn, then we need to give your sister a try, alright?"

He pauses for a moment before nodding in agreement.

I catch a glimpse of Trinity's pleasant expression. She's enjoying the sight of her children's fixation with the shifter, both who are completely unaware of the intensity of the situation they just endured.

Abbi takes her turn helping me shift gears before we pull up to the house.

It's the strangest feeling. Having the woman that I love, and her kids whose safety has been my main concern for the last year, pulling up to my house with me. Even though it's a strange feeling, it somehow feels even more natural. Like I've slipped right into a place where I was always meant to be.

There's a bark when I turn the truck off. Both kids sit up on the bench seat to see where we are.

Abbi's curious expression turns to excitement when she squeals, "Sugar!" She looks at me with surprise. "You kept your promise!"

"Of course I did," I smile at her. "I never make a promise I can't keep."

I open the door and stand near the truck as Abbi rolls over Tuck to get to me first, so I can help her down. Tuck does the same without skipping a beat. I pull the bag of S'mores ingredients from my truck bed. Then follow them to the fence and open the gate so they can play with Sugar. Who is just as happy, if not happier, to see them.

I look back to share the joy of the moment with Trinity, but she's still sitting in the truck. So I drop the sack, and secure the gate before jogging over to the passenger side to open the door for her. Only when I swing the door open, I'm met with a sight that hits my chest harder than a wrecking ball.

Her eyes are glowing as green as a neon sign. I slip my hand under both her knees in one swift motion and slide them to the edge of the bench seat so she's facing me. Then I pull her against me to hug her. "It's okay," I say. "Everything is going to be okay now. I promise."

She nods and gulps on her...*sob?* She's sobbing.

I pull away from her to see that tears are streaming down her cheeks. Her eyes are greener than I've ever seen because she's *crying*.

"Trinity," I whisper. "You're crying."

She cracks a laugh that's mixed in equal parts of relief and shock.

I kiss her tear-streaked face. Once on one cheek, then the other side, then against her mouth. "You're laughing and crying."

Her glowing eyes connect to mine. "I'm happy," she cracks another laugh. "Never in my entire life have I been happier than I am in this moment. Watching you be a better father figure to my children in two minutes than West was for their entire lives." With her arms draped over my shoulders she turns to look out the front window of the truck. "This house, Abbi, Tuck, Sugar, me," she faces me again and more tears roll out of her beaming eyes, "and *you*." She presses her mouth to mine, then, "It's better than anything I could have dreamt up on my own."

I couldn't have said it better. She just put all the feelings I've been having into words for both of us.

I press my forehead against hers. "Do me a favor?"

With her laugh, she says, "Anything."

"Move in with me. Marry me." I hear a short inhale from her mouth, when I say, "And let me be more than a father figure to them. Let me raise them with you. Let me be their dad."

EPILOGUE

Trinity

August 1999

"Are you sure you don't want me to drive you?" I say, helping Abbi slip her arm through her yellow Beauty and the Beast backpack strap.

She shakes her head. "No, Mommy. I want to ride the bus with my friends."

She opens the front door and pats Sugar's head on her way to the gate. I follow her out and through the gate. Then we begin the long walk down the path where the bus will pick her up by the road.

But she turns around with her hand up before we make it very far. "Sorry, Mommy, but mommies aren't allowed at the bus spot."

"Abbi, it's your first day. Aren't you a little bit nervous?"

She shakes her head. "I don't get nervous."

The front door swings open and Knox is jogging towards us with a camera in hand. "Hang on girls," he says with a proud smile. "Can't forget the first day of school pictures."

"Where did you find that?" I say. "That's my old camera from high school. The film has probably expired."

He shakes his head and raises the camera up in his hand as he reaches me and kisses the side of my face. "I found it yesterday in the box of photos from your parents' house. I bought film at the hardware store, so hopefully the battery still works."

My eyes widen, then he gives me a cheeky smile, letting me know that he's joking and had already replaced the battery too.

Abbi puts one hand on her hip. "Two pictures, Dad." Then she poses with a beaming grin as if she's modeling for the cover of a J.C. Penny's magazine.

I don't know when I got used to her calling Knox *Dad* but looking back now I wouldn't have her call him anything else. Especially since she hasn't seen West since shortly after the accident.

If the gunshot wound had been fatal, I think West would've gotten the easy way out. Especially since his life is a whole lot worse now. The bullet missed his artery behind his temporal lobe and instead severed the nerves and muscles holding his eyes in place. He's completely blind.

After West recovered from the gunshot wound. He was arrested for child endangerment, drug possession, and a slew of other illegal activity. People started coming forward with various crimes West committed against them, and his charges continued to rack up. I guess people weren't so afraid of him once he couldn't see them anymore.

Because of the many charges, and because he was uncooperative in court he was sent to prison for twelve years without parole.

Abbi doesn't talk about him much anymore. Especially since the last time she saw him, he decided to say, "Quit calling me your daddy. I was never your daddy." That left her heartbroken and confused for a few days. But Knox filled that hole in her heart quickly. I love that about him. And I love that about her, she's incredibly resilient.

"Okay, Dad," she says with a giggle, when he lifts her in his arms and kisses her cheek. "You're making me late for the bus spot."

He lifts his chin curiously. "Bus spot? What's a bus spot?"

She wriggles from his arms, and he sets her down. As soon as her feet touch the ground, she's running in the opposite direction of us when she calls out, "Bye! See you at the bus spot after school!"

Knox stands behind me then slips his arms around my waist and hugs my back against his chest. Leaning his chin against my shoulder, he says, "You didn't correct her when she called the bus stop a bus spot?"

I release a bittersweet exhale. "No, I couldn't." This moment is bittersweet because my baby girl is happily running off to spend the day at school without me. But because she's so determined and independent, I know she's going to make a great leader one day. And that makes me proud of her.

"I wouldn't have corrected her either. We'll keep her young as long as we can." He kisses my cheek. "If only there was a way to give them a perfect childhood. One where our mistakes didn't affect them."

His statement comes out pained, so I try to turn to face him but he holds his arms around me so I can't.

"Look," he says, nodding at Abbi.

I face the direction he's motioning toward and hold my breath. Not purposely but instinctively, because the bus arrives and all I see is Abbi's yellow Beauty and the Beast backpack bouncing as she jumps up the steps onto the bus.

My eyes sting as the bus drives off with a piece of my heart.

My eyes do that now. They sting a little bit right before they well with tears. Sometimes it's a deep burn and a lot of tears. Sometimes it's just a sudden sting with one tear. That's what's happening now. It's just a short sting with one tear that drops down from my eye. But it's the good kind of stinging.

"Heyyy," Knox says, still holding me from behind. But now instead of resting his chin against my shoulder, he's craning his neck over my shoulder to inspect my face. "She'll be back at noon. It's only half day kindergarten."

I laugh as I turn into him. "I know. But soon it will be all day first grade. Then it will be fifth grade graduation, and then eighth grade promotion. Then she'll be eighteen and—"

Now he's laughing. "It doesn't happen that fast. Especially if you're as intentional of a mother as you are."

When we face each other, I look up to see his eyes shining. They must be stinging in the way mine were doing a minute ago, since there's a spark to them I've only seen twice before. When I said, *I do*, and when he adopted Tuck and Abbi after West gave up his parental rights. And something about his watering hazel eyes reminds me of Abbi when she's trying not to cry.

"It's okay," I say in a quiet voice with my smile, "it's only half day kindergarten. She'll be back at noon."

He laughs at my repeated phrase and hugs me for a long time. Then when he pulls away, he digs in his back pocket and pulls out a photo. He's holding it high enough that I can't see it.

He folds his bottom lip into his mouth as he gazes at the picture for a moment. "You know, I've wished it was me. I wished I'd known you before. So many times, I wished I had woken up next to you after one of those parties in Abilene when I was at the police academy. I wished I had woken up next to you and never left. And I wished that I had been your one-night stand." He shakes his head and hands me the photo.

"What's this?" I say, confused about why he's saying all this while showing me a picture.

"It was in the box where I found the camera yesterday. I went through some of your old photos thinking I might get a sense of what you were like as a kid."

It's a photo from when I was seventeen. I'm at Brent's house. He's the one that lived behind my house and had the biggest parties because his parents were never home. Maybe Knox is showing me this photo because he recognizes Brent's house. Which is barely visible in the sea of people holding beer cans and disposable cups behind me and my friend Lara.

With a deep inhale he takes the photo from my hand and points to the back of a dark-haired guy. He's wearing a dark blue cutoff sleeve t-shirt with the words POLICE ACADEMY printed across the back. Then, sliding his finger down the length of the guy's arm, I realize what Knox is showing me. Because the guy has a tattoo that's covering half his arm. It's the same tattoo covering the top half of Knox's arm. The same flames engulfing the house. The same woman on his deltoid. The same tattoo, because it's the same guy.

My mouth is open when I turn to look at Knox. "It's you."

"With half my tattoo. But, yeah, it's me at the same house party as you."

My eyes are shifting between his as my heart rate begins to speed up with uncertain excitement. "Could it be possible that we were together that night?"

A relieved grin spreads across his face.

I release a puff of air out of my mouth. "Would it be such a wild idea to think you were my one-night stand? That you could be..." this time the puff of air that comes out of my mouth is mixed with a laugh. "That maybe you're Abbi's real dad?"

He scoops me in his arms and kisses my neck. "I am Abbi's real dad." He sets me down and brushes his thumb against my jawline. "And I'm Tuck's real dad too." His eyes gentle with his grin. "That's the truth. I don't need any more confirmation than what I feel for them. And nothing will ever change that truth."

There's a quiet yawning sound behind Knox. "Daddy?" Tuck says, trying to open the gate.

Knox meets him at the gate and instead of unlatching it he just reaches over it, pulling Tuck up into his arms. "You just missed your sister catch the bus, buddy."

I meet them near the gate. "How'd you sleep?" I say, running my hand over Tuck's messy bed head.

He yawns again, then leans his head against Knox's shoulder and blinks heavily. He's like me and needs a few minutes to wake up before he talks to anyone in the morning.

I open the gate, so we can return inside, but I catch a glimpse of the diseased sassafras tree in the yard. The one Knox refuses to cut down.

He stops with Tuck still resting his head against his shoulder. "What is it?"

I bite my lip curiously. "The tree."

He takes a step so he's standing next to me. His eyes look in the direction of the tree. Then a smile spreads on his face as he nods his head to the side, indicating for me to follow him. "I wanna show you something."

I follow at a quick pace as his strides are hurried. Rushing us toward whatever he so eagerly wants to show me.

We pass the diseased tree, that somehow doesn't look so diseased anymore, and he takes me through a heavy wall of trees. I tuck my head under a branch as we continue toward an open area where the sunlight is beaming, even though it's barely eight o'clock in the morning. Then he stops to face me, adjusting Tuck in his other arm. But Tuck begins to wriggle until Knox sets him down to play.

With his grin, Knox fans his hand out to the side. "This," is all he says.

I shake my head with my narrowing eyes of confusion. Looking around for whatever *this* is.

"This tree," his eyebrows rise with excitement. "It's a sassafras tree."

I inspect the tree. Sure enough, it's a small juvenile sassafras tree with a lot more life in it than the towering one on the other side of the wall the willow trees formed. The wall that has separated this sassafras tree from the dying one. "You're going to have to elaborate," I throw my thumb over my shoulder toward the house. "I won't be able to think straight until I finish my cup of coffee."

"I planted it last year." He laughs and approaches me, slipping his arm around my shoulder, pulling me into his side until he's able to kiss the top of my head. "Did you know that trees can share their roots?"

Tilting my face, I look up at him. He's staring at the little sassafras tree with a look of wonder.

"I didn't know that," I say.

He rubs my arm with his thumb, as his voice grows gentle. "As long as they're the same species of tree, they'll share their roots if they need to. One tree in the sunlight can share its nutrients with a struggling tree stuck in the dark shadows, where the sunlight doesn't reach. The healthy tree can revive the depressed tree back to life." He drops his chin, so our eyes meet. "The diseased tree was never diseased. It was only struggling and needed a little help to overcome its difficult environment."

I look back at the miniature thriving sassafras tree. It's full of life and apparently healthy. Its leaves are a luscious green with only a few bright crimson leaves from the approaching autumn season. All it took to resurrect the other tree was for this small tree to share its life with it.

The dampness returns to my eyes when I blink. "They kind of remind me of us. Helping each other, in the same way you shared yourself with me…reviving me back to life. We're like the sassafras trees."

He turns slightly to pull me to his chest, tucking my head under his chin. "We're *just* like the sassafras trees."

The End

RESOURCES

Domestic violence is not a topic I write lightly about. I wanted to bring awareness to this silent issue that gets overlooked too often. And in some cases, it's looked over until it's too late. Sometimes victims of abuse need help. And sometimes that help is a friend making a phone call for them.

If you or someone you know is suffering from domestic abuse, please reach out by texting **BEGIN** to **88788**

Or call 1-800-799-7233

Let's be LOUD about this problem.
No one should be silenced by an abuser.

FREEBIE JUST FOR YOU

Receive a free copy of one of my
eBooks when you subscribe!

Scan the QR code or visit
www.aurorastenulson.com

DON'T FORGET TO REVIEW

Thank you for your review!

Scan the QR code and
let everyone know
what you think about
Like the Sassafras Trees

A NOTE FROM THE AUTHOR

This section is meant to be read after the story. It contains spoilers.

This entire book was inspired by the horrific events that took place in my mom's early adulthood.

What a brave woman, right?

From the first time she told me about writing HELP on the condensation of her ex-husband's car window, I wanted to share her story of courage. And she gave me the okay to do just that. My only hope is that I wrote it in a way that reflects the complications that follow abuse, the problems that still occur in our judicial system, and the unbelievable strength it takes to overcome adversity when a person is isolated and without resources.

I know every situation is different when it comes to domestic abuse. And for my mom's circumstance, she was able to get out by the skin of her teeth. And I'm so impressed by her bravery and ability to grow from an atrocious experience.

This story wrote itself because so much of it was pulled from real life, believe it or not.

Like the part where Tuck pulled the trigger of West's gun...that was inspired by an incident that happened when I was five. My brother was three and we were playing on the floor in the living room. Our babysitter had fallen asleep on the couch and my dad had left a shot gun and a rifle on the floor. My brother got my attention and said, "I pull it," near the guns on the floor. I told him not to pull the trigger, but he insisted nothing happened when he pulled the trigger before. So I watched him pull the trigger for the last time. Our babysitter jumped up yelling, "*Whoah! Whoah! Whoah!*" at the sound of the gun fire. Thankfully no one was hurt, except for the carpet that was left with a burnt streak leading to a hole in the side of our house.

The setting of this story was in Mount Vernon, Texas which is a real-life, quaint, little town that I visited with my sister. During our visit, when I saw the historical remodel of their city hall and spoke with some of the locals, I was intrigued by their town. And when my sister and I wore out our welcome at M.L.'s and ordered drinks at Steve-O's at closing time, I *had* to write about this place!

Although the events in my mom's life took place in the early 80's, I chose the late 90's as part of the setting because the 90's holds my childhood, and it was easy for me to pull "historically accurate" information from my mind.

The parts about the blood-types were inspired by the way in which my mom found out her "dad" wasn't her biological father. She and my dad (who was a doctor) had a conversation about blood types once. She told him her blood type along with her parents. My dad said, "That's impossible. Your dad isn't your real dad." My mom called up my granny, who told her the truth and gave my mom her biological father's contact information. I remember driving twelve or so hours to visit my mom's real dad on his ranch. When we were having dinner together, even though I was a little kid, I was so infatuated by the resemblance between my mom and her dad's facial features, their shared hazel eyes and brown skin, and the fact that they even shared a birth mark along with my little brother.

The entire first chapter was a slew of true events that happened to my mom. She really did survive having her head beat against the kitchen floor. Only, unlike Trinity, she didn't have anyone show up and peel her off the floor in her second chapter.

And like Trinity, my mom's first husband took their kids and drove off to another state. But he never brought them back, and he didn't treat them half as well as West treated Abbi and Tuck. By manipulating the system and his parental rights, he obtained full custody. I remember seeing my sister maybe four times before she turned eighteen. But despite living on opposite sides of the country, she's one of my best friends. I truly believe nothing can separate the bonds between sisters, not even dysfunctional fathers.

My mom never did paint her first husband as a villain either (like I did in this story). She only ever spoke truth about him without emotion attached to it. And I believe she was able to do that because she forgave him in her heart. Not forgetting what he did or making excuses for his behavior, but accepting he wasn't going to change and forgiving the actions of the broken boy that never healed inside the man she married. Her strength has made me see how weak her first husband is. Weak people are selfish. Weak people lash out violently. Weak people point fingers. Weak people twist the truth. Weak people can turn an entire town against their victims. And weak people never own their wrongdoing.

The parts of West that were controlling, abusive, fake, petty, and alcoholic, were inspired by my mom's first husband. The only difference is that West finally received some consequences for his actions.

The parts of West that were charming, intelligent, and obsessed with Trinity were inspired by my dad. I never saw two people so madly in love in the most dysfunctional way. I can imagine it was confusing for my mom to be in a relationship with my dad when she just came out of a physically abusive relationship with her first husband. Although my dad wasn't physically abusive, his words could be very harmful. And the pain of someone's words can take longer to heal from than a broken bone.

My dad once hung xerox photos of my mom around town. I remember in the photo, she was sitting on a couch with a couple of men. What no one knew was that those men were my uncles. My dad had drawn little thought bubbles above their heads with profanities. It takes an incredibly smart, hurt, and manipulative person to twist the truth so heavily like that to try and make someone look bad. Much like the way West acted towards Trinity at the end of the story.

My parents separated when I was nine and divorced shortly after. And my mom only ever said good things to me about him. Like, *you get your green eyes from your dad*, and *you're so creative, just like your dad*. I knew he was imperfect, but she made a point to teach me that he also had good qualities that he gave to me. I can't say the same for my dad. He once told me that he couldn't be around me after the divorce because he didn't want to say anything bad about my mom to me. And honestly, I'm grateful to both of them. Because my dad choosing not to be around me in his unstable mental state, saved me from enduring greater trauma if I had been around him. And my mom focusing on the good, taught me that perspective has a huge impact on our circumstances.

I re-connected with my dad when I was an adult. It's very healing to love and accept someone without setting an unrealistic expectation for them. And because of a healthy perspective, I had a great relationship with my dad in my adult life—even though he was pretty much the same as he always was. He passed away a few years ago from COVID. But just a couple of months before he died, he was able to finally talk about my mom with me in a positive way. Sometimes growth takes a lifetime.

It's inspiring to see that my mom was able to become the strongest version of herself by growing from her relationships.

My brothers and sisters and I all got a patient, kind and loving mom. But because of our birth order, the mom I grew up with was wiser and different than the mom my older siblings had. I remember my mom as determined, educated and hard-working. She had boundaries and standards, and she wasn't afraid to use her voice. Especially when she saw someone wrong another person.

When I was a teenager, she remarried. I think her past relationships helped her choose a husband that was unlike her previous marriages. When she married my stepdad, I was able to see what a normal family looked like. My adolescents was full of fun and adventure because of my stepdad. And my favorite part of their marriage was that *home* was a safe place. Witnessing that normalcy inadvertently taught me what a healthy relationship looks like. And I really wanted to show that between Trinity and Knox too.

You'll be glad to know that my mom is happily cared for and very loved in her marriage now. When she's not working with a client in one of her therapy sessions, you can still find her rescuing butterflies and dragonflies from the dog bowl outside. She's fulfilling her dreams of changing a nation for the better, and empowering survivors of domestic violence every day!

ACKNOWLEDGEMENTS

To my husband, Kyle, thank you for being my hot best friend and favorite guy in the whole world. You're the love of my life and am thankful for the space you give me to create characters, settings, and plot twists. And I'm thankful you support me in getting these stories out of my head and into everyone else's minds. Half my life with you, and I can't believe that I get to continue *growing* in love with you every single day!

Thank you to the people of Mount Vernon that listened to my sister's and my laughter while we hung out at your restaurants well past the time we should have, watched as we took selfies in your town square, and walked by us as if collecting cicada exoskeletons was as normal as gathering Easter eggs on Sunday morning.

Thank you to my writing coach, Barbara. You are one of a kind and I'm grateful that you patiently repeated yourself every time we met until the information clicked for me—I'm a slow learner.

Thank you to Brooke for reading this story, sharing your insights, and making it better.

Thank you to my incredible team of ARC readers, and Beta readers. Your enthusiasm is contagious and keeps me motivated!

And to Ramy and Jo, thanks for pouring into your students. I've learned so much from your mentorship, knowledge, and advice in self-publishing.

Jai and Aims, thank you for scribbling your edits into the margins of my manuscript. I love to read your banter. And even more so, I love you both!

Des and Evan, I love you both so much and am so proud to watch you grow together, especially in your brotherhood. You fill up my heart and make me crazy at the same time!

Sisters, I wouldn't be me without all three of you. Sasha, when I was younger, I lived vicariously through you, learned from your mistakes, and always wished we were a little closer in age so I could hang out with you without being annoying. Amie, thanks for being my Wister and walking through each day with me—*you know what I mane*. Sandi, thanks for taking my writing seriously (even before I did), and spending two days of your vacation to read my manuscript (even though we were supposed to be doing more important stuff). I'm glad we can all be best friends in our adulthood, even though I can still be annoying and immature.

God, thank you. You know why.

And finally, to my mom, thank you for allowing me to share your story. Thanks for jumping into my stories before they're ready and giving me encouragement. Thanks for giving me the best version of you when you raised me. And thank you for always smiling, it's contagious and you make everyone's day brighter when you do. I love you!

AUTHOR BIO

Aurora Stenulson is an America author who primarily writes romantic suspense, women's fiction, contemporary, and YA. She lives with her four children and wonderful husband on their homestead in Wyoming.

To learn more, visit www.aurorastenulson.com

Instagram @aurorastenulson

Email aurorastenuslon@aurorastenulson.com

www.ingramcontent.com/pod-product-compliance
Lightning Source LLC
Chambersburg PA
CBHW031943260626
47157CB00017B/2089